THE RUBY MAGICIAN

THE RUBY MAGICIAN

BOOK ONE

D. R. Hudgins

Podium

Podium

THE RUBY MAGICIAN

CHAPTER ONE

Ardwyn was mystified at the sheer number of people walking about in the sprawling city of Alestead. He was standing just inside the entrance past the massive open doorways, dumbstruck at the sight. His entire company's horse riders could've fit through them, all six of them, riding side by side. All kinds of people walked through those doors, from nobles and their vassals to commoners wearing their entire life on their back. They walked through the door from different cultures and cities, though once past that grand entrance, all were the same. No matter their history, on the other side of those pillar-like door frames, they now shared something, one aspect to make them equals.

They were visitors, merely tourists, come to see the tower and the Climbers that challenged it.

A woman bumped into Ardwyn, barely noticing him, her eyes wide and head turning quickly, trying to see all that the grand entrance to the city offered. He readjusted his backpack straps, the weight nearly throwing him off. The woman kept walking, gaping with an open mouth, just as struck as Ardwyn at the city around them.

Ardwyn stopped to look at her, intending to chastise her for her rudeness, but quickly saw what actually drew her attention in the distance. The tower was even larger than he had assumed. It stood taller than the mountain range behind it that was rumored to strand at least a dozen people a year, yet it was thin and circular like a winding staircase in a castle. Granted, he had not seen many of those, only the ones at the lord's castle he once guarded years ago, but he mused at how their tower appeared to this one like a cat to a dragon.

The tower was named Alistair, and it was the lone magical tower in Jahnin. It was as glorious as it was dreadful.

Ardwyn shook his head, focusing. He looked around at the droves of people, watching them, taking note of where they were headed. Some were forming lines to the side further into the city, where stations were set with tents and small lines formed for new Climbers. Most, though, were headed straight toward the tower, seeking out the shops and attractions in the city, funneling through the streets like ants in a line.

It was nearly suffocating, the amount of people here, and Ardwyn tried to take a closer look at the people rushing to get inside. There were locals, citizens who'd decided to take residence in the tower's city and procure businesses. He recognized them from their carts with freshly procured supplies or trade items for their own shops. He remembered hearing that Alestead was a place of commerce and business, the people exchanging food, drink, equipment, and all manner of goods due to the high wealth exchanged by both the tower's explorers and tourists.

He could tell the Climbers apart from veterans and rookies, too, as those wide-eyed with wonder and curiosity were also filled with a healthy dash of fear and anxiety, just like him. They mostly blended in with the crowd, but Ardwyn was able to spot them with some effort. They sprinkled through the people, all ending up at the lines that gathered by the tents deeper past the gates.

The veterans he recognized easily, as they carried large weapons on their backs or sides and armor or clothes that looked outlandish and impractical. Plus, tourists either avoided them out of fear, or stopped to bother them with questions and admiration.

Gooseflesh ran across Ardwyn's arms upon seeing the veteran Climbers. They were who he aspired to be. He had come to the tower in the hopes of gaining a similar level of fortune and fame. His heart beat quicker, and he took deep breaths to steady his nerves.

The city of Alestead was a marvel, just like he had heard. The tower was set on the edge of the mountain range behind the city, and the city itself formed a half circle surrounding the magical spectacle that rivaled any capital city in the country. Ardwyn knew it would take weeks before he would even be able to explore it all, and likely three times longer to be used to the layout.

He took a deep breath. He had the time, though—he wasn't going anywhere else for the foreseeable future.

Continuing to make his way toward the rookie lines, he saw the crowd slow down. There were several lines now, with dozens of people waiting for their entrance. The stations were set equidistant from each other, small kiosks where officials gated further entrance.

Ardwyn saw several lines that were moving faster. These were for veteran Climbers, he assumed, as they all flashed something to the official and quickly moved past the rest. Other lines were slow, full of those without equipment to explore the tower, and from their stations came periodic cheers or sorrowful yells.

"Wild, isn't it?"

A woman, older than Ardwyn, had her arms crossed standing beside him. He jumped, not expecting her, and not having noticed how close she was. She wore fur-covered armor from her neck to her boots, and her auburn hair matched the color and was pulled back in a braid. She had a quiver on her back where feather-fletched arrows stuck out. Ardwyn noticed they weren't all the same color.

"That's one word to describe it." Ardwyn had to stop himself from staring in curiosity and admiration.

"Don't worry—you'll get used to it. If you survive this crowd, that is." She flashed a wink. Her face was warm and inviting, her freckles looking like tattooed dots on her face. She extended a hand. "Name's Marcy."

Ardwyn readjusted his backpack, trying to redistribute the weight, before grasping her hand and shaking it. It was strong, rugged and firm. He felt the calluses from her palms, and it reminded him of his time greeting men out in the fields at war. It was an archer's grip.

"Wyn. Nice to meet you, Marcy."

"You as well." She looked around, peering through the crowd. She took a deep breath and exhaled loudly, as though she were smelling something fragrant and fresh.

"The lines," Wyn said, as he noticed her shifting gaze. "They're going through their harmony, aren't they?"

Her gaze moved to him, where she eyed him up and down in a second.

"Yeah, they are. You're well caught up. Not many know about the harmony process."

"Really? I figured everyone would be excited to find out their class!"

They both turned and looked at one of the harmony lines, where shouts and yells suddenly erupted above the normal chatter. A group of people were laughing at someone, a man, young and energetic, who had just finished being harmonized. He threw his hands up in the air in dismay.

"Not everyone," Marcy said, laughing. "People want to choose their class, but it isn't that simple. The harmony shows them what the tower wants them to be, but I guess you already knew that." She pointed to the line of rookies. "Some, like him, aren't too happy about the outcome."

"I guess that's true, though the whole process is incredible. You'd think people would appreciate whatever they got. Do you have to follow your class, though?"

"No, not exactly. Though it's expected you do. It determines your mentor, if you can cast spells, and even the skills you'll gain in Alistair. If you choose a different class than you harmonized with, it'll be *much* harder to improve and hone your talents."

Wyn nodded, trying to solidify her words to memory. "And why would you want it to be harder when you're already facing the tower itself, right?"

"My thoughts exactly," Marcy said, and jokingly punched him in the arm.

Wyn smiled, thankful she was friendly and helpful. He made a quick mental note to find her again, if possible, to see if she'd be willing to help him in the tower.

"There's still a lot I don't know. I only knew of the class harmony, and a bit about the tower and classes. Not much about the rest." Wyn looked around, seeing the different Climbers merge into Alistair's base on the other side of the stations. There had to be dozens, and more of them would enter before the day was over.

"That's alright. You'll learn what you need before you enter the tower, and figure out the rest with a good party."

"I appreciate it," Wyn said. "You've been a great help. I hope to see you inside!" Wyn extended his hand first this time, hoping it wouldn't be too difficult to find specific Climbers once inside.

"You too," Marcy replied, accepting the handshake. "I'm a Ranger, by the way. Specialize in archery. I'd be glad to party up for your first trip in if you decide to enter today or tomorrow. Wouldn't hurt to have a friendly face for your first time, after all. Too many deaths lately."

Wyn nodded in agreement. He had heard about that. It dissuaded some people from becoming Climbers. Even his sister and father didn't want him to go. But the appeal of riches, glory, and power was too much for people to completely stop applying.

He also was delighted to hear she would accompany him on his first trip in the tower. He took a deep breath as he felt his nerves settle a bit, though his heart kept racing.

"Too true. Thank you again, I'll be sure to look for you inside. But I should probably go ahead and get in line!" Wyn smiled, one last pleasantry to offer, before joining a line to harmonize. It wouldn't be too long, thankfully, as he quickly counted about ten people in front of him, though a new source of anxiety was growing within him.

His military training served him well for fighting. He'd be fine in a combat class, if not excel in it, as most ex-military would—Fighter, Rogue, or Hunter would all be useful. His heart raced as he took another step forward, one step closer to deciding his fate. Just to prepare, he had studied some basic magic principles, in case he had a class that offered some magical abilities, like the Sorcerer or many different kinds of Magicians.

He didn't want a completely magical class, as he felt like his background would be wasted, though he wondered if it could give him an edge over other people? Mages normally didn't engage in combat. Not directly, at least. If he was skilled in wielding weapons and had more training than most, which he did, maybe that would be a valuable trait to a fully magical class?

Unless the growth of spells, skills, and procurement of items based on the Climber's class didn't account for things like that. Breaking out of the norm for the class was generally frowned upon, and he didn't need to research that bit of information—it was generally known.

Wyn wasn't sure about it all. Regardless, he thought about the potential of becoming a master in his class. A skillful, dexterous Rogue. A tough, strong Fighter. A perceptive, nimble Hunter. An intelligent, spell-slinging Magician or Sorcerer.

No matter what class he would receive, he would immerse himself completely. It was imperative to succeed, to climb the tower and gain the rewards it offered. Arabelle and their father both relied on him, and there was no other choice for him to take.

He heard a woman loudly clear her throat, drawing out the noise for emphasis. He blinked, lost in thought, and realized he was now next in line.

The woman behind the small desk in front of him waved her hand like she was a teacher getting the attention of a distracted student.

"Are you ready yet?" she said, her voice gravelly and hoarse. She was older and frail-looking.

"Um," Wyn said, stammering, "yes, ma'am, I believe so. What do I do?" He pulled off his backpack and placed it on the ground, thankful the weight was off his back.

He looked down at the desk in front of him and saw a number of odd items. Taking up the majority of the desk was a large, beautiful and ornate box. It was open, and it was full of gray sand. A palm-sized opaque orb rested beside the box. In front of the woman lay a blank piece of parchment, though no quill or ink was to be seen.

She picked up the orb and handed it Wyn. "You hold this, then watch. Easy."

He subconsciously grabbed it carefully, like someone would hold a delicate, expensive piece of jewelry. It was smooth and well worn, cloudy in appearance, drawing Wyn's attention to it by what felt like a command. The orb's cloudy appearance began to move, shifting and swirling like a rolling thunder cloud. Wyn wasn't sure if he was supposed to see anything at all in the orb or just hold it, but he didn't care in the moment. He had never held something so magical in his life. The sand in the box, once still, now shifted in unison with the clouded orb, a sort of magical communication forming.

Wyn couldn't decide whether the orb or sand was more interesting, then settled on watching the sand, witnessing runes and symbols eventually take shape. They would show in the box, take hold for a few seconds, then shift again, disappearing, like the moles that would peep out of their holes on the farm back home.

He laughed to himself at his mental comparison. He left the farm, but he surmised the farm would never leave him.

He was brought back to the present as more symbols formed in the sand. He recognized some of them. One was the basic runic foundation for magic—a circle with a triangle set inside. It represented the base for writing spells, a form of connection with intended spells and magical energy. He remembered reading it while preparing for the tower, just in case he could cast magic.

A sinking feeling formed in the pit of his stomach, as though the magical objects caused that, too. He wondered if it meant he would be given a magical class, or if this process itself was magical.

Another symbol flashed, though he couldn't recall what it meant. It was a circle with a square set in the middle, identical to the one with a triangle inside it though simply a different shape. There were many more that appeared, more complicated than the basic ones, and he was unsure what they meant.

Just as soon as it began, or so he thought, it stopped. The sand became calm once more, and the orb no longer had swirling clouds within it. The woman picked up the parchment in front of her and began writing on it, using a quill she pulled from behind the desk. If there was any ink on it, Wyn couldn't tell, as she wrote in a flurry and didn't stop to dip it in any inkwell. He carefully set the orb back down on the desk, waiting for her to finish.

She stopped writing abruptly and hid the quill as quickly as she revealed it. "Congratulations! Your class has been chosen."

Wyn blinked. "Wait, just like that?" Wyn's heart raced again, his anxiety and excitement reaching new heights as he was left in suspense.

"Just like that," she replied with a smile. She folded the parchment and handed it to him. "Please proceed past the gate and report to the guild hall." She motioned to someone behind her, who rushed out from the tent and grabbed his backpack. "Your belongings will be ready for you at the guild hall, where you'll be given a key to your room and information about your mentor. Good luck! You, especially, will need it." She waved him off once more, already looking past him for the next person in line.

Wyn, barely hearing any words she said, walked past the gate with his parchment in hand. He wondered what she meant by saying he'll need luck, but guessed she said it to every rookie who entered the tower for the first time.

He looked down at the parchment and opened it, having already forgotten about his backpack in the wonder of the events that just unfolded. Inscribed in fancy letters on the top half of the page was information that he had no idea how it had been revealed to the woman or anyone.

He read it several times, finding himself in awe of his new status.

Ardwyn Thatcher
Citizen of town Rywood
Resident of Jahnin

Tower Alistair: Climber
Class: Ruby Magician
Growth: Any
Passive Skills: Lucidity, Armored Spellcasting, Spellcasting (Ruby)
Active Skills: Dyadcast, Speed Up

Wyn smiled and tried to steady his shaking hands. He folded the parchment and put it in his pocket.

He remembered reading about Magicians, or more commonly called Mages. They were one of the two base classes for magic users, though their focus varied greatly depending on which elemental branch they were.

Ruby was not one of the elemental branches. It was a rare class, able to utilize a mixture of both spells and combat skills that afforded the Climber variety. Or, rather, that's what the basic information books said. Hopefully his mentor could shed more light on the class, as well as have him ready to climb today.

After all was said and done, Wyn felt excitement rise within him. The tower was a few blocks away, and his entrance ticket was punched. Plus, he wasn't just any Mage. He was a Ruby Magician.

CHAPTER TWO

Wyn snaked through the crowd, avoiding the new Climbers. All of the rookies were carrying their parchment like it was made of gold, which to them it might as well be. It had their newly minted information: their name, class, background, and skills. He still didn't fully know what most of it meant or why it was there, but he hoped his mentor would help guide him.

He just had to find them first.

The new Climbers all migrated toward a large building that appeared to be at least ten stories tall. It occupied its own space on the corner of a street on the way deeper into the city toward Alistair's base, though he assumed all streets eventually led deeper toward the magical tower. All of the people who had been harmonized now sought their next step like Wyn.

The entrance to the building mimicked the entrance to the city—pillars for doorframes with two large wooden doors filling their gap. It was smaller here, obviously, but the resemblance was purposeful and uncanny. In large letters above the doorway read GUILD HALL.

Wyn quickly realized there weren't just rookies in the crowd, either. He could tell the veterans apart from the rookies easily, as they walked with the same air and stride as earlier outside the city gates. None of them carried their parchments openly, and instead wore their weapons and armor like trophies.

The inside, no surprise to Wyn, was also grand. There was a large staircase at the far end of the hall, opposite to the entrance that was incredibly wide, easily able to accommodate five men walking side by side. It led up through multiple floors, branching off either direction, where he could see hallways and doors many floors up.

The staircase sat to the left of a desktop that spanned the entire back wall. The back wall was filled with shelves of bottles of alcohol, obviously serving as the bar when it wasn't so busy. Several people stood behind it, all running around, managing people who waited for their help.

Scattered in the middle of the hall were tables, steadily filling with people, either eating and drinking or just talking, likely planning out their day or simply catching up. Wyn overheard several conversations as he walked in, all discussing some element of the tower and the climb.

To the right of the hall was a large stone hearth, where a man was bent down trying to light the fire. There were doors on either side of the hearth where staff entered and exited. Coming through into the hall they were flying from table to table, carrying trays of food and beverages. They all wore a sort of uniform—black pants, formal white shirts, and a blue apron. They had varying degrees of flair to each of them, some shirts short sleeved and others buttoned, though all their aprons were adorned with silver trimming and a symbol of the tower Alistair on the chest.

Wyn felt a tap on his shoulder. "Can I get you anything?" A woman carrying an empty tray was smiling at him. She was middle-aged, slightly plump, and cheerful, with kind eyes.

Wyn realized he was just standing right inside as Climbers brushed past him in either direction. "I'm okay, thank you," Wyn said, smiling back. "I'm just looking for information about my mentor."

"Oh, yes! So you're a Climber," the woman said, tapping the tray with her fingers as she held it. "The managers are behind the desk next to the staircase. They'll help you find your mentor!" She was exceptionally positive, bouncing a bit, and Wyn couldn't help but keep smiling.

"Thanks, again. Do you normally have a lot of customers?" Wyn was nervous. He felt dumb right as he said it.

The woman laughed. "You could say that! We have new Climbers every week. This was a large amount, though! It's probably for the festival tomorrow night. Everyone wants a reward or recognition. Or just to enjoy it!"

"That's right. I almost forgot! I've heard they're quite the spectacle for Climbers and tourists alike. I've never attended one myself."

"You'll have a great time! Just don't overindulge, especially if you plan to start the next season right away." She giggled a bit, her hair bouncing off her shoulder and falling behind her. Her smile quickly faded, though, and she sighed. "You're right, though. It also celebrates all of the Climbers' accomplishments, both in life and death."

Wyn nodded, fully aware of how serious it is to climb the tower. "I'm sure the festival brings more business, here, too."

"It does, yes. Though I do wish I could have regulars more than tourists and newcomers. No offense!"

"None taken."

"I just . . ." She paused, looking down. "I hate to get to know a new group of people and find they lose themselves, or leave, or . . . die in the tower." She immediately lost her glow as a sour expression crossed her face.

"I'm sorry." Wyn balled his fingers into a fist. He had lost friends when he served in the military, so he understood to a degree. It was never easy. Impossible, even, for more than most.

"Well, no matter," she said, quickly smiling again. "I don't mean to greet you so negatively. I do hope your time here is long and fulfilling!"

Wyn returned her smile, finding it infectious. "Me, too. I'm Wyn, by the way. I'm sure I'll be back and see you again."

She gave a soft smile. "You better! I'm Wendy. When you come back, ask for me!" She gave a wink, then darted off as quickly as she came, running back behind the closest door beside the hearth.

Wyn walked over to the desk and looked for someone who wasn't busy helping another Climber. The crowd was thicker now, the noise well above average conversation. Some were talking to the guild staff for information, others were trying to get their attention, and some still were yelling just to be heard.

A shorter man, tanned with cropped black hair, ran up toward the desk in front of Wyn. He was wearing a similar outfit to the waiters and waitresses, being part of the guild, though instead of an apron he wore a vest with the same symbol of Alistair on the chest.

"Let me guess, looking for your mentor?" The man was looking around, his forehead glistening with beads of sweat. He was being summoned left and right.

"Umm, yes," Wyn said, flustered.

"Hand me your parchment. Quickly, please!"

Wyn held up his parchment, then began to hand it over. The man grabbed it so fast he nearly snatched it, scanning it quickly.

"Your mentor is Daniel. He's on the third floor." The man began to walk away, looking for another person to help.

"How will I know which door?" Wyn said, yelling back at him. Who knew how many doors or rooms were in this building? Was he supposed to knock on each one?

The man looked back and simply pointed to his hand. He was already taking another Climber's parchment.

Wyn looked down at his own magical paper. What did he mean by that? He looked it over, reading the words again. This time he noticed something he didn't see before. On the top right, stamped like a seal, was a symbol. It was a magician's hat, red in color, laid over a shield that covered a sword and staff in a cross shape. It appeared like a coat of arms, a symbol of royalty.

Here in the tower, classes *were* royalty. They were the means to gain access inside. And he realized he had his ticket.

Wyn made his way upstairs, giddy with newfound excitement. He thought of Daniel, his mentor. He wondered about his knowledge, his skills, even his appearance. He imagined a strong, tall man, though smart and intelligent, who wielded the skill set to fight in close quarters but also cast magic when needed. He wondered how popular being a Ruby Magician, or Red Mage, would be, considering they were rare. The ability to be flexible with his own skills to overcome any obstacle would surely be valuable.

As he thought and walked, he found himself on the third floor, daydreaming while climbing the stairs. The hallway snaked around the open floor of the guild hall's entrance, and he started to his right. The doors didn't have numbers or names, but rather symbols. And there were many more doors than he thought.

He noticed on this floor there were mostly magical doors, as he passed other classes' symbols. He saw a staff over a magical rune, the same foundational circle around a triangle that allowed the user to cast spells. He assumed that would be a Magician's door. He also saw some with elements on them: a ball of fire, a snowflake, a lightning bolt. He passed by one that had an incredibly complex magical symbol, a large circle with many other shapes and lines inside it, and he hurt his head trying to figure out what it could represent.

He passed by several Climbers also looking for their door, checking their parchment and looking for their symbol. Some of them exchanged nervous glances and anxious smiles, while others simply ignored each other. Who knew what would happen next? Fortune, glory, and power could be introduced on the other side of that door. Death, ruin, and shame could, as well.

Finally, at the end of the hall, he came across his door. He checked his own symbol, then checked the door again, and sure enough, the Ruby Magician's symbol was there, though it wasn't what he expected. It was older, splintered in places, more worn and dusty than the others. Was it more commonly used? Maybe it was opened quite a lot? He thought he remembered reading that Red Mages were more rare but maybe not. He grabbed the cold doorknob and turned it to open.

He had no idea what to expect on the other side of the door. A grand room, a simple room, weapons and armor on racks or a bookshelf with knowledge and spellbooks. He was excited and anticipated anything and nothing at the same time. What he saw, however, was *not* what he expected.

Inside was an apartment, and Wyn stepped right into the den. The low lantern light offered little visibility, but what he saw was out of a nightmare. He first saw a small bookshelf to his right, with a few books lying on their sides or sprawled open, and cobwebs filled the majority of the empty space. The middle of the room had a small rug, stained and dingy, with a wooden table set on top. The table was filled with dirty plates, bottles of alcohol, and a rag thrown on top of it all like a cherry atop a trash can sundae.

The smell of ale and old food smacked Wyn in the face. He gagged and tried to hold back his breakfast. He immediately hoped he had stumbled into the wrong room, but deep in his gut he knew he was, unfortunately, in the right place.

Two armchairs sat to the left in the room, less stained but torn in random places, and a bearded man was cuddling a bottle of ale while he slept. He jolted when Wyn gagged, and woke up.

"Mrmm, hello? Who's there?" His eyes were bloodshot. His words slurred.

"Hi," Wyn said, offering a sad excuse for a smile. He breathed through his mouth so he wouldn't smell the room. "I'm looking for Daniel. I'm a new tower Climber."

"You are? Really?" The man got up and dropped his ale, though none spilled. The bottle clanged against the ground, hollow and empty. He gained some composure, and his words sounded more sober. Barely. "Alright. Wait one moment." He walked off, further into the den, where a hallway sat behind a wall. Wyn hadn't noticed it before due to his gagging and disgust.

The man jumped back out into the den, now haphazardly dressed in a red robe and hat, his right arm not fully into the sleeve and the hat covering his left eye. He was taller than Wyn thought, slightly above average, though he had a gut that betrayed his indulgence of food and drink. He looked as though he left his prime several years ago.

Wyn jumped back in surprise, smacking the door behind him with his back.

"Ta da! Hello newcomer! Welcome to, umm," the man said, hiccuping several times between words. He pulled out a ripped piece of paper from somewhere in the robe. "Welcome to the Ruby Magician's den! We at the guild would like to thank you, umm . . ." He stopped, then turned the piece of paper over in his hand. "The rest is here somewhere. I don't know where, though. Ha! That's embarrassing!" He laughed, and hiccuped several more times.

"*That* is what's embarrassing?"

"I'll find it eventually. Anyway! I am Daniel! I'm the Ruby Magician mentor for tower Alistair. I'll be your mentor! Welcome!"

"Yeah. You already said that." Wyn looked over the filthy room. He instantly regretted coming to the tower, and had a sinking feeling he would die a quick and painful death.

"Well, once more for emphasis," Daniel said, smiling. He walked into the den and sat back down in his chair. "Please, have a seat. And what's your name?"

"Wyn," he replied, and brushed off some crumbs from the chair. Thankfully it wasn't as dirty or stained as the other. He sat on the edge delicately.

"Great to meet you, Wyn." Daniel stared at him, smiling again.

Wyn stared back, not knowing what to say or do.

"Oh, yes," Daniel continued. "Can I see your parchment?"

Wyn waited a moment, unsure if he wanted to part with it so quickly and to someone so questionable, but eventually offered it. Despite it being his, it appeared as though it was customary to have officials casually review his newly acquired paper.

Daniel took it and looked it over. He nodded several times, twice raising his eyebrows.

"Rywood, aye? You must have some farming in your blood. Makes sense with your lightly tanned skin and broad shoulders. Though you don't have the bulk of a young farmer your age. And *Lucidity*! That's a useful skill! Not every Ruby Magician has that right away."

Wyn perked up, ignoring the slight. "Yes, actually, I do come from farmers. I remember reading that some skills are given immediately and some are earned in the tower. I thought maybe that skill was standard?"

"Yes, yes, and no. I think that's right. *Lucidity* is a special passive skill usually earned in the second tier for our class. It will serve you well, though, if you make it that far." His face grew sour. He looked at the bottle of ale he dropped earlier, picked it up, then threw it back down when he felt it was empty.

"I plan to make it *very* far, thanks."

"Don't they all." Daniel handed him back his parchment, then got up from the chair with effort and walked back to the hallway.

Wyn stared at him in disbelief, his jaw open subconsciously. His mentor, whom he had been looking forward to meeting and imagined was a great Climber and person, was a drunk and cynic.

A cork popped in Daniel's direction.

Wyn set his jaw and clenched his teeth. "Look, I didn't mean to interrupt your day plans or anything, I just need you to mentor me. Or whatever needs to happen in order for me to go into the tower."

Daniel came back out, now holding a new bottle of ale in his hands. He took a quick drink, then appeared oddly more at peace. He sat back down in his chair.

"Most Ruby Magicians don't come here. They either choose a different class, find some other work, or leave." He was hiccuping less than before, and waved his ale bottle around while he talked. "The ones that do stick it out don't understand how to *be* the class. I haven't had a new Climber in . . ." Daniel looked up at the ceiling. "Almost a year."

Wyn swallowed hard. He wondered how long his mentor had been in Alestead and how many negative experiences he'd been through. "Why do they leave without giving it a chance?"

Daniel sighed, then took a small sip of his drink. His slurring was hardly noticeable now, and his movements were less sporadic, though still slow. "People don't like a class that doesn't specialize in something specific. A Ruby Magician's specialty is *variety*. Options. Flexibility. Our growth," Daniel said, pointing to Wyn's parchment, "is any. We don't focus on strength or toughness like a Fighter, speed or quickness like a Rogue, or pure magic like a Sorcerer or other Magicians. That variety doesn't appeal to people who need to play a role inside Alistair to succeed."

Wyn thought on that. "I'd imagine the ability to do several things, though, would be helpful. Like you said—flexibility. That could be useful in the tower where the floors change and environment is unexpected."

Daniel tilted his head. "Sort of." He took a large swig of his beer. "Though when Climbers go into the tower, they form parties, of course. They expect specific roles in those parties both to maximize their chances of survival and to face obstacles they find."

"I knew that. And roles, too. Like someone who can heal and support, someone who can cast spells or shoot arrows, and someone in close combat. A well-rounded group."

Daniel pointed at Wyn with the top of the beer bottle and smiled. "Exactly. You've done your homework!"

"If I want to succeed, I needed to know the basics. I thought so, at least. I still have some questions I was hoping you could answer, though." Wyn realized he had fully settled back into the chair during their conversation as his focus shifted to the dirty room. He immediately sat up and scooted closer to the edge of the chair again. He felt contaminated.

"There is so much I am unable to tell you that you must learn on your own in the tower. It's that simple. However, there are some basics I can teach you first to help you in the beginning. And you must know these before risking your life." He took another long drink from the bottle.

Wyn nodded, holding his breath for a second as he wanted to keep breathing through his mouth. He felt sick to his stomach. "Then can we discuss it downstairs? No offense, but it's absolutely disgusting in here. I think I might throw up."

Daniel furrowed his brow and looked around the room. His cheeks flushed red, and he cleared his throat.

"Umm, yes, you're quite right." He popped up from his seat and began to grab the dirty plates from the tables. "Meet me downstairs in the guild hall. Order some food—that will help. I'll be down before long!" He hurried back behind the wall with dirty dishes in hand.

Wyn didn't hesitate. He held his breath, jumped up, and ran out the door.

CHAPTER THREE

Wyn settled at a table by the roaring hearth in the guild hall. It was quieter, with less of the hustle and bustle of the rookie Climbers, far different from the rest of the hall. Most of them had likely found their mentors, who probably weren't drunk and didn't live in garbage, though, so they still had an advantage.

Wyn took a deep breath. He shouldn't be too critical of Daniel. The man had a history, and Wyn just met him. He made a mental note to be more gracious with the older drunk.

There were several groups still in the hall, nearly all of them dressed like they were going to climb. Obviously not new Climbers, they either sat and laughed at the newcomers or silently talked amongst themselves. Wyn grew antsy, ready to dive into the tower himself. He knew it was a challenge, and felt as physically prepared as he could be, but he also knew there was more to this experience than just pure training.

Daniel could offer that. Information, knowledge, expertise. It would be crucial—necessary, even—to know more about the tower Alistair. Plus, not to mention, he needed more information about being a Ruby Magician. His excitement and anxiety both grew.

Wendy, still delivering food and drink, saw Wyn and came over to him. She was still chipper and pleasant.

"Hello again, dear! Would you like something to eat or drink?"

Wyn heard his stomach rumble. She had oddly perfect timing.

"Gods, yes. A pitcher of water, two cups, and . . ." Wyn trailed off, and looked around the room. Other tables had assortments of large platters of food of a variety and amount that would make any noble jealous. If that kind of food was commonplace, there was no need to be stingy. "Maybe a platter of bread and fruit, if you don't mind? My mentor should be coming down soon."

"Excellent! I'll place it on his tab." She trotted off back toward the kitchen, leaving as quickly as she came.

Wyn immediately saw Daniel coming down the stairs. He was dressed in his red robe and hat, though a bit more presentable than before. He appeared to have at least washed his face and combed his beard, and he looked more like a mage. His hair was graying as some glimpses of it popped out from under his hat, but it only added to the wizened older man look.

Wyn had a brief glimmer of hope seeing him more cleaned up. Maybe this wouldn't be so bad, after all.

Daniel sat down opposite him at the table. He looked around nervously.

"Alright then," Wyn started, "let's get right to it. I know the basics of the classes and party roles. That the tower floors change every day, like a different pathway to the next floor, so no two days are alike. I know there are monsters inside it, and defeating them is necessary to climb the tower."

Daniel repeatedly tapped his finger on the table. "That's the basics, yes."

Wendy, as if on cue, returned with what looked like more food and drinks than she should be able to safely carry. She sat down a large pitcher of water and two cups, and a heaping plate of bread, cheeses, fruit, and assorted meats. She also brought a mug that Wyn immediately smelled was ale. She put it directly in front of Daniel, and he swore she winked at him.

Daniel smiled and grabbed the mug first.

Wyn's mouth watered seeing the food all laid out before him. He grabbed a handful of cheese and some grapes and began making himself a plate. If this was life as a Climber, he could easily get used to it.

"First, I want to apologize," Daniel said. "I haven't taken my role seriously or kindly. I have had a certain . . . history . . . of students, you see, and don't enjoy the prospect of another. No offense." He held the mug gingerly in his grasp but didn't drink it.

Wyn nodded, then popped a grape into his mouth.

"But this is a fresh start," Daniel continued. "A clean slate, if you will. So I will be better."

"Alright. Thank you."

Daniel nodded and took a deep breath before pushing the mug away forcefully and grabbing some food for himself.

"Let's start with classes and roles," Daniel said. He poured himself some water from the pitcher and made a plate of food while talking. "Your first lesson!"

Wyn munched on a mouthful of food. "But I already know about them." He didn't realize how hungry he was, barely stopping to swallow before talking.

"Yes, but you also didn't know why Ruby Magicians aren't popular."

Wyn nodded, reluctantly agreeing, now more amenable with food.

"So, since that's the case, let me explain further—it won't hurt to be reminded. Now, parties have specialized roles to diversify, yes. A standard party is one primary healer, one support class, and three to four damage classes." Daniel paused to swallow his mouth of food. He absentmindedly reached for the mug of ale, decided against it, then grabbed his cup of water instead.

"Optimal diversification would be a mix of ranged and close combatants," he continued, "as well as spell casters and non spell casters. Not to mention you have the Mappers and Packers."

"The Mapper helps trace the route taken, and the Packer helps collect items and carry equipment." Wyn wagged a piece of bread while he spoke.

"Yes, but they can have classes as well." Daniel smirked while taking another sip of water. He plucked a few more grapes from their vines, too.

Wyn stopped before grabbing more food and looked at Daniel closer. "Huh. I didn't know that."

"See? There are some things for you to learn still! Yes, they have classes, and usually serve as support. But their reasons for being Mappers or Packers vary wildly, and it's more of a discussion that your impatience won't enjoy."

Wyn chose to ignore the slight. "That's interesting. So why aren't Ruby Magicians popular? You still haven't completely answered that."

"Ahh, yes." Daniel set down his cup. It rang hollow, and he poured more water into it from the pitcher. "So within the specific roles of a party are specialists. Alistair is unforgiving, and you want to be as proficient at that role as possible. Fighters deal damage and endure, Sorcerers deal damage with spells, Diamond Magicians heal and support, Rogues deal damage quickly. That is their focus." Daniel refilled his cup and smiled wide, waiting for emphasis.

"Ruby Magicians are able to do all those things!" he continued, taking his arms out wide in excitement before restraining himself by clearing his throat. "Like we said, flexibility is helpful. However, we aren't as efficient as someone who *specifically is designed to do that task*. We can do them all, just not, or ever, as well. When people look for party members they find specialists, not generalists."

Wyn scrunched his eyebrows together. "So because we can't heal as well, or protect as well, or deal damage as well, we aren't as appealing?"

Daniel sighed. "That's right. If a party wanted ranged spell support, they'd find a Topaz or Garnet Magician or try a Sorcerer. Not a Ruby Magician."

"Well that's complete bullshit." Wyn forcefully stabbed a hunk of sausage with a fork.

Daniel spilled some water from his mouth from Wyn's sudden cursing. It sloshed into his beard, and he wiped it with a napkin.

Wyn took a deep breath. "I'm sorry to be crass. That's just hard for me to grasp that a class here is considered useless."

"I know, Wyn, but you'll see. Sooner rather than later." He stared past Wyn, caught in the moment. He cleared his throat after a few silent seconds, refocusing his thoughts. "Yes, well, to continue. About tower Alistair itself. All you need to know, for now, is about the floors themselves."

"I remember reading about it. Different towers across the world are all different. The tower here, Alistair, has twenty floors, and they are all the same for one day, then change their path the next." He spoke as though reciting a lecture given when asked by a teacher.

"Sort of."

"Wait, that's not true?"

"No, it is. But it's more complicated. The floors are split in groups of five based on difficulty. Floors one through five are the easiest, and fifteen through twenty are the hardest."

"That makes sense." Wyn crossed his arms, taking a break from eating. He was finally getting the information he sought, and wanted to be as present as he could.

"Every fourth floor is more difficult, having tougher and more monsters. Those are floors four, nine, and fourteen. The final floor in each tier is an advancement and recovery floor, no enemies or obstacles. They're popular meeting and relaxing spots. The twentieth floor is unique and always changes, but hardly anyone truly knows about it. However, what most new Climbers don't realize is that the very first floor in each tier is easier, making good locations to repeat over and over. As long as it's a compatible floor for the group, of course."

"Farming, right? For money, items, weapons, class growth?"

Daniel scrunched his face and scoffed. "Yes, though I *hate* that term. We aren't farmers. We are *Climbers*. We seek things in the tower: glory, treasure, camaraderie. We don't *farm* things. Whoever coined that is a fool."

Wyn couldn't help but smirk. He remembered reading and hearing about the term *farming*, which is what appealed to Climbers so much. Repeating floors over and over again, like a farmer continuously reaps their crop. Slang was popular, and he was exposed to it even in rumors and books in his preparation before coming. Obviously Daniel was exposed to it, too.

"Anyway, to continue," Daniel said. He also stopped eating, though the platter of food was nearly empty. "Each floor has a sort of final challenge before the next, and each group of floors carries a theme. So if you enter the first floor, and see it's makeup is a castle, you can expect the next four floors to be climbing further into that castle, gradually more difficult than the last, with the fourth floor in the group being the most difficult challenge."

"Okay, so there would be difficult monsters at the end of each floor to defeat, with the final one being the hardest?"

"You would think," Daniel said, smiling again. He eyed the mug of ale and reached for it, though stopped himself, writhing his hands together like he was washing them. He began tearing into the last bread loaf. "The final floor in the group is a surprise. But it isn't always monsters that present the challenge inside for the other floors. Sometimes it's a puzzle against the tower itself. It's actually very clever, though dangerous if you aren't ready."

Wyn grabbed the last cut of ham to add to his plate. "That's good to know. Thank you for the information."

"That's why I'm here, after all. To prepare you to not die."

"I thought it was to help me succeed to climb the tower?"

"To me, your mentor, they are one and the same." Daniel sloppily finished his loaf, and Wyn watched as crumbs fell all over his beard and robe. "Another point of interest with the floors are that the themes change every month. Though that also means they are the same for one month, which is why Climbers come out in larger numbers at the end of the month. Like now."

"Really? I figured it'd be toward the beginning of the month in order to practice the new season?"

"Some veteran Climbers do that after they took a break, sure. But rookies are informed to come at the end to take time to prepare for the following season. I'm surprised that wasn't told to you."

"I didn't exactly seek the information at a guild, so no, I didn't know that. But that means whatever theme the first set of floors are now, being the end of the month, they'll stay that way today and tomorrow, until after the festival. Just the floor's paths will change each day?"

"Precisely!"

Wyn took one final bite of bread. He had been skeptical of how much the platter would fill him, but it felt as though it was food made for four instead of two. He relaxed back in his chair, his stomach fuller than he would've liked.

"I appreciate you helping me, but I'd like to get right into the tower. Today. I'm ready to explore it already!" Wyn sat back up, forgetting about his stomach. His heart was racing.

Daniel laughed a brief, high-pitched chirp. "That's rich! You just arrived, Wyn. Why would you want to start now? There's more preparation to do. Most rookies take at least a week before they enter Alistair."

"There's no practice quite like the real thing, right? I could find a group willing to take me, or you come with me, and I'll see for myself. Easy."

Daniel's face went as red as his robe and hat. "I won't be going into Alistair. I'm sorry, Wyn. But if you're absolutely certain about going today, some veteran Climbers are taking rookies out for their introductory climb this afternoon. It happens before the season change as a safer first experience."

Wyn's eyes went wide. "That sounds perfect! You should've started with that. What do we need to do next, then?"

"So eager! A lot, actually. You still need to place your mark and learn some important things about your class, your skills, and spells, too."

Wyn thought of Marcy when he first entered Alestead. She was a veteran, though happy and excited to climb the tower. He suddenly had the urge to find her and ask if he could join her party. His cheeks flushed unexpectedly.

"If you want to climb this afternoon, we need to move along. It's a lot to cover in a few short hours."

Wyn placed his hands on the table, shooting up. Daniel spilled his drink again and stared at him wide-eyed, huffing.

"Then what are we waiting for? I didn't come here *just* for a lesson. I came to seek out riches in that tower, and by the gods I'll find it!"

Daniel laughed while wiping water out of his beard.

"I envy the excitement of youth! I'm reluctant, but I can't stop you. Let's head to the training hall, then. We need to place your mark, and you need to learn about magic. Meet me in half an hour." He got up from the table, straightened his hat, and placed some coins down on the table. He bowed to Wyn, bidding farewell.

Wyn returned the bow with an added smile. Finally, his luck was starting to turn.

After Daniel walked off, Wendy came over to pick up the tray and dishes. Wyn waited for Daniel to be out of earshot before talking to Wendy. He didn't want to be rude.

"So you seem to know him. Daniel, I mean." Wyn looked down and noticed Daniel had left a gold coin and three silver rounds. His breath caught in his throat. Why would he leave such a ridiculously large payment?

Wendy talked while she cleaned up their table. "Of course! I know all of the mentors here. But Daniel is special."

Wyn perked up, trying to wrench his eyes from the coins. "Why is that?"

"Well, a Ruby Magician isn't a popular class. He hasn't trained a new Climber in I don't know how long."

"He told me that earlier."

"After his last Climber," Wendy continued, "he would just drink and stay in his room. He loathed coming out to meet new Climbers who just got their class. Those who would get Ruby Magician wouldn't follow through after the last one, even though there weren't many at all. It's rare, you know, like a Summoner or Samurai." Wendy finished cleaning, quickly pocketed the coins, and finally wiped the table dry, ready for new patrons.

"I can't believe they wouldn't at least try. Who would come all the way here then just give up?"

"I'm not sure. But they usually end up being employed by the guild in some other way, or try their hand at something different. They're definitely out there, though, shamefully keeping their selected class a secret."

"What happened to the last Ruby Magician?"

Wendy looked Wyn in the eyes, her mouth contorted in a sad smile. "It's not my place to say the whole story, but they went in alone after no group would take them. They died inside Alistair, and Daniel blamed himself."

Wyn felt his stomach drop. "That's awful. Well, I'll be sure to be more sensitive about that. And him. Thank you, Wendy." He decided not to push the subject anymore. If Daniel wanted to talk about it, he'd let him in his own time.

They both heard another group clank their tankards on the table, several in unison, and watched as beer sloshed all over the table and floor. Laughs and guffaws flooded the room.

"I believe I'm needed. Good luck, Wyn! I hope to see you soon!" She smiled her infectious smile once more, then darted off.

Wyn was one step closer to climbing the tower, one step closer to his goal of getting the wealth he and his family needed. He would be a great Red Mage, the best one Daniel had seen, and prove them all wrong.

Father and Arabelle needed him. They needed money, and a lot of it. He vowed he would do whatever he could to make that happen. Sticking with his class seemed to be the quickest way to climbing as long as a group would take him. But he could prove his worth one way or another.

Unfortunately, though, Wyn had no idea how to even get to the training hall.

CHAPTER FOUR

Wendy, gods bless her, was able to direct Wyn out of the guild hall to the training hall. Thankfully it wasn't far, but still—in their excitement Daniel forgot to tell him where it was, and Wyn forgot to ask.

The training hall ended up being down the street closer to tower Alistair's base. It was large and unexciting, a contrast to everything else Wyn had seen so far. Though it didn't have the grand pillar entrance or even the cozy feel of the guild hall, its sheer size was impressive in its own right. It had the look of four or five buildings smashed together, because in a way it was. It was at least four stories tall and held an entire side of the street, dwarfing any other building Wyn had seen since entering the city.

Unsurprisingly, there was more traffic flowing in than the guild hall, a solid combination of new Climbers coming to train with their mentors, many in groups. There were veterans as well, sprinkled in amongst the people though in less numbers here than he'd seen so far. They were the ones with audacious gear and the focus of many stares.

Wyn shuddered. He thought of rain, his company moving up a muddy hill toward an unknown enemy on the other side. They slipped and trudged slowly, as quietly as possible, the rain helping mask their noise of rattling armor and weapons. His helmet clouded most of his vision and he despised it for that, though was also grateful for the protection.

He shook his head and took a deep breath. He needed to focus—he was no longer on the front lines of war. He was in Jahnin. He was home.

Well, sort of.

He took another deep breath and walked toward the doors.

Wyn followed a crowd of Fighters. He guessed they were Fighters since they wore the same military clothes he'd seen before—a long-sleeved fitted black shirt and black pants, with the patch of Jahnin's coat of arms sewn into the left breast.

It was a stag with a silver head and antlers, and was bright in contrast to the black shirt. The same symbol of the tower he'd seen with the guild members was directly below the stag head.

There were over a dozen of them being led by two mentors, a man and woman, both tall and well-built. Wyn wondered if they were related or maybe a couple, or even just two friends who happened to both be Fighter mentors sharing similar body types.

Though there were some in the group Wyn's age, the group was more on the younger side, basically teenagers who chose to become a tower Climber rather than another profession. They all looked the same age as his sister, like some of the fresh soldiers he led in the war. It reminded him of his own time as a recruit in the military, young and foolish, seeking companionship and a new life.

He laughed and smiled, followed by a sharp feeling of shame. The memory and nostalgia thankfully faded quickly.

Wyn tried to keep to himself, but it was difficult. He stuck out like a sore thumb compared to the others. He was dressed in casual clothes: a short-sleeved undershirt and red jacket, which he now saw as ironic because of his class, and his trusty leather boots. He caught some wayward glances from the nearby group of Fighters, and he tried to ignore the lingering stares.

"Welcome, new Climber! I'm assuming you're meeting your mentor here today?" The woman mentor spoke to Wyn, her voice booming over the relatively subdued chatter of the crowd. She was taller than Wyn, taller than most of the Fighters, even, and her arms were impressively bulging through her tight-fitted black shirt.

His cheeks flushed. "Umm, yes. He said to meet him here."

She nodded and moved on, trying to tend to other Climbers like a shepherd to their flock of sheep. Wyn looked around, hoping to see Daniel soon so he wouldn't have to talk again. This was surprisingly awkward. Wyn didn't know if it was because of his less popular class or a new environment, but he hadn't felt this way since his early days as a soldier.

It was hard to spot Daniel, too, because Wyn was lost marveling at the hall itself. It was larger than any training hall the military had as the ceiling was several floors high and the training room was one large room for a wide range of activities. There were sections full of targets and dummies with multiple racks of weapons, equipment, and people to try them out. One entire length of wall had various obstacles of ropes, pits, walls, and more that Climbers were facing at various points.

"Ahh. Coming to show off a bit, eh?" The male mentor spoke this time, his voice equally as loud as his partner. He smiled and flexed his arms a bit. Some of the Fighters laughed, some snickered.

"I bet he's a Sorcerer. He looks as lost and dumb as one!"

Wyn couldn't tell who said that, but it came from the middle of the crowd. More of them laughed this time, louder than before.

He hoped the mentors would discipline them, make them have respect for the other Climbers. Unfortunately, he was wrong. The two adults laughed loudest.

One Fighter on the edge of the crowd didn't laugh. He was scowling at the rest of them, arms crossed and shaking his head. He began to say something, but the male mentor cut him off.

"Come along, now, Fighters. We have *actual* training to do. Let the little Sorcerer go!" He laughed to himself, and the rest of the group joined in like school-yard kids.

The lone Fighter stayed behind as the rest walked off toward the section of the hall full of racks of equipment and training dummies. He was as tall as Wyn, appeared to be similarly muscular, if not more so, and looked to be a bit older than the rest of the group. Wyn immediately wondered if he was also a soldier.

The Fighter walked over to Wyn, still scowling. "Sorry about them. They're immature and misguided. They don't understand the value of making friends here, apparently." He dropped his scowl and offered a charming smile. A sword was strapped on his hip that had runes running all along the sheath, and a shield was attached to his back.

"Obviously not," Wyn said. "But I appreciate that. And I'm a Ruby Magician, not a Sorcerer."

The man winced. "I wouldn't tell them that. They'd make fun of you more, honestly."

"Probably so. But I don't mind. I'll be just fine." Wyn felt his confidence grow-ing, though also wondered if it was a front. Maybe it was the excitement of the day and of what was ahead, but he was getting more and more used to saying he was a Ruby Magician. It felt right, despite what others thought.

The Fighter eyed him up and down and smiled again. "I think you might be right! I'm John, by the way. John Gallows." He extended his arm in a greeting.

"Wyn. Nice to meet you." He returned the greeting and clasped John's fore-arm. Wyn still wondered if he was ex-military, though didn't think it was the right time to ask. It was a customary greeting to grasp arms with your peers and bow to superiors, but many people adopted the greetings who weren't involved in the military, either.

"You too. Maybe I can go and set the others straight before my climb this afternoon."

Just then, Wyn saw Daniel standing by a rack of weapons in a corner of the large hall. He had a few targets and training dummies beside him. He caught Wyn's eye and waved, at first excitedly, then reined himself in.

"There's my mentor," Wyn said. "I hope to see you again this afternoon if I can help it."

"That'd be nice. Good luck!"

Wyn moved through the crowded hall, avoiding Climbers and their training. He heard clashes of weapons all over the room, and could see the occasional arrow flying at a target. He noticed several guild members on standby just in case, all wearing the same uniform as before though with additional royal blue overcoats and the tower symbol on their chest. As Wyn looked around he noticed they were scattered around the hall, all observing, though whether for talent or protection he wasn't sure.

He thought back to his time in the military with his company. He was back on that hill, smoke covering his vision, hearing far-off clangs of metal and yells of men. He remembered his company cresting the top of the hill, happy to cross the last barrier before they could join the fight, despite feeling ragged and tired. They were weighed down by caked mud on their boots and armor drenched from the rain, though they were ready to fight.

"Wyn? Hello?" Daniel said.

Wyn stared at nothing, his mind distant.

Daniel grabbed Wyn's shoulder and shook him gently.

Wyn, reacting on pure instinct, grabbed Daniel's wrist and twisted, using his body for momentum in self-defense. Daniel rolled with the movement, surprisingly agile, and grabbed Wyn's arm back, bringing Wyn down to the ground beside him. They both lay there staring at each other, Daniel wondering what had happened and Wyn's mind blank.

Wyn realized what had happened and immediately let go, scrambling away from his mentor on the ground in the process.

"I'm so sorry, Daniel! I . . . I wasn't thinking." His breathing was quick, but several deep breaths helped him calm down. His mind wandered yet again, and he had reacted as if he was being attacked.

Wyn repeated his phrase to himself to center his mind. *I'm in Jahnin. I'm home.*

Daniel slowly stood up and brushed himself off. "It's alright."

"No, it's not alright. I attacked you unprovoked," Wyn said. "It was reckless!"

Daniel studied him for a moment. "You were in the military, weren't you?"

Wyn returned his stare, his face blank. He didn't know if it would benefit him more to tell the truth or lie, though his lack of response answered for him.

"It's not uncommon, you know," Daniel said, continuing, "for ex-soldiers to come to the tower. But your neatly cropped short hair, your attentive pose, the way you speak, and your observance of the environment tells me you might not have been a simple soldier."

Wyn stood at attention and took one more deep breath. "You're right." He didn't want to share much more than that. Not yet.

Daniel slowly nodded, understanding. "As I said, it's alright. We all have pasts. Though we didn't come to discuss that, did we? This hall was built for training, and that's what we must do!" He walked over to the weapons rack beside a training dummy. It had all sorts of basic weapons, and nearly all of them Wyn had seen or trained with at some point. They were wooden training weapons, too, of course, as expected.

Wyn followed silently. Based on Daniel's reaction, maybe he really was the mentor he'd been seeking.

"Now," Daniel continued, "before we get to the basics of magic, I want to see your capabilities in combat. Being a Ruby Magician means having different tools at your disposal, both magic and weapons. We are capable of doing nearly anything well, if not exceedingly well, despite what most think. So, as your mentor, I have a task for you."

Wyn took another deep breath to suppress his smile. If there was anything he was confident in, it was his combat abilities. "Yes, sir."

"Daniel is fine. No need for formalities," Daniel said, offering a warm smile. He patted the weapons rack beside him. "Now! I want you to choose three different types of weapons to attack this training dummy. I want to see what you favor and what you're comfortable with." Daniel picked up a short sword and twirled it around his wrist. He didn't look at it, only at Wyn, and exuded confidence and skill he hadn't shared before.

Daniel walked over to the dummy and stood beside it. It was wooden and lifelike, having a torso, head, and arms, though they were all rectangles or squares of wood pieced together. It stood on a base, firmly planted to the ground, and had a shield as its left hand. Daniel patted it on the back, and Wyn noticed a strange aura radiating away from the impact like smoke from a flame.

His heart skipped a beat. Daniel just used magic.

The dummy suddenly jerked, the head and arms moving in quick flashes, and Wyn stepped back in surprise. Daniel laughed.

"Haven't seen a magical training dummy before?"

Daniel then gave his short sword to the dummy. It reached with its empty right hand and grabbed it. Wyn hadn't noticed it had fingers before, or any capability to hold a weapon. Then, as suddenly as it jerked alive, legs sprouted out of the base, almost as though it was a plant breaking free from a pot. It then waited, still as a statue, and Daniel backed away to provide some space.

Wyn wondered how skilled the dummy was in combat. If it was magically enhanced to wield a weapon and be able to fight back, it likely was a worthy sparring partner.

Wyn walked to the weapons rack. He had trained on nearly all of the weapons, sure, but he *did* favor a few. The military encouraged certain weapons anyway, and his company wasn't the type who used clubs or maces.

He looked back at the dummy, then decided to match it weapon for weapon.

Wyn picked up a shield he knew he'd be comfortable with, an average size round shield. The weight felt good. He then looked for the right sword. Most of his experience was with a slightly longer short sword rather than a more stout weapon that required two hands to adequately wield. The reach and length balance, along with the lighter feel, served him better than the more common longsword, too.

He didn't see one, though, and settled on a wooden longsword. He hooked the shield onto his left forearm and felt confident with the straps, then picked up the sword.

The dummy quickly strode toward Wyn the instant he picked up the sword. It didn't waste any time.

In the moments during its approach, Wyn tried to study it. Its stride wasn't too long, though it was more smooth than he expected from a wooden enemy. The arms were a bit shorter as well, and he began to estimate the distance it would be able to reach.

Wyn readied himself and stepped away from the rack. The dummy swung down first on the offensive, and Wyn easily blocked the strike with his shield. He felt the recoil but maintained his grip. He moved his shield to the side to open up for an attack, then swung his own wooden sword in retaliation. He was faster than his wooden opponent, but it raised its shield at the last second and blocked it sloppily. He noticed it recoiled back more than he did, staggered from the blow.

He smiled. It wouldn't be nearly as hard as he expected.

Wyn drew back and stabbed forward this time, faster than before, and the dummy wasn't able to keep up. It took the hit to the torso and stopped, then backed away to where it started and waited, as though it was following unknown commands.

Daniel walked up to the dummy and slapped it on the back again. Another aura of magic plumed away from his smack. "Good! You're quick and precise, fitting for a trained soldier. You obviously need something more challenging!" The dummy jerked again, then loosened up its stance a bit. It swung its sword in a circle, ready for the next round.

Wyn had a feeling the next match was going to be much more challenging.

He walked over to the rack and placed his equipment back. He knew what he was going to pick up but thought about the order. He left the shield behind this time, choosing the battle axe and picking it up.

The dummy moved faster this time, its stride more fluid and purposeful. Wyn tried to surprise it and struck first, swinging the axe down with both hands to the approaching dummy. To his own surprise, the dummy sidestepped and blocked it with the shield, brushing the axe aside and opening Wyn up to an attack. The dummy began to swing the sword in a diagonal slash, though Wyn dropped low and ducked under the swing, sidestepping to the left. There was a brief moment where the dummy was open and exposed, and Wyn knew that was his chance.

He reached to his lower back for a dagger that wasn't there, ready to strike quick. He grabbed nothing but air.

The dummy, whether sensing the opportunity or simply following preset moves, slashed out horizontally, following the momentum of its first swing. It struck Wyn in the side. It wasn't a hard hit, thankfully, as the instant Wyn felt the wood hit him, the dummy stopped with surprising control. The wooden combatant sensed it had won and backed away to its starting position yet again.

Wyn cursed, frustrated. He was used to a dagger on his low back for those exact moments. Caught up in the excitement, he had forgotten to equip one.

Daniel smiled again. "Not a bad choice! Though it appears you're also used to having a secondary option to your weapon. That's good. We'll have to remember that."

Wyn threw his axe on the ground and turned back to the weapons rack. He saw exactly what he wanted—a spear. He grabbed it and turned, not waiting for the dummy to charge him. He spun it with both hands, twirling it around in the air. He wanted to feel it, sense the weight and length. He stabbed the air a time or two in front and behind him. It was solid and felt just like one with an actual metal spearhead.

To his surprise, the dummy didn't charge. It instead started to circle him and crouched lower than before in an unfamiliar stance.

Wyn stepped forward to close the gap, still twirling his spear. He felt lighter on his feet than with the other weapons and more confident, too. He reached a distance he knew would be enough and struck out, half stepping with his front foot to gain a few extra inches.

The dummy blocked it with its shield and smacked it away, similar to the axe. Wyn recovered easily, spinning it as the dummy pushed it to the side, able to maintain control. The dummy then attacked again, this time leading with a flat horizontal swing. Wyn ducked and made sure to carry the spear with him, striking the butt of the spear into the dummy's leg. He backed away, thinking he had won.

To his surprise the dummy continued to advance, readying another swing. Wyn was confused but decided to keep going—no sense in stopping now.

The dummy stabbed forward, extending its wooden body for more reach, and Wyn used the spear shaft to block it to the side. He spun around it quickly, hoping to stab into its side, though the dummy hopped out of reach almost *too* fast, avoiding another strike.

Wyn felt alive. He nearly forgot the thrill of fighting and sparring. Using a spear afforded him more reach and maneuverability, and he valued the tactical advantage that was usually under appreciated. He loved this part of his training and using his own talents while wielding a weapon. It was *invigorating.*

He moved toward the dummy for one final attack, spear at the ready. This time he performed a series of strikes, all stabs, at various points toward the dummy in quick succession: the right leg, torso, left arm, and head. The dummy did what it could to dodge or block, but it missed the final strike, taking a wooden spear point directly to its wooden head.

It stopped, stood tall, and backed toward Daniel in defeat.

Daniel walked over, slowly clapping. Wyn let the butt of the spear rest on the ground and held it proudly by his side. He was breathing a bit harder than before, but not quite out of breath—his experience served him well to keep his stamina up. It was mostly out of enjoyment and adrenaline.

"We know what weapons you'll use in the tower, now. That was impressive!" Daniel patted Wyn on his shoulder like an approving father. The older mage looked more open and inviting than he had when they first met.

"Thank you, Daniel. It *felt* good, too! I always favored the spear. I love the reach and feel of a weapon I can use quick." Wyn walked to the rack and placed the spear back.

"Not many people use a spear, but it is a worthy weapon," Daniel said as he walked back to the dummy. He patted the dummy on the back one more time, and another aura of magic flowed from his touch. The dummy shortened, its legs collapsing back into a base. It looked like a regular training dummy now, funny and awkward with its wooden body.

Daniel pulled a flask out from under his robe and took a quick swig. His face scrunched in disappointment. "Now Wyn, are you sure you want to explore the tower today? There's another introductory tour tomorrow afternoon, as well. You don't have to rush, you know." Daniel looked around the hall at other rookie climbers and their mentors, all training. The sounds of thumps and thuds radiated through the hall, everyone sparring with wooden weapons and each other.

Wyn smirked at Daniel trying to sneak a drink. "It's just a brief climb, right? If the veterans are leading us it should be easy. It seems as safe as could be."

Daniel paused and sighed. "That's true. But nothing is safe in the tower, Wyn. If nothing else, remember that. Always be on guard. Always be ready for anything." Daniel stared intently at Wyn now, his brow furrowed and demeanor unwavering.

Wyn took a deep breath. "I will. But I still would like to go. After you teach me magic, of course."

Daniel laughed. "Wyn, I couldn't teach you everything about magic if we had weeks. Months, even."

Wyn looked confused. "Then how are you going to teach me what I need to do before the first climb in a few hours?"

"Because I'm going to teach you magic for a Ruby Magician! And, thankfully for you, magic is simpler and more straightforward when using your tower mark."

"Right. I almost forgot about the mark. It's to help use magic and skills, right?"

"Yes. But we need to go apply it." He took another drink from his flask, quickly and discreetly. "Follow me, please." Daniel then walked off toward a door in the wall Wyn hadn't noticed before.

Magic. A large part of the appeal of the tower. Wyn had heard it was easier to use as a Climber, but he didn't know exactly how. It was rare to see magic in the military, but those who could wield it were revered by the soldiers and officers alike.

If only his company could see their captain now.

CHAPTER FIVE

Wyn stood, holding his left forearm. He had decided to apply his mark on his inner arm so he could see it when he wanted but hide it fairly easily with a coat or sleeve. The mark wouldn't be large, at least, though Daniel told him it could be as big as he wanted, such as on his chest or back, or small if he wanted it on his hand or face.

He wondered why in the hells someone would've wanted it on their face, but then he thought about people and how strange they are.

Daniel went on to explain to him that the mark allowed the casting of magic and using skills in the setting of the tower, outside of more complicated means throughout the rest of the world. "The mark acts as a focus," he had told Wyn, "and magic needs a focus to transfer raw energy into purposeful casting." Wyn followed, or at least he thought, though it wasn't easy. He needed Daniel to explain it again or a different way several times.

He was glad it was only *part* of his class as a Ruby Magician and didn't make up the *entire* class. If he were a different Magician or Sorcerer, which was completely focused on magic, he knew he would need *much* more time to study it enough to be useful.

Daniel told Wyn that runic circles helped make up the components of a spell, and that they served as the foundation for the specific creation. They could have multiple layers of varying designs and complexity. If letters helped form words, then runes and their variations helped form spells. It made up the language of magic to cast what was intended. Basic spells only needed basic runes, and higher-level spells needed more circles of runes that added to their complexity.

That made sense to Wyn, though he knew it would get complicated fast. Training wasn't just going to involve physical improvement anymore. He'd need to train his mind as well.

Daniel and Wyn were in a private room in the training hall. Apparently there were many of them for more specific studies or meetings. This room was large, almost as big as the guild hall where they shared breakfast, and he figured it was because it helped contain the casting of magic.

The area was lit by multiple torches set in sconces on the right, and the midday sun shone bright through windows on the left. Wyn wondered how there were windows in here when he felt like he was in the middle of the building, but he didn't dwell on it.

There was a small desk beside a bookshelf with various books, a large table for writing and making notes, and targets at the other end of the room. The table had several stacks of pages, mostly blank, a few quills and inkwells for notes, and many smooth stones for paperweights.

"Magic is not nearly as easy outside the tower," Daniel said, continuing his lesson, "but we don't need to discuss that now. The mark is your class mark and matches what was provided to you on your parchment. Can you set in on the table?"

Wyn obliged. He unrolled his parchment and set it down. Daniel then placed some of the stones on the edges to keep it from rolling back up. There, at the top right, was the symbol of the Ruby Magician with a runic circle behind it. There were four small circles set within the runic circle at each corner, so if you drew a line to connect them, a square would be formed inside.

"The runes behind your class mark are specific to you. It is your foundation for performing skills and casting magic. The combination of skills is different for each person, and you can choose any sort of spells allowed by your class."

Wyn nodded along, understanding some of it, but didn't want to interrupt. Not yet, at least.

"Your Ruby Magician skills come from the same pool as mine, though we obtain them at different points based on our experiences and performance in the tower. The runes on your mark allow those skills to be more basic or more advanced, no matter when you obtain them.

"For example, you have the skill *Lucidity*. That is a special skill, and one that you should study further. But for now, at your beginning stage, it only allows you to accumulate mana. And slowly, at that."

"Wait," Wyn said, deciding it was time to interrupt him. "I have several questions. Mana is the energy we have for magic, right?"

"That is correct."

"And, from what I read, it's a pool of energy that is finite but can grow as I grow in my class. Different from my energy to move or swing a weapon, too."

"Yes! Your pool is different from anyone else's and will increase in time. Our magical energy pool is different from our physical energy, such as what we need for our muscles or organs to function. It's also different from our spiritual and mental energy as well."

"That . . . seems complicated." Wyn rested his arms on the table, still standing but quickly growing impatient. His head hurt.

"As I said, it can be. And honestly is! But just trust me on this. When you're tired physically, your muscles ache, your joints hurt, and you want to rest to recover. Or eat," he said, patting his stomach and smiling. He then patted his coat higher up and grabbed his flask. He took another drink, this one longer, and set the flask openly on the table.

"I know that all too well," Wyn said. "The military made sure to make *that* energy pool seem never ending. Or at least make us get used to the pain of when it *was* empty."

"So your physical stamina is high. That will serve you well, as I've said before! When you're tired mentally, you have difficulty focusing, your emotions are less in control, and you can develop headaches."

"Like I have now." Wyn rubbed his temples. His mental stamina wasn't *nearly* as impressive as his physical endurance. He ran, fought, and worked out constantly, but he wasn't forced to read or study in the military.

"Mana is similar. You will know when your pool is low, and your mark will tell you, too. Not everyone recovers mana passively like you with **Lucidity**. It takes food, rest, and a mental break."

Wyn nodded along but didn't respond. He was getting more and more mentally drained.

Daniel smiled and laughed that chirped sound again. "Then let's move this along." Daniel walked over to the desk and opened its top drawer. He pulled out a strange stick and inkwell. It had a diamond at the base and a sharp point at the other end. The inkwell was glowing.

Wyn perked up immediately. He didn't like the looks of that.

"The mark, unfortunately, is a magical tattoo of sorts. I'll need to place this on you for you to channel the tower's magic."

Wyn, excited but reluctant, rolled up his left sleeve. He pulled out a small stool from under the table to rest and laid his bare arm on the tabletop. He sat and thought about what he could focus on to distract him. Plenty of soldiers got tattoos during service, and he accompanied them more than once for support. This was no different.

Well, this was completely different and no ordinary tattoo.

Wyn wasn't helping himself during the situation.

Daniel set the tools on the table. "It won't take long. I don't have to stab you repeatedly for it to take like a regular tattoo, either. I just have to draw it on while the magical ink and pen do the rest."

Wyn exhaled loudly, relief leaving him in a rush. "Okay. I'm ready."

Daniel grabbed the pen and inkwell to ready them for the mark.

"Wait!" Wyn shouted, startling Daniel. He nearly tipped the magical inkwell over. "I almost forgot. What about the skill **_Lucidity_**?"

"What about it?" Daniel snapped back at him. He checked the inkwell to make sure none of it spilled. "You nearly made me drop this!"

"I'm sorry!"

Daniel took a calming breath. "It's alright. What about **_Lucidity_**?"

"You said it allows me to accumulate mana. How? And it can do more than that? Not to mention I don't even know how to use a skill!" The moment of relief from before vanished, and anxiety quickly replaced it.

"So many questions," Daniel said, and set the diamond-studded pen down on the table. "**_Lucidity_**, at its most basic form, allows mana accumulation slowly while the skill is being used. It's a passive skill, so it's used at all times. You activate skills by focusing on them and using your mark, similar to a spell. You'll see."

"If you say so. I still don't fully understand."

"That's alright. You'll figure it out in due time! Now quit putting it off. I figured you for more courage than you're letting on."

Wyn shook his arms and stretched his neck. Daniel was right—he needed to get over this fear of the unknown and _act_. He placed his arm back on the table and braced himself, tensing. Daniel said it wasn't bad, but he saw how his soldiers reacted when actually getting the tattoo. It wasn't a sight you forget.

Daniel chuckled, taking another drink from his flask. "You won't need to do that. Just watch."

Wyn gulped, hoping Daniel wasn't getting too drunk to do this right, but had a feeling his tolerance was much higher than the average person's.

Daniel traced the mark on Wyn's parchment with the pen. He did this carefully and slowly, and Wyn figured he was practicing so he wouldn't mess up on his arm. The diamond began to softly glow white while he was tracing. He then dipped it in the ink, and the point changed color to a bright red glow. He took it to Wyn's arm and began to trace the mark, slowly but steadily.

Wyn still winced when the pen touched his arm, but realized immediately it was a blunted tip, pointed for accuracy and not for piercing the skin. Daniel was just drawing on his arm like he said. No sharp needle or stabbing involved.

As Daniel worked over his inner forearm, Wyn noticed the drawing was slightly crooked and lopsided. An intrusive thought entered his mind about him not being able to use his skills or magic from this drunk man's shitty mark as the lines would be wrong. Thankfully the magic was truly magical, and the lines corrected themselves into a smooth and perfect copy from the parchment.

It only took Daniel a minute before the mark was finished. The symbol of the Ruby Magician, in all its glory, was now stamped on Wyn's arm. He felt power rushing through him. His adrenaline spiked.

His parchment and mark began to glow in unison. It was the same shade as the point when it magically connected—blood red.

"What's happening?" Wyn looked at his parchment closer, and the glow slowly faded, including his mark on his arm.

"The mark took, connecting itself to your parchment. Remember that parchments are pieces of paper directly from the tower itself. This is how magic is so easily used inside Alistair, as a connection was formed between you and a literal piece of the tower."

Daniel grabbed some other pieces of paper on the table and drew on them with the same pen. Wyn saw he was drawing his unique mark in the top right corner at the same location as his piece of parchment. Daniel copied it onto four total pieces of paper. They all gave off the same red glow before dulling down to resemble a perfect red stamp.

"These will guide you as you climb the tower. Thankfully there's seemingly no shortage of extra sheets from Alistair for Climbers to use." He wrote titles on all the pieces of paper—**SPELLS** on two of them, then **CLASS** and **ITEMS** on the others. "As you collect items, equipment, weapons, or anything, really, it will magically appear here. It's tied to you now, evidenced by your mark stamped into the paper."

Daniel shuffled the papers neatly and handed them to Wyn. He grabbed them gingerly, not knowing what to do with them.

"I'll give you some beginning equipment and help copy a few spells. It is our job as mentors, after all, to start you off properly. Fold those papers up with your parchment and keep them on you at all times."

Wyn followed his instructions.

"Now," Daniel continued, "I want to give you a few basic spells to start."

Wyn's heart was racing. "That's very kind of you, Daniel. Thank you. I honestly have no clue where to start with magic."

"Yes well, it would be a disservice if you didn't have any starting out. All classes who cast spells start with a few given by their mentors. You may find a few more in the tower to use, but most are here in spellbooks. You'll want to choose your own, of course, based on your group and preferences, but these will serve you well for now."

Daniel walked over to the bookshelf and pulled out a book. He hefted it back and plopped it on the table. Wyn read the cover—*Beginner Spells for Tower Alistair*. It was a simple, unassuming book, but if it gave him spells to use, it was one of the most powerful objects he had seen yet.

Daniel casually flipped through the pages. They were covered in runes and magic circles and contained paragraphs of information. Wyn wasn't reading them too carefully, but he could tell they weren't overly complicated. Nearly all the spells he could see at a quick glance were made up of a few runic shapes and circles at most.

He wondered what the more advanced spells looked like. They probably held pages and pages of information per spell, and he shuddered at the thought of sifting through them for study and use.

Daniel stopped flipping through the book toward the middle. "This book holds dozens and dozens of spells, but *you* can't hold too many. Not yet. We have to select our spells wisely as Ruby Magicians, but know you can change them out if needed. All it takes is a spellbook where the runic foundation is held. I have a few copies in my room of this book, and you're free to take this. I'd encourage you to look through it when you have the opportunity."

Wyn was shocked. Becoming a Climber held one surprise after another, and he wondered if—or when—it would ever end. Here was a spellbook, an artifact of untold value, which was just given to him. He could hardly believe it.

"Let's discuss a few that would be most beneficial to you. It's easy to change out spells but time consuming. You need several hours of focus followed by practice to use a spell efficiently, especially for the more complex spells."

"This is amazing," Wyn said quietly, almost at a whisper. "I've never dreamed of anything like this. But how do I know how many I can use at a time?"

"That's a good question. Ruby Magicians would be too powerful if we could use as many spells as other Magicians or if our mana pool was as large. At least I'd like to think so . . . But your mark and parchment will tell you how many you can prepare and store at a time."

"How?"

Daniel pointed to Wyn's magical pieces of paper. "Hold your new parchment labeled **SPELLS**. It will react to your mark."

Wyn eagerly picked up his new piece of parchment. It began to glow at his touch, and he noticed there were four spaces for spells. At least it *looked* like there were four places he could copy a spell, though it was more intuition than certainty. It wasn't obvious, and he wasn't sure how he knew—but in his gut he knew he could prepare four spells.

"I'm not entirely sure how, but I think I have room for four."

"Intuition of your mark. You'll find that occurs more as you gain experience, too," Daniel said as a matter of fact. "But that's great! So we should find four spells that suit your needs most. What do you feel you could benefit from?"

Wyn thought on that. He knew his combat ability was more than qualified, but was limited to close range. Maybe something at range would be helpful? Then he thought about improving his physical ability, too, to make himself even more capable. There were so many avenues he could take it was almost overwhelming.

Daniel gave Wyn some time. This wasn't an easy decision.

The older Magician took his flask and drank from it. His face scrunched up from the liquid's taste. Then he did it again. He tapped his fingers on the table waiting for Wyn to decide. "May I give some suggestions?"

"I don't know the exact spells, but I know what would be helpful. Something to improve my combat ability. Something to stay alive, of course! Something to help my teammates, too."

Daniel's face relaxed into a wide smile. "Excellent ideas! There are several spells you could use. **Cure** heals wounds, **Arcane Aura** protects you, **Magic Weapon** improves your weapon's damage and durability. There are damaging spells as well, which would be beneficial for ranged ability, too."

"Won't most other magical classes have those and use them? Aren't I looking for something helpful but different?"

Daniel thought on that a second. "You have a point. Yes, any Diamond Magician worth your time will prepare several variations of healing and protection magic. And the other elemental Magicians will have damaging spells galore, either direct or indirect."

"So something that's similar but not exactly the same. It would admittedly be easier after forming a group. But can we look at the different spells together for now?"

"Of course! And I know you're still wanting to join the introductory climb today. We have only a brief amount of time to find, select, and copy your spells before you'll need to go."

Wyn agreed. Daniel showed him the book and explained to him different spells—sections of the book for different categories of spells, their descriptions, and occasionally different variations of them. It was hard to narrow his list down to just four. He thought of changing it in the future, and knew he would several times, but for now he wanted a good variety.

It took about thirty minutes, but he finally found the ones he wanted.

"Are you sure?" Daniel was tired but satisfied. It had been a long day already. It was invigorating teaching again, but he wasn't used to it, not to mention he was reaching his peak drinking alone time.

"I am. So I need to add them to my parchment next. I just use the pen and ink, and my mark will do the rest?"

"In simple terms, yes. You just write in the spell by copying it! In the tower you say the spell, and your mark will do the rest. At least for now."

Wyn thought about how much time he had. He checked the lone clock in the room over on the desk. The climb was at three in the afternoon, and it was currently one. "I'll need to copy these quick. The climb is in two hours!"

"Go ahead, then, and I'll gather some things for you while you work. I'll be back in an hour."

Daniel left the room, and it was suddenly very quiet. The only noise came from the torches, their flames crackling like sharp whispers in the dead of night. It was oddly comforting, reminding him of the various camps he and his soldiers endured throughout his service.

Wyn began right away. He wanted to make the introductory climb today. He *needed* to. His family couldn't afford for him to wait much longer. It was a fast decision when he left his military company only last week, visited home, then came to Alestead to pursue climbing the tower. He knew it was the only option to help his family and refused to allow any time to change his mind.

He felt hopeful that these spells would help, but his anxiety continued to grow. He still wanted to practice them, too, but knew that would be cutting his time close. Combat was known to him—fighting and killing. He hated it, but convinced himself before he came that killing monsters in a magical tower would be easier than men in a war.

Magic and spells, though? It added tools to his belt, sure, but he didn't like the thought of being unprepared in a deadly place. It weighed on him like a suit of armor that didn't fit.

Still, it didn't overcome his desire to climb, and climb quickly. He would learn on the fly and do what he could for now. That was something he was good at, at least.

The magical papers on the table didn't deter him. He grabbed the sheet labeled **<u>SPELLS</u>** and started copying.

CHAPTER SIX

This is *maddening.*" Wyn stood at the base of tower Alistair. The actual entrance, not just the guild hall or the city. Before him was the opening, the same opening he'd seen throughout Alestead and the one that welcomed him in earlier this morning—two large pillars, wide and glorious. It was the exact image of the entrance to Alestead, only he knew these were the original while the others were simply copies. Something about the slight dullness to the stone that showed weathering over the years and the pockmarks that littered it like freckles wasn't here on these pillars. The pure magical radiance that the tower released kept these stone barriers in pristine condition.

Wyn craned his neck to look up at the top, and he wasn't even close to seeing the peak. Not that he could, considering there were clouds hovering in the sky and the tower was higher than the clouds, but still. Even the width of the mighty tower was abnormally large, being easily as round as several buildings. The tower seemed evenly cylindrical with various windows and decor spiraling up its length, but it also didn't seem to make sense. No support structures were anywhere to be found, and the building felt as though it should fall over from its sheer height. The only explanation for its strange and unrealistic appearance was that it was completely made of magic.

No castle Wyn had ever passed or even heard about came close to matching the sheer scale and awe of Alistair. He looked back down at the entrance in new-found amazement. It was no wonder people were captivated by the tower's allure. And that was only what the outside held.

There were fewer Climbers coming to the tower than came into the city. Wyn still noticed a handful, many accompanied by what looked to be their mentors or other veterans. The rookies wore more simple clothing and gear, and the more experienced Climbers had more elaborate equipment. It was nearly time for the scheduled climb.

Back in the training room, Daniel quickly taught Wyn the basics of his magic with a few spells to practice, which he promised wouldn't consume too much mana. He said *Lucidity* would recover them before he started his climb. Thankfully Wyn picked up on them relatively quickly, though he was by no means as comfortable as his combat ability.

"Just say the name of the spell, and the mark does the rest," Daniel told him. Sure enough, he was right.

The spells were listed in his parchment—the names, runes to cast them, and their descriptions. The mark worked by summoning those runes when called on, using mana to cast it. It was a complicated concept, but Wyn accepted both that he had a limited understanding and that it would work in the tower. He thought this because it worked in the room at the guild hall, and it worked well.

"It is something, isn't it?" Daniel wasn't as in awe as Wyn. He'd seen it many times before, and while Wyn was in awe in some ways, Daniel was in awe for different ones. The elder mage had experienced the tower. He *felt* the impact of climbing it, both good and bad.

Though all he could focus on right now was the bad with his new apprentice.

"I'm ready." Wyn gripped his spear tight with his right hand. Being here felt *right*.

"You say that," Daniel said. "You won't ever be ready. Not truly. But you're *prepared*. And that's as good as you can hope for." He pulled out his flask of seemingly never-ending alcohol and took another drink.

Wyn looked at Daniel. He knew, deep down, something had happened to him. Not just losing students or prospective future students. Some other bad experience or culmination of experiences that changed him. He opened his mouth to ask but thought better of it.

In time he'll share when he's ready. Now isn't that time.

"Thank you, Daniel. I mean it. You've done *so much* for me to get ready to climb today. I don't know how to repay you."

Daniel smiled. "I'm your mentor. It's my job to help! But I know one way you can repay me."

"Survive? Come back and have a beer with you after reaching the top?"

"Yes, but also no," Daniel said, and patted Wyn on the shoulder. "Actually repay me. I think 150 gold crowns should cover it."

Wyn's jaw dropped. "What?! *150* crowns? It took over three months to make that in the military!"

Daniel paused but quickly laughed and hiccuped at the same time. The alcohol was finally catching up to him. "I'm only kidding, Wyn. I would never ask you to repay me. I want you to succeed, of course, so I'll give you whatever you need!"

Wyn's heartbeat returned to a steady pace. He was surprised Daniel was able to catch him off guard. He obviously still had a lot to learn about the man.

"If I do have the opportunity to repay you, consider it done. I *am* thankful for what you've done for me in a short period of time." Wyn adjusted his leather jerkin, another gift from Daniel. It covered his shirt and protected him without restricting his movements while also not interfering with his spells. Daniel informed him earlier that most mages can't cast spells in armor reliably, which limits their protection—another benefit to the Ruby Magician that goes unnoticed by most Climbers. He couldn't wear heavier armor, but that was fine with him. It was too restrictive anyway with his more mobile fighting style.

Daniel pulled out another small object out of his inner robes. Wyn thought it was simply another flask until Daniel handed it out to him. "Here, one final gift. I want to make sure you are *completely* prepared."

Wyn grabbed the object. It was a small vial of a deep-red liquid.

"It's a healing potion," Daniel said. "A basic one, but plenty for the first floor. Use it in an emergency."

Wyn had only seen these in the military, where they were provided for his superiors in times of war. He immediately wondered if they were commonplace here. It made sense that they were, considering how magical the tower was and the people who traversed it, but still, Wyn was surprised to be holding one.

Daniel also provided him a spear and dagger, both standard issue and basic, but kind gifts nonetheless.

Wyn had sheathed the dagger in the small of his back under his backpack—his preferred place. He checked it was snug, then checked again, and adjusted his pack's straps one more time. He only had the basics inside—a water canteen, some dried food, and now the healing potion. Daniel had offered the pack and supplies for his quick trip, and Wyn didn't feel right not taking them when offered. Plus, Daniel recommended he climb light so he could get used to the experience as a whole. It was a climb that only would take a couple of hours at most, and only the first floor at that.

Wyn pulled out his parchment from a pocket on his pants. It was the piece labeled **SPELLS**. He quickly looked it over once more, trying to familiarize himself with the information.

__Ice Shard__: A damaging spell that allows you to fire a sharp chunk of ice the size of a dagger in the direction you point. This could pierce the target or coat them in ice. Consumes a small amount of mana.

__Arcane Aura__: A protection spell that coats the user or target in a magical shield of armor. Currently provides basic protection that will last a short amount of time. Consumes a moderate amount of mana.

__Regen__: A healing spell that will heal the user or target over a period of time. Heals basic wounds, not able to cure diseases or remove poisons. Currently takes more time to heal and consumes a less moderate amount of mana.

Magic Weapon*: A utility spell that coats a weapon in magic for a small amount of time, increasing damage, durability, and overall effectiveness. Consumes a less moderate amount of mana.*

Wyn stared at the parchment for a moment. He used them all in the training hall, but he silently cursed himself for not finding out more about them. How much is a small, less moderate, or moderate amount of mana? From the first spell he cast to now was about an hour. He foolishly took some sips of a weak mana potion Daniel brought in order to help recover and be completely ready. Of course it restocked his mana pool, but he didn't track anything about how much mana each spell used. There was no true sense of his capacity or ability to cast spells in the brief time he had. And, the spells that lasted longer he also ended early to save time, but now he regretted not having a better idea of how long they lasted.

His stomach dropped. He felt less prepared than he did before, like he was wading into combat with a weapon he didn't know how to use. Which in a sense was exactly what he was doing.

He took a deep breath. Then another. He was experienced and level-headed, having trained for years to expect the unexpected and adjust himself on the fly. Plus, this was more of a training exercise than anything truly life-threatening. He folded the parchment back up and placed it back in his pocket.

Climbing the tower was the entire reason why he came. The best training was jumping right in, and he needed to get out of his head and jump.

Wyn adjusted his gear, ending with his new robe and hat. Both were the most unique gifts of all, at least according to Daniel. They were the signature look of Ruby Magicians, and it was customary, Daniel said, to wear them proudly and respectfully.

The robe was a high-collared coat and the hat a magician's hat, wide-brimmed with a loose center. Both were blood red. It was a nice contrast to his dark gray undershirt and stained leather jerkin, though he felt funny wearing the hat. Daniel told him it was a rite of passage to wear it for his first climb, and that veterans wore far stranger gear that offered magical boons. These were as ordinary as socks, but who was he to argue?

"Good luck. I mean that." Daniel offered his hand.

Wyn took his hand, shook it, and offered a smile in return. "Thank you. It'll be great, I know it!"

Daniel quickly walked away, obviously not one to linger. He headed back to his room to find a drink until Wyn returned. He couldn't go with him into the base of the tower. Most other mentors were at least escorting them inside, but he couldn't. Not again.

Wyn was nervous but ready. He walked through the entrance and inside, ready to face Alistair. He joined the mass of other new Climbers, almost all of them nervous along with him. He expected a few snickers and laughs from his outfit but found only whispers, likely not even about him.

It wasn't a long walk past the large pillars, though it was equally as intimidating and awe-inspiring inside the tower as from outside. The main hall wasn't as large as Wyn thought it would be, though it was strikingly beautiful. He had never seen anything like it, even in noble castles he'd protected in the past.

The walls were made of smooth stone, set perfectly from floor to ceiling. There were large stained-glass windows in the walls, all depicting different scenes. Some were of trees and nature, some of war with conflicting armies. They were *massive*, easily as tall as buildings, and Wyn wondered why he didn't notice them from the outside and how someone was able to construct them. Each one ended before the ornate domed ceiling of intricate patterns of stone, though to Wyn's surprise he could see the top. It was still the tallest room he'd ever seen, but the tower obviously spanned much, much taller than this ceiling appeared.

At the far end of the room was a series of connecting desks and people behind them, all guild workers. Some were walking around carrying objects here or there, and some were standing still, though all had tasks to do. Further behind them were storage compartments and various doors that other staff members were using, entering and exiting beyond the room into unknown areas.

To his left and right were open doorways and hallways that extended past the main room into more unknown places. Wyn *knew* those were the way to the actual adventuring part of the tower. The desks and guild staff were probably there for information or help.

The rookie Climbers were gathered in the middle of the hall. Together with their mentors there were probably thirty or forty of them, and the room still looked as though it could hold more, probably over a hundred people.

As Wyn looked around, he noticed about a dozen Climbers standing to the left of the desks. They were wearing extravagant gear—full packs, weapons, and armor that were definitely *not* basic. He assumed they were the leaders for their climb. They looked tired and beaten. One woman's armor in particular was covered in a green, almost fluorescent substance. She had a quiver on her back and a bow slung around it. Her armor was made of furs over leather, and the more he stared the more he recognized her.

It was Marcy.

She caught him staring at her and smiled and gave a small wave, quick as a flash. Wyn couldn't help but return both.

"Wyn! You made it!" A voice rose up from the hushed crowd, surprising several people. One rookie jumped and dropped their staff. Wyn, most surprised at all, looked around for the source.

A man cheerfully pushed himself through the crowd toward him. It was John, the Fighter from the training hall. He had his sword sheathed on his left hip, and his shield was attached to the outside of his backpack. He was holding a helmet in the crook of his left elbow and wearing padded armor, a popular choice of protection that gave more defense but was still more maneuverable than heavier plate armor.

Wyn breathed a sigh of relief. "John! I guess you made it, after all!"

John trotted up beside him. His mentors weren't around, thankfully. "I couldn't miss it. I'm too excited to wait and sit it out! Most of the other Fighters wanted more training, but I *knew* I was ready. I've been ready for a while."

"I felt the same way. Were you in the military, by chance?"

John's face scrunched up. "No. Why do you ask that?"

"Well, you said you've been ready for a while. And you seem more mature than most other new Climbers. I figured you'd have combat training or experience somehow?"

"Ahh," John said, adjusting his backpack strap. "I've been training to be a Climber for months, now. Nearly an entire year. And that's outside of lessons and study. My entire family are Climbers!"

"You're not serious," Wyn said, eyes nearly popping out of his head. "That seems dangerous for a family business!"

"It is. But rewarding," John said, smiling again. "My father and mother met while climbing Alistair, then they left after a while to start a family. Me and my siblings caught the bug."

Wyn nodded. "I can understand that. Everyone has their own reasons for being here, I suppose."

John sighed and peered through the crowd, darting his head back and forth. "You're telling me. Good or bad."

Wyn looked at him. His sword and shield did look different from others he saw in the crowd. He only caught a glimpse of both in the training hall, but now he really studied both. The sword had an ornate hilt, and the sheath had gold trim. He realized the hilt perfectly matched the runes on the sheath, which were also laced in gold. The shield had an aura similar to the brief bits of magic he'd seen, as though the air around it shimmered and shifted.

John grabbed the handle of his sword as if he knew Wyn was examining it. "This was my older sister's. She retired a couple of years ago after climbing to floor 17, and it was one of her magic swords she found inside Alistair. She offered it to me to use on one condition."

"What's that?"

"That I find a weapon to pass down to my little sister in the same way! She wants a bow, though. What crazy fifteen-year-old wants a magic bow for her birthday?"

Wyn just stared at him. He absolutely did not know the answer.

"So were you in the military? Interesting choice of a spear there," John said, pointing to Wyn's weapon.

Before Wyn could answer, one of the veteran Climbers walked to the front of the guild desks and climbed on top of it. He was a large man, both tall and wide, and wore black chain armor. He had a large axe on his back and a belt across his waist full of potions in varying size bottles.

Wyn was struck with how easily he was able to climb on top of the desks. The gear looked heavy and the armor awkward. He wondered if it was part of his class growth or something else.

"Good evening," the man said, and his voice boomed over the crowd. Everyone was already mostly silent, eager and anxious to climb, but now you could hear a pin drop it was so quiet.

"I am Xander," the man continued. "I am a Barbarian and veteran Climber of tower Alistair. I'm here to help guide all of you on your first climb, along with others who are experienced and capable to lead you safely. They are very generous to give their time and expertise to all of you!"

Xander was animated with his speech, smiling awkwardly and waving his arms around. The crowd was silent though, not sure what to expect or how to respond.

Wyn couldn't help but wonder how he was a Barbarian, either. He hadn't heard of that class before. Of course there were other classes out there, but there were only five choices to start. Obviously more could be found or earned.

"Are you not excited or ready for your first climb!?" Xander yelled. His powerful voice carried through the hall, echoing off the walls. Some of the rookies jumped in surprise.

Wyn shot a side glance at John, who also glanced over at him. They smirked at each other. John then beat his chest with a fist twice. Eagerness and confidence poured from him.

Wyn gripped his spear tight and banged the butt on the floor twice. He used to do it to signal his comrades he was ready for battle, and they would return the beat with their own weapons. Memories flooded his mind of laughter followed by war cries, friendly shoves in the barracks over meaningless games, followed by gritty, dirty fighting to be the one standing rather than dying.

He remembered the excitement before the bloodshed.

Alistair didn't seem too foreign from war. Regretfully, he was in his element.

CHAPTER SEVEN

Xander, standing on the desk by himself and towering over the Climbers, was as loud with his voice as his appearance. Though his effect was *too* effective, as he wanted responses, but he only managed stunned and scared silence.

He cleared his throat, which seemed just as loud. "As I was saying, there are some rules we must follow. We will split you all into groups of six led by a veteran. We have already mapped all of the first floor and cleared some of the monsters for today. Our goal is to have you proceed to the final challenge of the floor safely, though you still need *some* challenges! We're here to keep you alive but not do it for you. At least not from here on out.

"Also, any drops and rewards that occur during our first climb will be given out on decision of your group. If you are unable to make a decision or you simply don't care, your leader will decide and have the final say. Now! Let's split up into parties and find your teammates!" He pumped the air with his armored fist, striking a pose. There was a moment of awkward silence.

The large group of Climbers moved slowly, not separating at all but growing louder with conversation. Wyn looked over at John, who was giddy with excitement.

"Well?" Wyn said, nervous to ask but wanting to jump on the opportunity. "Would you want to be in a party together?"

"Absolutely!" John replied. "I'll help keep you alive, after all. That pointy stick will only get you so far." He laughed. Wyn did not, though he couldn't help but smile.

"I think I'll be fine," Wyn said. "And to answer your question, yes, I was. Seven years, actually."

John's eyes went wide. He stopped perusing through the crowd and looked Wyn up and down. "Whoa. You fought in the Great War? And made it out in one piece?"

"Sort of. I wasn't in it the whole time. It's a long story." Wyn's cheeks flushed. He shook his head, trying to keep his focus on the present and not dwell on the past. He was thinking about his unit and allies, the good times they shared, and the bad times they suffered.

"Fair enough. But I guess I don't need to worry about you, then. I take back what I said about it," John said, pointing to Wyn's spear. "You could probably use that better than most. Plus, I'm curious to see your magic!"

Wyn paled. Maybe he should stick to his combat only for this climb if he meant to keep friends and not embarrass himself.

John looked around at the other rookies. Most of them had started to pair off, and he noticed the mentors had left too.

Wyn quickly realized it as well. "Let's finish getting a party together first. Do you know anyone here?"

"Well, yeah, I trained with a bunch already. And there one is," John said, and ran over to another Fighter. They bumped forearms in a friendly, informal greeting.

The Fighter was taller than both John and Wyn, and stout. He wore chain mail under a shirt with a coat of arms on the right breast, though Wyn couldn't make it out. Which was odd, because he was familiar with most emblems of the country. The Fighter had two war axes on his belt, one looped under each arm. He was just as big as the veteran Climber who climbed on the desks, though not nearly as flashy or well equipped.

Wyn walked over, eager to meet his potential new teammate.

"I'm Wyn," he said, and extended his hand out for a greeting. "Nice to—"

"Oh, shit, you're that Red Mage, aren't you?" the man said, cutting Wyn off mid-greeting. "John, why are you so nice helping out the needy?"

Wyn balked as he was rudely cut off, and he felt as though the voice sounded familiar.

"Easy, Lionel," John said. "He's a good guy. And experienced. We'll be fine!"

"Ugh." Lionel sighed. "I'm always having to do the work. You'd be more useful as a Sorcerer," he said, pointing his thumb toward Wyn. "It's your lucky day, Red Mage, to be paired with me and John."

Wyn instantly remembered. His voice was the voice of the person who ridiculed him in the training hall, the Fighter that made the comment about his class. And now he was in his party.

"Yeah, we'll see," Wyn said. "I think I can handle myself."

Lionel laughed. "Oh, I'm sure you can, Mage."

Wyn started to reply to him, but stopped. It wasn't worth a response—his opinion didn't matter. They'd work together now, but he'd move on in the future. It was a necessary evil for this one climb.

"Anyway," John said, patting Wyn on the back, "we need a couple more. Hopefully a Garnet or Sapphire Mage to round us out? We can power through this tower in no time at all with one or two!"

"Shouldn't we have some healing or protection?" Wyn said. "And we still need three more for a group of six."

"Look at the Mage, thinks he's so smart," Lionel said, looking around the room. "Most are already partied up. We're too damn late."

One of the veteran Climbers came over to them with a rookie Climber trailing behind. They both were Magicians of some sort, Wyn could tell, as the veteran wore gray robes lined with yellow patterns interwoven in basic but beautiful designs. He had a book lashed to his side in a leather sling like a sheathed weapon. He was also walking with a staff that had a gnarled top with a topaz gem set within it.

There was no telling how much that gem was worth. Easily several hundred crowns. Selling it could feed a family through an entire winter, and this young man carried it around for a weapon.

Climbers were very, very different breeds of people.

The rookie, who Wyn saw was a young woman, wore a robe and carried a staff herself. Her hair was dark and curly, and she seemed well put together though simple overall.

It was as though she was trying to blend in with the other rookies, looking plain and boring despite her barely cracked leather boots and well-hemmed clothes. She obviously had money, likely a merchant's daughter. The staff she carried didn't have a jewel set in it, and she had a dagger sheathed on her side, so she didn't have the background like John.

"You three need to round out your group," the veteran said. He had a husky voice, despite being about the same age as Wyn, and clearly enunciated his words. "We've already placed the rest of the rookies in groups of six."

"Damnit," Lionel said. "Do we need to split up and join a different group? 'Cause I'm alright with that."

Wyn glared at him.

"No," the veteran said. "I have a rookie Diamond Mage here. Her name is Tasha." He waved his hand back toward the rookie to introduce her, and she shyly stared at the ground. "She will join our group."

"*Our* group?" John stepped in. He extended his hand to Tasha. "I'm John, by the way. This is Wyn and Lionel." He pointed to each of them when he said their names.

"Yes, *our* group. I'm Cedric. And we'll have an extra veteran with us since our group is short."

"There really aren't any other rookies for a group, huh?" Lionel asked. He kept scanning the other Climbers in the room, though Wyn wasn't exactly sure why. It could've been any number of reasons, though he was only half paying attention to the current conversation. He must've *really* not wanted to pair up with them.

"Afraid not," Cedric said. "But here she is."

"She?" Wyn asked.

Another Climber walked over to the group. She was obviously an archer, with a quiver on her back and a bow slung around it. The fletched feathers on the arrows were made of several different colors. Her armor was furs over leather, and it was covered in a strange green substance.

"Good afternoon, rookies," Marcy said, cool and confident. She winked at Wyn. "I'm Marcy."

John introduced himself again, and Lionel simply shrugged her off. Wyn was not getting a good impression of him, and something didn't sit right about him. It wasn't just that he was rude, but something deeper he couldn't place.

The rookies in the room all began to walk further into the tower, escorted by their veteran guides for their climb. Wyn was getting restless and excited, and apparently he wasn't hiding it well.

Marcy cleared her throat in the silence of the group. "Well, this isn't awkward at all. Hopefully all of you will open up some when we get inside. I don't want to be carrying all of you through the whole damn floor." She patted Wyn and John on the back before setting off to lead the group.

John, Lionel, and Wyn smiled. Tasha gulped.

"I like her," Lionel said. "I guess this is it, then."

"Good," Cedric said, ignoring Lionel. "Let's proceed to the portals. Marcy and I will show you the entrance and exit into the tower's actual challenges."

The rookies followed behind as Cedric and Marcy led them. The other groups had already begun to file off in the same direction, and they seemed to be last. They walked past the guild desks and into one of the wide, large hallways. It had the same look as before—stone walls and stained-glass windows, though both on a smaller scale.

At the end of the hallway was a smaller room, with multiple portals floating in the air, all scattered about. They were as big as a door but oval shaped, seemingly able to take a person in one at a time. Wyn had never seen anything like it, but he immediately noticed they were *beautiful*. He stopped to stare at the closest one. It was shimmering like a brilliant gemstone and radiated a heavy aura of magic. It was thick in the air and clear in color. Wyn was in a trance.

"This is an entrance portal," Marcy said, and ushered in the rest of the group around the one portal.

The rookies were staring at it, all with differing feelings. Cedric and Marcy simply smiled at each other.

Cedric cleared his throat. "We'll step inside this to start the true interior of Alistair."

"How does it work?" Wyn wanted to reach out and touch it but was terrified. And mystified. He was feeling many emotions.

"There are many portals to enter different floors of the tower," Cedric said. "Each floor has several portals, too. The difference is each portal will place each group at a different starting location on the floor."

"So will we all be scattered at the start?" Tasha spoke up. She wasn't feeling many things. She was just scared.

"No. Since you are all in a party, you'll start in the same place. The tower will separate parties from each other to give you all a bit more room to roam, so to speak. But you can still find other parties inside. It's strange, I know, but that's the tower's magic. Check your parchments."

The rookies took out their papers. Wyn noticed something interesting on the main page toward the bottom.

PARTY: 6/6
Alistair's Base

He had no idea how or when it showed up, but sure enough, it was there in ink, as clear as if he wrote it in himself.

The others must've seen something similar. They were all silently reviewing their own parchments.

"So you can see and check the new status," Cedric said. "You'll get changes like that on your parchment often. The tower keeps updating it periodically."

"Like what?" Tasha asked.

"Like the number in your group, your task at hand, or if you've cleared a floor. Oh, and a summary of your potential growth and rewards when you leave the tower and return here."

"A summary?" Wyn asked. "What do you mean?"

"Oh, I got this one," John said. "Correct me if I'm wrong, but after you spend time in the tower and then leave to return to the base, you get updates on your class growth and any treasure the tower rewards you with. You show your papers to the guild members at the desks where we walked in, and they pay you! I think."

"Yes, you're correct," Cedric said. "The tower chooses how to reward you based on your performance, though growth typically only applies to class upgrades. As I said, it's strange. You'll find out for yourself before long."

"My growth says *any* though," Wyn said. "What exactly does that mean?" He remembered Daniel mentioned all Ruby Magicians had "any" as their growth, but he didn't explain much further.

"Sounds about right," Lionel said, trying but failing to keep his voice low.

Wyn ignored him. He wasn't sure if he was scoffing at Wyn for not knowing or because of his growth being "any." Either way, the guy was an ass.

"Not what you'd hope," Cedric said. "Sorry, Wyn, but *any* growth means all of your characteristics have the potential to grow, but none will grow as quick as others like yours, Lionel." He looked over at the Fighter. "You essentially have the ability to grow in anything but *specifically will grow faster* in those three traits, and have future skills available that relate to them. When your growth is any, your skill progress is slower, and future skills could be anything, making your skill set potentially too broad to be specifically useful."

Wyn's smile instantly faded. The next instance of what made a Ruby Magician less popular and desirable showed up like a slap in face. It was nice to hear that his class could grow as he climbed, but if he was spread too thin with his potential growth, he'd fall behind others who were more specialized. Yet another reason why the Ruby Magician was less desirable that Daniel warned him about. It was hard to hear.

Lionel laughed, hearty and excessive. "That makes perfect sense! A Red Mage sucks like a Sorcerer. Too bad."

"But don't worry," Marcy said. "It still depends on how you use your class, Wyn. You could be the best class on paper but still make poor decisions or not be a team player," Marcy said, eyeing Lionel.

Wyn inhaled and exhaled deeply. His resolve to prove other Climbers wrong about his class was strengthened. Even if he obtained skills that didn't completely work in his favor, he'd use them to the best of his ability and make himself useful. It would be a challenge, but he was up for it. He'd faced worse and overcome them. His family depended on his success, and he wouldn't fail them.

"True," John said. "And he was in the Great War, so I'm going to stick close to him!" He inched himself away from Lionel a bit.

The others looked at Wyn. Cedric and Marcy sized him up, and Tasha's eyes went wide. Lionel simply narrowed his eyes and stayed quiet.

Wyn felt his cheeks flush from the sudden attention. He didn't particularly like having so much focus on him, especially when it came to his time in the war.

"How about we move on and try out the floor," Cedric said, seemingly reading Wyn's mind.

"Loud and clear," Marcy said. "The day isn't getting any shorter, after all!"

Wyn smiled and took another deep breath to calm himself. "You're right. I'm ready!"

"Looks like we got to party up after all," Marcy whispered. She smiled to him, then stepped into the portal. It swallowed her, or maybe allowed her to enter. Wyn wasn't sure which. It was a strange but exciting sight.

Wyn reached out with his hand at the portal to follow her. He didn't exactly know what to expect but he was confident—more than he had been in some time. He felt the pull of the portal and stepped inside.

CHAPTER EIGHT

Wyn immediately felt nauseous, like he was shunted out of reality and brought back a second later.

Which, to his surprise, was exactly what happened.

When he stepped through the portal, he didn't know how he would feel, though he was glad he at least kept his lunch down. When Tasha came through she began throwing up almost right away. Almost was key here, considering she was able to hold off long enough to step out from the portal's entrance and throw up a few feet away from where the others came through.

Lionel came next, followed by John and Cedric last. The rookies all took a few minutes to adjust, their heads and stomachs swimming.

"That was very uncomfortable," John said. He was holding his head as a headache pierced his skull. "No amount of preparation was enough."

"Exactly," Marcy said. "Which is why it's important to have these first-time climbs guided."

"I can see that," Wyn said. He took a few deep breaths and steadied himself. It didn't take his body long to settle back down, but he certainly didn't feel ready to fully engage in a fight at the moment.

Then he looked around.

"By the gods."

Wyn realized he was standing at the edge of a field. Behind the group was a small village surrounded by a wall made up of wooden logs. There was a well-worn road leading from the village toward a sparse forest of trees. Wyn realized they were standing by the road. The treetops and limbs were swaying with a slight breeze, and some patches of tall grass further into the field were leaning with the wind. The sun was high in the sky. Wyn noticed a small fire smoldering on the edge of the forest where the road lead deeper into the woods.

None of this was right.

"How in the hells is this possible? It should be late afternoon, not midday." Wyn tried to look further away. He could see clouds above him mostly covering the sun, and far away behind the village a mountain top crested high above the terrain.

A minute ago he was standing in the tower base, and now he felt like he was in another location entirely. Not only that, but this was far too grand to be fully inside the tower.

"The tower teleports us to a realm of its design," Cedric said. He was walking ahead toward the campfire. "Or at least that's what the researchers believe. No one knows *exactly*, but it makes sense."

"But the point," Marcy continued, "is that the tower is choosing a challenge for us. So for this month, the goal of the first floor was to find a little girl from the local village who got lost in the woods."

"How do you know that?" Lionel asked, then unsheathed an axe and inspected it. He looked at Marcy from the corner of his eye.

"Your parchment tells you," Tasha replied. She wiped her mouth with the sleeve on her robe in one hand and held her parchment in the other.

Wyn pulled his out from his pack and looked at it. Sure enough, continuing on from the information from the party and floor was new writing. It read exactly as Marcy told them, though more like a wanted poster in the town square.

"I didn't ask you," Lionel said. "I asked the Archer."

"I'm not an Archer," Marcy said. "I'm a Ranger. And you should be kinder to your teammates, especially the one who can save your ass."

Tasha tried and failed to hide a smirk. Lionel openly scowled.

John walked over to the campfire along with the rest of the party. He began to take the shield off his pack and attach it to his left forearm. It was dark gray, nearly black, and runes were etched along the edges. "Is that why you have green goo on your armor?"

Marcy sighed. "That's enough questions for now. You all have to learn this stuff on your own, after all. I won't tell you *everything*."

Cedric laughed. "So that means we'll shut up now. We have a few hours to accomplish our goal in order to be back in a reasonable amount of time. We'll help make sure you don't die in the process, but you should start trying to figure out what to do."

The group waited around the campfire, the rookies not sure about their next move. The smoldering logs weren't lit, and instead gave off a pitiful smoke that rose from cinders. It made a good point to commune, though, as the two veterans stood to the side silently.

Wyn took a deep breath and closed his eyes. He had to focus, and the fact remained that they had a task and a path to accomplish it. They needed to find a little girl, apparently, and the road that connected the village to the woods was an obvious starting point, as well as the old campfire. This was a good starting sign, and he wondered if other signs in the woods would be as easy to spot.

"Hey guys," Lionel said. "I found something." He stood by the edge of the woods away from the campfire. He was holding something in his left hand. "It looks like a little girl's ribbon."

"That's good," Wyn said. "It's definitely a clue. We should keep to the road and head into the woods. It'll probably form into a trail or something similar."

Lionel huffed. "No shit, it's a clue. And I found it! Catch up, stragglers, or I'll leave you behind." He laughed and pocketed the ribbon. He stepped backward with a slight skip and mocking smile, then disappeared after entering the woods.

"What an ass," Tasha said. "Do I *have* to keep him alive?"

"Unfortunately, yes," Wyn said. "We're better off sticking together. We'll accomplish our goal faster that way and stay safe." He eyed Lionel as he said it, trying to convince himself of those very words. Something felt off with him around, and he made a mental note to keep an extra eye on the arrogant Fighter.

Tasha sighed. "If you say so." She grabbed her staff and set off to follow Lionel. Cedric began to follow them as well, staying true to his word to keep silent.

"Think we'll be alright?" John asked, and he fiddled with the straps on his shield again.

"Yes," Wyn said. He grabbed his spear and secured his pack. "I do. We'll be fine as long as we work together. Climbers do this all the time."

"That's the spirit," Marcy said. "Stay confident and positive." She elbowed John in the side for emphasis.

"You're stronger than you look," John said, wincing.

Marcy's smile grew wide. "Just you wait."

Suddenly Tasha screamed. Marcy unslung her bow lightning-fast, and the three of them ran into the woods behind the others. They weren't too far past the tree line, but just enough to where John, Wyn, and Marcy couldn't immediately see the situation. A short trip into the woods and the trees were suddenly denser, and the sunlight didn't shine near as bright.

After a few seconds of running, they saw Lionel hacking into something on the ground with his axe. Tasha was beside him using a free hand to cover her mouth from the scream. Cedric was standing off to the side with his staff at the ready, away from Tasha and Lionel but staring intently further into the woods.

"What in the hells happened?" John said, unsheathing his sword as he ran behind Lionel.

Lionel stopped hitting whatever he was hitting with his axe. "*That* happened."

John looked down in front of Lionel at a pile of green goo and dark black bits. Lionel's axe was now green, dripping with the slimy substance. His armor was speckled and blotched in areas of it, too.

John bent down to inspect it closer. "Is that what I think it is?" A long, hairy appendage twitched once, and John fell back on the ground with a yelp, dropping his sword.

"Yeah," Lionel said. "A spider the size of a small dog! It came down from the tree beside Tasha. I just started hitting it."

Tasha held her staff close to her chest. She wasn't screaming anymore but was as white as a sheet and completely still, breathing soft and deep.

Wyn looked over at Marcy. She was calm and collected, unfazed at the situation. "That's what you're covered in, isn't it? You cleared these out before we came inside?"

Her face twitched a bit as her muscles worked to keep her thoughts from expressing themselves, but the faintest hint of a smile curled on the corner of her mouth.

Wyn walked over to the group. "So there are spiders here. It's darker here, too, even though we're only a bit into the woods. It's reasonable to assume it'll get darker the deeper we go, too."

"Just our luck," Lionel said. "I didn't bring a torch or lantern."

"Me either," Wyn said. "And you know there are probably other things here, too. We *have* to stick together so we can be more prepared."

"We *are* together," Lionel said. He wiped his goo-covered axe on his pants.

"No," Wyn replied. "You and Tasha went ahead, out of our vision."

"So? I handled myself just fine. Her scream scared me more than this piece of shit."

"Which is great, and I'm sure you can handle yourself with a bigger one, too. But what if there were five of them instead of just one?"

Lionel glared at Wyn. He shook his head and took a deep breath. "Yeah, alright, Red Mage. But who put you in charge?"

"No one! And I'm not trying to be the leader. But for now we need to have a plan and stick to it. We're here to beat the tower, not argue."

John grabbed his sword and stood up. "He's right, you know. That's why we came to Alestead! So let's work *as a team*!"

Tasha cleared her throat. "Yes. Let's do it." She seemed to relax a little, though kept her staff close to her chest.

"All of you are ridiculous," Lionel said. "Whatever."

"Alright!" John said, swinging his sword in an arc. As he did, it lit up in flames, runes on the hilt activating the magic inside. The other rookies recoiled from the sudden burst of flame. "Onward!" As he yelled he stuck his flaming sword up and forward.

The flame from the sword lit up the area above them. The sudden burst of light and heat made the previously hidden hanging spiders shriek and flail. The noise was eerie and unnatural, like high-pitched squealing and chittering. There were several close ones that had started to descend before the others, following the first that was felled by Lionel. Their hairy legs jerked away from John's flame, scurrying helplessly in midair while suspended by thick strings of web.

Tasha screamed again.

Wyn reacted quicker than the others. He raised his left hand in front of him and thought of the spell he wanted to cast. The brief review of magic and spells with Daniel suddenly seemed laughably inept, but Wyn hoped to the gods it would work.

"*Ice Shard*!" Wyn yelled, and *felt* his mark activate. He could see it glow out of the corner of his eye under his sleeve, too. It was an incredibly odd but invigorating feeling.

A series of magical runes instantly formed in the air in front of Wyn's left hand the moment he said the spell. They were the copied runes for the *Ice Shard* spell, and a sharp, pointed slice of ice flew directly away from his hand. It was fast, too— faster than arrows from a bow and possibly as fast as those from a crossbow.

The shard of ice crashed into the spider closest to Tasha, dangling from a singular web strand above her. It pierced its main body, and the momentum took it further back into a tree, pinning it like a nail. Its legs curled as it went still.

Lionel acted nearly as quickly, though his efforts to strike at the nearest spider were in vain. He tried to swing his axe high in the air to strike it, but it was too far out of reach, even with his height. He swung upward several times, hoping to hit it as it lowered.

John, initially shocked at seeing the many spiders, snapped out of his inaction. He saw the closest spider and swung his sword at it, activating another rune on the sword. The flame that coated the sword's blade lashed out, growing several feet in an arc. It caught two spiders on fire. They began to shriek and cry continuously before falling from their web, the connection breaking from the flames. They fell in a fiery heap to the ground.

The other spiders stopped their advance and retreated back into the treetops, their black bodies blending in with the leaves and dim light. The woods became silent, save for Lionel cursing and the flames from John's sword crackling.

Cedric walked over to Wyn. "Not bad! That was an impressive cast."

Wyn briefly heard a chittering sound and thought the spiders were waiting up in the trees to attack again. A loud *thwack* came from Tasha's direction, followed by more thumps and pounds.

Wyn looked over and saw Tasha was beating a spider with her staff, green spider's blood flying everywhere. She was groaning with the effort. Random shrieks filled the air, but whether from the spider or Tasha was impossible to tell.

He ran over beside her along with Marcy. Cedric went to check on John and Lionel.

Tasha's robe was now a splotchy bright green, and beads of sweat formed into streaks on her forehead. The spider was a mashed pulp beside her.

"That's unconventional," Marcy said. "I like it!"

"It was quieter than the others," Tasha said. "I never saw it. It fell on my shoulders, and I knocked it off in a panic."

"It's alright," Wyn said. "You took care of it."

"But my shoulder and back hurt," Tasha replied, and turned her back to them. "I think it bit me. Is it bad?"

Both Wyn and Marcy winced. Tasha's robe was cut, and she had puncture wounds on her shoulders and upper back like shallow stabs from a knife. The wounds slowly bled, and large welts already formed around them.

"You've been bitten a couple times," Marcy said. "We need to heal you. Nothing serious, though."

She began to reach for her pack, but Wyn caught her wrist. He briefly saw that her mark was on her left hand and wrist and had two outer runic circles.

"Let me," Wyn said. "We have to be the ones to do this, right?"

Marcy nodded and stepped around to where Tasha could see her. She held the Mage's shoulders and looked her in the eyes. "Wyn will heal you. You'll be fine."

Wyn set his spear against the closest tree and thought of his next spell. "**Regen**," he said, and again felt the mark activate. The runes appeared in front of his hand and hung in the air, emanating a soft white glow that seemed to spill out onto Tasha. There was a radiating aura that started at her back and shoulders, then transferred to her whole body. She looked like a gently radiating white firefly. The wounds stopped bleeding right away, though Wyn guessed it would take the entirety of the spell's length to heal her. He didn't know if it would fully heal her, but it should at least close the wounds.

A smile flashed across Wyn's face subconsciously. It was strangely funny— here he was, in a magical land inside a magical tower, casting magic.

Wyn suddenly thought that maybe he should be timing the spell to see how long it lasts. It had only been a few seconds so far, and he began counting in his head to get an idea of the spell's length since the description was vague.

Another thought occurred to him. He pulled up his sleeve to expose his mark. It was radiating magic, giving off a similar glow to Tasha. Less than half of it was dull and gray, as though it wasn't being used.

Tasha relaxed her body, physically relieved by Wyn's spell. "That already feels better!"

"You didn't choose **Cure** as your healing spell?" Marcy said, letting go of Tasha's shoulders. She walked around Tasha to look at her back.

"I figured most healing Mages would prepare it, so I chose something else," Wyn said.

"Not a bad idea, but you'd be surprised how useful an instant healing spell is," Marcy said, satisfied with Tasha's back. She looked over at Wyn's mark. "Did your mentor tell you about your mana reserves?"

Wyn thought about that for a second. "Not entirely. I rushed him to get ready to climb today. I believe I remember him saying, 'You'll figure the rest out.'"

Marcy laughed. "Of course he did! Typical. Well, we don't have an exact measurement of our mana. But you just *know*. Like an intuition."

"He did say it was like how we know our mental or physical energy stores. Like when they're full or low."

"Something like that. But your mark is glowing because your spell is still working. It does that with skills, too."

"What about passive skills?"

"Depends. But every class is a bit different, so your mentor was right—you really will need to figure it out for yourself. I'm not familiar with Ruby Magicians."

Wyn sighed.

"I think I'm better," Tasha said. "Thank you, Wyn." She stopped glowing right then.

Wyn blinked, remembering he was trying to count the time. He figured it lasted about three minutes, though wasn't exactly sure. He wondered if spells could even have exact times, or if they varied depending on different factors.

Marcy checked her back again. "It looks great! Can't even tell what happened!"

Wyn looked down at his mark. It was still glowing. The outer runic circle wasn't glowing now, but only the center image. It was slowly radiating inward, becoming softer and dimmer like the dulled bit from earlier. At least half of his mark was still glowing, and he wondered if **Lucidity** was already working.

It must be, but he needed more experience to truly figure it out. There's no way he'd learn it all now.

"Everyone okay over here?" John asked, as he, Lionel, and Cedric joined the rest of the group.

Marcy and Tasha filled them in as Wyn was still distracted with his mark. He wasn't fully listening.

Tasha waved her hands in front of Wyn's face. "Hello? Wyn?"

"Yeah, sorry," Wyn said, and dropped his arm. "Still trying to figure out magic and my mark."

"Aren't we all," John said. "But let's go. We can do it later when spiders aren't plotting our demise."

Wyn picked up his spear. "Fair enough. Do we know where to go?"

They looked around. It was even darker than before. A small sliver of light permeated through the trees, though it was much darker in the denser forest.

Tasha held up her staff. "***Torchlight!***"

The end of her staff glowed like a bright lantern, much brighter than a torch, and the group shielded their eyes for a moment.

It was incredibly effective, though.

"Sorry," Tasha said. "We need a light, and we need to get going."

"And that's where we need to go," John said, and pointed with his sword again.

There was a small path leading deeper into the woods split by trees, which was a bit more worn than the undisturbed forest floor. It was a clear trail though not very wide.

"Then get on with it," Lionel said. He waved his axe. "I'll lead. Tasha, you should be in the center so we can all see. I don't care about the rest of you." He immediately set off toward the trail without waiting for a response.

Wyn looked at the others and shook his head. At least if something attacked, Lionel would be hit first.

CHAPTER NINE

The surrounding woods were eerie with the absence of light and the strange transition from the side of the village to a darker forest. It was as though they stepped into a new place altogether, not the woods set next to a village that seemed normal. These woods had a creepy feel to them, danger falling from the trees or wherever else the tower decided.

It was exactly that, though. A new, magical place that the tower presented to the group of Climbers, a challenge to overcome and push through. Wyn was still mystified and impressed all at once.

He stopped to feel the leaves and trees, and they felt so *real*. He had wondered if this was going to feel fake or something would be off, as though the tower had created a fake image or copy of the real world to populate its residence, but it didn't feel that way at all. It was *alive*.

"Strange, I know."

Wyn jerked his hand from the tree in surprise and whipped his head around. Cedric was standing behind him smiling, his staff in his right hand.

"This whole place is nothing like you thought, is it?" He had a sly smile on his face, and was failing to suppress it.

"Not at all," Wyn replied. "It's so *real*."

"It's because it is. It's as real as it gets."

Wyn thought about that for a second. "I guess I didn't think much about what was *in* the tower, only what I could gain from it. I knew it was dangerous, but still."

"Some people believe the tower actually holds this environment, that it changes for a new season every month into something different so people can't exploit it for too long," Cedric added. "So you climb the tower literally after each floor, hence the height."

"And others believe different," Lionel said.

Cedric turned his head sharply, eyes wide. He quickly settled down. Lionel was standing behind him, listening quietly.

"What do they believe?" John asked. Everyone was listening at this point, eager to learn more about the tower. Marcy was the only one not interested, holding a small splinter of wood and absentmindedly picking her teeth.

"They believe the opposite," Lionel continued, "about the environment here. That the tower actually transports people to another place. An entire plane of existence, actually."

"Whoa," John said. "That's . . . hard to imagine."

"I'll say," Tasha chimed in. "How can one magical reason be crazier than the other?"

John scrunched his face. "Huh. I'm not sure. That's a fair question, to be honest. But why would the tower be so tall, then?"

"Because of what it represents," Lionel said. He was inspecting a tree, the same one Wyn was standing beside. He ran his hands up and down the bark as though he was familiar with it. "It's a monument. A marker of a challenge for those deemed strong enough to find true meaning and prove themselves worthy."

Cedric narrowed his eyes. He glanced over at Marcy. She was standing against a tree but tossed her toothpick to the ground. Her arms were crossed, and she nodded. He nodded back.

"I know, I know," Tasha said. "That's the goal of all Climbers—climb the tower, survive, claim your rewards."

Lionel jerked his hand from the tree and cleared his throat. "Exactly. Which surviving isn't easy with all the monsters and traps here."

"Oh, those spiders weren't that bad," John said. He waved his sword in the air. "We handled them just fine!"

"That sword of yours is something else," Lionel said. "It's no fair that you're a decent Climber, too."

"If you're not careful, Lionel, I'd say you're starting to like me."

Wyn suddenly heard a low growl from the darkness further down the path. It wasn't loud, but it was obvious, specific in its nature. He looked into the dark woods but couldn't see too far past Tasha's magical light. The shadows and darkness were oddly heavy, and based on his experiences it shouldn't be this dark at this time.

Just as Cedric and Lionel both said, though, the tower was different. Even the environment was not normal. Wyn knew he needed to be more on guard here than ever.

Another growl echoed the first.

"There are other things out here besides spiders, John," Wyn said. He grabbed his spear and readied himself. "I heard growls in the thicket. Get ready!"

Lionel raised his axe. "I've been ready. Stay behind me, and you won't get hurt."

Wyn stared at him. Then, uncontrollably, he stared *through* him. His mind wandered, and he lost his focus.

". . . stay behind me, sir, and you won't get hurt! We can't afford to lose you!" A hollowed voice came from a far away time. A blurry man dressed in armor and holding a sword and shield stepped in front of Wyn. The scene was like looking through still water, murky and unclear, sounds muffled and dull, but he could still make out what was said.

"No!" Wyn yelled back, trying to stand up from a kneeling position. He failed, falling back to his knees. He looked down and saw a bloodied, dirty arrow shaft sticking out from his stomach, the white feathers clean and pristine. The arrow was as clear as the morning sun, a point of clarity in the haze of memories.

The soldier guarded Wyn with his shield, standing tall and towering over him. The sky was orange with the setting sun, the land around them muddy and littered with bodies, both humans and horses either lying still or frantically writhing about.

It didn't make sense. They were supposed to surprise them, not the other way around. It was a setup? How? The enemy knew they were coming, and they were ruthless.

The orange sky turned dark. Wyn looked up as a large flock of birds silently flew over them, the messenger of death signaling he was coming.

"Stay down, sir! Please!" The face of the man was clearer. Only it wasn't a man. He was no more older than a boy, barely seventeen, his first engagement in war. Wyn looked past him at the sky, at the fast-moving birds.

No, they weren't birds. They were arrows.

Their silence quickly faded as dull thumps hit like a barrage around them, screams and cries responding everywhere. The loudest was in front of Wyn, as the boy blocked most with his shield but not all.

Wyn finally gathered the strength to stand in the mud. The boy then lost his strength and fell on his shield. Wyn looked down, arrows littering the muddy field like flowers of death, their white feathered fletching like morbid daisy petals. Several were sticking out of the boy, who was now silent, quiet and still. He had used his shield to block Wyn, and where he couldn't block him, he used his body to shield the rest.

The scene faded into a cloud as quickly as it came. Wyn was knocked on his back, shouldered from a tackle by a large wolf. He looked up from the ground, aching and pained, and saw a canopy of dark leaves and limbs from trees, not an orange sky. He shook his head. Immediately in front of him was a wolf growling and snarling, its teeth bared as bloody saliva dripped from its mouth.

Wyn could feel the hot air it breathed on him, the smell of a canine's breath—pungent and real. He snapped back into reality instantly, the gravity of the situation cloaking over him in warm, dangerous air. He saw a flash of sharp teeth and knew it was over.

Wyn closed his eyes softly, accepting his fate. The fate stolen from him not long ago in a muddy field of death and daisies, a time borrowed and short-lived.

A loud thunk hit flesh. He shot his eyes back open in surprise. He thought of the field, the many arrows that penetrated man, beast, and earth, and recognized that gruesome sound.

Only he was here in the tower, about to be eaten by a wolf. Suddenly, though, the wolf fell hard to its side, blood seeping from its neck.

A bloodied, dirty arrow shaft stuck out from its neck, the colored feathers clean and pristine. Both arrow and beast lay still.

"Get it together, Wyn!" a far-off voice yelled.

Wyn looked around. Marcy was standing about thirty feet away, her back to a tree. She had an arrow nocked and drawn, though she stared hard at Wyn.

"Get off your ass, I said!" she repeated, and loosed an arrow at another wolf.

Wyn saw the arrow fly into a gaping mouth scarily close to Tasha's arm, the very arm that supported her staff—the group's sole source of light. She whimpered and closed her eyes, scared, though the wolf fell midair with an arrow protruding from its skull.

Wyn took a deep breath and audibly blew out hard. He was dead weight, almost literally. He didn't want to fail another group, and needed to focus. His eyes darted around the area, scanning the situation.

Tasha was standing in the middle of an open area of the magic forest, her staff glowing and giving off light. It was bright but not overly bright like the sun—it offered as much brightness as a torch, but it reached further than a torch ever could, its magic working to light up their area. The wolf Marcy slayed with her arrow lay beside her, and she was shaking, her staff vibrating with her nerves and sobs.

She was terrified, and Wyn didn't blame her. The setting was chaos, and outside their circle of light was darkness and more unknown dangers.

Cedric stood at the edge of their light peering deeper into the forest. It was as if he saw further despite the darkness, looking for other threats. He very well could see past there, his skills unknown to the rookie Climbers. Marcy was standing on the opposite side on the edge of their light, the two veterans sandwiching the rookies in a protective manner. She had already fired two arrows, felling a wolf with each one, and had a third ready.

John was waving his flaming sword around, using it like a torch to ward off the wolves. It was working, thankfully, as three wolves had him surrounded but weren't openly attacking him. They were crouched low and snarling at him, ready to attack, though hesitant from his deadly, magically flaming sword.

Wyn heard a sound he knew all too well—the slurping, wet sound of metal meeting flesh. Only it was exiting instead, and he turned his head to see Lionel pull his axe out of a Wolf's back. There was another dead wolf that lay beside him.

"You useless Mage," Lionel said. He took a quick, heavy breath and steadied himself. "Do something already—don't just stand there!" He trotted over beside John and began to swing at one of the wolves surrounding him, yelling as he moved.

Wyn clenched his jaw, angry at Lionel, though mostly for him being right—he was not only useless right now, but by not acting he was causing the situation to be even worse. His knuckles went white as he gripped his spear in anger, and a sudden jolt of pain erupted from his left arm when he tried to lift his spear. His robe was ripped and shoulder bloody. The wolf didn't just tackle him—it took a small chunk out of his shoulder.

Ignoring the wound, he ran over to Tasha to support her.

"Are you alright?" he asked her. She looked over at him, her eyes large and frantic. She was blinking fast and turning her head in seemingly all directions to check for danger.

She didn't answer him.

"Okay," Wyn said, "listen. We'll be fine. We need you, though. Just in case."

Silence.

"Tasha."

Her breathing slowed when she heard her name. She looked at Wyn, staring, and allowed her gaze to soften. She seemed to relax a bit. Her staff stopped shaking so heavily. Then, she gasped.

"Wyn, your shoulder!" Without a response, she pointed her bright staff at him. *"Cure!"*

A wave of refreshing energy washed over Wyn's left shoulder, followed by a tingling where the tissue and flesh magically regrew and reformed. He saw the same effect on Tasha's back from his own spell, but this effect was instant.

"Thank you," Wyn said. He moved his arm around, and it thankfully felt perfectly normal.

"You're welcome. I can at least do that."

"Yes, you can. And watch for people getting injured so you can heal them, too."

She nodded, and looked over at the two Fighters who were standing their ground. Or, more accurately, where Lionel was wildly swinging his axe and John was matching his chaos with a flaming sword.

Wyn chuckled to himself. It was absurd, but effective. At least for now.

Out of the corner of his eye he saw a wolf circling them. It was eyeing John, waiting for the opportunity to attack. John didn't see it as he was preoccupied with the wolves in front of him, having struck one down with his sword already.

Wyn patted Tasha's shoulder in reassurance and began to work his way left, slow but steady. He knew that if he'd be able to circle it himself, he could catch it off guard. He'd have to be quick, though, and quiet.

The ground was soft under his feet, as the grass was tall enough to soften his steps but not impede his advance. He crouched low and moved with purpose. He didn't want to move too slow in case the wolf decided to attack, but didn't want to alert it, either.

Luckily the tactic paid off.

Wyn was able to get right behind it before it closed in on John. He lunged quickly, launching off his rear foot, and jabbed his spear out with force.

He pierced through the wolf's haunches at an angle, feeling less resistance than he anticipated. The spear tip protruded through the wolf's left front shoulder, as Wyn staked it from its right side. He pulled the spear back, and the wolf fell in its place, dying immediately.

John sliced through another wolf, the magical fire searing the wound as he cut it. It whined and limped for only a second before John sliced down at another angle, following up his first strike.

The area of the woods went suddenly quiet, save for the sound of leaves and branches swaying in trees they couldn't see. Wyn breathed deep, settling his heart rate.

Both John and Lionel didn't look tired at all. Tasha was sweating more than all of them, though mostly from fear.

"I didn't know what was going to happen," Marcy said. She walked over to the group and still had an arrow nocked though not drawn. "Especially from you. I wasn't expecting you to freeze, Wyn."

Wyn's cheeks flushed. He looked at the ground and squeezed his spear hard. Truth be told, he didn't expect to freeze, either.

John flicked his sword and the flames subsided. He sheathed it to rest. "What happened?"

"I . . ." Wyn started, and paused. "I had a memory overtake me. From the war. When you said to stay behind you, Lionel, it drew it out of me. I'm sorry."

"You're a liability," Lionel said. "A weak Red Mage in class and a weak person in experience."

"Hey, that's not fair," Tasha said. "Just because he's not a popular class doesn't mean you can put him down!"

"He's a shit class, and he could get us killed, too," Lionel said. "Being in the war is not a good thing. Not if you clam up like that when we need help."

Wyn pursed his lips. He kept quiet, because he knew Lionel was right, unfortunately. Again.

"Well, he seemed to snap out of it," John said. "We'll be fine. Just try not to let it happen again, Wyn, okay?"

"I know," Wyn said. "I'm sorry. Truly. I lost my focus and realize now how dangerous it is here. Of course I won't let it happen again."

"Then it's settled!" Tasha said. "I mean, I froze, too. Let's just move on. If anyone got hurt I'd heal them."

"You're a White Mage," Lionel said. "You aren't supposed to fight. No offense. He's a Red Mage, and a veteran. He has both experience and a class that encourages fighting. It's inexcusable."

"I've seen things I'd rather forget, Lionel," Wyn said. "And I'm sure people have seen and experienced things in this tower, too, but it was war. Fought by soldiers that could barely be called adults. And no magic to heal them when they got hurt. At least not the grunts, anyway."

The group was silent for a moment.

"Still," Lionel said. "I'll take care of myself. I won't rely on you or anyone else. I don't trust anyone."

"Then your time here will be difficult and unpleasant," Cedric said. "Climbing the tower means working together. If you don't do that you don't succeed—period."

"We'll see about that," Lionel replied. "No obstacle here will stop me. Just wait."

"At least we took care of the wolves," John said. "So that's encouraging!"

"There's more out there," Marcy said.

"Wait, what?" John asked. "How do you know?"

"I'm a Ranger! That's part of my class. I can hear and see them. Is that scary to you?" She nudged him in the ribs with her elbow playfully.

Cedric laughed. "I've always been jealous of that."

Wyn looked at Marcy. She might've been joking around, but there was more to her than she let on. Cedric, too. So maybe he wasn't the one looking into the dark—she was.

John groaned. "Then maybe we should keep going? Let's stick to finishing the floor. There's an objective, after all. And it's not killing everything in here."

"Agreed," Wyn said. "We stick to the same formation. Keep going down the path deeper in."

Lionel immediately set out ahead of the group without another word. The rest followed, falling in line.

Wyn's gut still felt unsettled. Lionel wasn't team-minded, and though he didn't have much room to talk, Wyn felt he'd be a liability in the long run. The Fighter said he didn't trust anyone, and Wyn certainly didn't trust him.

The quicker they could finish the climb, the quicker he could move on from the guy.

"Come on," Marcy said, poking at Wyn. "We'll be fine. You, too."

Wyn smiled. As much as he wanted to get away from Lionel, he wanted to partner up with Marcy that much more.

CHAPTER TEN

Tasha had one hand on her knee, and the other held her staff. It was still lit from her spell but dimmer. She was breathing hard and sweating profusely, her robes damp and her hair matted to her head. She leaned against a tree for support but was reluctant to sit to rest, knowing she and the others would need to continue on soon and that stopping would make starting again that much harder.

The group of Climbers were taking a brief solace from following the trail deeper into the floor, trying to finish their goal of finding a little girl who was lost in the woods. They had been successfully following a trail led by various objects that a little girl would carry—a ribbon, a doll, and a little shoe. It was creepy, they thought, but it was their goal, nonetheless.

The woods were nearly pitch-black this deep, Tasha's spell being their sole light source. They couldn't see too far around them, so they protected her and kept her at their center. The sky above was almost completely covered by leaves and branches of trees, and it felt like night even though their sense of time was distorted and false.

"How are you guys not tired?" Tasha asked, stopping to breathe between every few words.

"**Resolve** is certainly helpful," John said. He held his sword at the ready and was scanning the woods. He forced himself to slow his breathing to combat his own fatigue, but he hardly seemed tired at all. "Plus I've been training for a while. You have to be prepared!"

"What is **Resolve**?" Wyn asked, leaning on his spear. He was also recovering from the trudge but felt good, his years of training having come in handy for the physical test of the tower. He was sweating, but his muscles didn't ache. He was thankful for that.

"It's a passive Fighter skill," Lionel said. "It improves our overall strength and endurance." He was inspecting his axe and didn't bother to look at Wyn. A dirty mixture of red and green blood covered his shirt. "Helpful for sure."

Tasha huffed and put her head down. She wiped the sweat off her forehead.

"Well, Tasha, you're doing great," Wyn said. "Thanks for the healing and light, too. Those wolves were nasty. I'll need to remember some better armor instead of this robe." Wyn looked at his left sleeve—or rather, what was left of it. It was shredded and his mark was exposed, though his wounds had been healed by Tasha when able.

His mark was still glowing as the passive skill *Lucidity* worked to slowly restore his mana. He had used more of his stores firing two more *Ice Shards* at wolves.

Lionel and John both had wounds that Tasha also healed, but they were the only others. Cedric always seemed to be in a position where he wasn't attacked, and the few times he came close Marcy took care of the beasts and spiders for him. To her credit, she picked the various enemies apart before they ever came close to her. She was obviously very skilled as each arrow was perfectly placed, which was extraordinary in the heat of battle. Wyn wouldn't have believed it if he didn't see it for himself.

John obviously felt the same way as he commented on her accuracy nearly every time.

"I thought you veterans were supposed to clear this place out?" John asked. "There are spiders and wolves everywhere!"

"We did," Cedric said, as he wiped his forehead of sweat. He was tired, too, especially after climbing this floor at least once. "The tower will always bring in new monsters. But we did thin them out. It seems like it's nearly back to the amount we started with, though. What do you think, Marcy?"

"I think you're right," Marcy said. "I wasn't planning to go through so many arrows this time. I only have about a dozen left."

"*About* a dozen arrows, she says," John said. "Even though you could kill twice as many monsters with those."

"So we've heard," Wyn said. He smirked at John and lightly slapped him on the back.

"Well, you should use them," Tasha said, standing up from the tree, "because I'm running low on mana. I want to save the rest for my *Light* spell. Unless you all want to finish this in the dark?"

"Oh, no," Wyn said. "It's very helpful. I can help heal from here on out, too."

"Not as good as her," Lionel said. "So how about we just kill things before they kill us? I think you're better at that than healing, anyway."

Wyn stared at Lionel with an open mouth. Did he just compliment him?

"I never really recovered from my mana from before," Cedric added. "But there's enough to finish. We aren't too far from the end. Let's keep pushing."

"What's that over there?" Tasha said, and pointed with her staff to a tree stump.

It was shimmering in the dim light, a faint green aura surrounding it. It was radiating magic.

"You lucky ducks," Marcy said. "That's a treasure chest!"

"Treasure?!" John said, nearly yelling, and ran over to the stump.

It was more obvious close up, and John knew it. It was a wooden chest that appeared like a tree stump, round with a flat top instead of a square body with a rounded top. He flipped it open without hesitation.

"Whoa."

Inside was a small collection of coins, jewels, and a small vial of liquid. The vial swirled with a light shade of blue.

"What's in it?" Lionel asked, and ran beside John. He looked inside and visibly deflated. "That's it? Money and a lousy potion? I want gear. Weapons and armor."

"How much is it?" Wyn said. He wanted to patiently wait for John to count it, but he was excited, too. It was strange to just find a small cache of items, but he wasn't going to complain. Any opportunity to help him obtain more coins was a welcomed one.

"What is the potion for?" Tasha asked.

"Settle down, children, settle down," John said, the most excited of all. "While I count the coins and jewels, why don't you figure out the potion?"

"I'll do it," Cedric said. "Save your mana, Tasha." Cedric grabbed the vial from John and inspected it. He grabbed his staff and said, "***Identify.***"

A large, magical rune appeared over the vial. It glowed a brighter blue, beautiful in color. It was hard not to look at the magical display. Cedric then pulled out a small piece of paper from his pocket and looked at it.

"It's a mana potion," he said, reading the results on his parchment. "That's not a common find!"

"I'll take that instead of my share of coins," Tasha said. She eyed the potion and was entranced by it. To a mage a mana potion would be invaluable.

Wyn didn't blame her for not wanting more of the cut. He felt envious for the potion.

"I'm fine with it," John said.

"Sure, whatever," Lionel added.

Tasha grabbed it and held it carefully, like a newborn kitten. She pulled her robes back to reveal a thick leather belt around her waist. There were loops and empty spots in them, and she placed the small vial in one of the loops.

Wyn couldn't help but stare, his envy growing. "Where did you get that belt?"

"My mentor bought it for me," Tasha said. "At a tailor's shop in Alestead. The same one that made my robe, actually."

"I'll have to see which one when we get out. I need some better gear." Wyn dangled his ripped left sleeve. He definitely needed some armor, let alone clothing. At this rate he'd spend all of his money just on clothes.

"Me, too. I don't think standard robes cut it. I need a magic set."

"Can you buy that?"

"Sure, but my mentor said it's better to trade for items at the trading hall. She's a bit biased against the shops, but I've liked them so far."

Wyn nodded, but was as lost as the new recruits he used to train. There was so much he needed to learn, and part of him wondered if it was a mistake coming in so quickly.

"Alright!" John said. "I've counted it up! There are fourteen gold crowns, twenty-one silver cloaks, and forty-seven copper boots. Plus a small ruby, onyx, and jade."

A strange wave of relief fell over Wyn. He was thankful the currency in the tower was their own, though it seemed odd to find it here.

"Wyn should get the ruby," Lionel said. "You know, since that's you and all."

"Lionel, are you being nice to me?" Wyn asked.

"No, 'cause rubies are shit," Lionel said.

Wyn sighed.

"But treasure is treasure," Lionel added. "And you did spear that wolf that nearly bit a chunk out of my leg. So thanks for that."

"You're welcome."

"Aww, look at you two," John said. He put his arms around both of the rookies. "Getting along and making up!"

"Bite me," Lionel said, and shrugged John's arm off his shoulders. "And give me my money."

"Alright, alright!" John split the currency evenly and handed out the spoils. The three rookies went about to store it in their packs. John looked back at Marcy and Cedric, who were whispering to each other and watching the woods. "And you two don't get any, right?"

"Right," Cedric said. "We got our share when we cleared this floor out to begin with."

"*Mostly* cleared," Marcy said. She winked at Cedric. "Have to let them have a *little* fun."

"You call this fun?" Tasha asked. "This place is horrifying. I had no idea this is what the tower would be like!"

"Surely you had *some* idea," John said. "I knew it wouldn't be easy but it's *exciting*. I feel alive!"

"Well, yes, that's true," Tasha said. "But seeing it in person is completely different. I just need to get stronger, I guess."

"You will," Cedric said. "Everyone does if you stick with it and climb smart. When you get reckless and make stupid decisions is when you end up hurt or dead."

"Same with life, honestly," Wyn said. He slung his pack around his shoulders. "The war was the exact same way. People died when they didn't think ahead or prepare. Though I'll admit sometimes it's just dumb luck, too."

Cedric nodded in agreement.

"The military is one thing, but the tower is pretty different," Lionel said. He put his axe back on his belt loop. "A spear isn't a popular choice, but you're not bad with it. Not many know how to wield it well."

Wyn inspected his spear for a moment. It was basic and bland, just like he was used to using, though a large part of him was curious about the magical weapons he'd find.

"We trained in many weapons," Wyn said. "It's the one I'm most comfortable with. That and the sword and shield."

"Now *that* is a truly great choice," John said, as he patted his shield. The runes flickered. He then closed the tree stump chest and sat on it. "I chose this combination last year and began training with it. It's the best combination of attack and defense, in my opinion."

"Why did you choose to climb the tower?" Wyn asked. He leaned against a tree opposite John. "I know you said your family climbed it and were successful. But surely they told you how dangerous it was."

"They did, yeah." John stretched before resting against a tree. "But it was basically expected of me. My dad was actually a shopkeeper and my mom's main supplier. They took their earnings and moved out to Veritas. He opened a general store, and she kept training. Then my sisters and me all came along!"

"Moving to one of the major cities with no previous land is impressive," Tasha said. "So you went into the family business, so to speak?"

"Sort of. They never forced us. My sister climbed higher than my mom, finishing floor 17 and taking her spoils back home. My parents were *so* proud, but not nearly as proud as me and Quinn, my little sister. But now she's rich and traveling all of Jahnin!"

"Wow," Tasha said. "She sounds incredible."

"She is. But why are you here, Tasha? No offense, but you don't seem like the type to be excited about climbing the tower."

Tasha paused, stiffening for just a moment before relaxing. "No offense taken. My father wanted to enroll me into Keyworth's—"

"The magic college?!" John interrupted. He threw himself forward away from the tree.

"Yes. He's a Wizard and wanted me to follow his footsteps. I didn't want that life."

"So you came to the tower and still became a Wizard?" Lionel asked. "That's the same thing. Only more dangerous."

"It's not the same thing," Tasha said. "I would've had to study for years at Keyworth's. Sitting in a classroom, reading textbooks, practicing magic on dummies and targets for years only to either join the Great War or teach back at the college. It sounds so . . . *boring*. At least here I can go at my own pace with something new every month."

"But it's not what you thought, is it?" Wyn asked.

Tasha sighed. "No. It definitely isn't. But I'm here, and I need to make the best of it! I just hope I made the right choice."

"I think we all feel the same way," Wyn said. "I know I do."

"So what about you, Wyn?" Tasha asked. "If you were in the military, you must've been paid well. You survived, obviously, and most survivors go home with *some* wealth, according to my father. Able to start a new life with plenty of cloaks and crowns to their name."

"I did, yes," Wyn said. "Make money, I mean. And I survived. Which not everyone can say, especially those in my company."

Wyn went quiet. His mind wandered back to the hill, but he forced himself to be present. No more mental wanderings.

"I lost some people. Allies. Friends. But my family back home are farmers. I didn't want that life, and still didn't when I came home. But my sister told me about some bad deals our parents made and that to keep our farm they went into some serious debt with people they shouldn't."

"I've heard of that before," Lionel said. "Thieves' guilds all over Jahnin demanding high interest for loans they know will ruin those who actually need the money. Forces them to do whatever the guilds want."

"Exactly," Wyn said. "Then our mom left us. Still not sure if she left on her own or was taken, though my father says she bailed the moment they were caught. I might not ever know the truth. At the end of the day, it doesn't matter since they were shitty parents and people. But my sister isn't fit to work the fields, and my father is too stubborn and foolish to do anything else. So I decided to try to make money the quickest way I knew."

"How much do you need?" John asked.

Wyn felt a hitch in his breath. "I'd rather not say."

"I'm sorry you're in this position," Tasha said. "But I'm sure it's not *that* bad in the grand scheme of things."

"Bad enough to come to the tower as a last resort? I left the military for this life. I could've stayed and been promoted, but my only shot is here. Nowhere else can get me the amount I need in the time demanded."

"How much, Wyn," Marcy said, more of a point than a question. She was standing by the tree line and keeping an eye out, but now she was invested in their stories. Wyn's obviously caught her attention. "Not to be an asshole, but desperate people do desperate things. Just how desperate are you?"

Wyn sighed. No sense in keeping it a secret. "75,000 crowns."

John spewed his mouthful of water all over the ground, and Tasha gasped. Even Cedric was shocked, fumbling his staff in his distraction.

"Yes. My father is a fool! First the banks turned him away, then the merchant guilds. He found the wrong person that put us all in this situation. Owed money and promised to pay it back, and the last two years have been awful for crops. He kept borrowing and kept borrowing. All of this happened while I was gone, and I came back to the news after he forced my sister to lie in her letters. I left for the tower right away."

"How long does he have to pay it back?" Lionel asked.

"Until the end of the year."

The group all looked at each other.

"That's not too bad," John said, finally breaking the silence. "That's nearly the whole year and still six more months. You can make a lot in that time! Maybe not the whole amount, but at least half if you're smart about it."

Wyn laughed. "I have to make at least 12,500 gold a month. They threatened him, John. First it was a warning—according to my sister, he came home bruised and bloodied and couldn't work for almost two months. Now it's an arm if we don't deliver. Honestly I couldn't care less about him, but he still has to work for my sister's sake, and I don't want them to turn their attention to her. Who knows what's next, but I can't let it go on."

The others were quiet. The forest was strangely quiet, too. It had perfectly emulated a real forest with all the sounds of wildlife scurrying about, branches falling from trees, animal calls and sounds. But oddly, in this very moment, there was an eerie hush around their small lit circle of the first floor.

Marcy stood up quickly with her ears pricked. She spun around and pulled an arrow from her quiver in a flash, nocked it to her bow and drew halfway.

"Something bigger is here," she said. "Not a spider or wolf—my ***Extrasensory*** kicked in."

Wyn looked at John, who simply shrugged his shoulders. He didn't know what that meant either.

Still, the group grabbed their gear and readied themselves.

"Is it the floor boss?" Lionel said. He twirled his axe in his hand and crouched.

"No," Cedric answered. "We aren't at the end yet. It must be a champion. That's rare." The topaz gem at the end of his staff lit up and began radiating magic.

"A champion?" Wyn and Tasha asked at the same time.

"It's the floor adding in an extra challenge," John said. He swung his sword and activated the runes, setting it ablaze. He raised his shield so he could just see over the top. "Monsters that are stronger than normal for the floor. My sister warned me about them."

Wyn steadied himself. They couldn't see too far into the woods due to the darkness, and Tasha's staff was effective but limited to a fixed point. John's sword helped to see with the magical flame, but Wyn needed to be ready.

Wyn, Lionel, and John all surrounded Tasha in the middle. Cedric and Marcy stood toward the edge of Tasha's *Torchlight* spell, and Cedric had his back to Marcy. Tasha was holding her staff and shaking again.

"It's alright, Tasha," John said. "Just stay in the middle to give us light. We can handle this!"

At the edge of their light, where the trees were dim and shadows were more present, was movement. Wyn saw a small tree writhe and separate like it was splitting itself apart. Bark and branches cracked as it took a different shape.

Then he saw another tree beside it do the same thing. Then a third.

The new trees moved toward the group slowly. They weren't wide or tall but changed their height to be the size of a person. Wooden arms and legs looked vaguely human, but something entirely different, too.

They were creatures born from the tower itself, not twisted beasts or insects. They crept closer, slowly, and came inside the group's light together.

They were wooden warriors, all wielding weapons—one a large club, one a sword, and one two daggers. Their gait was slow and jerky, though purposeful in their direction. Thick bark covered vulnerable spots like natural armor, wooden reinforcements that seemed to be part of them rather than accessories. Where a face should be was a blank slab of wood except for red glowing eyes that darted between each Climber.

The monsters began to separate, slowly attempting to attack them on different sides. They mimicked Lionel's crouched stance with their weapons raised.

Wyn didn't want to assume anything in the tower, not if he wanted to be careful, prepared, and alive. These enemies appeared smart with some degree of intelligence, not unlike the wolves with their tactics. The difference was these enemies wielded weapons and seemed far more durable and dangerous.

No more flashing memories, only action. This was a threat too great to ignore. Wyn knew what he needed to do. It was like he taught his company—strike first, strike swift.

CHAPTER ELEVEN

The wooden warriors oddly reminded Wyn of the dummy back at the guild training hall. They had similar features, wielded weapons, and were magically created. Unfortunately, that's where the similarities ended. Here they were out to kill, the tower's sadistic way of challenging its Climbers.

Wyn sidestepped to the left of the group, hoping to challenge one of the champions himself. The closest one was the one with a club. He knew it was a more favorable matchup with his spear being faster and him being agile, though he wondered about the skill of these new enemies. At first glance they certainly looked stronger and more capable than the beasts they'd been dealing with so far.

If they were too fast or too strong for them, he knew Cedric and Marcy would step in, but they'd still be in trouble. Not to mention the rookies didn't need to rely on the veterans to fight their battles—they were here to grow and learn, and they had to be able to do that even if the challenge was difficult.

The club-wielding tree monster homed in on him and matched his readiness, raising its club to strike. Wyn was crouched and held his spear in front of him, similar to Lionel though lighter on his feet. He started to slowly circle around the monster, hoping to keep its attention on him. The enemy also crouched and circled now, separating from the other two to focus on Wyn.

Wyn decided to strike first, hoping to get an early upper hand. He lunged out quickly, stabbing forward where the neck should be. There was no extra bark armor there, and he was hoping they had vulnerabilities like humans. His strike was aimed well, though the figure leaned back just out of reach to avoid being stabbed. It then raised its club overhead and swung it as Wyn dodged the swing with a quick side step.

The wind from the club tousled Wyn's robe. The monster was faster than he expected, and the club more than a mere piece of wood. He realized the weapon was a small tree, and the end was a gnarled mess of dirt, roots, and wood. It made a loud thud as it hit the ground, and dirt scattered about both from the tree-club and the ground after the impact.

It was obviously strong. Too strong. And quick. Wyn knew right away that if that strike connected he'd be knocked out or more likely dead.

An idea clicked in his mind. He took a step back to give himself some room and time. The spell would hopefully activate right away, but he wanted to be sure. After placing his left hand on his chest, he glanced at his mark. There seemed to be enough mana for the spell, as it was recovered just over halfway. His mark's symbol was still lit, gathering mana from **Lucidity**, though the outer ring was dull. He instinctively knew it was enough.

"**Arcane Aura**!" Wyn yelled.

A magical rune appeared in the air in front of him in a soft white color similar to his **Regen** spell. It hung in the air for a second, the circles of magic turning slowly, before rushing toward Wyn in a swarm. It covered him like a sheet, and the magic became an aura around him. A layer of armor was created from his spell, covering his torso, head, and thighs, though it weighed nothing. He radiated some light around him, too, being able to see his immediate area a bit better than before.

He nearly laughed to himself. While the danger was ever present, using magic really was special.

Just as the spell took hold the wooden figure stepped toward him and brought its club up for another attack. Wyn again dodged it as the club whiffed the air and missed him. He thought he might not need the spell if he was able to dodge it consistently, but he was cautious. He'd get tired before the magical creature would.

Wyn brought his spear up and stabbed into the figure's thigh. He hit his mark, though the spear thudded against it and bounced off as though he stabbed a tree.

Which, in a way, is exactly what happened.

The two continued their lethal dance several more times—club swinging and missing, spear stabbing harmlessly. Both were locked in a stalemate of ineffectiveness.

"Guys, I'm not having any luck over here!" Wyn shouted. "My spear is useless against its body!"

"Speak for yourself!" Lionel yelled back. He was locked into the fight with John against the other two champions. They were more successful on their end as John's flaming sword and Lionel's axe were both effective weapons against enemies made of wood.

John clashed sword with sword and shield, parrying the enemy's strikes with his shield and effectively striking back. His sword wasn't doing much on its own, but the magical flames radiating from the blade made large, burnt gashes in his foe. The armor was stripped away after a few strikes, sloughing off like melted wax. Even when John would miss with a direct attack, the flames would lick at the wooden body, catching fire here and there in a literal heated fight.

Lionel quickly gained the upper hand against his enemy as well. The dagger-wielding champion was quick, but his strikes were shallow, glancing off Lionel's chain mail with every cut and slash. His shirt was shredded, though. He would counter with his battle axe at well-timed moments, cleaving bits of bark off with each contact. The champion was fast and dodged with high agility, though Lionel was smart with his attacks and connected more often than not.

Both Lionel and John were good Fighters, keeping their edge intact. Tasha was holding her staff and keeping the *Torchlight* spell active, watching the fights around her nervously but keeping her composure. She took deep breaths to keep her nerves still.

"We might not be needed after all," Marcy said to Cedric, still holding a nocked arrow. They were both watching the group handle the champions. "They're doing fairly well."

"You know how it can change," Cedric said. "Keep your eyes out. We're still tasked with keeping them alive, after all. Even if we are supposed to let them succeed or fail as much as possible."

"Yeah, yeah. I know." Marcy kept looking around. Something felt *off*. Her *Extrasensory* skill was alerting her, but she couldn't quite make it out. They were already aware of the champions, but the skill was still activating within her.

"Ha!" Lionel yelled. A soft thump came from the ground as his enemy's arm fell, lopped off by his axe and a lucky swing. He took the opportunity to attack faster, and was able to chop off a leg on the same side. The champion fell, now off balance, and Lionel quickly chopped into it like a logger splitting a tree, except more carnal and barbaric.

Wyn, however, continued to struggle. This fight was dragging on, and he was aware of it. He was getting tired and had only splintered the armor on his foe, despite managing to luckily avoid all of the slow club swings.

That was true until his fatigue caught up with him.

He stepped to the side to dodge yet another attack when his foot caught on a lump of grass. The recovery was too slow, hindered by fatigue. He managed to avoid most of the club's force but still took the majority of the hit on his right shoulder, knocking him back several feet and onto his backside. The magical armor dissipated at his shoulder as it took the majority of the blow, but it still felt like he was kicked by a horse.

He took a quick, gasping breath. His arm was nearly numb, but he could move it, at least. A silent prayer went up to the gods it wasn't broken. The realization that the spell saved his life and prevented his torso from being smashed hit him nearly as hard as the club.

No need to dwell on that, though. He needed to finish this.

The tree monster had its club at the ready and was pacing him again, taunting him. Wyn's spear was near useless. He realized, here and now, the importance of a magic weapon and their effectiveness against the tower's monsters.

He looked at his mark through his shredded robes. It was still recovering mana but had enough after his **Arcane Aura** spell for one more, based on his intuition.

Wyn waved his left hand slowly over his spear and thought about the spell he wanted to use: **Magic Weapon.**

He didn't even need to say it. The mark protruded itself like before when he cast a spell, magic runes appearing in front of him and around his spear, covering it with magical light. His spear lit up a bright white, the same color as his magic armor, and gave off a bit more light in the dark. It hummed with magic and shimmered in the darkness.

The spell wouldn't last forever—Wyn knew he was racing against time. In fact, he didn't know exactly how long it would last, so he also knew he needed to be smart and act quickly. If the spell faded and his spear lost its magical ability, he'd for sure be useless against it.

He took the opportunity and decided on one last attack. If it didn't work he'd need to back off and let someone else handle it. He hated the thought of not finishing the job because he couldn't do it, so he decided to risk it.

He ran toward his enemy and swept its leg with his spear. His weapon was stronger, and he *felt* stronger wielding it. He hooked behind the foot and pushed it to the side, hoping to throw it off balance.

It worked.

The champion's foot slid to the right from the force of the spear, harmlessly bringing the club down awkwardly. Wyn swung the spear around and butted it in the stomach. He figured it wouldn't do much, but he was hoping it would tell him if the spell would be effective or not. He could back out now if it wasn't, or keep going if it was.

The shaft dug into the bark armor and beyond, piercing several inches into thick wood. The warrior doubled over and stepped back as if the wind was knocked out of it, if that was even possible.

Wyn saw a hole in its torso that was bigger than the shaft of the spear. Even though the hit was with the blunted end, the magical aura seemed to amplify the power of the weapon.

Seizing the opportunity, Wyn twirled his spear around and performed one more attack—slashing across the torso followed by a stab.

It was more than effective. The slash left a large, gaping gap of wood that Wyn felt was as easy as cutting through paper. The stab went straight through the champion's neck, well past the spearhead. Wyn's momentum carried him further than he wanted, and he stared at the monster face-to-face in its red eyes.

He watched as its eyes dulled and became a lifeless husk of bark and dirt that fell to the ground.

"Damn, Wyn," John said, walking over beside him. His sword wasn't on fire anymore. "What in the gods did you do? You're glowing!"

"It's a spell," Wyn answered. "And the magic on my spear is my spell *Magic Weapon*." He looked at his spear. The aura was still there, pulsing and vibrant. It felt alive.

"That's helpful. I wonder what it would do to a weapon that's already magic?"

"Huh. I don't know. I'll need to ask my mentor about that."

Wyn made a mental note to ask Daniel about the spell when he returned. His list of questions was growing quickly.

"You guys are amazing," Tasha said. She looked at the champion John slayed. It was a pile of harmless wood and ash, some parts still smoldering. "But that was creepy."

The fallen champion Wyn defeated began to glow. He and John readied their weapons, unsure of what was happening.

A small, dim glow of bright green was coming from the wooden body. It wasn't moving, but rather began to dissolve like acid. It only took a few seconds, and what was left underneath was a strange object and the source of the glow—a hunk of wood.

"What in the hells is that?" Wyn said. He bent over to look at it closer. It didn't seem dangerous, so he picked it up. It was truly a hunk of wood though it was radiating a small amount of magic.

"It's the reward," Marcy said. She walked over and inspected it while Wyn held it. "Monsters in the tower will sometimes drop items. This one is a common crafting material. Not too special."

"Says you," John said. "I can't wait to see what else we find!"

"Mine had nothing," Lionel said. The others jumped when he spoke, startling them. "I finished chopping it up and wanted to see all the fuss."

Marcy perked up again. She drew her bow, pulling the arrow back and anchoring it on her jaw. The others stood confused.

"There can't be more already," Tasha said. She stood in the middle of them to offer them light.

"Something else is here," Marcy said.

The woods appeared to be alive. The trees swayed and moved similar to before.

Wooden branches cracked and thudded against the ground, falling from something unseen. It was like a miniature, focused storm around them they couldn't see.

The group huddled closer together and drew their weapons. Cedric joined them in the circle, no longer standing back to watch them.

Something didn't sit right with Wyn. Marcy and Cedric looked like they were about to intervene rather than let the rookies fight. He wondered what was beyond their light.

More wooden enemies suddenly formed from the trees. They had varying types of weapons, though most of them wielded branched clubs or nothing at all. They slowly stood, stretched, and then crouched in an attacking position. They began to slowly move toward the group.

There were nearly two dozen of them.

"By the gods," John said. He lowered his sword. "I don't think we can take all of them."

"We have to try, damnit!" Lionel said. He raised his axe.

A bright light shot from Marcy's bow with a twang from her bowstring, startling the rookies. Wyn thought he heard her say something but didn't make it out.

The arrow flew quickly, striking one of the wooden monsters in the head. It caught fire immediately, his wooden head now engulfed in a harsh and powerful flame. It dropped to the ground as fast as it was hit.

It was a fire arrow. And a powerful one, at that.

Marcy drew again. Wyn saw the fletching right before she fired—red feathers.

She downed another, this time hitting it in the torso where its heart would be, if it had one. It began to catch fire and burned longer than the previous one, producing more light for the group to see.

"Anytime now, Cedric," Marcy said. "I don't want to shoot *all* my arrows!"

"I know, I know," Cedric said. "Everyone huddle together."

He raised his staff, and the topaz gem at the end began to glow. He pointed it at the closest enemy, not ten feet behind them.

"*Lightning Arc*!" he shouted.

Wyn stared wide-eyed as he saw a large runic circle, much larger than his own spells, appear at the end of Cedric's staff. A large flash of lightning formed and shot out from his staff even quicker than Marcy's arrow. It exploded the first enemy in a loud pop as wood chips rained down around what used to be solid wood.

The sound was deafening, like someone clapped right inside their ears. The rookies all flinched, barely following the bolt of lightning as it flew. The after-effect was more noticeable than the spell itself.

Wyn next saw two more arcs of lightning fly out from the now-charred corpse into nearby champions with a similar speed and clap of thunder, though a bit slower than the original flash. It continued several times, the arcs splitting away and forming new streaks, until all of the enemies were smoking husks of burnt wood.

The area was silent for a few moments. The rookies' ears were ringing from the sound of the spell. Marcy and Cedric, however, were used to the noise, seemingly unaffected.

"Show-off," Marcy said. She seemed to relax for the first time.

"Sorry everyone," Cedric said. "But that was unusual for the first floor to have not only a second wave of champions, but that many. I figured we would just get rid of them quickly and move on."

"Holy shit," John said. "I . . . wow."

"I'll say," Lionel said. He eyed Cedric up and down, gripping his axe harder. "What in the hells kind of spell was that?"

"A powerful one," Cedric said. "I wanted to make sure they were finished. Though, admittedly, it might have been a bit of overkill."

"You think?" Marcy said.

Wyn and Cedric both laughed. Tasha stared at them dumbfounded.

"Let's just get on with it," Tasha said. "Get me the hells out of here."

"I think some dinner sounds nice," John said. "Lionel, maybe some sparring after, too? I'll go easy on you this time." He mockingly patted the other Fighter on the back.

Lionel snickered. "I'd like that. You spar better than you climb." He grabbed John on the shoulder in a friendly manner, then jerked his hand back as though the gesture physically hurt him.

He shook his head and cleared his throat, ignoring the looks from the others. "Let's just find that trail again."

The group began to search for the path to continue on, except for Lionel. He suspiciously watched the group, never letting go of his axe. Wyn didn't bother to ask why—he was ready to move on and move away from him.

In minutes John picked up the trail and led the way. Lionel followed behind the group this time, keeping his distance. Wyn didn't mind, but something still felt off. They cleared the enemies, but he just couldn't explain what it was. Marcy seemed on edge, too, so at least he didn't feel like the only one.

Wyn sighed. Onward and forward. It wouldn't be long before they'd be finished, and he'd be able to sit down and think about the challenge the tower presented. He only hoped the final challenge wasn't too difficult—he had a long ways to go to be useful in this strange place.

CHAPTER TWELVE

A re we there yet?" John asked. He was getting impatient and rushing the trail toward the final area. They were back on track following the clues from the little girl, their current goal for completing the first floor of tower Alistair.

"Gods, I don't know," Tasha said. "I'm so ready to be out of these dark woods. It's creepy!" She was still holding her staff that was giving the group light. She had to recast it not long ago, though she was grateful it was a basic spell that didn't cost too much of her mana.

"We're almost there," Cedric said. He was toward the back of the group walking with Marcy. "And we've only been in here for a couple of hours. It took us longer than that to map it out and clear it today."

"I've been meaning to ask about that," Wyn said. "All of the veterans that are leading the groups cleared it this morning? The *entire floor?*"

Cedric smiled. "Yes."

"But it couldn't have been too difficult for all of you. I'm sure you've cleared much higher floors."

"Sort of," Marcy answered. "It depends on what you consider much higher."

"The tenth floor?" Lionel asked.

"Almost," Cedric said. "We're working on the ninth floor right now."

"Which isn't bad for our group," Marcy added. "We've only been together for a season and don't even have a guild yet."

"Hmph," Lionel grunted. "I've heard of better." His interest left as quickly as it came.

"That's pretty good," John said. "Most new groups take a few months to make it that far! And those that move past the tenth floor are usually only in guilds."

"Why is that?" Wyn asked.

"The resources needed to finish it safely," Cedric answered. "Those floors are larger and deadlier. More people means more skills, talents, and ability to bring in items and money. Not to mention sponsors and backers, too."

Wyn stopped walking. "You're kidding. People sponsor guilds? Like actually pay them to climb?"

"Well, yes. For clout and respect in their social circles, but also for special items from the higher floors. You'd be surprised."

"That's . . . believable, actually. I just never thought about it."

"The guilds that are sponsored are the guilds that last. As long as they keep producing quality climbs."

"Who cares," Tasha said. She threw her free hand up and sighed with great exaggeration. "We can talk about all of this back in the city. What's going to be at the end of the floor so we can get back?"

"It can be several different things," John said. "But it's a major obstacle that separates one floor from the next. A difficult puzzle, a monster boss. Even just finding it is sometimes the challenge."

"Or a combination of those," Marcy said. "As you'll find out here."

Tasha bumped into Lionel, who had stopped walking. She was listening to the conversation and not fully paying attention to where she was going.

"I think this is it," Lionel said. He looked out of the woods into a clearing. It was strangely lit as a series of dim lights were scattered around the edge of a wide, curving tree line. They couldn't tell exactly what they were, but the lights made the area visible enough to where Tasha felt comfortable stopping the light spell from her staff.

The clearing was a large open area set in front of the mouth of a cave. There was short, almost manicured grass with large rocks scattered about, and a strange red magical shimmer covered the mouth of the cave.

"What is that red aura?" Lionel asked.

"It's the entrance to the second floor," Cedric replied.

"Why is it red?"

"It's closed until the first floor's final challenge is complete. Then it will turn white and open, allowing you to enter."

"But the floors are open to all groups. What's to stop a guild from powering through the floors and rushing a rookie group with them?"

"Don't forget your parchment," Marcy said. "We're in a party. Unless our party faces and defeats the challenge it won't open for us. The tower will continue to provide a final test as long as there is a party willing to challenge it, so there could be an endless number of final tests."

"At least at higher levels," Cedric added. "We're doing that in a way, now, by guiding all of you through the first floor. But if you don't grow with your experience and skills, you'll eventually become a liability to yourself and your group."

Some groups of other Climbers stepped out from the edge of the forest. They all appeared battered and worn, having faced other paths through the first floor to come to this ending. They were standing and waiting.

"Maybe we should go out, too," Wyn said.

"Already ahead of you," John said, as he stepped out into the clearing. "I want to be a part of the group to clear the challenge! So even if you guys hang back I'll get us through. That's how it works, right?"

"It can, yes," Cedric said. "As long as someone in your party helps overcome it. But you all should pitch in. It'll make this go smoother and hopefully with fewer injuries."

The rookies all stepped out, with Lionel and Wyn walking further into the clearing beside John. Tasha stayed behind them to offer support but didn't want to be directly in the fray.

Wyn noticed Lionel wasn't his usual confident self. He was changing his gaze between the other groups and the portal constantly. He played with the axe on his belt nervously with his fingers, like he was itching to use it. That wouldn't have seemed too odd, considering their situation, but Lionel seemed to have kept his nerves in check the whole time. Something was off, but Wyn couldn't pinpoint what it was.

"What now?" Lionel said. He drew his axe and began to spin it in his hand. He rocked back and forth between each foot.

He looked . . . paranoid. Wyn was thinking about asking him what was bothering him but was distracted. He was eager about what would happen next, too.

"We wait for the challenge to present itself," John said. He drew his sword.

Other parties that surrounded the clearing were similarly gearing up for their challenge. Whatever the challenge was going to be would have a difficult time with nearly every rookie present. It seemed like all of the Climbers from the guild hall just a few hours ago were standing here.

Wyn suddenly felt a rumble beneath his feet. The ground shook, the earth under them vibrating as the scattered rocks began to shift and move. He steadied himself to keep his balance.

In the middle of the clearing popped open a hole. It wasn't big, but it was definitely noticeable. It started to grow bigger as the earth around it rose, pieces of rock and dirt falling over each other having nowhere to go. The energy rising from beneath then exploded above ground, and several shouts and yells came from the Climbers.

A large, hairy leg popped through the hole. Then another. And another. A bulbous, huge body followed, and a spider the size of a horse crawled out of the hole.

Then another followed behind it.

They dwarfed the spiders they'd killed so far. They began crawling out into the clearing, two identical arachnids moving steadily but with obvious force. Their fangs looked to be the size of daggers, and their legs were long and thick like crooked, ugly, black trees. The only saving grace was that they appeared to move slow relative to their size, their legs working in an eerie tandem.

It would take them a minute or two to crawl to the closest group of Climbers, but some of them began rushing toward the spiders with a battle cry, eager to finish the floor. More groups quickly followed suit.

"Not again," Tasha said. "I *hate* spiders!"

"At least there are only two of them," Wyn said. "And look how many there are of us!"

Immediately two more spiders of identical size came out of the hole.

"You just had to say something, didn't you?" Tasha said.

"Let's go already," Lionel said. He began to charge the spiders with the rest of the Climbers, leaving John and Wyn behind.

"He's brave, I'll give him that," John said.

"I guess," Wyn replied. "Still, he's not entirely wrong. You ready?"

"As I'll ever be. Tasha, stay behind us. Make sure we don't die, okay?"

"You'll be fine," Tasha said. "Plus, the veterans are watching over us. This is meant to be practice, remember?" She smiled, though nervousness came across more than confidence.

The three followed behind Lionel heading toward the fight. Several groups had already met the spiders, and the clash of weapons and arachnids began. Screams of horror and excitement came from all over, and the shrieks of the four spiders joined the symphony of battle. The many Climbers with their weapons, skills, and magic were able to overpower the spiders and their size and strength, working together to fight them with relative ease.

Wyn was joining his party in attacking one of the monsters, a combination of distracting strikes and powerful blows hitting the enemy on all sides. When Climbers would be thrown back or hit they would be healed almost immediately, as both rookie and veteran mages were healing them to make sure they weren't anywhere close to sustaining an actual threat of death.

Wyn stopped and pulled back, wanting to watch the spectacle around him. Another party had joined theirs to attack this spider, and he knew they were going to easily kill it. He noticed the veterans were also firing magic from the back lines, helping the rookies when possible. He took special notice of Cedric as he saw his staff flash, followed by vines from the earth grab hold of the legs of the spider they were facing. It held it in place long enough for the rookies to finish their onslaught and defeat it.

He remembered his time on the hill in a far away time in a far away land. Their company was outnumbered, running toward a guaranteed defeat that they didn't know at the time. It was a slaughter, and his soldiers were on the receiving end.

For a brief moment he pitied the spiders and the tower's attempt at defending itself against a small army of intruders.

Then he thought of what the tower was. It wasn't an opposing country and army, with its own beliefs and clashing ideas fighting oppressors. It was a challenge, a means of proving oneself by climbing and showing their worth in a place that could never be truly conquered.

Wyn shook his head and snapped back to reality. Regardless of the means, he was still fighting and could get hurt or die. Shouts of victory rang out around him as four large bodies were cut and beaten and slain, and Climbers reveled in their quest's end.

"What a rush!" John said. "That was incredible!"

"It doesn't seem so bad after all," Tasha said. "What do you think, Wyn?"

Wyn saw Marcy and Cedric walking down to meet them. The parties were all hugging and celebrating with each other, happy to finish their introduction to tower Alistair. Who knows what they met and found on their way here? It was all different, and tomorrow the path here would be different, too. It was an odd feeling.

"Wyn?" Tasha said.

Wyn caught a glimpse of Lionel staring at the portal to the second floor. It was now clear, though the aura that showed it was a portal was still there. It was enticing, a call to keep climbing and face another challenge. He felt it. It was magnetic, drawing him in to see what was behind it. He believed Lionel felt it, too.

Or so he thought.

"Wyn?" Tasha repeated. "Hello?" She waved her hand in front of his face.

Wyn blinked several times. "Sorry," he said. "What did you say?"

"Never mind," Tasha said. "I'm just glad we're done. Now how do we leave?"

"Good question," Marcy said. "There are magic keys that will return you to the base. Or, when you step through the portal to the next floor, you can choose to return to the base instead."

"Really? I didn't know that," John said.

"Yes. The tower will sense your will. If you want to stop and go back it'll send you back. If you want to keep going, it'll take you to the next floor."

"But once you're there," Cedric said, interrupting her, "you either have to have a key to return or finish the floor. It's a risk if you're unsure of what to do."

"Do you have a key?" Wyn asked. "Maybe we should use that." He thought of what he wanted. Did he want to go back? It was hard to tell. What if he went through and the tower accidentally took him to the next floor?

His heart skipped a beat. He decided he didn't want to take any chances.

Marcy laughed. "I get it. You're drawn to the next floor. We've all been there."

"I agree with Wyn," Lionel said. "You should use your key." He kept eyeing the portal and the rest of the parties.

"I used mine earlier today," Marcy said, "when we cleared it the first time. I didn't bring a spare."

"I have mine still," Cedric said. "Here." He took a large, almost ridiculously large, key out of his robes. He walked over to an open area and pushed it forward into nothing like he was pretending to open a door. When he turned it, though, a portal that was big enough to walk through opened in the space. It was the same color and appeared exactly like the portal that led to the next floor.

"Here you go," Cedric said. "Easy as that."

Wyn looked around. The other parties also had veterans who opened portals back to the base. It didn't seem like any of the Climbers there wanted to step into the portal that could lead to the next floor. They steadily walked through them, all returning after their successful first trip into the tower.

"Thank the gods," Tasha said. "I'm ready for a warm bath and dinner!"

Before they stepped through the portal, Marcy's ears perked, and the hairs on her arm stood on end. A shiver ran down her spine, and she froze.

Wyn saw her and knew something was wrong. She looked the same as when the champions showed up not long ago. The final monsters were defeated, though—why was she sensing danger?

Cedric noticed her, too. He frantically looked around for another threat, another monster to fight and defeat. Nothing stood out, as though it was a false alarm.

They were wrong.

John had a sudden look of confusion and jerked forward with his chest. Lionel stood behind him and dropped his axe.

"John?" Wyn said.

John put a hand to his back and coughed. Blood spewed out of his mouth before he fell forward on his hands and knees. Lionel quickly grabbed John's sword before he completely collapsed onto the ground.

There was a dagger embedded in John's back nearly to the hilt.

Lionel started sprinting toward the portal to the next floor, John's sword in his hand.

"NO!" Wyn yelled, and immediately ran after him. His mind started to return to the hill, but he suppressed the memory in a fit of rage.

"Heal him!" Marcy yelled at Tasha. "And get him back to the base!"

Tasha stood, frozen. She was too shocked to move.

"NOW!" Marcy yelled. She was already running after Lionel, though she lagged behind Wyn. In a swift motion she nocked an arrow and fired it quickly while running. It was awkward and misplaced, and the situation wasn't the best for firing arrows. It zipped beside Lionel, barely missing him but alerting him to an attack. He ducked in response, hoping to avoid another attack.

The arrow may have missed him, but it did slow him down. He was almost at the portal, and Wyn and Marcy made up some of the distance. She drew another arrow but realized they wouldn't reach him before he went into the portal. Instead, she redoubled her efforts into catching up to him, hoping her next shot would be on the other side when she could properly aim. If she stopped now, she'd never make it to the next floor to help Wyn or before Lionel could escape.

Cedric, choosing not to run, already had a spell prepared and pointed his staff. He hesitated. His only spells were meant to harm, and only for monsters, at that. What did it say if he attacked a person? Though Lionel already betrayed them and tried to kill John. That was reason enough to retaliate.

In his time of indecision, Lionel was too far gone and almost at the portal. Wyn and Marcy were directly in his line of fire as well, making it impossible to accurately hit the Fighter.

"Damnit," Cedric said. He looked at Tasha and John. "Tasha, stabilize him before he dies!"

"I can't," Tasha said. She was staring at John on the ground. "I . . . I don't have enough mana."

Cedric bent over and held John. He was unconscious and barely breathing. Cedric pulled his hand away, now covered in blood. They were the only Climbers left in the tower, the others already back at the base. No one else could help him.

Tasha suddenly gasped. "Wait! I do have enough!" Her free hand shot to her belt and pulled out the mana potion she acquired earlier. She uncorked it immediately and drank.

Pulling her staff up she spoke her spell—"***Cure!***" They both saw John's body relax a bit. She repeated the spell again, hoping it would heal him further. She reached down for the dagger, but Cedric grabbed her hand.

"No," he said. "Let the medics handle it. Just keep him alive."

"The bleeding stopped, at least," Tasha said. "I can keep healing him for now."

"Good. Then we will take care of Lionel." Cedric looked toward the portal. The open area in front of them was empty except for the spider carcasses.

Cedric helped drag John toward the portal, Tasha holding on to John to the best of her ability. He pushed both rookies into it, and they vanished without a sound.

Then Cedric was running toward the floor portal without another thought. Marcy and Wyn would need his help. He couldn't let Marcy and Wyn go by themselves. Whatever happened on the other side with Lionel wasn't the final straw—they would still need to finish the floor since they didn't have another portal key.

Two veteran Climbers and a rookie against a traitor and another floor of the tower.

His mind was already made up. He felt the pull of the portal as it whisked him to the second floor.

CHAPTER THIRTEEN

Wyn tolerated moving through the portal much better his second time. It was a stranger sensation since the first, almost like a delay, not quite as fast as before. As though the tower was taking an extra second to decide where to send him.

His desire to chase Lionel to the second floor easily overcame his desire to leave, and he found himself standing inside the mouth and entrance of a large cave. A wave of fatigue washed over him since he stopped running.

He looked around between breaths and was immediately thankful he could see, not standing in pitch-black darkness. The cave was lit by clumps of glowing moss and various mushrooms scattered on the walls that spread from the ground to the very top of the ceiling. They emitted a soft glow, all varying in color, and the shimmer was similar to the treasure chest they found on the previous floor. There were also holes in the roof of the cave where beams of sunlight pierced the room, adding to the brightness, though it was still darker than out in the open. He could see better than he did with Tasha's **_Torchlight_** spell, and much farther, too.

Lionel stood at the far end of the cave that seemed to lead deeper inside. He looked relaxed, almost peaceful, despite just stopping from a complete sprint. He faced Wyn with one hand by his side and the other holding John's sword.

He didn't assume a threatening pose. Wyn thought he might've attacked him right away, but he was just standing there.

"What in the hells did you do?" Wyn yelled. "You bastard!" He raised his spear, ready to attack. He started running toward the Fighter, trying to close the distance before he struck.

"I did what I had to do," Lionel said. His voice was different. Calm, purposeful, soft. "You had your objective, and I had mine."

Wyn gripped his spear hard, his knuckles white. He stopped his advance. "What are you talking about?"

Lionel scoffed. "There's so little you understand about this world. About this tower."

"Like you know more? You're a rookie Climber! We're here to work together against the tower, not each other!"

"No!" Lionel yelled. He pointed John's sword at Wyn. "You're wrong! I am here to *defend* this tower. Climbers have always been in the wrong, Wyn. You'll find that if you keep climbing."

Wyn was caught off guard. He didn't understand what Lionel was saying. It didn't make any sense.

Lionel reached into a pocket with his free hand and pulled out a key. "If you survive, that is. I was starting to somewhat warm up to all of you. But it had to be done. I finally saw the truth, and maybe one day you will, too." Lionel smiled. "Praise Aliyar!"

At the same time, Marcy emerged from the portal behind Wyn and tumbled forward in a controlled roll. She rose to her knees with her bow readied and an arrow drawn. Lionel's smile quickly turned sour.

Lionel opened a portal with his key and stepped through right as Marcy released her arrow. He seemed to duck at the right time, avoiding a lethal blow, but wasn't able to avoid it completely. It grazed him right as he disappeared inside the portal. Marcy's arrow clanged against the wall of the cave and the portal behind Lionel vanished.

"You didn't try to stop him?!" Marcy yelled. She grabbed Wyn's collar and pulled him close to her face. She was seething, her cheeks and nose flushed red and eyes wide. She had a feral look to her with her goo-coated fur armor and crazed expression.

Wyn raised a hand in surrender. "I was trying to stall and talk to him first. He said, 'Praise Aliyar,' and that he wanted to defend the tower and not climb it. It didn't make sense."

Marcy let go of him. She yelled, and the cave returned her scream several times over.

Wyn looked at her and the empty space where Lionel just stood. He could hardly believe what happened. He was caught off guard with Lionel's change of demeanor and words. Maybe he should've just attacked him instead, but he wanted an answer to his actions.

A realization suddenly hit him. How were they going to get out of the second floor?

Cedric appeared in the cave, entering through the same portal like Marcy. He looked around, his staff raised and glowing. His eyes were large and his moves sporadic.

"Where is he?" Cedric asked. His voice cracked.

"Gone," Wyn replied. "He used a key and teleported out."

Cedric cursed. Marcy laughed.

"What in the hells is so funny?" Cedric said and whipped around to Marcy. She was crouched at the other end of the cave entrance.

"At least I snagged him on his way out," she said. She turned to face them, holding an arrow. The tip was blood red.

"So he's hurt," Wyn said. "He'll likely heal."

"Probably," she said. "But it's *something*. That bastard."

Cedric sighed. "And I'm too late. I'm sorry."

The three stood in the cave for a moment, all processing the events. Everything happened suddenly at once.

"We lost him," Wyn said. "There's nothing to do about it now. Cedric, how was John? Did you see him?"

"He should be fine," Cedric said. He set his staff against the wall and sat down, folding his legs and resting his head on the wall. "Tasha was healing him. He should be stabilized, and she'll take him back through the portal I opened. The guild's infirmary will take over from there."

Wyn breathed a sigh of relief. "Thank the gods."

"Thank Cedric and Tasha," Marcy snapped. "*They* did it. *Not* gods."

Wyn stared at her. "You're right. Thank you, Cedric. And I'll thank Tasha later."

Marcy sat down beside Cedric. She straightened her legs and relaxed. "I'm sorry, Wyn. I don't mean to be an ass. I'm just frustrated! And tired."

"It's okay," Wyn said. "I get it. But now I can't help but wonder how do we move forward from here?"

Marcy and Cedric looked at each other, bags under their eyes and shoulders slumped.

"I just used my key back on the first floor," Cedric said. "I don't have another."

"We all know I don't have one," Marcy added.

"Okay," Wyn said. He set his spear against the cave wall and folded his arms. He was too anxious to sit and did his best planning while up.

"This was not a smart decision," Cedric said. "It won't end well."

"Downer," Marcy said. She lightly punched him on the thigh.

Wyn took a deep breath. "Let's talk this through. There'll probably be another group sent after us once word gets back, right?"

"Maybe," Cedric said. "But the odds of them porting here is far too low. The tower starts parties at different locations for a better challenge."

"Strike that one, then," Marcy said.

"Alright," Wyn continued, "why don't we wait until morning, then? We camp here, wait for tomorrow when the next batch of Climbers enters the tower. The chance of one of them coming here or us meeting them in the floor increases."

"That won't work either," Marcy said. "The tower resets itself with a new day. A new layout of the floor, a new set of monsters, different rewards. We don't need to be in the tower when that happens."

"Why is that?"

"It's the reason people don't camp overnight here. When it shifts, this small alcove could be where the boss is. Or at the bottom of a lake. Or in a volcano. Or in a horde of enemies. Or sucked into the void when the actual shift happens. No one knows because the Climbers stupid enough to try it have all died."

Wyn stopped pacing and stared blankly at her. "Shit."

"I'll say," Marcy said.

"Strike that one, too," Cedric added.

"Last idea, then," Wyn said. "And I think it's our only option."

"I was afraid of that," Cedric said. He closed his eyes.

"We finish this floor," Wyn said. "And quickly, apparently, since we'll all die when the tower changes. At least we have several hours."

Cedric kept his eyes closed. "How? I'm nearly spent of mana. After clearing the first floor the first time and helping you guys I don't have half my mana left. I'd be next to useless."

"And I have less than half my usual arrows left," Marcy said. "Just over a dozen. Like Cedric, I have about half my mana, too. And no offense, Wyn, but you're not exactly an experienced Climber. Only three of us in poor condition tackling a floor? Even for just the second floor it's not good odds."

"Maybe not," Wyn said. "But I'm experienced with fighting. And I'm damned determined not to die here. If you two back me up, I believe I can lead us to the end."

Cedric and Marcy simply stared at Wyn. Marcy chuckled.

"You're confident, Wyn," she said. "I like that." She stood up and wiped her hands on her fur-lined pants, smearing green spider goo everywhere. "But you have a non-magical spear, limited magic, and used quite a few spells on the first floor."

"True," Wyn said. "Sort of. I currently have four spells." He looked down at his forearm and noticed his mark was glowing but mostly dull. The time between casting his last spell at the champions and now was enough for *Lucidity* to regenerate most of his mana.

Wyn was thankful for it—it truly was an incredible skill.

"And, my mana will be fine. I'm over halfway full."

Cedric stood up. "How? You cast several spells just an hour ago. It takes food and rest to recover mana. Or a potion. You should be nearly spent!"

"It's my passive skill—*Lucidity*. It lets me naturally recover mana over time. I don't have a large pool like you two, but my mark tells me how little or how much I have, thanks to that skill. And right now it's saying I have over half of my mana available."

"Damn," Marcy said. "That's pretty useful. You can be smart about spacing out your magic with other things and essentially never run out."

"That's the hope."

"What are your spells and skills?" Cedric asked. "Marcy and I know ours, of course. We've been climbing for a while together, so we know how to manage when we're low on resources. But I'd like you to share your abilities so we know what we have available."

Wyn smiled. They were trusting him. Even if they were veterans they knew they had to work together. Hope swelled up in his chest that they'd get out of this hellish situation.

"I have *Ice Shard*, *Arcane Aura*, *Regen*, and *Magic Weapon* for my spells."

"*Regen* is good," Marcy said. "Just be smart about when you use it."

"And *Magic Weapon* can solve your non-magical spear problem. This might work after all."

"That was my thought, too," Wyn said. "I took more utility spells thinking I'd be better served that way. I'm hoping it'll pay off now."

"What about your skills?" Cedric said. He reached into his pocket and pulled out a small piece of folded paper. He looked it over for just a second and folded it back up.

"*Lucidity*, as I mentioned," Wyn said. "Also *Dyadcast* and *Speed Up*."

"*Speed Up* is straightforward. I'm not sure I know the other one. What does it do?"

Wyn flushed, and his heart skipped a beat. He realized he never finished reviewing his skills with Daniel. A resource he had available wasn't put to use because he wanted to rush into the tower. A pang of regret resonated within him. Like with his spells, he could read them on his parchment, but he wouldn't know the full capabilities or applications. Not yet.

He pulled out his parchments and looked them over. Rifling through the pages, he pulled up the paper labeled **CLASS** and looked at it. Sure enough, there was a brief description of both *Lucidity* and *Dyadcast*.

"*Lucidity*: *Allows passive recovery of mana. Your mark will show the current status of mana and is a guide to your expected amount of recovery time from empty to full. When your mark fully glows, you are empty and currently recovering. When your mark is dull and gray you are full. Current time to fully recover: 3 hours.*"

"*Dyadcast*: *Allows you to cast a spell twice for only one and a half the mana cost. Speak the skill followed by the spell to engage the ability.*"

Wyn read them out loud to Marcy and Cedric. He stared at it for a second longer. Shame crept up within him, now—he should've looked at this before he stepped inside the tower. This information was important and crucial to his suc-cess. The fact that he was just now learning about it was embarrassing.

"Not too bad, not too great," Cedric said. "At least compared to others, hon-estly. Sorry, Wyn."

Wyn held his head up and squared his chest. Based on what Daniel told him, he knew the Ruby Magician's skill set and abilities wouldn't be the most efficient. But he was damned if he wasn't going to make the best of them.

"It's alright," Wyn said. "I'm going to prove it's better than you think. You'll see."

Marcy smiled. "You must've been popular in your company. You seem to be a pretty positive guy."

"I learned that you have to be," Wyn said. "Especially when you're young and facing the likelihood of dying."

"And you're wiser than most," Cedric added. "Most rookie Climbers can't see that. They're too bold and make stupid mistakes."

Wyn briefly thought of his own conversations with Daniel earlier in the day. How he wanted to rush to get into the tower rather than take his time to learn his abilities in a controlled environment. It was a bold and stupid mistake, the exact thing Cedric was saying he *didn't* see in him.

"I wouldn't count myself out of that category, yet. But all I know is that we can definitely make it through this floor if we work together."

"You're right," Marcy said. "I believe we can, too."

"Alright," Cedric said. "Let's get a plan. According to my parchment it's cur-rently 7:12. We have some time, but we don't need to be distracted. We're a small group, low on mana and resources, and need to find the best way to the boss so we can open the portal and return to Alestead."

"And be smart about what we do," Marcy added. "We aren't looking to grab rewards, here. Only move forward. We're on a clock, and the odds are still against us."

"True," Wyn said. "But what skills or magic do you two have? Since we're laying everything on the table." Wyn couldn't suppress a smile. He was dying to know their abilities.

Marcy laughed. "It's not worth the time to go over everything we can do. Let's just say I will shoot things with arrows, Cedric will shoot them with spells, and you will stab them with your spear. On top of healing, if needed."

"She's right," Cedric said. "But I focus on lightning spells, obviously, and have skills to support the strength and mana efficiency of those spells. To be brief."

Marcy threw her pack on the ground. "And mine support ranged attacks, improve my senses, and overall just make me more of a badass."

Wyn's effort at trying to get them to share their abilities wasn't totally fruitless, but still disappointing. "That's something, I guess. Do you have any magic items or weapons, at least?"

Cedric held his staff out in front of him. "My staff and robe are magical. I can cast a few basic attacking spells without using mana, and it can amplify my magic, simply put."

"And my bow is similar," Marcy added. "I can increase my accuracy, use it to cast some arrow-specific spells, and make standard arrows magical. You should find a weapon like that at some point, too, by the way. If we make it out of here."

"Oh, and our packs are magical," Cedric said. "They can hold more than normal."

Marcy sighed. "And the rest we left back at our stash. This was supposed to be an introductory climb, remember? I didn't want to bring anything extra with me outside of some snacks and an emergency kit."

"Which," Cedric added, "in hindsight, was foolish. We won't make that mistake again."

Wyn took a deep breath. "Okay, then. I have another idea."

"Let's hear it," Marcy said.

"I'll scout ahead for a bit while you two rest to recover some mana. I won't engage with anything but will note the paths ahead. Then, in an hour, we start and push through."

"I won't even fight you on it," Marcy said. She reached into her pack and pulled out a blanket and rations. She lay down on the cave floor and began eating, handing some rations to Cedric. Using her pack as a pillow, she pulled the blanket up like she was going to sleep. Cedric did the same beside her.

Wyn turned and looked deeper into the cave. It was lit by ambient mushrooms on the wall and ceiling and gave off dim light, which was enough for them to see without another source. It wasn't lit as well as their space due to the beams of light from the ceiling, but at least they'd be able to see. He noticed the path immediately veered to the right, though, so he couldn't see too far.

Using his spear as a walking stick, he began to walk into the cave to explore.

He stopped mid-step as a thought struck him. The tower had objectives for them on each floor. Maybe the objective for this floor could give an idea about what lay ahead?

Wyn pulled out his parchment. There it was, magically imprinted:

Quest: Your search for the girl leads you deeper into the unknown. What lies within? Is she still alive? Is she worth this much trouble? Keep pressing on to find out. Fair warning, though—something doesn't want you here. Good luck.

Wyn folded it up and put it away. He chuckled a bit at the near-absurdity of it all. The description was definitely ominous, and completing a quest in the midst of surviving here was ridiculous.

He thought about the objective at the last floor and trying to find the little girl. He didn't remember any more clues but figured if he were to keep climbing the floors he'd find more. It seemed as though there was a large, connected puzzle between each of the floors inside the tower. As though the entire twenty floors laid out an adventure rather than random challenges.

Excitement grew once more despite his current situation. He understood the appeal of being a Climber with only the smallest of exposure. The taste was intoxicating, and he wanted more.

But now wasn't the time for that.

Wyn checked his mark. It was still recovering mana, of course.

He had an idea.

Placing his hand on his chest, he immediately cast ***Arcane Aura*** on himself. The same showings of mystical armor appeared over his Ruby Magician robe gifted by Daniel, and he matched the same glow from the moss and mushrooms on the cave wall.

He checked his mark again. It showed less than half of his mark recovering mana but more than a third. So, one cast of his armor took about one-third of his total mana. Using the time they had until they started exploring as a group, he could be able to track more precisely how long the spell lasts.

He tapped his spear against the ground and stood at attention. Being caught off guard here would spell death for all of them, and he'd be lying to himself if he said he wasn't nervous. It was one thing to be out in the real world, but here he felt even more exposed and at risk.

Wyn took two steps forward, and the moss on the wall changed color—what was just a soft green quickly turned to a shimmering purple, and the plants shifted like they were alive.

Two steps in, and he was already questioning just exactly how far he should go.

INTERLUDE: LIONEL

Two months prior . . .

Flir scratched some notes on a small pad of paper. The sounds of sparring—punches and kicks landing, grunts of effort and pain, and weapons echoing off each other—were melodious, like a sweet song. It relaxed her. The training hall was bustling with Climbers, all eager to continue practicing in order to maximize their chances of succeeding in the tower. The newer Fighters held most of the hall as they were the most numerous of the rookie classes, and she watched over them along with her partner.

"Samuel doesn't seem too bad," Flir said, not taking her eyes off her notes. "Good strikes with a club. Strong. Not too bad footwork."

"Good family, too," Dirk said. "I believe they're minor nobles outside Fyrewatch?"

Flir's eyes lit up. She quickly made another note on her pad. "Excellent! We could . . . *persuade* them to sponsor us. I could use a new set of armor. And I'm still missing a water helm to complete the set."

"Come now, Flir, think of the Climbers. They need some things, too."

Flir looked at him, and he looked back. Both smirked and chuckled quietly to themselves.

"Maybe a potion or two," Flir said. "Where would they be without us leading them to greatness?"

"Hmm. Quite right. Alright, who else have you noted?"

Flir sighed. "The stock this week is slow. This season has not been productive for us. But a legacy Fighter named John seems promising."

Dirk raised his eyebrows. "A legacy's here, and you're just now mentioning it?"

"It's the Gallows."

Dirk moaned. "No wonder. We won't squeeze even a copper boot out of him."

"Which is why I haven't said anything. But, I will say he shows potential. Good sword and shield skills, good endurance compared to most rookies. It's obvious he's trained for a while before coming."

"What are his skills and growth?"

Flir scribbled more notes with fury. "He hasn't shared them."

"What?" Dirk snapped. "We're his mentors. We should know all of his information!"

"He said he doesn't want it known just yet. It's driving the others mad."

"Has he not practiced them during sparring bouts?"

Flir smiled. "No. He's beating his opponents without them."

Dirk nodded. "Not bad. And even though I hate it, it's not a bad idea keeping them secret with this much competition. I'm surprised he's held his own without them, though. Maybe he already has a passive skill?"

"Maybe. But the only other rookie to give him trouble is Lionel." She tapped her quill on the paper several times. "He's our guy."

"Lionel? Why?"

Flir flipped a few pages over and handed them to Dirk. "Take a look. He's a bit older than the rest, but still young. Tall. Well-built. A temper like a bull!"

Dirk read over the pages. The notes read how Lionel preferred using axes, overpowered his opponents with brute force, and was reckless with his attacks but almost always won his matches. He tended to go too far when pushed, but was noted to be more than capable.

Dirk looked over the recruits and frowned. Flir was right, of course. But she didn't take it as far as she needed. "I think they'd want him."

Flir felt her heart skip a beat. "Shit. I really don't want to see her again."

Dirk smiled and patted her on the back. "I'll do all the talking. Don't worry."

Dirk stepped forward and clapped his hands together several times, gathering the training Fighters. He smiled his best charming smile and praised them for their efforts.

"We're done for today, unless anyone wants to prepare for the rookie climb tomorrow. If so, there are more preparations to make, but please break for some food or rest and meet back in two hours. Lionel, could you please stay behind?"

Murmurs swept through the small crowd. They slowly split apart, all going their separate ways. A tall Fighter stepped forward, a wooden training axe in his right hand. His arms were bruised, and his hair was plastered to his head with sweat.

"Yes?" Lionel said. "Did I do something wrong? If Annie doesn't want an actual fight she shouldn't be a Climber. It wasn't my fault—"

Flir raised a hand. "It's not about that. We've taken notice of your abilities. You're good."

Lionel straightened up and relaxed his grip on the axe. "I know."

Dirk smirked. "See? He's perfect."

"Perfect?" Lionel asked. "For what?"

"You'll see," Dirk said. "Follow us."

Dirk turned while Flir waved Lionel on.

Lionel stood still, confused. The two mentors were obviously up to something strange, and he had no idea about their intentions. He was clearly a much better Fighter than the rest of the lot, so it likely had something to do with a secret boon or training.

Well, he wasn't better than John, but the sword and shield Fighter had an unfair advantage from his family and prior training. Lionel was confident he'd surpass him in a season or two.

The two middle-aged Climbers silently led Lionel out of the training hall and toward another part of the city. Lionel hadn't been in Alestead long and was still getting used to the layout, but he knew where they headed was not a commonly traveled area. Regular citizens made up the vast majority of people walking about, and it wasn't nearly as busy as the primary street or trade district. The houses were more cramped and on top of each other, too, like a shanty town. No one seemed to be too poor, though, as he didn't notice a single beggar on the cobblestone street or anyone running around in cloth sacks or pitiful clothes. It was likely the housing area for the various workers at the tower or markets.

"Where are we going?" Lionel asked. They had passed multiple streets and turns, and his patience was wearing thin while his nerves were growing. The number of people they passed were lessening with every turn, too, to the point where now they hadn't passed anyone.

"Be patient," Dirk answered.

Lionel scoffed. He hated roundabout answers, and hated being patronized even more. If these two weren't his superiors he would've raised more of a fuss or started pushing back by now. There was obviously some deeper, secretive thing happening, but he was annoyed how they decided to go about it.

This didn't seem like it was worth the trouble, and Lionel started to look for a quick escape.

"We're close," Flir added. "Just one more side street."

True to her word, the trio turned once more into a dead end. There were no homes or doors here, only the shadows from the tall buildings and barely any light from the early afternoon sun. It was dark and more shaded than lit.

Lionel immediately stopped and took a step back. "What is this? What are you two doing?" He raised his fists like he was ready to fight, and quickly stepped toward Dirk.

"My, my, he's feisty," a silky smooth voice said further down the alley.

Lionel stopped his advance and whirled his head to the sound of the voice. He squinted, but was unable to see in the shadows.

Dirk and Flir stepped to either side of the alley away from each other.

"We have a new recruit," Dirk said. He folded his hands behind his back. "He's very promising."

"Recruit?" Lionel asked. "I don't want to be in some damn group."

The voice from the shadows laughed. It was deep but oddly still feminine. "You say that now. Every Climber has to be in *some* group."

Lionel looked at both of his mentors in turn, but they stayed resolute, looking down the alley as though they could see the person clear as day. Flir gave a quick glance back, but her expression was unreadable.

Light steps clattered on the cobblestone as a woman emerged from the darkness. She wore a sleek robe with dress shoes, adorned with various jewelry on her hands, wrist, and neck. Her straight, long hair was as black as night and smooth without a single strand out of place. Her green eyes seemed to pierce Lionel's soul, and her smirk seemed to invite him back to her bed.

Lionel's heart raced. She was alluring, but out of place. Her appearance didn't match the situation or environment. Someone looking like her was the last person he expected to step out from a dark back alley.

This was *not* good. But, they wanted something from him. So he had the upper hand.

"I'm Marianna," the woman said. "And you are?"

"Lionel."

"Lionel. Your name suits you. Strong, confident, brash. We need people like you, young man."

"Who is we?"

Marianna's smirk deepened into a smile. "We are a select group of Climbers with a very special task inside Alistair. We don't invite just anyone to join, either."

"So you're part of a guild, then? Already had my information from these two and liked what you saw?" Lionel gestured to his mentors but only saw empty space.

His heart raced. Those two bastards must've sneaked away when Lionel was busy focusing on the woman. He suddenly felt very exposed but also trapped like a caged animal. She didn't seem too dangerous, but those were always the type of people to guard against. Their motivations were usually deeper than what they let on, and Lionel felt like this was that exact scenario.

He was vulnerable, and that wasn't a feeling he particularly enjoyed.

"Not quite a guild. And yes, we heavily invest resources into any potential member—can't have just anyone join us, after all."

Lionel took a step back. "I have a bad feeling from you. Like . . ."

"Like power?" Marianna finished for him, cutting him off. She held out a hand and summoned a small orb of water that slowly began to swirl. It was perfectly round and constantly in motion, almost mesmerizing. "The ability to defeat your enemies with absolution? Crush those who oppose you?"

Lionel stared at the orb now, her words flowing through him like a siren's song. The orb grew to the size of a large melon, though maintained its allure.

"Yes," Lionel whispered, almost absentmindedly.

"Prestige? Fame? Known throughout the country for your deeds and wealth even the highest of nobles would envy?"

"Yes."

The orb continued to grow, now the size of her torso as she held her hand out further from her body.

"This is a small portion of power you could obtain. Even as a Fighter."

Lionel scowled at her, shaking off the trance-like display. "Even as a Fighter? Lady, warriors are better than damned Mages in every way. Your little spells won't do much when you've run out of mana. That was a neat trick, but not good enough for me."

Marianna chuckled and decreased the size of her water orb back to fitting in the palm of her hand. "I could do so much with this little orb of water before you could even react, and no one else has this kind of spell or skill. Don't underestimate the power of magic, boy. It's how anyone, *even Fighters*, accomplishes what they do, but me and my group more so."

Lionel folded his arms. "I don't need a lecture. If you're asking me to join your magic group or whatever, count me out. I'm done." He turned and walked away, ready to get out of this twisted recruitment. He had no interest in what she was selling.

Marianna sighed and released her water orb, causing the water to disappear as vapor into the air. "He's more bullheaded than I thought. Wait, Lionel. We aren't a group of magic users."

Lionel stopped and turned back around. "Then what are you?"

"I can only reveal a little. You'll have to agree to join to find out the rest."

"That's a terrible deal."

Marianna laughed again. "If people only knew what we offered, they'd be trying to kill you right now for the chance."

"You haven't mentioned shit. That's not a very convincing argument."

"I guess not for you. But do you know who the last person to complete the twentieth floor of Alistair was?"

Lionel shook his head. "No."

"That's because the city's guild doesn't announce who completes the tower. They don't want the masses to know how rare it actually is to finish all twenty floors, and how many Climbers die on the last tier trying to win it all."

"We all know the risks. So what?"

"So, our leader was the last one to finish. And the rewards he received are far, far better than any amount of gold crowns or magic items you could find."

Lionel's heart raced again. "What did he earn?"

Marianna smiled. Her hook was back in place. "Power. And plenty of it."

"Good for him. Why would I care?"

"Because the power he received allows him to share it with others. You could be far greater than any normal Climber, no matter what kind of rare class you obtain or magic items you find. This is true, undiscovered strength that Climbers such as yourself only dream to hold in their hand."

Lionel felt a strange surge of power suddenly rush through him. Was that her? Or did he only imagine it, hoping what she said was true? He desperately wished for her to be right. He craved—no, needed—power above all else.

"How do I know you're telling the truth?"

Marianna waved him to her. "Come, show me your mark."

Lionel hesitated.

Marianna scoffed and pulled the edge of her dress back, exposing her entire left leg up to her bare hip. The mark of some class Lionel didn't recognize composed the center, and four rings of runes surrounded the symbol.

Lionel blushed, then realized what he saw. Four runic rings were rare, showing she had a class upgraded three times allowing her to climb all the way up to the fourth tier.

Maybe she really is telling the truth.

"I've been a Climber for some time, but I wouldn't have four rings without the very power I'm offering."

Lionel walked up to her and took off his outer shirt. Staring at her, he unbuttoned the top of his under shirt and pulled it to the side, exposing his Fighter mark on his left chest.

Marianna gingerly placed her hand on his mark and closed her eyes. A swirl of arcane runes formed around her, creating a faint blue aura.

"Interesting," Marianna said, her eyes still closed. "This wasn't your chosen class, but you've decided to be marked as a Fighter anyway."

"How did you—"

The swirling runes around Marianna circled and swept down her arm toward Lionel, settling on his mark.

Lionel felt his breath catch and recoiled. A wave of cold washed over him like jumping in a frozen lake, and his breathing rapidly picked up. He tried to step back but found that Marianna's hand was magically attached to his mark.

"What are you doing?" Lionel asked, his voice cracking. He tried to suppress a rising feeling of panic, but stopped resisting when the cold turned warm with a euphoric sensation.

The blue aura dissipated, and the woman let go of his mark.

"There. And that's only a fraction of what you could obtain."

Lionel looked at this chest and saw his single circle had more runes lined within it. They contrasted the Fighter's red runes and slowly faded to black over several seconds. He still only had one runic circle, but knew he was just granted a boon.

"What was that?"

"That was a small enhancement. I can't grant you the full amount of power, but I was able to pass along a minor boost. To establish trust."

Lionel squeezed his hands into fists over and over. "I feel . . . I'm not sure. What's the enhancement?"

Marianna winked at him. "Something fit for a Fighter, of course! Your strength and endurance are permanently increased beyond what a first-tiered Fighter should possess."

Lionel flexed and moved his body, eager to test the amount of improvements. "That's incredible. I already feel it."

"So you see now that I'm serious. We want you, Lionel. And we mean business."

Lionel's smile faded. It could be too good to be true, but he couldn't deny this feeling. This power. It was intoxicating.

"Alright. How do I join?"

Marianna placed her hands behind her back and dropped her smile. She stood straighter, displaying a commanding presence that didn't match her previous appeal.

"We are not for the weak. We will demand you to do things you may not like but are necessary. You will be ruthless. You must be willing to do what others shy away from to accomplish a greater purpose."

Lionel's face crept into a smile. "That's the best thing you've said yet."

Marianna smiled once more, though it was not as alluring as before. It was . . . menacing. "You say that now, but we'll see if you can stomach it. Your task for entry requires a sacrifice."

"A sacrifice? I have to die to join?"

"No, you fool." Marianna's voice cracked into a deeper, harsher tone. She visibly softened, trying to maintain her composure. "You must sever the bond of an ally and prove your level of cruelty."

Lionel clenched his jaw. How in the hells was he supposed to do that?

The woman walked up to Lionel and cupped her hands around his face. She stared deep into his eyes, past the surface and further into his being. Magic runes began to swirl in her irises, and her words felt as though they were echoing in his mind.

Lionel couldn't look away. He was completely focused on her and her alone.

"We must introduce you to our beliefs. Our meaning for Climbing."

Lionel didn't blink. Her eyes were hypnotic, both commanding his attention and showing him truth. "Yes."

"Your first lesson. Have you heard of the great Aliyar?"

CHAPTER FOURTEEN

This place is a maze," Marcy said. "Twists and turns everywhere. There are so many paths to keep straight!" She was leaning against the cave wall and smacked it with her fist.

"I know," Wyn said. "And we haven't faced anything. This spear is more of a walking stick than a weapon."

"At least both of you have one," Marcy replied. She stuck her lip out and huffed.

"You're just pissed you can't remember this floor's challenge."

Marcy didn't respond.

"Which doesn't make sense. How can either of you two not remember an entire floor?"

"Because we rushed through this floor almost a month ago," Marcy said. "The first day of the season we finished the first, second, and third floors, then never looked back. Can you remember what you ate for a day a month ago?"

Wyn shook his head. "I don't think that's a fair comparison."

Marcy kicked a rock into the cave wall, hitting a small mushroom. "I don't care. After enough floors changing every day and the entire environment changing each month, they start to blur a bit."

Cedric was quiet. He had his own parchment in one hand, turning it around and looking at it from different directions periodically. There were scribbles from him mapping out the floor, but it was chaotic and incoherent.

"It doesn't make sense," he said. "We've been in these tunnels for half an hour! I keep drawing them out, but it's like it doesn't end."

"I know," Wyn said. "I'm confused too."

The tunnels had been winding and varied greatly, branches of paths splitting the further they went. They had backtracked dozens of times, looking for anything that resembled the right path or changed scenery. The tunnels all looked the same with the same glowing plants and elevation, and they were easily disoriented.

Wyn just stared at a mushroom that was glowing purple. It still moved ever so slightly, like it was waking up from a deep sleep.

"Let's just keep moving," Cedric said. "At least there aren't any monsters. If we come to another branch, we'll just keep mapping it out. You know it has to end at some point."

"Yeah, yeah," Marcy said. "This whole tower is a monster. One huge, cunning, damned monster." She stormed off further down the path. Wyn and Cedric followed behind her.

"By the gods!" she yelled. "Another branch!" She stood between a fork in the tunnels not one minute after they stopped. She kicked the cave floor again, this time causing dirt to spray onto the wall.

"Which way should we go?" Wyn asked.

"Who cares," Marcy replied. "We'll be coming back here to try the other before too long anyway." She started off to the left path.

Cedric sighed and followed her, trying to carefully draw a new tunnel on his map. Wyn waited behind. He knew if they didn't try something different, and soon, they'd be lost in the floor and never make it out.

Wyn began to follow them but quickly stopped. He raised his spear instinctually. He saw movement out of the corner of his eye, though he wasn't sure from where. He scanned the other tunnel and the one they just entered for any signs of a threat.

Then he saw it. A mushroom on the wall shook itself, releasing a bit of the purple magic it used for light onto the ground. Then another, in the same tunnel Marcy and Cedric were walking down, shook itself and dropped its magical purple dust, too. More followed suit, silently releasing their spore magic behind them.

Wyn wondered how they didn't notice it before. It was nearly silent and behind them, and they never thought to turn around while exploring the tunnels.

He stared for a minute while Marcy and Cedric rounded the tunnel. The first mushroom's dust was slowly disappearing. It didn't take long for the others to disappear, too. That was how they missed seeing the dust on the ground when they backtracked. By the time they returned, the evidence was already gone, magically disappeared.

A thought entered his mind. Maybe the mushrooms gave off different colors, too? Could the color help determine their path?

Wyn rushed forward to follow the pair of veterans.

"Wait!" Wyn yelled. "I think I found something!"

Marcy and Cedric stopped abruptly.

"What is it?" Cedric asked.

"I believe the mushrooms are telling us which way to go!"

"Oh gods," Marcy said. "You didn't eat one of them, did you?"

"No, of course not," Wyn said. "But hear me out. I think we need to start from the beginning."

Both Cedric and Marcy let out an audible sigh.

"I know, I know," Wyn continued," but when you start walking down a path they release magic spores. These have been purple. There could be other colors, too!"

"It makes sense," Cedric said. "Different paths for different groups to go through so they wouldn't interact. That *is* something the tower likes to do."

"Fine, fine," Marcy said. "I can already tell he swayed you, Cedric. Let's go. We're wasting time." Marcy immediately set back toward the tunnel they walked down. Then she stopped.

"But we'll need your map. I can't remember how to get back."

Cedric laughed. He walked ahead of Marcy and led the group back to the entrance without another word.

"Is it working?" Wyn asked. He had decided to take the lead down a hall so Marcy and Cedric could see for themselves. He picked a random tunnel, one they had mapped out, and began walking down it.

He heard Cedric laugh and Marcy curse.

Wyn smiled. It must've worked.

"The mushroom is letting out a blue powder," Marcy said, having caught up to Wyn. "We just need to find tunnels that are blue, right?"

"I believe so," he replied. "Though both of you have way more experience in the tower than me. I'm just assuming, here."

"Most of the tower is an assumption," Cedric said. "At least until you rerun the floor a time or two. Though any other floor could be, and usually is, wildly different."

The three of them continued down the tunnel, each turning back to watch the mushrooms. It was an odd sight—they would vibrate and shake to release their magical spores like a dog shook water off its coat. The blue substance coated the tunnel floor but would disappear before too long. They each marveled at it, especially the veterans who knew they had seen quite a bit but were also surprised each time something new came up. Such was Alistair—a new obstacle, enemy, or both, all under the guise of a magical tower releasing its power into the world.

"Didn't both of you say that certain things in the tower can be valuable?" Wyn walked over and picked up the blue dust on the ground. It felt like light, fine sand as it fell through his fingers. He was surprised how much the mushroom made and dropped to the ground.

Marcy walked beside him and inspected it. "Yes, but we aren't here to collect items, remember? We need to worry about finding a way out, not making money."

Wyn let the spores fall through his fingers. It vanished as it hit the ground, and the rest of the pile disappeared, too. "I know you're right. I just can't help but wonder."

Cedric put a hand on Wyn's shoulder. "Let's get through the floor, and you can wonder about making money and gathering items on another climb. Remember—priorities."

Wyn nodded. He knew they were right, of course. Time was of the essence, and he didn't want to be the reason for them to be too delayed. Still, the tower was enticing, and he could already feel the appeal of wanting more and more here, whether that be money, items, or clout. Like a moth to a flame, he needed to be careful and guarded, and know when to approach or stay away.

In minutes they were at a crossroads with multiple paths before them, branching tunnels of six possible paths to take. They all looked identical. Cedric pulled out his paper he had been using to map out the floor. He looked at it carefully, turning it over multiple times for different views.

"That's odd," he said. "These don't match up with the ones we had before. We never had six possible options."

"Do you think the tower changed the layout so quickly?" Wyn asked. "Can it do that?"

"If there's anything I've learned," Marcy said, "it's that it can do anything— but it does tend to follow set rules. Maybe since we have a plan and figured out a path to the end it showed us the right options of tunnels."

"That's more likely," Cedric said. "Before you learned about the mushrooms, Wyn, we would've just endlessly wandered around these caves. The tower is showing us the way. In a sense."

"Then let's go," Wyn said. He stepped into the second path from the left. He walked about ten feet into it then stopped to look back to the mushrooms to see if he chose correctly. Cedric and Marcy waited, watching eagerly.

A mushroom shook itself and released yellow spores onto the ground.

"Okay, then," Wyn said. "Let's choose another path." He began to walk back toward the others. Suddenly more mushrooms began to shake and loose spores, more yellow dust falling onto the tunnel. The amount was definitely more than before, and it was thicker than the blue spores, like sand pouring from an open hole.

Wyn stopped. He wondered if it was a trap.

The spores began to grow from the tunnel floor, quickly rising and forming a mushroom shape then morphing into something vaguely humanoid. A large mushroom cap formed its head, with a stalk-like body and appendages that were thin like sticks. It grew a long spear in its right hand similar to Wyn's. Where its face should've been was a mixture of various types of mushroom caps, with glowing yellow eyes staring right at Wyn.

He raised his own spear, ready to fight the obvious challenge. It was definitely a trap, though it appeared to be straightforward.

Wyn thought about his spell—**Magic Weapon**. He raised his spear and readied himself to attack the mushroom, hoping it wasn't a waste to use his mana like this if his regular spear worked fine. He also didn't want to waste time or energy, and wanted this dealt with quickly. If his spear had the same effect as the wooden champions without the spell, it'd be detrimental to getting through the floor. And that's if he came out completely unscathed.

He didn't want to chance it. At least his mana would recover.

Wyn first swept the mushroom's leg, severing it and causing it to teeter over in a heap. From there he stabbed it in the face directly below the eyes, shoving his spear hard. The spear tip hit the rocky ground with a loud pang behind the mushroom's head. It was odd—he thought it would be more durable, but it felt like he was stabbing into a firm lump of dough.

He pulled the spear out of the mushroom and left a gaping hole where its face used to be. It quickly dissolved back into a pile of yellow dust. The other piles of yellow dust around them disappeared, too.

"Not bad," Marcy said. Her and Cedric were just standing there watching Wyn. Her arms were folded, and she had a smirk on her face. "For killing a plant, at least."

"The spell might've been too much," Wyn said. "But I wanted to make sure."

"At least your mana can recover without resting," Cedric said. "We should be fine, but I definitely think it was unnecessary. Let's just find the right path, already. I have a bad feeling about this floor. Something feels unfamiliar."

"Always so negative," Marcy said.

"Realistic, actually," Cedric said, correcting her. "You know that."

Wyn was a bit frustrated with himself, but it couldn't be helped. Better to be safe than sorry, at least, and how could anyone predict the abilities or strength of a magical mushroom? Maybe next time warranted a test without the spell first.

The rookie trotted back toward them and went down the next path. He repeated what he did before—he walked in about ten feet, turned to watch for the mushrooms, and waited. This time, however, he readied his spear right away. The spell was still active, and he wanted to take advantage of the time.

The mushrooms lighting the cave shook and released a green powder in a similar amount and density as before.

Wyn heard Cedric sigh. He chuckled thinking about the two veterans being impatient while he fought some weird mushroom monster.

The dust began to grow like before, except this time the monster looked different. Its mushroom-cap head was smaller, but its body was taller than the yellow mushroom. It was stockier and seemed stronger, too. Joints and muscles helped form its shape, and it looked much more humanoid. It didn't grow a weapon but flexed its body, stepping toward Wyn right after forming.

He was shocked, but only for a moment. He knew to expect the unexpected, but it was amazing the amount of weird he had found here so far.

Rushing the enemy, he swiped diagonally at the monster, slashing down across its body. Surprisingly, the mushroom dodged it, quickly ducking under the attack. It was more nimble than the last colored mushroom. Not having a weapon was going to be its downfall, as Wyn's reach with his spear gave him the obvious edge.

Wyn back-stepped as the monster tried to close the distance. He wanted to use the best strike to end it in one blow and needed to use his weapon's advantage. Spears weren't typically used to slash at enemies, and were most effective to stab and pierce armor. The magic coating on the weapon, however, at least gave it different means to cause damage.

Taking his spear in a wide horizontal arc, he opted to hit it whether the blade struck it or it bluntly knocked it away. To his pleasant surprise, a large gash formed across the monster's torso, and its top half collapsed forward in its momentum.

It was easy, oddly, and a bit unsettling the power that magic wielded. The mushroom disintegrated back into dust.

"Damnit," Cedric said. "I should've known it wouldn't be this easy."

"What do you mean?" Wyn asked. "That wasn't that bad."

"Wait until there are more of them. And deadlier."

Wyn wrinkled his eyebrows. "Fair point. But how about someone else pick the next path?"

"I'll go," Marcy said. She skipped a few tunnels and went for the far-right path. She walked forward like Wyn and stopped to turn around. The mushroom shook and blue spores fell.

"How about that," Marcy said. She chuckled to herself. "Let's go, boys."

Wyn held his arm up, confused. "How did she get it first try?"

"I've learned it's a gift," Cedric replied. "It can sometimes be an annoying one, but a gift nonetheless."

Cedric and Wyn followed her, all walking through the tunnel deeper into the cave. None of them recognized the new path, especially Marcy, though she wasn't exactly trying to remember them. Cedric was mapping out their paths on his parchment. Though whether it was truly to find their way back or keep his hands busy Wyn wasn't entirely sure.

While they walked down the cave, Wyn still couldn't believe his situation. The books, the rumors, all of his preparation didn't do the tower justice. The magic was far beyond anything he'd seen or heard about. Portals, items, equipment, classes, skills, spells—it was nearly overwhelming.

Wyn remembered that Lionel mentioned the name Aliyar. He wondered if he was the creator of the tower or someone influential in its early days? Was he a mage, a god, or one of the first ascendents to complete it?

Daniel would know the answer. When he made it back—and he was determined to make it back—he knew he needed to take a breather and learn more about the tower. His mentor would have a good sense of direction about what to research for learning more.

The three came to another branching while Wyn was deep in thought. Now only four options were presented for the next tunnel.

"That's a good sign," Cedric said.

"What is? Only having four paths instead of six?" Wyn asked.

"Yes. Though be on guard—it'll be harder and more challenging." Cedric raised his staff, and the tip began to glow softly.

"I'll lead this time," Marcy said. "Maybe we can skip one of those challenges." She began to walk down the far-right tunnel, walked ten feet in, and turned around.

Wyn was quickly learning Marcy must've been the braver Climber in their group. That, or she was the reckless one. She didn't seem to be bothered by difficult decisions or shy away from a challenge. It was impressive, really.

Immediately after Marcy stepped into the cave tunnel three large stalagmites erupted from the ground and attached to the ceiling, forming bars that separated her from Wyn and Cedric. The stalagmites had an orange color to them mixed in, appearing like a light clay.

Marcy cursed. "I wasn't expecting that. Cedric, what do we do?" She felt the earthen bars with her hands then grabbed and shook one. It was solid and unmoving.

Cedric also ran his hands over the stone bar, then the wall and ground around the immediate area. "I don't know. There doesn't seem to be a release or similar."

He and Wyn watched as mushrooms outside the tunnel began to shake, and orange dust dropped onto the ground. It had a similar consistency as before. A mushroom began to sprout from the ground, smaller than before but wide and round. Beady eyes glowed orange under its mushroom-cap helmet, and there were additional caps on its torso and joints that looked like armor.

It was very close to looking ridiculous if it wasn't trying to kill them.

"Damnit," Cedric said.

Wyn readied his spear. Thankfully it was still glowing, but it wasn't nearly as bright as before. A dull glow barely emitted any light, and he hoped it lasted at least through the fight. It hadn't been but maybe ten minutes since he cast the spell to coat it in magic.

As Wyn lowered his spearhead to charge the mushroom, another sprouted behind it, identical in appearance. Then another.

"You just had to say something," Wyn said.

Cedric raised his staff, but Wyn put his arm out, blocking him.

"Save your mana. We'll need it." He steeled his nerves and charged the first mushroom.

CHAPTER FIFTEEN

Wyn knew his spear was going to lose its magical boost soon, and he didn't want to waste the time. The orange mushrooms were in their way and needed to be eliminated. Quickly.

Unfortunately for Wyn he found their cap armor was sturdy, though the monsters themselves were slow. They didn't wield weapons like the yellow mushroom and didn't move quickly like the green one, but he knew if he got caught by a blow from them it would be incredibly strong.

Well, he didn't know for a fact, but he assumed based on their armor and bulk.

His stabs at the armor were effective, though not as much as the last round of enemies. It was only from the spell, too, as the mundane metal spear tip was nearly useless. He was finding more resistance with each stab, and his attacks were only damaging the outer cap due to the magic radiating from his weapon. Unfortunately, even that was fading.

The fight further emphasized his need for a magical spear. When he returned, it would be the first item he'd look to obtain.

He sidestepped the first mushroom and went for the second, which was several feet behind it. He swept the second's leg, cutting a shallow gash under the cap that protected what he assumed would be a knee. It stumbled but didn't fall, and Wyn tried to expand on his attack with another strike. The mushrooms were thankfully moving slow, like they were trudging through water, which gave him additional time to maneuver himself.

He turned to the back of the first mushroom and saw an opening. There was no armor on its back, and it was completely exposed. He stabbed it, happy that his magical spear tip went much farther than before. It was dense, but still not resistant to the magic coating the metal spear.

When he pulled out his weapon he followed it with a quick slash, opening up the mushroom's back and causing it to fall. It collapsed into a large pile of spores.

He then noticed Cedric in front of him, his staff raised and pointed at him, while a runic circle appeared in the air.

Cedric was casting a spell. And he aimed it directly at Wyn.

He couldn't hear what he said as his focus was on the current fight, but he began to yell, hoping some magic in the tower didn't cause Cedric to turn on him or have him think he was an enemy.

Helplessly he raised a hand toward Cedric, hoping a peaceful gesture showed he wasn't going to attack him. Right as he did two things happened at once. One was a heavy thud at his back that felt as though an angry mule or a mean drunk smacked him hard undefended. The attack was enough to make him lurch forward and fall to the ground exactly like the mushroom he just attacked.

The second thing that happened was that several small yellow streaks flashed out of Cedric's staff, flying in several directions but mostly where Wyn was just standing.

Only the magical shots didn't go for Wyn. They went wide around his space.

Wyn lifted his head from the ground to see, wanting to visually follow the magical lines, and saw the second mushroom monster standing directly behind him with a raised stalk leg ready to attack him again.

The yellow streaks all flew into it at once, and magical lightning erupted from the mushroom at the points of impact. It stopped mid-attack, paralyzed and smoking, and crumbled to dust as it fell to the ground.

Cedric was attacking the mushroom, not him.

Why would he even think his ally would do such a thing?

Wyn's back ached and stung when he tried to lift himself. He paused, hoping there wasn't any major damage, but when he twisted his back he didn't find any worrisome effects.

Wyn's cheeks flushed with heat. He looked at Marcy, who simply smirked and nodded. Both shame and embarrassment welled up inside him, for questioning Cedric and for his own mistake, respectively. He wasn't looking much like a leader here in the tower. The experience he had leading his company in the war would only take him so far.

Immediately two of the stalagmites retreated down halfway from the roof of the cave. The middle one stayed tall. Marcy inspected it more, and tried to climb over one side but failed after several attempts.

Cedric reached a hand to Wyn to help him up. "I know how it looked. You're not the first to think I was attacking them."

"I'm sorry," Wyn said. "I'm still getting used to this place. And magic, too."

"I understand. I won't try to critique you on fighting—you're much more experienced than most Climbers, especially rookies. But you have to expect the unexpected here. *Always* be on guard. You just never know here in Alistair."

Wyn remembered Daniel telling him the same thing. Obviously the experience of a veteran Climber was worth more than any gold crowns or magic items he'd find. They were right, of course. He needed to trust them more for the tower's challenges and his own assumptions less for his survival.

"But don't be too hard on yourself," Marcy added. "You're still getting your feet wet. At least you didn't freeze like on the last floor."

Wyn grimaced. "I know. I'll be better. But how are you going to get out of there?"

"I have an idea about what's happening," Marcy said. "I think you killing those two monsters moved these two bars."

"And the third?" Cedric asked.

Marcy looked back toward her hallway. It was empty, though she had a hunch it wouldn't be for long. "I think there's one more to kill. On this side of the bars. Another test from the tower, separating us."

"Like we need that," Wyn said. "We're only three people down here as it is."

"The tower knows it, too," Cedric said. "It adapts as Climbers enter it."

Marcy began walking down the tunnel, though she wasn't in a hurry like before. She took careful steps, checking her surroundings as she went. Wyn could've sworn at one point he saw her sniffing the air.

She stopped about halfway down and quickly drew an arrow from her quiver. About twenty feet in front of her another mushroom began to sprout from the ground. It was the same orange color—caps began to expand in size like before in areas of potential weakness for armor.

Before it even materialized fully, Wyn heard the Ranger mutter a spell right before she loosed her arrow—"*Ignite*."

Wyn's eyes went wide.

A complex, green runic circle appeared at the very tip of the arrowhead, and it caused the pointed tip to light up like a torch. Not just any torch, though, but a large one—it was at least the size of a campfire. The arrow flew toward the orange mushroom in a red line, leaving a trail of smoke behind it. It hit the enemy directly in the chest, piercing its cap armor.

The arrow sank in for a second, and it set the entire plant on fire. It barely even stood to fight before succumbing to Marcy's attack.

"You don't see Rangers often," Cedric said. "Their abilities are quite a sight."

The third stalagmite barring the tunnel began to retract, and when it met the others halfway down they all moved toward the cave floor. The entrance was opened, and Marcy was able to exit.

"I guess that wasn't the way either," she said. "Now we know what will happen if we pick the wrong way."

"So I'll pick next," Cedric said. "Wyn can stay back and help handle the two that pop up, and I'll take care of the one that shows up in the tunnel."

"I won't argue," Wyn said. "Are you positive that's what happens, though?"

"Not entirely, but I have a hunch," Marcy said. "The tower tends to follow a pattern with puzzles like this. I'm sure once we get through this tunnel and to the next it'll be harder but similar. Just like this one was compared to the last tunnel."

That explanation made sense to Wyn. So far, the tower had shown a certain pattern. First there was just one enemy, the tunnel wasn't barred, and there were six possible paths. Now there were three enemies, the tunnel required them to be defeated to proceed, and there were four possible paths. The mushroom monsters were all formed the same way, too.

Even though this was his first trip into the tower, Wyn was able to get a better sense of the progression. He only imagined how confident Climbers became with more experience as they completed the floors over and over.

Cedric began to survey the other tunnels. He checked each one, taking his time to pick the tunnel he wanted to try.

"So a Ranger," Wyn said. "I don't remember that as a class option."

Marcy chuckled. "I started as a Hunter. Ranger was my second-tier class upgrade, but you don't need to worry about that right now." She held up her bow and inspected the bow string, plucking it gently. It vibrated a bit then quickly went still.

"Why is that?"

"Because getting to the second tier isn't our focus at the moment. Living to see tomorrow is."

Wyn relented. Of course she was right. His curiosity was getting the better of him, though.

"Humor me. What makes your class stand out?"

Marcy stared back in his eyes, seemingly looking beyond them. Her gaze was piercing.

"Alright. There aren't many classes that are more ranged outside of pure magic. Some Fighters and Rogues specialize in ranged combat, and of course there are Magicians and Sorcerers. But I'm a sort of magical hybrid focusing on a bow."

Wyn laughed. "You sound like a Ruby Magician, just ranged."

Marcy scrunched her face up. "Huh. I guess you could say so. But my spells are specific and different from your options."

"I guess that makes you more desirable, then. That's good for you."

Marcy patted Wyn on the back. "You'll find a group like I did. Who knows, you might've already found a couple of members with Tasha and John."

Wyn thought about that. Maybe Marcy was right. What the three rookies went through, culminating with Lionel's betrayal, created a sort of bond, in a way. He'd certainly ask them to group up when he got back.

He still wanted to ask Marcy, too, even if she was in another group. But he needed to find the right way and time.

"Alright," Cedric said. "I think I know which one I'll try."

"Finally," Marcy said. She began to walk over to Cedric and the tunnel he chose. "I'm ready to get out of here and find Lionel so I can kill him."

"And make sure John is okay," Wyn added.

"Don't worry," she responded. "He's fine. The guild medics are second to none."

"And, like I said," Cedric added, "Tasha was healing him when I ran after all of you. He made it back. Let's just focus on ourselves."

Marcy and Wyn nodded.

Cedric was right, of course. Wyn was realizing he must've been the voice of reason in their group. A tactician, too. If he wasn't the leader, he was definitely someone they turned to for direction.

The three stood outside the main hub of tunnels. Cedric walked to the far-left tunnel this time, then stopped. He shifted his feet and went to the tunnel beside it, second to the left.

Marcy chuckled. "Always superstitious."

Cedric ignored her and walked into the tunnel. All three of them waited for a second, and nothing happened.

"Huh," Cedric said.

No mushroom shook its powder, and no bars erupted from the cave floor to seal him off. There was only silence.

"What does that mean?" Wyn asked.

The three Climbers then heard a sound further into the tunnel. It sounded like stone moving against itself, something shifting further down they couldn't see at the entrance. *Something* was happening though they weren't sure what.

"I'll go take a look," Cedric said. "You two just wait here. It'll only take a minute."

Wyn felt a bead of sweat roll down his neck. He knew Cedric could handle himself, but he *hated* the thought of him going in alone. He wanted to interject and say he'd follow him but ultimately decided to respect his request and stayed behind.

Cedric walked down the tunnel and disappeared around a bend out of sight. Marcy and Wyn waited impatiently.

"So Rangers aren't too popular, then," Wyn said, breaking the silence. "Ruby Magicians aren't either. Obviously."

"That's not a question, just a statement," she said.

"You didn't let me finish."

She nodded, conceding.

"Have you seen another Ruby Magician? Is it really *that* bad?"

"Why does it matter?"

Wyn took a deep breath. "In the military we respected rank. Someone higher up could give orders without question, and we'd follow them. We looked up to them."

"Of course. Makes sense."

"I was a captain. I led a company of men who looked up to me and relied on me. They respected me. I earned it, too."

"That's great. But then something went wrong, didn't it?"

"Yes." Wyn looked at the ground, breaking eye contact. His shame returned, and he closed off.

"I'm not going to push you to talk about it. I'm sure it's not easy."

"Thank you."

"But what's your point with all this?"

"My point is that in the military camaraderie and working together was crucial. Those leaders were useless without soldiers to listen and act. It takes trusting people to accomplish a goal. The same goes for here. To really climb Alistair you need a group that's rock solid. Together."

Marcy plucked her bowstring again, keeping her fingers busy. She let Wyn go on, not wanting to interrupt.

"Which is why what Lionel did was unforgivable. But do people really not trust others because of their class? He ridiculed me just because I'm a Ruby Magician. I don't care, honestly, because I know my abilities—but have you seen that here?"

Marcy drew an arrow and twirled it with her fingers. "Yes, unfortunately, I have seen it."

Wyn wasn't surprised. Just disappointed.

"The main classes all find their place in one way or another," Marcy continued. "Fighters are the most common and the most general. They have many different kinds of skills they can use for enhancing their physical abilities. Magicians, in their different forms, are the strongest magic classes and typically focus on spells that either hurt enemies or help allies. Look at Diamond Magicians like Tasha or Lightning Wizards like Cedric."

"You keep calling him a Wizard. Is that his class upgrade, too?"

Marcy smiled. "Yes. He was a Topaz Magician."

"I don't know if I'll ever figure this out."

Marcy laughed. "You're being too hard on yourself. Classes are specific, yes, but also generic. Rogues are generic physical attackers. Sorcerers are generic magic users. You just happen to be one of the classes that falls under both."

Wyn didn't answer. He didn't know how.

Marcy took a second before elaborating. She scrunched her face and brought her hand up to her chin. "Think about it like this. Generic classes can be helpful because there are a lot of them and they are varied. You can have a dozen Sorcerers all with different skills and different spells to cast, and they will seem unique despite being generic."

"Like one focusing on the fire element, or one focusing on ice?"

"It could be that way, yes. Or one Sorcerer having skills and spells to support area-based magic instead of targeting a single enemy."

"Okay, I think I'm catching on. And on the other hand, Fire Magicians, for example, all cast fire spells and are basically the same?"

"In a way. Though they're called Garnet Magicians. They're based off the gem that helps provide the elemental magic. The difference in the gemstone Magicians, though, is that they're immensely helpful by being so focused."

"That's the secret, then."

"In a party of six people, let's say, you want roles to round out your group. It's good to have a variation. It's also good for that one person filling that role to be great at what they do. And on the higher floors it's necessary."

"So a Ruby Magician, as an example, being both generic and specific, is nei-ther? And *not* useful?"

"To most people, yes."

"To most people. My mentor told me that, too." Wyn smiled. "I'm guessing you don't fall under that category?"

Marcy smiled back. "No, I don't. Because my class is also considered not very useful."

Wyn laughed. "No way. Don't make me try to feel better."

Marcy furrowed her eyebrows and stopped smiling. "I'm serious. Why do you think there aren't many of us? We're seen as *not useful*. When given the option, Climbers don't take Ranger."

"That doesn't make sense. I've barely seen you use your skills and you're incredible."

Marcy's cheeks flushed. "I'm grateful to be in a group that thinks the same thing. Which is what you need to do, Wyn. Find people who see your worth. Prove them right and then prove the masses wrong."

Wyn thought on that statement. She was absolutely right—just because people think Ruby Magicians aren't helpful doesn't mean they aren't. Variety is useful, and having a group to utilize that like Marcy's group would be his key to success.

John is someone like that. Tasha, too.

A rush of cold flooded through Wyn's body.

"John," Wyn said to no one. "He agreed to team up even knowing my class. I have to make sure he's okay. I want him in my group."

"He'd be lucky to have you," Marcy said, and tapped her arrow on Wyn's arm.

"Maybe your group needs some more variety," Wyn said. He smirked, and twirled his spear in a flashy display.

Marcy laughed. It was hearty, loud, and warmly comforting. "Maybe so! You need some better gear, though. You can't be taking on even the lower middle floors with basic weapons and no armor."

"This should help with that," Cedric said.

Both Marcy and Wyn jumped, startled by the Wizard. He was standing at the entrance of the tunnel holding something in his left hand.

"What happened?" Wyn asked. "And what do you mean?"

"Oh, it was a dead end," he replied. "But at least at that dead end was a chest!"

"What happened to *focus on the task and don't be distracted by loot*?" Marcy said, mocking him.

"We're doing alright on time," Cedric replied. "I checked. Plus, Wyn is right. We'll make it out of here fine."

"Well, spill it already," Wyn said, "What did you find?"

"Some silver cloaks, a few gems. The basic monetary rewards. But this—this was more special. And you should have it, Wyn."

Cedric then held out a dagger. It was simple—black and silver, plain, and sheathed. It looked to be an ordinary dagger. Except it was not, as it had a blue aura around it.

"Damn," Marcy said. "A blue weapon on floor two? That's pretty rare."

"What's the importance of that?" Wyn asked. He took the dagger from Cedric. The faint blue aura was captivating, like his eyes were drawn to it.

"Magic weapons and armor have a certain amount of magical power to them based on their aura," Cedric said. "Green is the most common and least powerful."

"Next is blue," Marcy added, "followed by purple, then orange."

"But besides the aura, it doesn't look all that special," Wyn said. "No offense."

Both Marcy and Cedric chuckled.

"What's so funny?"

"It hasn't been identified yet," Cedric said. "Once it is, its appearance will reflect its true, magical nature."

Wyn opened his mouth to respond, but Marcy cut him off.

"And before you ask more questions, just put it in your pack. No sense in Cedric using his limited mana to identify a weapon that may not even help us right now. Let's just stick with what we know, and you can identify it back at the base. Alright?"

Wyn already had his pack open and placed the dagger inside. "Alright. And thank you, Cedric. I'm sure this is worth quite a lot."

"Don't mention it. This is your climb, after all. An atrocious one, mind you, but still."

Wyn nodded. "How about I check the next path? It's my turn, and there are only two left." He turned around and walked to the next tunnel in line to try.

"Do I see smoke coming out of the end of that tunnel?" Marcy whispered, trying to look down the cave path where Cedric explored.

"I don't know what you're talking about," he replied, smiling. He followed Wyn to look for another path.

She accepted his reply without another word.

CHAPTER SIXTEEN

Two more tunnels left here," Wyn said, standing with his arms folded. "The far-left one and this one. Second to the right."

"I went through that one," Marcy said, pointing to the far-right tunnel, "and it was a bust."

"And mine had a chest but still not the way through," Cedric added. "So yes, that leaves these two."

"You had a bad feeling about the far-left one, didn't you?" Wyn asked. "That's why you changed your mind at the last minute?"

"He's just neurotic," Marcy said.

Cedric shot her a harsh look. She failed to suppress a laugh.

"Well, I'm trusting him," Wyn said. "I'll try this one."

Wyn held his spear at the ready and walked through. Wanting to not enter too far, he stopped a few feet in and waited. He turned around and shrugged to Marcy and Cedric.

After a few seconds a mushroom shook itself out of the entrance, and red dust fell to the ground. Stone bars shot up from the ground separating the group again, and Wyn quickly stepped further back into the tunnel a few feet to avoid being impaled.

"Damnit," he said. "I thought I had it. This is wasting our time!"

"It's a step forward," Cedric said. "Now we know the other tunnel is the correct one. We just need to focus and take care of the mushrooms quickly and efficiently. Get ready." He raised his staff, and the topaz gem began to glow with a pale yellow light.

A mushroom began to form in front of the veterans and by the bars, rising from the ground. It was fiery red, thin like the yellow mushroom, and had cap armor similar to the orange one, though not as large as either. Overall, it was a bit short, maybe four feet tall. While it was smaller, it looked more dangerous than the other colors. It moved fluidly as it rose from the ground like a flickering flame, and smoke trailed from its head like dark, dirty hair.

Then another identical mushroom rose directly in front of it.

Wyn was only a foot away, the bars separating him and everyone else. The red mushrooms were facing Marcy and Cedric and weren't focused on him. They didn't even acknowledge him at all. He was thankful, too, because the heat they gave off was immense. He felt hot even with the bars between them and a few feet back. Direct combat would be difficult, and both Marcy and Cedric were better equipped to face them anyway.

"*Earthen Trap*!" Marcy said, nearly yelling. She bent down and placed her hands on the ground, palming the stone floor. A large magic circle appeared and covered the ground between her and Cedric and the two flaming mushrooms.

Cedric raised his staff and pointed it at the mushrooms. "Come on, you bastards!"

Wyn began to yell out but stopped himself. What would he even say? They were two veteran Climbers who had likely been in similarly difficult situations and managed themselves just fine. They weren't his soldiers, and he wasn't their captain. He needed to let them handle it themselves and stay on guard for his own safety.

He turned and looked down the tunnel to see if any other mushroom had formed like before. All he saw was an empty cave path lit by mushrooms on the wall and ceiling. During the last attempt to find the exit one formed on Marcy's side of the bars, so he figured another could be here, too.

Taking a deep breath, he began to slowly walk, staying vigilant so he could strike quickly.

A loud clap echoed off the walls, like a heavy rock suddenly slapped against stone. He turned quickly and stabbed with his spear. There was nothing there, though he saw what caused the noise.

The two mushrooms had charged Marcy and Cedric but were now caught in a rock-like prison. Chains made of stone held them in place in various areas—their necks, arms, legs, and torso were all shackled. The spell Marcy cast held true, and they tried to writhe and free themselves but weren't able. Flames erupted from their heads and bodies, licking at the magic chains, but were seemingly useless. The spell was strong, and apparently too much for these weaker enemies.

Cedric stepped forward to the two mushrooms and extended his staff, arcing his body back away from the heat and partly covering his face with his free forearm. "*Forked Lightning*!" he yelled, casting a spell.

Instantly lightning burst from his staff, arcs flying out in multiple directions. It pierced the mushrooms and the rest of the tunnel, too, jolting out wide. The electric bolts bounced around the tunnel entrance, looking like lightning caught in a bottle.

The two mushrooms froze in place as lightning coursed through their bodies, their flames expanding before snuffing out. They dissolved in a pile of ash just as the lightning spell dissipated around the cavernous room.

Two of the bars lowered just like before, the one in the middle staying still.

"Your turn," Marcy said, yelling down the tunnel.

Wyn knew what that meant. His heart raced, excited but nervous. They easily dealt with their enemies—would he be able to handle himself just as easily?

He turned, focused back at the task at hand. He knew another would be showing up but didn't know when or where. It shouldn't be long. Strategies bounced around in his head about the best way to combat these flaming enemies.

His spear's reach afforded him some distance, but there wasn't much room in the cave tunnel to maneuver his position. He could keep backing up to the bars but would essentially trap himself. That would be a death sentence. Trying to skirt around the enemy could be possible, but the room was much narrower on the sides, not to mention he ran the risk of being burnt.

Ranged attacks would be best, like how Cedric and Marcy handled it. Unfortunately Wyn only had two means of ranged attacks: casting **Ice Shard** or throwing his dagger. He was never one to throw his secondary weapon, and the odds of it harmlessly hitting the flaming mushroom with the hilt or flat of the blade was far higher than an actual pierce with the tip or cut with the edge. That left his spell, but it was an ice spell. How would that be effective against a flaming enemy?

Maybe Cedric could identify his new dagger quickly through the bars. There was still a chance it held some effect that could help him. But would he even be able to use it correctly? He barely knew how to use his spells, and he spent time with Daniel telling him exactly what to do to even get to his current point. If he relied on it and it failed, the dagger itself could hurt him, or he'd be burned alive by these fiery creatures.

About twenty feet in front of him he saw a mushroom shake its dust to the ground, and a red flaming mushroom began to emerge. It was writhing like the others in its formation, the incarnation of living flame.

Wyn quickly thought about how the magic would react to each other. Hopefully the elements didn't interact *too* much—it was magic, after all, and his spell could hopefully overcome the typical idea of ice melting under fire. The monster forming in front of him was magic, too, though, so that theory was highly unlikely.

He looked at his simple spear. The **Magic Weapon** spell had worn off a good while ago. Would a standard metal spear point and wooden shaft be enough against magical flames?

The mushroom was almost fully formed. Wyn quickly brought up his left forearm and checked his mark. **Lucidity** had recovered some mana but not that much. He had just under half remaining, and the thought of using it for testing theories didn't sit well with him.

He had only one option left. If he could quickly strike the flaming monster, position himself for attacks and defenses fast by moving away to avoid the heat and fire before they overwhelmed him, he'd stand a fair chance.

He opted to use his **Speed Up** skill and hope for the best.

The mushroom finally finished growing itself into its final flaming form, and locked its beady, smoking black eyes on him. The effect was unsettling, like a demon had formed directly from one of the deep layers of hell and rose as a perverse fungus.

Wyn decided it was time. The more this was drawn out the worse it'd be for him. He still wasn't exactly sure how to engage the skill, but he hoped it was similar to his spells—say it with intention, and the mark did the rest. "**Speed Up**!" he yelled.

A soft red glow began to envelope him. It was much duller than his **Arcane Aura** spell and red instead of white, but still obviously magical. A rush of what felt like adrenaline overtook him. He did *not* have the same feeling with the protective spell. They were obviously different, but it was striking how this skill made him feel.

The mushroom began to move toward him in a hypnotic pattern. It was beautiful, almost like a dance, as flames licked out of its core body in swirls. There was no weapon in its hands, and Wyn could hardly tell if it even had hands. But it didn't matter with this enemy, as being too close would bring about scathing heat and burns, and any direct contact would be dire.

Worse, what other kinds of magic did it have? Could it cast spells or throw fire at a distance, or was it strictly a close-range combatant? Wyn had no desire to find out. This monster needed to be killed *fast*.

Moving his feet to reposition, Wyn felt his legs pulse forward much quicker than he thought. It was jarring, and his body matched the quickness when he awkwardly shot himself forward. He lightly jumped back and forth, then swished his spear in the air, testing his new ability with a few movements. To his satisfaction and surprise, he was moving at a greater speed than he imagined, able to move his weapon and body faster than ever.

The red mushroom began to hop down the cave, frolicking like a child. It was strangely unassuming, like it was playful rather than trying to kill him. The flames were not harmless, though, and Wyn could feel the heat rising as the monster came closer. Using his newfound speed he pierced his spear forward, aiming in the middle of his enemy. The weapon lashed out quickly, but his body was adjusting to his new speed. It was invigorating, though Wyn had no idea how long the skill would last. He needed to be prudent.

As the spear tip lunged out, the entire metal head went into the monster. Wyn didn't quite know what to expect. He felt as though he would've been surprised whether the monster was gaseous like fire without a true physical form or had a solid body that only radiated fire. Thankfully for him the latter was true, as he felt resistance in the torso give way to his weapon. When he pulled his spear free, the monster jerked, obviously damaged by the attack. He was glad he could hurt it but hopped backward as the heat was nearly too much to bear even being several feet away.

The spear head was barely glowing red as though he quickly exposed it to a fire, which in a way, he did. Wyn could also see the end of the spear's shaft was discoloring, and he figured too many attacks would char the wooden portion of his weapon, making it useless.

This further emphasized the importance of dealing with this enemy quickly. If he stalled too much, he'd be weaponless and *then* burned to death.

Wyn took several more strikes against the enemy as he seemingly flew around the cave tunnel, moving like a whirlwind. The monster returned his movements in kind, slinging small globs of fire at him left and right, though Wyn was moving too fast to be hit. His theory was unfortunately right about the monster having more abilities, and long-ranged ones at that.

Still, it was truly a beautiful fight, like two dancers playing the role of fighters on a stage.

Thankfully the red mushroom was slowing down, the spear strikes working to kill it. It was oddly shrinking in size, the flames dying out and reducing both their intensity and heat. The tallest flames coming off its head weren't even reaching Wyn's waist.

He was close to finishing it, and was glad. The fight felt like it was raging on, though it couldn't have been thirty seconds—Wyn's speed increase made it feel as though he was speeding through time. It didn't help that he felt like he was fighting in a furnace, and several patches of holes formed in his robes from stray streaks of flame.

He sidestepped once more around the monster, repositioning to its back for a better strike. As he did, the mushroom leaped toward him in a desperate maneuver. It lashed out with a fiery hand to cut him or punch him, Wyn wasn't sure which. But the contact would be awful regardless.

Wyn was able to cut it down with a large slash, but the body of the mushroom kept rushing toward him. It struck him directly in the hip and leg, and he gasped from the initial impact. The mushroom lost its flames and turned to dust, but not before scorching Wyn's waist and right leg down to his shin. He yelled in pain, his robes singed and pants underneath completely burned away, exposing his leg.

Wyn patted the smoldering embers, hoping he could put out the fire before it caused worse damage. It felt hot and ached, the cool cave air torturing his new burn. Not to mention each pat caused sharp pings of pain from his leg to his brain.

This was his fear. Injury at this point in their climb would not just be detrimental to finishing the floor, but could cause a permanent injury. Would his healing be able to address severe burns? What if he passed out from pain beforehand?

The spear clanged to the ground. Wyn dropped to the cave floor soon after, the pain unbearable. He had been hurt before, but nothing like this. It wasn't normal fire but magical fire, if that even made a difference. He was afraid to look at his leg but decided to anyway. It was important to know the extent of his injuries, if he could heal completely or if he'd be dealing with something far worse.

The skin was charred and swollen, and who knows what the muscle and tissue was like underneath. When he tried to bend his knee it felt as though he was being stabbed by thousands of tiny needles, and he couldn't move it much at all.

At least he wasn't bleeding. The burned skin cauterized whatever deeper wounds he had.

Wyn took a deep, shaky breath. This might be the end. ***Regen*** was a powerful spell, but he didn't know its capabilities or limits. The thought instantly crossed his mind that he might lose his leg if he even survived.

What in the hells did he get himself into?

CHAPTER SEVENTEEN

Marcy and Cedric rushed down the tunnel the instant the stone bars were gone.

"What happened?" Cedric asked. He got his answer when he walked in front of Wyn and saw his leg. "Shit. I was hoping we would get through this unscathed."

Wyn laughed, which was a strange feeling. Seeing Cedric still focused on the task of finishing the floor was oddly comforting, like this was an injury that was possible to overcome. It gave him a sense of hope.

Then Wyn felt the pain in his leg, again, causing that small flicker of hope to snuff out.

"Not now, Cedric," Marcy said. She quickly dropped her pack on the ground and rummaged through it.

Whether by subconscious decision or the skill expiring, Wyn's magical aura faded. He gritted his teeth and breathed heavily. The loss of the magical boost to his physicality made him feel even more helpless than he was.

"I'm sorry," Wyn said through gasps. Each hitch in his breath caused movement, which made his leg jolt with pain. "I didn't have much of an option. I thought **Ice Shard** would be useless."

"You're right about that," Cedric said. "Being made of the fire element, ice is weak to it. It would've been a waste of mana and could've been even worse. That was the best call you could've made, unfortunately."

Marcy glared at the Wizard. "We don't need a lesson right now, Cedric." She pulled her hand out of the pack along with a medium-sized corked jar of some type of cream. It looked like it should hold some type of spread for the dinner table rather than the middle of a deadly tower.

"Learning opportunities are always . . ."

"Cedric, damnit, *shut up*," Marcy snapped, cutting him off. "And save your breath, Wyn. Try not to jerk so much."

Cedric started to reply but quickly closed his mouth, stopping himself from continuing his lecture.

Wyn wasn't listening too well, anyway. His leg still felt like it was on fire, and a portion of his charred knee began to ooze. Or at least what he thought was his knee. It didn't resemble much of a leg anymore, to his horror. It was more of a large lump of unidentifiable flesh.

His thoughts began to push back to the war, where bloodshed was rampant and death welcoming. The view was hazy as Wyn fought to stay present. He shook his head and focused on the pain. Oddly, it helped ground him to the situation at hand.

Marcy had already popped the cork on the small jar while Wyn was lost in thought. The cream was yellow and waxy, and a strong aura exuded out from the jar. It wasn't as strong as Tasha's spells or Wyn's **Arcane Aura**, but it was more noticeable than the potion.

Wyn shot upright from the ground, then cursed at the pain. "Shit!"

"Wyn, I said to stop moving!" Marcy said. She scooped a bit of the magical cream up with her fingers and reached over to Wyn's leg.

Wyn caught her wrist. "Save it. My mentor gave me a healing potion."

Marcy smacked Wyn's hand away. "*You* save it. It won't work as well as this for this injury."

That was all Wyn needed to hear to find some comfort that he'd be all right. If Marcy was turning away a health potion, then it either wasn't as serious as Wyn thought, or her magical cream was just that good.

He leaned toward the latter based on how his leg looked and felt.

Wyn immediately closed his eyes and clenched his jaw. He knew the application would hurt—salves on burns always did. He remembered the soldiers who suffered burns from oil fires and flaming arrows and their screams when the medics tended to them. They said it was the contact with the burned flesh that felt like being stabbed with a hot iron.

Only pain never came. Relief flushed over him instead, reminding him of the bath houses outside Caryn. He remembered the soothing feel of lotions and creams on him after the baths, how his chapped skin drank the moisture with rejuvenation before setting back out into the sun with his company.

He snapped open his eyes. The bath houses and company men were not here— he was in the tower, fighting for his life and the life of others.

It still surprised Wyn how magic was seemingly infused in everything here. At this point he expected it to be inside the food, too, served on literal silver platters. But the salve that Marcy applied worked like a spell to heal him, whether it was one or not.

He finally gained the courage to look at his leg where Marcy was still applying the medicine. The cream was still glowing, nearly as bright as the mushrooms around them. He was sure that it was magical. The pain steadily went away, and his skin returned, like she was wiping a new layer back onto his leg. It wasn't fast, though, and the process took several minutes, even if it felt like it took hours.

"That's amazing," Wyn said. He moved his leg. It felt perfectly fine now, even though his pants exposed him almost up to his groin. The weakness and tingling sensation were both gone.

"It's a Ranger spell that can be stored," Marcy said. She jammed the cork back onto the jar and placed it back in her pack. "It would never be useful in the heat of a fight, but it's great for down times. And it's stronger than potions for elemental injuries."

"Now look who's lecturing," Cedric whispered.

"It's perfect," Wyn said. "Thank you, Marcy."

Marcy reached out for Wyn's hand to help him stand. He grabbed it, and she easily yanked him to his feet. He was a bit taken aback at how strong she was, and made a mental note to stop using his preconceived notions and experiences to try to understand this new world.

"At least it was minor," Cedric said. "All things considered. Some monsters in here can rip limbs off. You got lucky."

"Minor," Wyn said, shaking his head in disbelief. "But I know I did." He fingered the singed edges of his robes and pants. "I really need to get some better gear. This is pathetic."

"This wasn't expected, though. No rookie Climber would have magical gear on their first trip into the tower. Not average ones, anyway."

"Cedric's right," Marcy said. "And you're doing great. Well, except for the parts where you aren't. But don't worry."

Wyn knew she was teasing him, but hearing it out loud stung more than he thought. "I think I need to stay in the first few floors for some time and not rush it. As long as I can find a good amount of gold that way."

Cedric penned some notes onto his map. "You'd be surprised about what you'd make doing that for a season. It won't be as much as you need, but you can increase the number of climbs to help offset that. But, Wyn, that's one of the wisest things I've heard today." Cedric patted him on the back.

"Don't mind him," Marcy said. "He missed his true calling as a teacher."

"And having a magical weapon is basically required," Cedric said, ignoring Marcy. "All Climbers have one, and those who engage in combat often have several. That way you won't have to rely on your spells and skills and use valuable mana inefficiently."

"Especially for a Ruby Magician who needs to use everything," Wyn said. He flicked his right foot and felt the cool air rush over his now-barren leg. At least his boot was still mostly intact so he wouldn't have to walk or fight lopsided. "And maybe several pairs of clothes, too."

Marcy and Cedric laughed. It felt good to hear it, and they all warmed up at the lighthearted feeling despite their situation.

That was the camaraderie Wyn missed the most with his company. The laughter and bonds formed in the midst of chaos and destruction.

Marcy walked out of the tunnel back toward the entrance. "But let's move on to the final fork, shall we? I don't want to press our luck with time," she said, not turning back. She waved her bow in the air like she was summoning them to follow her.

Cedric pulled out his small piece of parchment again. "It's 9:41. She's right. We still have some time, but I'm exhausted, too. I'd rather not delay anymore." He began to follow Marcy hurriedly, catching up to her.

They were right, of course, and Wyn knew it. Based on Marcy and Cedric's information they should be nearing the end of the floor. It didn't feel much worse than the first floor regarding the combat, though the enemies were more magical. Of course that made them more dangerous, especially for a new Climber like Wyn who wasn't familiar with the knowledge of magic, the elements, and monsters that are made of them both.

The maze leading through the cave was another challenge to overcome, and Wyn could see how each higher floor would pose different sets of challenges rather than pure fighting. This floor was a maze-like puzzle in addition to bouts of combat. What would the eighth floor look like? Or the fourteenth?

Wyn put that out of his mind. There was no sense in worrying about that when he'd never face them. Not now, anyway. By the time he was ready to challenge those floors, this season and environment would be long gone.

He jogged behind them, catching up to the veterans. They silently walked back to the beginning of the forked tunnels to traverse the only one left—the far-left tunnel.

Wyn thought about all of the possible challenges he'd face in the tower. Of course combat was ever present, but based on this floor Climbers would need a good head on their shoulders, too, in order to face non-combat related issues. Having magic was an obvious bonus as well, as he was sure there'd be tougher magical enemies and terrain in his future. The luxury of choice he had in choosing spells he could use was as much of a boon as any. Entering the tower with a good balance of spells, magical equipment, and Climbers to wield them all would make for a powerful team that could achieve great heights.

Thinking about this only solidified his resolve that Ruby Magicians were helpful rather than a handicap. Having combat related skills like melee classes and being able to use spells like magical classes was the best option for the unexpected. He could maintain a variety of tools at his disposal in order to keep his relevance. A store of weapons here, a cache of armor there. There'd be no doubt with his future team about his worth.

But it was all worthless if he couldn't earn the money needed to pay off his father's debts. Earning coins to send back home was the ultimate goal, after all. Being the best Climber possible in his situation was the means to achieve that goal.

Wyn made a vow to himself that he would do what was necessary for his family.

"So much for your bad feeling," Marcy said as they all stepped into the last remaining tunnel. They all turned around and saw two mushrooms shake their blue dust onto the ground, the tower's signal that they were finally on the right path.

Cedric made a face at Marcy, sticking out his tongue and crinkling his face. She laughed at him and pushed him away from her. He laughed, too, a high-pitched cackle Wyn wasn't expecting. It was jarring coming from the stoic Wizard, but Wyn was unexpectedly delighted that Cedric of all people made a noise like that.

The three made their way through the tunnel, knowing full well they were getting closer to the end. It was progressing into a sour feeling, and they all felt it—they were happy they were doing fairly well but upset at why they were here in the first place. They wanted to confront Lionel more than their fear of the consequences of going to the next floor without a key.

But they were here now and doing what they could to survive.

"I want to take the next one, too," Wyn said. "Whatever happens I can manage. I know I can."

Marcy and Cedric exchanged glances.

"We will all take the next one," Cedric said.

Marcy nodded her head. "Right, because it'll likely be the final path."

Right then they came upon their next fork. It was far shorter than the previous tunnels between forked options, but the mushrooms continued to light their path. Only now the fungi were becoming more sparse, their multicolored glow lowering down to more of a dim light.

Before them now were two possible tunnels to choose. They could see down each about twenty feet, but then they both curved off, hiding what was further down the path.

"So this is it," Cedric said. "Our last path."

"Either the right way," Marcy said, "or the very wrong way. That's usually how this works at the end."

"I'd imagine it's deadlier if we choose wrong," Wyn said. "So maybe two should go instead?"

"No," Cedric said. "We stay together. We can't afford to be separate if we choose wrong."

"Exactly," Marcy agreed. "From here to the end. Whether we choose right or wrong, it's as a group."

Wyn nodded. They had a point, and he wasn't about to argue. This wasn't a basic scouting assignment or patrol. This was far, far different, and the value of keeping together as a group was apparently paramount.

Marcy sat down at the fork and set her bow beside her. "Might as well rest for now, though. There's a lot riding on this."

Wyn thought for a moment. "Cedric. We only have a couple of hours, right?"

Cedric pulled out his parchment paper. "9:56."

Wyn checked his mark. He had little more than a third of his mana remaining, which likely wasn't enough for two spells if he needed to use them. "How much of your mana would you recover if you rested for an hour?"

Cedric scratched his chin. "Some, but not a lot. Maybe a fifth?"

"About a fourth for me," Marcy added.

"Then I say we rest for an hour and then pick. We'll have more mana, and we have the time, especially since this is the end. We can afford it."

Cedric sat down beside Marcy. "That would give us only an hour to finish the final room. A calculated risk I'm willing to take." He closed his eyes and set his head against the cave wall.

"I'll be nearly at full," Wyn said. "But can you talk and recover mana at the same time, or does it take concentration?"

"Concentration," Marcy said, closing her eyes. "Sort of like meditation."

"So I guess trying to remember what the final area consisted of would be too distracting?"

Marcy threw a small rock at Wyn that bounced harmlessly off his chest.

"Maybe something in the room will spark a memory," Cedric said, not opening his eyes. "But for now, we empty our minds and prepare."

Wyn took that as a statement to leave them alone. Which was fine by him, as he didn't need to concentrate to recover his mana. Meditation never came easy to him anyway. He was happy once again that *Lucidity* allowed him to recover his own mana without the need to rest. He wondered if he could recover more if he joined them, but he was restless. It would be fruitless to try to sit still so close to the end.

And yet, the camaraderie was important as well.

Wyn ultimately sat down opposite them beside a purple mushroom. Not ten seconds later his stomach growled. He realized he hadn't had food in hours. He opened his pack for his water skin and rations and snacked for a few minutes, enough to curb the hunger but not too much to overfill.

His attempt at resting was failing quickly. He tried taking deep breaths to still his mind but was unable to tear himself away from the cave. Finally, he decided to take a look around. *Lucidity* would recover some of his mana, and he made peace that it would suffice.

The mushrooms here were moving ever so slightly, impossible to tell unless you took the time to stare at them exactly as Wyn was doing. They would gyrate as though trying to escape the wall and ceiling, and seeing them all move like that was a bit off-putting. No dust was falling from them, though they continued their luminescent glow in various colors with blue being the most dominant. The spectacle of movement and many colors made Wyn uncomfortable and nearly sick.

He looked down the tunnels and noticed the left tunnel was now glowing a dim yellow. The light began to grow slowly, a different, stronger light than the mushrooms. Wyn stood up to try to get a better angle. The light was warm and inviting, and he felt a strange sense of calm while watching it grow brighter with each second.

Before he realized it, he walked over to the tunnel entrance and slowly stepped toward the light. He stopped, not wanting to go alone. Cedric and Marcy would be furious with him if they knew he went down it without them.

"Guys, look at this," he said, but squinted his eyes now due to the brightness. "I think we need to—" he started, but stopped. Marcy and Cedric were gone. The tunnel was empty, the mushrooms no longer gyrating. The space was still and void.

The yellow light was pulsing now, giving off a strong magical aura. It seemed to call to him, drawing him in to see what it was.

Wyn couldn't resist the urge. He stepped forward and began to walk into the light.

CHAPTER EIGHTEEN

The instant Wyn stepped into the tunnel to find the source of the light he regretted it. He didn't walk twenty feet before the light became too bright, shining big and bold like the sun, forcing him to cover his eyes with a hand and then close them when it was still too much.

It was an odd feeling as his mind wasn't thinking clearly. Deep down in the back of his mind he knew he shouldn't be going anywhere without his teammates, let alone toward a mysterious bright light. Still, his legs were seemingly moving on their own as the light drew him in.

He could see the light through his eyelids for only a second, an afterimage of the blinding light. Before long he noticed it was thankfully starting to fade. He gingerly opened his eyes and saw the light was now gone, but his vision was clouded from the experience. His eyes needed to readjust. It took him almost a minute of hard blinking and nervously looking around in fear before he could make out any details.

He now realized, to his horror, that he was no longer in the cave tunnel. Instead, he seemed to be in a small cabin.

Wooden walls surrounded him, simple and plain. Bookshelves lined the walls to his right, and a small countertop with a wash basin sat on the left wall. There was a square wooden table in the middle of the room, two chairs sitting on either side of it. It was empty. Hanging on wood columns that accented the space were lanterns that offered light so Wyn could see. The light was soft yellow—the same yellow that beckoned him in the first place.

There was a single door to his back and no windows, and he was alone.

As Wyn looked around he noticed it wasn't as simple or boring as he first thought. He walked over to the bookshelves and saw not books, but jars of liquids set all across it, murky colors of green, brown, and yellow clouding the insides.

They looked old and dirty, like someone from decades ago filled them from a swamp or some similarly disgusting water.

He picked one up and shook it a bit, the brown water swirling inside. A rattle echoed off the glass. He couldn't make out exactly what was inside, but it looked almost like small bones.

"Welcome, Ardwyn," a voice said, scaring Wyn. The words were drawn out, the voice hoarse and old. He jumped back, startled, and dropped the jar onto the ground. It shattered, and the liquid spewed all over Wyn's robes and boots, the bone-like objects scattering on the wooden floor. Wyn looked around the room to find who spoke to him and said his name.

"Hello? Who's there?" He stepped over the glass and walked to the table. He narrowly avoided stepping on the small bones from the jar, and didn't realize they were inching toward his boots like worms on the floor.

It didn't seem anyone else was in the room. Not that he could see, at least. The space appeared empty and eerily silent, but he had no idea about what magic resided in this place. The sound of the glass jar shattering still echoed in his ears.

"Please sit down," the voice said again, and Wyn jerked his head around. There was now a woman sitting in one of the chairs in the middle of the room, her fingers steepled together as her arms rested on the table. She had a sly smile on her face, and her gray hair was wiry. Her skin was wrinkled and gray, like she was wearing makeup made of dust.

Wyn cautiously stepped over to the table but didn't sit down. "Where am I? And who are you?"

The woman chuckled. "Always so many questions. You're in the same place you've been. And I am an Avatar of Alistair. Won't you please sit down?"

Wyn felt like he was in a dream. For all he knew he was—maybe the mushrooms in the cave put him in a sort of hallucinogenic trance? Were Cedric and Marcy in similar situations?

Wyn grabbed the chair. It felt real. The grains of the wood were splintered and rough, and when he pulled it out to sit it was heavy. He sat down opposite the older woman.

"Thank you," she said. She gave that sly smile again. It felt . . . odd.

"Avatar of Alistair. What does that mean?"

She laughed this time. It was more of a cackle, really, and Wyn's hair stood on end hearing it. "No one seems to know anymore. It means that I am a part of the Great One. I was created to carry out whatever is needed, and have been granted the magic and means to do so."

Wyn made it a point to remain as calm as possible. He didn't want to seem antagonistic or threatening, and right now it felt as though she only wanted to share information. But he felt very strong and very serious power from her deep inside him. "The Great One. You mean the tower?"

"Not THE tower, the Great One! And you will refer to her as such!" She raised her voice at Wyn, sending spittle across the table with her words. She pounded her palms on the wood when she spoke, and Wyn jumped in his chair. He could've sworn her eyes were glowing yellow when she lashed out.

It struck him that she referred to the tower in another name he hadn't heard, not to mention calling it "her." He'd need to tread very lightly and carefully choose his words.

"I'm sorry," Wyn said. "The Great One. You're . . . her . . . Avatar, then."

"Yes," she replied, her demeanor calming down and her sly smile returning. "I change with the seasons. Currently I reside on a higher floor, but she wanted me to see you."

Wyn's heart raced. There were several points in that sentence that he picked up on immediately. This Avatar was a higher floor creation—definitely a strong enemy, maybe a boss. If the tower sent her, that pointed to it being potentially sentient.

But, above all, why was he so special?

Wyn took a deep breath. "She . . . wanted you to meet me. Why? I'm a nobody. A rookie. I just came here today, after all."

"The Great One sees all and is a part of all beings and things here. Your class, magic, and abilities come from her. Items, currency, even some foods are born here, their magic stemming from the Great One and being sent out into the world. She knows much more than anyone gives her credit for."

Wyn didn't know what to say. How could he? Was this normal? He didn't even know what normal meant in the tower, if there even *was* a normal. Was this supposed to happen to Climbers and be kept a secret? His mind was racing, and he was having difficulty focusing.

The old woman smiled. "I know what you're thinking. So many questions running through your mind. But it's okay, child, you don't need them all answered. And some will be answered soon."

Wyn just stared at her. He didn't know if he should speak or just listen at this point.

She stared back at him for a minute. They were both locked in, her mysterious and vague and him nervous and confused. A bead of sweat ran down his forehead. He knew deep down he wouldn't have the ability to fight her. If she truly was a being from the higher floors, she could kill him with relative ease. It wouldn't even be a fight. It would be a slaughter.

"The Great One wanted me to meet you for encouragement. What happened today wasn't exactly . . . *typical* within her walls. It was unexpected, even for us. But there are forces at play here outside your understanding. It would be wise to not interfere."

Wyn perked up. "So it's a warning, then? Steer clear of this since I'm too weak to do anything?"

She shrugged her shoulders. "In a way."

Wyn quickly switched from being nervous to being frustrated. He did his best to keep his expression subtle.

"Now, now, don't be offended," she added. "You still have much to learn and much room to grow. And the Great One sees that you will grow very well."

Wyn obviously didn't do well with subtlety. The Avatar's words were unexpectedly encouraging, and he honestly didn't know how to respond.

"Be patient. Do what you came here to do. Grow, acquire magic and wealth, and then . . ." her sly smile grew wider and more menacing. "And then, we will meet again."

Wyn's heart skipped a beat. "Why are you telling me this? Even if it is a warning. And it sounds like you're encouraging me to defeat . . . the Great One. And you."

She cackled, and the sound made Wyn's skin crawl. The noise was piercing and harsh. "Don't forget your true purpose. You aren't here to *defeat* the Great One. That's impossible. You are simply here to pass her tests and take what she offers you."

"What do you mean? I thought the purpose was to conquer . . . her. Climb to the top and . . . well, I don't know. Win?" Wyn felt ridiculous the instant it came out of his mouth. He honestly didn't know what happened when Climbers reached and finished the twentieth floor. So few of them actually made it.

The old woman tilted her head to the side and furrowed her brow. "You must not know much about the Great One and her magic. How she came to be. How her brothers and sisters are?"

"No. I don't know."

The old woman let out a sigh. "Always so naive and uninformed, these children. I'll make it brief since I don't have much time. The noble and wonderful Alistair was the name given to this Great Tower by Aliyar, one of the gods who brought magic to the world by means of a special space . . ."

For a second Wyn was distracted hearing the name Aliyar again. Apparently they're a god, and he made a point to look more into them.

". . . He wanted to test the citizens of the world by trials to determine their worth. Even I don't know exactly why, but we were created to push people and advance them. And advance them we have."

"Through magic?"

"Of course."

"So that still doesn't answer me. It sounds like I'm still trying to defeat the tower since it's a trial."

The woman jerked her head slightly from Wyn's words. "Have you studied in an apprenticeship or undergone training in your life?"

"Yes. I was in the military. They exposed us to general educational classes and combat training." Wyn was honest. No sense trying to lie.

"That explains your resourcefulness and confidence for your first day." She smiled again. Wyn shivered.

"So," she continued, "think about it like this—when you had a test in your education or training you were graded in some way about your performance, no?"

"Yes."

"So you weren't trying to defeat the actual test. You can't. There's nothing to beat or kill. You were only displaying a performance about your abilities. And then others did the same with the same material."

Wyn thought on that. She was right, after all, as he processed it. It was a strange way to consider it but it made sense.

"This trial you are experiencing is similar. You cannot *defeat* the Great One. You can pass her trials or die trying, and you are only here to determine your worth. From Aliyar's perspective."

"This is a lot," Wyn said. He rubbed his temples. He was getting a headache with everything piling on from the course of the day topped with this new information.

The old woman sighed. "You are right. Which is why I shouldn't reveal more. You will find out more in your time here and continue to face challenges. However, don't forget—stay the course and don't interfere."

Wyn felt a heavy pressure from her when she finished. The room grew dark as the various sources of light flickered and dimmed. She smiled, and they returned to normal.

He was frozen, afraid to move. This felt even more surreal—just how powerful was she?

"Oh," she said. "One last thing. She wants you to have a reward. For the trouble caused."

Wyn perked up. "Yes?"

She waved her hand, and he felt a strange force in his pocket. It seemed to come from his parchment.

"The Great One wanted you to have a new skill. Exclusive to you."

Wyn could hardly believe it. A new skill exclusive for him? Was it normal to obtain skills easily like spells? He pulled out his parchment labeled **CLASS** and looked at it. There, at the bottom of his skill list was a new entry—***Tower's Blessing***.

Tower's Blessing: *A gift from the Avatar of Alistair. Provides one additional spell slot that may be used from any class at your tier that uses spells.*

"That will make your arduous journey slightly easier," the woman added. "Not by much, but it will grow in time."

He couldn't believe it. He felt exactly what she offered—blessed. One, for not attacking him and simply talking, and two, because he was getting a boon that he imagined no other rookie Climber possessed.

"Wyn," she continued, "one more thing." She walked over to the bookshelf and grabbed a small jar that she easily palmed in her hand. Or rather Wyn thought she walked, because it was hard to truly tell. She was fluid with her gait, and her long, ragged gray robe covered her legs, masking the truth. It looked as though she was gliding on air. Regardless, she came over to Wyn and showed him the jar.

There were small mushrooms inside the glass jar and a small chain on top of the lid. The mushrooms resembled the ones he'd seen so far in the cave, only tiny. She shook the jar, and the mushrooms bounced around, releasing their spores that lit up the area around him in an orange glow. It wasn't as bright as a torch, but the effect strangely carried further around the room. The mushrooms in the jar settled down but the spores swirled around like falling snow caught in the wind. The light was impressive for the size of the magical object.

"The blessing was from the Great One, and this is from me. Shake this jar, and you'll have light for a few hours. You can use the chain to secure it to yourself similar to a chained lantern."

Wyn took the jar and attached it to the front of his pants. "But won't it break? It's glass. It looks fragile." He played with it while it hung around his waist, giving it a brief tug to test the chain. Only now did he realize there was a faint blue glow to the item.

The old woman laughed again. "Silly child. It's a magically reinforced object! If you manage to break it you'd be the first."

Wyn blinked hard. It felt strange being called a child. Was he not the first owner of the jar?

She rapped her knuckles on the wooden table. "But our time is up. Remember my words, Ruby Magician. Take care."

Wyn saw the same light as before behind him. It was alluring, drawing him in again. He began to walk toward the light nearly subconsciously, his legs carrying him without him controlling them. Before he completely reached the light, he heard her speak one last time behind him, almost as an afterthought.

"And, Wyn, mind the colors. You won't make it out whole, I'm afraid."

Wyn turned back, unsure of her words. His legs carried him forward, though, and before he could reply he was engulfed in the light. The cabin and the old woman disappeared as the light overtook him once more.

Wyn felt the room spinning. He looked around, startled that he was back in the cave tunnel. His head throbbed, and he felt disoriented. The cave provided some support as he reached out to steady himself, but his knees buckled slightly, wobbling uncontrollably. He decided to give in and sat down on the cave floor as softly as he could, resting himself. The cold floor helped ground him to reality, and he closed his eyes to refocus.

His eyes shot open. Marcy and Cedric. Where were they? His head wasn't throbbing as much, thankfully, and he noticed there was a path leading left. Maybe it was the beginning of the two tunnels that forked, where he started walking when following the light? He stood up and walked over to it.

Sure enough, he was right. It was the start of the fork, the final decision that either led to the final room or a wrong path. He didn't find Marcy and Cedric, though. They were just here, he remembered, resting to recover some mana.

It didn't make sense. Nothing made sense.

He heard footsteps, shoes stomping on the ground loudly. Someone was here, and they were running. He wondered if it was his teammates, or maybe some straggling group that stayed late to tackle this floor?

Cedric and Marcy suddenly appeared from the tunnel from the previous fork, the last area they overcame. They were sweating and running.

"Marcy, Cedric—" Wyn started but was cut off from Marcy tackling him and pushing him against the wall.

"What in the hells did you do?!" she yelled. She seemed frantic. Her eyes were wide, and she was breathing hard, likely from running. Or so Wyn thought.

"What do you mean?" Wyn asked. He held his hands up pleadingly. The cave wall was digging into his back, and Marcy was holding his lapel, keeping him pinned. He tried to shift his torso for comfort, but she held him firmly.

"You've been gone nearly an hour," Cedric said. He was breathing hard.

Wyn's heart dropped. An hour? He was talking to that old woman for barely fifteen minutes! There's no way that was right.

"We've been running up and down these tunnels looking for you," Marcy said. She let go of Wyn a bit but still held on to him. "We didn't want to chance going down one of the final tunnels, but we retraced our steps. It was like you disappeared!"

"I'm so sorry," Wyn said. "I saw a light down the left tunnel while both of you were meditating. I went toward it to get a better look before I was suddenly gone! Both of you disappeared. It was like I was teleported somewhere else."

Marcy let go of him. She waved him off and turned away. Cedric was still recovering, doubled over with a hand on one knee, though Marcy had basically recovered.

"That was incredibly dumb," Cedric said, taking another drawn out breath to help settle himself. "You shouldn't have taken even one step . . . toward either tunnel without us." He was leaning on his staff for support. He looked worn down.

Wyn nodded. "I didn't think I stepped into it at all. I was about to warn both of you before it happened. But I was only gone for a few minutes, then I came back."

Cedric took one more deep breath. "Even if it *felt* like a few minutes it was much longer here. It's eleven o'clock."

"That doesn't make sense. Though I'm realizing it's a ridiculous effort to try to make any sense of this place."

"Not true either," the Wizard replied. "There are *some* rules."

"But there are also some things we don't fully understand," Marcy added. "Are you alright? What happened in those few minutes?"

Wyn thought about it for a second. Should he tell them? Would they think he was crazy? It seemed crazy even by this tower's standards. He flinched, expecting a scolding for not thinking to call it "the Great One" or "her."

He laughed. He trusted them. Of course he would share it.

But not yet.

"You won't believe me, but now might not be the best time for it. I'd rather get out of here first."

"At least tell us *something*," Cedric said. "And what is that on your belt?"

"It's a magical jar like a lantern. It was given to me."

Marcy and Cedric looked at each other. "Maybe it *would* be best to wait to tell us when we get out," Marcy said.

Wyn laughed. It felt good to laugh.

CHAPTER NINETEEN

S o the left tunnel is the wrong one, then?" Wyn asked. The three Climbers all stood at the final fork, deciding on their next move.

"Maybe," Cedric said. "We still don't know for sure."

"But this is the one where you saw the light?" Marcy asked. "You're sure?"

"Yes," Wyn answered. "It took me to a room, sort of like a cabin where I met an old woman. I don't remember going into the tunnel at all."

"A cabin with an old woman," Marcy said. "What was it like? Describe it."

Wyn paused for a moment to think. "It was simple but creepy. All of the furniture was wooden, and there wasn't much of it. Plain and unassuming. There was an empty table in the middle of the room, a small kitchen on one side, and a bookshelf with strange jars on the other. I felt like I was in a hunting cabin instead of in a magical tower."

Marcy and Cedric exchanged a quick glance. Wyn caught the look.

"What?" Wyn asked. "Does that sound like something you've heard of?"

"Did she attack you?" Cedric asked.

"Like I said, it wasn't bad. She sat down at the table and just . . . talked. Though what she said was *weird*. And made hardly any sense."

"That sounds like floor 9," Marcy said. "Remember what that Cleric from the Alistair Junkies said during the floor planning a few weeks ago? That the ninth floor was just a field and a witch's hut and they lost three members?"

"Yes," Cedric said quickly. "I remember. They said it was one of the hardest final floors of a second tier they've had in many seasons. That the floor boss was a witch—cunning, devious, and cruel. They were recommending guilds to only take their best groups and for the others to skip it."

"Wyn," Marcy said. "Did the woman look like a witch?"

"What does a witch look like?" Wyn responded. "I can't say I've ever met one."

"You ass. You know—creepy, old, hermit-like?"

"Well, that does describe her. But that could be anything in this place. Or any village crazy lady."

"Did she have gray, wispy hair?" Cedric asked. "Thin and fine? Grayish skin? Moved like a ghost? Cackle that sent shivers down your spine?"

Wyn's face paled. Her sickening laugh rang out in his head, and he felt a wave of goosebumps shimmer over his arms. "Yes. That description matches her exactly."

Marcy whistled, long and drawn out. "You met the boss of a much higher floor. They were saying she likely should've been the next tier boss, too. The head of floor 14, not 9. What in the hells happened?"

"Now isn't the time. Just know we talked, and she gave me this magical jar. Shouldn't we focus on getting out of here first?" Wyn wanted to share with them what he learned, but not yet. Though he wanted to keep his new **Tower's Blessing** skill to himself. He didn't want to give off the impression he was being given handouts immediately after becoming a Climber.

"Probably," Cedric said. "There can be time to figure out how you managed that when we're done, but we absolutely need to discuss it. For now, maybe we should try the other tunnel?"

"I say yes," Marcy said. "Since you both want to avoid the more interesting topic of conversation. But we need to be smart in our approach. We didn't recover as much mana as we needed."

Wyn felt a pang of worry strike his stomach. "I'm sorry. How much did you recover before you looked for me?"

"Hardly any," Cedric said. "And we spent some looking for you. Some of the tunnels weren't searched, and we tried them. We had to fight back."

Wyn felt even more guilt stir within him. He didn't blame them for searching for him as he would've done the same thing. A team member suddenly disappears—in this environment of all places—and you look for them. No question. He was sure they started right away, trying to make sure they didn't potentially lose another rookie in this death trap. And then they spent even more precious resources to find him.

He clenched his jaw. He'd be damned if he wouldn't make it up to them somehow. A gift, or loyalty, or *something.*

A renewed sense of purpose flushed out the guilt and took over his emotions. He wasn't as tired as them, had plenty of mana, and knew he needed to take the lead. Marcy could hold her own, but Cedric seemed as though he was wearing thin. They needed to finish this floor, and fast.

"But we'll be alright," Marcy said. She patted Wyn on the back. "Nothing we can do about it now. Let's move ahead and finish this damn thing. I'm tired and ready for a bath."

Wyn chuckled. Cedric again laughed hard, high-pitched and brief. Wyn laughed harder after hearing it, forgetting his strange laugh.

The three smiled, finding a moment of solace, camaraderie, and confidence in a desolate place. This was a familiar feeling to Wyn, though in his experience it was always the enjoyable times of companionship before hardship came to light.

"So this one, then," Cedric said, pointing his staff to the right tunnel. "Let's go down it together."

"Together," Wyn echoed. "I like that."

Marcy pushed the men on, all three stepping together in a line. They just fit down the width of the cave tunnel walking arm in arm. They didn't hesitate, stepping into and continuing down the tunnel that could be either correct or very wrong.

Nothing happened. The three kept walking, silently, anxiously, further down the mushroom-lit cave path.

Wyn stopped, which forced the veterans to stop, too. He nearly forgot how to confirm the tunnel they chose was right. The blue mushroom should be shaking itself to show the path the tower designated was theirs from beginning to end. He turned around and looked out for the sign.

Not ten feet away a blue mushroom gently shook its cap, scattering blue spores onto the cave floor. Several more followed suit, looking like a grim celebration that they'd made it to the end but would still have to face the final test.

Wyn turned back, and Marcy and Cedric were smiling. They knew this was it, the final walk before whatever it was that held them from returning to Alestead and getting out of their situation. There were several things Wyn needed to do right away, and he felt as though he wouldn't have the time to do it. He needed to make sure John was all right. And to check on Tasha, too, after dealing with the immediate aftermath of Lionel's betrayal. Then there was resting, eating, and celebrating their victory beyond the first floor.

It might not feel quite like much of a celebration after what had happened to them, but it was important to do nonetheless.

"Did the witch give you any advice for the last room?" Cedric asked.

Wyn stopped walking. He froze, her words coming back to him like a slap in the face. "Only one thing."

"Well, don't tease us," Marcy said. She nudged him in the ribs playfully.

"She said to mind the colors."

"Hmm," Cedric said out loud. "That vaguely rings a bell. And the entire cave has been a color puzzle, too."

"And," Wyn continued, "that we wouldn't make it out whole."

Marcy and Cedric's smiles were instantly wiped away. They looked at each other worriedly, then back to Wyn.

When the witch first told Wyn that last sentence, he barely registered what she had said and truly didn't know what to make of it. Maybe she was blowing smoke, or maybe she was just trying to scare him. But thinking back on their conversation, she was incredibly honest and forthcoming, not teasing at all. After Marcy and Cedric revealed her true nature, he was even more convinced.

He knew, without a doubt, she was right. The only problem was the extent of how right she would be.

The three walked to the end of the tunnel, silent and anxious once more.

Based on the previous tunnels, they knew it wouldn't be long before they were at the final room. The last two paths had only taken a few minutes to walk, a brief stretch in the cave maze that the tower laid before them as a challenge. Now, they walked at least twice the distance of the previous tunnels, and Wyn wondered if it was deliberately laid out longer.

Regardless, he didn't have too much time to wonder as the tunnel started to open up into a large square room. They stopped immediately before crossing into the room, except for Wyn, who noticed the veterans waiting and awkwardly stepped back mid-stride to stand with them.

"Okay," Cedric said. "This is it. We have very limited information," he noted, pointing to Wyn. "Though we can take what we've encountered so far as a sort of warm-up to this."

"Something with colors," Marcy said. "Which is obvious, if you think about it, considering the different mushrooms and their colors so far. So that was a basically useless clue. You bet your ass it'll be a harder puzzle of some kind."

"I think you're right," Wyn agreed. "But still, we need to keep that in mind about colors. You two are the experts here, but I want to do the heavy lifting. So to speak."

"Wyn," Cedric started, "that's nice and all, but you're right—*we* are the experts. We need to be the ones to lead."

"But you both have much less mana than me." He pulled up his left sleeve and looked at his mark. It was hardly glowing now, about one-third of his mark showing his mana recovery. "I'm mostly full. I can do more if needed! Or at least hold off anything that tries to attack us while you two figure out what we need to do."

"It's not a bad idea," Marcy said. "I can back you up, and if we get into too much of a bind, Cedric can take out several at once as a last resort." She looked at Cedric. "Just focus on the puzzle and try to figure it out to move forward. We can handle the enemies."

"Gods, I wish I had my potions," Cedric said. "It was *so* stupid not to bring them."

"You're the one who said it was only a rookie climb," Marcy said. "Remember? *'I don't need potions, it'll be easy! I don't need my circlet, or robe, or boots—it's a cake walk.'"*

"Don't remind me," Cedric said. He put his hands on his forehead and shook his head. "I'll know to never do that again. Always treat the tower like I'm facing the highest challenge."

"Exactly like Faye used to say. She knew what she was talking about, after all."

"Who's Faye?" Wyn asked. He kicked some dirt nervously.

"She was our former leader," Cedric said. "She was a veteran for two seasons before she led our current party for two more. Then she was recruited to one of the top guilds."

"I think she made their lead party, too," Marcy said. "Which isn't surprising."

"Really?" Cedric said. "I didn't realize that. Good for her! She was a great Druid."

"*Is* a great Druid," Marcy corrected. "Just not one for *us* anymore."

"Did she leave on bad terms?" Wyn asked. He was more interested now, curious about other classes and Climbers.

"No," Marcy replied. "We knew she would go on to be in another guild. It was only a matter of time. She's a great Climber—skilled, smart, and team-focused. But we lost some definite confidence and power when she left."

"And we've been trying to climb back ever since," Cedric finished. "But we'll get there."

"Exactly." Marcy gave Cedric a smile. He returned one to her.

Wyn couldn't help but smile at their interaction. It was contagious and encouraging. In a sense they looked more like allies at war than Climbers in Alistair, and truthfully, they were.

"Alright, you two," Wyn said. "No time like the present." He stomped the butt of his spear on the ground, readying himself.

"True," Cedric said. "We have a plan. Let's stick to it the best we can."

"Ladies first," Marcy said. She began to walk into the room, striding carefully. She drew an arrow and nocked it to her bowstring, readying herself to draw and fire at a moment's notice.

Cedric held his arm out for Wyn, inviting him to go next. Wyn started but then stopped. He pulled up his left robe sleeve and held his arm out to Cedric, touching his shoulder.

Cedric furrowed his brow, unsure of Wyn's intention. Wyn smiled and patted his shoulder reassuringly.

"***Dyadcast: Arcane Aura***!" Wyn said. He felt the skill take effect on top of the spell, the magical energy surging from his mark. His class symbol appeared on the ground below him, and a second one appeared under Cedric. It started from the ground and moved up, enveloping both of them in the familiar magical aura. The symbol morphed into another one with a single circle, the runic makeup of the ***Arcane Aura*** spell. The skill and spell covered them in a magical haze, forming into a soft white suit of armor over their own clothing.

Even Marcy turned around and watched him cast it, curious at his skill.

"Thank you, Wyn," Cedric said. "That skill is definitely something. I've never seen that spell used in a sort of double-cast." The Wizard moved his body around, twisting and turning his torso and arms freely. He stood a bit straighter with the armor around him, confident and secure.

"I'm glad you're impressed," Wyn said. He felt useful for a change. "But let's get this going while it's still active. Based on the experiment at the start of the floor, the spell should last about ten minutes."

Cedric nodded his agreement and followed behind Marcy. "I hope that's enough. And I'm ready to get out of this place, too."

Wyn followed behind both of them. He quickly looked down to inspect his mark while they were still safe. Nearly the entire mark was glowing—the Ruby Magician hat, shield, sword and staff were gently pulsing magic, and the singular runic circle was dull. *Lucidity* was working, and by his mark, needed nearly the entirety of his mana before it would completely recover, or just under three hours. He figured he would have enough for an *Ice Shard* spell only, and not even right now. It would be some time for him to recover enough mana for a single cast.

This had to work. He still had years of combat experience and training to rely on.

The three Climbers cautiously walked further into the room. They each looked back at the entrance and noticed it wasn't barring them off. At least the entrance was still a possible escape.

But it didn't matter. They had only one possible way out, and that was forward.

The room was massive, as Wyn figured it would be. It was nearly as big as the training hall where Wyn first met John and then sparred with Daniel. What he didn't expect, though, was the sheer amount and size of mushrooms that grew out from the cave walls and randomly through the cave floor and ceiling.

The mushrooms created an assortment of varying colors. They all pulsed and emitted a bit of light, blanketing the final room in a strange rainbow. The Climbers could see everything easily, but it was a bit disorienting, too.

Wyn noticed there were a few colors he hadn't seen in the tunnels before. Pink, white, brown, even some multicolored mushrooms were scattered around the ones he recognized. He wondered what kind of mushroom monster would emerge from those.

"Here we go," Marcy said. She was standing at the opposite end of the room. Wyn realized he was standing directly in the middle of the large cave, staring at the mushrooms coating the area. Marcy and Cedric had been busy in their time, having fanned out to search for the objective.

Wyn felt again like a true rookie. Despite his experience and training he still found himself caught in moments of wonder, difficulty focusing on the task before him. He hoped it would be easier as he gained experience as a Climber, but he couldn't help but chastise himself for these moments.

"What is it?" Wyn asked. He had jogged up to them to see what they stopped to investigate.

Marcy was standing at a stone pedestal that held a large bowl. They were both dark gray. The bowl was also stone, and there was a small circular hole in the middle that appeared like it drained deeper into the pedestal. It looked like something that belonged in a temple, though Wyn hadn't had much experience there.

He looked over to Cedric and noticed he was standing in front of an opening. There were a series of stone bars, similar to the ones that they had encountered on their winding journey here. Three were vertical, and three were horizontal, all the size of a small tree.

Behind them, though, was their prize. The portal to the next floor floated there, bright red, beckoning them to touch it so they could exit. It was a tease, literally barred off from them until they could solve whatever puzzle the tower laid out.

"So this was probably open earlier today, after some groups cleared it, right?" Wyn asked, pointing with his spear at the portal.

"Yeah," Marcy replied. "But it closes quick, resetting itself for the next group. Otherwise you could get carried through the whole tower, which defeats the purpose."

"That makes sense. There's no spider bosses here, though, so that's something."

"Marcy," Cedric said, inspecting the bowl and pedestal. "Do you remember the color puzzle on floor 6?"

"Gods, yes. I *hate* that floor."

"Well, I have bad news. I think this might be similar."

Marcy groaned and smacked her forehead with her palm.

"Why is that so bad?" Wyn asked.

"The puzzle," Cedric started, "involved having to light colored flames in a specific order to continue on. If you made a mistake, enemies would appear and you'd have to start over."

"That doesn't sound *too* bad."

"It took over two hours," Marcy said. "And nearly drained us of our resources at full capacity. As other groups joined us, more enemies joined, too. It was awful."

Wyn nodded, trying to understand the difficulty. "Well, how do we start, then? There's only a gray bowl and no other colors."

"Based on our previous trials, the assorted mushroom enemies we faced, and the massive amounts of colored mushrooms here, it's safe to say this will be similar. I feel like this floor might be coming back to me."

Wyn still wasn't convinced. It just seemed . . . *boring.* Granted, there wasn't much information to make that conclusion, and he needed to trust their experience. If there were only a few mushrooms like what they faced, they stood a good chance while Cedric remembered what to do.

Marcy suddenly perked up and wheeled around, facing the entrance. She drew her bowstring, anchoring the arrow to her cheek. She steeled her gaze and straightened her torso, readying herself.

Wyn was slower than her **Extrasensory**, and he turned to see what alerted her. Three yellow mushrooms had vibrated and shaken on the wall beside the tunnel where they entered, and they released their spores onto the cave floor. Mushrooms began to sprout from the dust, all yellow like the ones they first fought on the floor.

Wyn smiled and readied himself beside Marcy. He remembered that they weren't so bad, being slow and soft. They had weapons but were manageable. Plus, there was a fair distance between them, giving him plenty of time to counter with an attack.

Marcy cursed.

The mushrooms grew larger than the ones they had fought previously. They expanded at least three feet taller and wider, more like trees than mushrooms, looking much more intimidating than before. He could see their yellow eyes glaring at him from across the large room. One wielded a spear like him, another an axe, and the third had two swords, one in each hand.

Wyn immediately stopped smiling. This wouldn't be nearly as easy as he thought.

CHAPTER TWENTY

Wyn waited just a second to see how the mushroom enemies would move. They charged the Climbers, running across the hall toward them. It would only be a few seconds before they met them at their speed.

Not only were they bigger, but they moved faster than before, too. He found himself both surprised and not surprised at the outcome, as this was the final floor after all. He was warned it would be harder, but it was still jarring to see them appear so much more formidable.

Wyn decided to act quickly in order to catch them off guard. He focused on the one in the middle, the one leading the charge who wielded a large axe. The weapon was easily as big as Wyn.

He decided to take two quick steps forward at the same time as it approached. He stabbed forward and up with his spear, aiming at the top of its chest, hoping to succeed in his plan to take it down fast. In a brief moment of panic he was afraid his mundane weapon wouldn't do any damage, afraid their outer layer was tougher, too.

Thankfully the monster had its axe held high wanting to strike down, and after being caught off guard stopped its attack in surprise. Wyn used his spear as a lever and aimed up and to his side, trying to use the monster's momentum to his advantage and cast him off like throwing hay with a pitchfork.

By the gods, it worked.

With great difficulty he flung the mushroom off to his left, away from Marcy and Cedric. It was definitely heavier and tougher than before, but it was easier to stab and haul than a soldier in full combat gear. Even though his spear wasn't magically coated, he noticed how the entire metal head of the weapon pierced the mushroom's body, and he easily pulled the weapon out before stabbing its downed head in two quick successions.

He smiled, silently thanking his time on the farm for the maneuver. He certainly didn't learn that in the military, nor would he want to use it there—he would've been stripped of his rank and laughed out of service. He could only imagine the verbal lashing he would get for trying something like that in battle.

The mushroom began to dissolve on the ground just as before, and Wyn was thankful it wasn't too much harder than last time.

He turned, ready to face the others, before realizing there weren't any others. He looked around the room and saw Marcy standing, her bow now relaxed with no arrow drawn.

Two piles of mushroom spores covered the floor not too far from where she stood, arrows poking out from both of them.

She downed them both before Wyn finished off his one. He didn't know if he was completely focused on his own fight or if she was just that skilled. The twang of her bowstring and firing of her arrows never even crossed his ears.

Wyn nodded with his head, small but firm, reassuringly. She returned a similar nod before walking over to the piles of yellow spores and picking up her arrows. Wyn noticed she inspected them, twirling them in her fingers and bending them slightly, like the archers he had in his company.

One of the arrows she tossed to the ground, the rest she placed back in her quiver. Two were kept in her bow hand, a technique Wyn wasn't familiar with.

"Now what?" Wyn asked.

Almost like the tower was answering him, a large pedestal grew out of the far corner of the room. It looked like the one beside the portal though it was slightly smaller. A stone bowl sat at the top, and it wasn't gray but completely yellow.

Cedric ran over to Wyn and picked up some of the mushroom spores without saying a word.

"Cedric? What are you doing?" Wyn looked around the room. He didn't realize it before, but there were more pedestals, all different colors. Were they there before and he missed them? But wouldn't Marcy or Cedric have mentioned them earlier?

Cedric, with a handful of yellow mushroom spores, then ran over to the newly risen pedestal and dumped the spores into it. The pedestal began to glow from the bottom up, like it was filling up with a magical, glowing substance.

Which is exactly what it was doing.

Soon, though, it stopped. It was only glowing about three-quarters of the way up the pedestal. It stayed that way and didn't rise anymore as the spores had filled the pedestal only a portion of what it could completely hold.

"Bring more spores!" Cedric yelled. "And hurry!"

Wyn looked over at Marcy, who looked at him at the same time. There was only a brief pause before they each scooped up as much of the spores as they could. Marcy put away her arrows and slung her bow on her back in order to use two hands, and they both awkwardly trotted over to Cedric.

They lost some of the spores on the way over, but there was still plenty to add. They dumped it all, hoping it was enough.

The entire pedestal was now glowing, and one of the bars that blocked off the portal turned yellow and began to retract.

"It worked!" they all said in unison.

"I remembered!" Cedric said, his face beaming with pride despite their situation. "A new wave will come soon, but I'll make sure to get the leftover spores unless I need to intervene!"

A mushroom shook right beside their head, and red spores now began to fall.

They stepped back, drawing their weapons to attack and to give themselves some room.

"Get ready," Cedric yelled.

Wyn looked across the room. More mushrooms had shaken all across the room, and now four more mushrooms began to rise.

Two were green, one was red, and another white.

Wyn quickly thought back earlier in the floor. The green mushrooms shouldn't be too bad, but those two red mushrooms would be downright deadly. He had no idea what a white mushroom could do.

His spear began to quiver, but a few deep breaths steadied his hands.

Cedric stepped forward and raised his staff straight toward the ceiling. "***Electric Bolt!***"

A large rune appeared above Cedric's staff, intricate patterns and swirls of magic confusing Wyn and disorienting him. It looked powerful just from the runic makeup alone.

The same magical missiles Wyn saw before streaked out of Cedric's staff and arced their way toward the mushrooms. This time, however, the streaks of lightning were larger and faster, confirming Wyn's guess this was a strong spell. The first one hit the red mushroom right beside them, and the impact burned a large hole in its chest. It stopped the red mushroom's advance, which was an impressive feat as the monster was their height and size. Smoke plumed from both the creature's head and the now-empty torso.

Before it could react too quickly, Wyn took advantage of the moment and stepped over to it, slicing across its chest with his spear. It opened more of its body up, the lightning crackling through its armor and into its fire-like body. These were upgraded, too, having cap armor over their bodies at strategic locations for additional protection. Wyn attacked once more at the closest distance he could stand, hoping to fell it before it fought back or burned him again.

He was thankful he had his magical armor this time. He could barely feel the heat emanating from the monster, even now that it stood eye to eye. After his second slash, the mushroom fell back in a smoke puff, dissipating into ashes on the ground.

Wyn looked around the room and saw the other mushrooms similarly falling down, all except for the white mushroom. It was stocky and short but bulbous, looking like a clean blob of dough with a ridiculously large mushroom-cap head. It absorbed Cedric's lightning attack and looked to be unscathed.

It was standing still, at least. It didn't seem to want to attack them. It had strangely small, beady black eyes that didn't seem to fit its larger body. It wasn't looking at any of them in particular, just . . . staring at the cave wall.

Seeing the mushroom was unsettling. Wyn felt a shiver run across his spine. It was odd, and he didn't have any idea what else it could do, adding to its mystery.

"Don't just stand there, Wyn," Cedric said, "go take the spores!" He went over to the closest red mushroom and gathered it, then looked around the room for the colored pedestal. He began trotting toward the one colored red.

Wyn snapped out of his complacency. Cedric was right. They needed to be efficient and move fast.

He started toward the other mushrooms then paused. He saw Marcy hesitate, too. They stood about thirty feet from the piles of spores, but that wasn't what they were concerned about. The other mushrooms were fairly close to the white mushroom, and they were still unsure of its abilities.

"Let's go, but be on guard," Marcy said.

Wyn snickered. "Like you even have to say it."

He held his spear at the ready and sidestepped in an arc, hoping to keep some distance from the white monster while closing in toward the piles of spores they desperately needed. Marcy was doing the same on the other side. They both gave it a wide berth, hoping to keep their distance and avoid unnecessary fighting. Time didn't seem to be as much of a concern anymore, but efficient mana usage and energy expenditure was critical.

The mushroom wasn't focused on them, keeping its gaze in the same direction. It seemed more like a statue than an enemy and had yet to move an inch.

Marcy and Wyn met in seconds, quickly grabbing as much of the spores as they could carry while being cautious. They both grabbed a handful of green spores and looked around.

"Do you see the pedestal?" Wyn asked. He saw Cedric run to a far-off corner and stop. The pedestal lit up red, a similar amount as the first one, and one of the bars began to glow red, too.

"There," Marcy said, and began to run toward a different corner of the cave.

Wyn followed her, trusting her vision more than his. He couldn't completely make out the colors, and his focus was being pulled in several directions. His hope was that when the pedestals held at least *some* spores they'd light up, becoming easier to see within the sea of colors.

He ran over to it, though he lost most of the spores along the way. Multiple curses left his mouth.

Marcy dumped her share into the bowl, able to carry more with two hands than Wyn. He quickly realized he had a decision to make. He could leave his spear and carry more spores, but he'd be without a weapon if something happened while he was transporting the material. If he took it, though, he limited his ability to carry more of the spores to add. Any second more mushrooms would form, and Wyn couldn't think of a good alternative.

He decided to keep his spear for now in case he needed to defend himself. It was the cautious decision, believing he could always get more spores for another trip rather than being without a weapon.

Marcy followed him, quickly realizing they needed much more to fill the green pedestal as their current haul wasn't even half of the amount required.

"I might have to be the one to do this," she said, speaking between huffs. "You can't carry very much!"

"I know, but I don't want to leave my weapon behind!"

They made it back to the piles and grabbed more, still eyeing the white mushroom. It continued to stay still, facing the same direction it was before.

Where were the next set of mushrooms? Surely, Wyn thought, they would've come by now.

Both Climbers took their new share of spores back to the green pedestal and poured it. It filled nearly full but stopped. The bar in front of the portal was still closed off.

"Damnit, we still need more," Wyn said. He set his spear against the pedestal this time, opting to be more efficient with gathering the spores. He could easily grab more with two hands to scoop and decided to take the risk this time, mushrooms be damned.

Without another thought he started back toward the pile again, nearly in a sprint now. When he got there, he realized the green pile was duller than before. Where it previously was a bright green it was now nearly gray, the color draining from the pile.

The magical aura dissipated from the spores, and it looked like a pile of gray sand.

Wyn looked at Marcy, confused as to what was happening.

"It's a different color," Wyn said. "Think it'll still work?"

She sighed. "No, I don't think so. Looks like we have a limited window of time."

Wyn cursed again. He had made two wrong decisions back to back, and they missed out on completing part of the puzzle due to his mistakes. This process wasn't nearly as easy as he thought it would be.

Cedric had moved to the portal, inspecting the door. "We're doing well so far!" he yelled. "We just need to keep getting the spores!"

"We need to be fast, too!" Marcy yelled back. She held up a handful of the spores and let it pour out onto the floor. "It won't be good after a minute or so!"

Cedric moved toward the other pedestals. "Here is the blue one. And here's an orange one!" He was moving along the room quickly, pointing out the various locations for Marcy and Wyn to note.

Wyn saw more mushrooms shake and release their spores. Marcy drew another arrow, readying herself. Wyn stood in the middle of the cave without his weapon, the exact situation he wanted to avoid. He immediately ran to the green pedestal to grab it.

He looked around the room to see where the mushrooms would be growing, but there weren't any obvious signs yet. Cedric was standing beside him now, staff at the ready, while Marcy stood in the middle of the floor.

"I don't like that mushroom," Cedric said. He used his staff to point to the white mushroom not far from Marcy. "I have a bad feeling about it, and I can't remember what they do."

It was facing Wyn and Cedric, now. It was still expressionless and not moving its body, but it wasn't facing the same direction as before.

"Strange," Wyn said out loud. "It turned."

"That's part of why I don't like it. But new plan—let me and Marcy kill the enemies, and *you* get the spores."

"What? Why?"

The mushrooms were forming, scattered all across the room. There were multiple colors again, and Wyn thought it looked like a deadly and perverse rainbow. There were more of them, too, nearly ten by Wyn's estimation.

"Because we can kill them quicker and from further away. I have enough mana for one more wave, so this needs to be it. Just be fast! We'll help when we can!" He raised his staff again and pointed it at the closest mushroom. It was a mere fifteen feet away, glowing orange and growing fast. Like the last wave of enemies, this one was slightly bigger than the orange one they fought earlier in the caves. Wyn knew it would be seconds before it reached its full height and closed the distance between them.

A large rune formed in front of Cedric's staff followed by a ball of crackling lightning the size of his head. It flew toward the mushroom with the speed of an arrow, quick and precise.

It smacked into the chest armor of the mushroom, dispersing into webs of crackling energy that seared the mushroom all over its body. It immediately roasted into plant ash.

Wyn felt the hairs on his arm rise and his skin tingle from the lightning attack. Thankfully his magical shield armor still shrouded him, and he shuddered to think of the effects of being so close to a spell like that without it.

Cedric took his staff and pointed it at another mushroom, casting the same spell again. It hit its mark a second time, and again the enemy was reduced to mushroom spores. Wyn couldn't help but marvel at Cedric's magic. War was one thing, smashing into each other with swords and shields and arrows flying like a flock of birds. But this? This was an entirely separate beast, and it was difficult to not be awestruck at the power of magic.

He snapped out of his wonder when he saw Marcy shoot a magical arrow like earlier, nearly exploding a mushroom on the far end of the room. The sound crackled and popped loudly, shaking him from his lost focus.

He realized Marcy and Cedric were more than holding their own. They were basically playing with the plant monsters, conserving their resources but still easily dealing with the situation. If this kept going, though, they'd be out of mana and in a dire spot.

Wyn left his spear beside the green pedestal and ran over to the orange spores that Cedric first annihilated. He began to pull the spores on the ground together into a pile and tried scooping it up, disappointed at how little his cupped hands could hold.

He took a deep breath to think. Rushing himself was only causing mistakes, and he needed to jump ahead of the situation rather than react after the fact.

An idea entered his mind.

He dropped the spores back to the pile. He nearly forgot about the Magician hat Daniel gave him, as it was surprisingly a good fit on his head—but now he needed it for a specific reason. He put it on the ground and began shoving spores inside it to use as a makeshift bowl.

He remembered where the orange pedestal was, and locked in on it. It was on the other side of the room between two corners at the left of the portal and right of the entrance. Unfortunately there was chaos separating him from the pedestal, but he was determined to be useful and this was his designated role at the moment.

His magical aura flickered and dulled slightly. A soft curse left his lips. Did he cast his armor spell too soon? Doubt tried to cloud his mind, but he forced those thoughts away. He needed confidence and focus now.

Carrying his spore-filled hat as though his life depended on it, he rushed across the room without another moment of hesitation.

More than just his own life rested in the balance. This wasn't the first time that was true, and Wyn wanted to be sure this time he'd succeed.

CHAPTER TWENTY-ONE

All around Wyn was chaos. It could've been worse, of course, but he certainly didn't feel that way in the moment.

Arrows flew like quiet bringers of death, strategically placed to be able to bring down mushroom after mushroom with the most efficiency possible. Wyn recoiled as another pop of crackling energy echoed off the cave walls, the smell of burnt plants filling his nose.

His companions were doing their part. Wyn was doing his. He kept his head down and just ran, holding his spore-filled hat so nothing would fall out. It wasn't the prettiest hold or run, since he still held on to his spear for emergencies, but it was the best he could do. The orange pedestal wasn't too far, and he did his best to ignore the impulse to check his surroundings and focus on his task.

Marcy and Cedric obviously worked well together. What would their situation be like if they both were more close-ranged Climbers?

Wyn pushed the thought away. He was thankful for their abilities and teamwork. Maybe, just maybe, when they made it out, they'd be willing to group up and continue climbing together.

Without a single mushroom focusing on him, Wyn made it to the pedestal and dumped the contents. It was more than before, and it filled up over halfway. He smiled, happy that it filled more than he and Marcy together were able to carry with their hands. The strategy paid off. It could take just a couple of trips, maybe less if he filled his pockets, too.

Silence filled the room. It was a strange contrast to the pops of Cedric's magic, twangs and thuds of Marcy's bow and arrows, and loud crashes of giant, monstrous mushrooms. They had succeeded again for the second wave of enemies, and Cedric and Marcy took them out with relative ease.

But at what cost?

The three Climbers wasted no time.

"Fill your pockets!" Wyn yelled, trying to save time. "Take as much as you can!"

They ran around the room gathering spores where they could, filling pedestals with their respective color and trying to be efficient. Cedric was using his robe pockets to fill with spores, grabbing and scooping as much as the dead fungi would offer. Marcy was shoveling spores into her pack, gathering plenty of the material but was moving slower. Between the three of them gathering, transporting, and dumping the spores, they worked more effectively than the last wave of enemies.

In the middle of them running around the room, however, they each noticed something. Two more white mushrooms had spawned, and all three of them were unmoving in the room. It was like they were glued to the ground though able to turn as a whole, resembling movable statues.

Marcy was the one to point out what they each were thinking, yelling it out while they kept filling pedestals. "Cedric, they're following you!"

It would've been more eerie if they weren't white and round like a child's toy, but the Climbers still wondered what their purpose served. For now, though, they were merely distractions, not engaging in the fight and not posing a threat.

As the next minute rounded off, the remaining spores dulled. Wyn was in the middle of pouring blue spores into the pedestal when some of it went dark, and the pedestal stopped filling with color. He cursed.

When he looked around the room, though, he realized they had completely filled the orange, green, and yellow pedestals. They partially filled the purple, red, and blue ones. The portal was that much closer to being freed, and relief washed over him seeing more bars that kept the portal locked away retracting. This was their most successful wave yet, and Wyn guessed it would take only one more round if the correct colors fell for them to use.

The three Climbers met in the middle of the room, huffing and breathing heavy. Cedric leaned on his staff for support while Marcy took big breaths arching her back, both hoping to calm themselves down after nearly sprinting around the room. Wyn could feel his own fatigue set in as sweat dripped down his cheek and neck.

Both of the veterans looked utterly exhausted. Wyn understood, though. They'd climbed the tower all day and were still doing the majority of the fighting despite his intention to lead them. Marcy had bruises all over her exposed skin but was seemingly unhurt. Cedric's robes covered his body so Wyn couldn't tell if he was injured, but his lack of magical armor revealed that he'd taken some blows during the last wave. The aura still covered his head, hips, and left leg, but was gone everywhere else.

"This needs to be our last shot," Cedric said. "This armor won't last past the next round, and I'm nearly out of mana."

"Same here," Marcy said. "I only recovered three arrows and have enough mana for about two spells, depending on which I use."

Wyn checked his forearm. He was still recovering most of his mana as they'd only been in the final cave room for a short time. No spells or skills would help him for this next wave.

"New strategy, then," Cedric said. "We only kill the colored mushrooms we need and avoid the others unless absolutely necessary. Marcy, you and I take out the red ones. Wyn, handle the blue. They're resistant to magic but weak to physical attacks. And if you can, use your *Ice Shard* spell on the purple ones—they're the opposite, resistant to weapons but weak to magic."

Wyn shook his head. "I don't have enough mana for that yet. I can do my best to distract the other colors and take on the purple ones while you two focus on the red and blue."

"Shit," Cedric said. "Once I use my mana, I'm useless. I have no charges in my staff or any way to recover."

Marcy pulled a large knife from her boot. "I'll do what I can with Wyn and save the arrows for the big baddies. Cedric, call it out."

Wyn stared at the two Climbers for a moment. "Call it out?"

"Climber terms," Cedric said. "Being the eyes and ears for your team when you need to solve a task."

"You were military, Wyn, you should at least infer that," Marcy added.

Wyn sighed. "There are plenty of differences, you know. And I absolutely don't know everything."

"You're such a rookie," Marcy said.

"Focus," Cedric said. "We have three colored pedestals left and the large gray one, too. I can't remember how it plays into the room, but I do remember we need to use it. Hopefully we can figure it out sooner rather than later."

Wyn knew climbing the tower would be difficult, but he never imagined the amount of thinking required to progress. Of course he should've known there'd be one more piece to the puzzle on this floor. He hoped one of them would figure out the final piece before it was too late.

Wyn heard, rather than saw, the mushrooms shake their spores. There were so many across the room it was audible, like a waterfall of sand being poured onto the stone floor.

The three Climbers braced themselves. By the sound and looks of the spores falling they expected about a dozen or so to emerge.

They were wrong.

The spores on the ground collected together, forming larger piles than before. Mushrooms began to grow from the ground, rising like large stalks that looked more like trees. Seven new mushrooms formed in total. One was white and was the size of the others, making four of those strange creatures.

The other six were huge, at least ten to twelve feet tall, completely towering over them. They made the last wave of enemies look small in comparison. Two yellow mushrooms and one each of red, purple, green, and blue were scattered around the room.

The colors they needed were there. All they had to do was survive the others.

Wyn had trained for years to harden his body and resolve. There was no way in all the hells he'd let this be the end.

He raised his spear and readied himself to charge. There really wasn't any choice but to attack and to attack fast.

"Wyn, distract them while Marcy and I take out the red and purple!" Cedric yelled.

Wyn stopped his advance. He had ran directly at the closest green mushroom, and it faced him ready to fight. But now that Cedric called for a change of direction he needed to divert his strategy.

The easiest way would be to have them chase him around the room. Would it be that easy, though?

One of the large yellow mushrooms lumbered forward toward Wyn, dragging a large yellow sword on the ground behind it. The monster walked right behind the green mushroom, who was still focused on him.

Apparently it would absolutely be that easy.

Wyn started jogging away from Cedric and Marcy in an arc, hoping to pull the attention of the majority of the mushrooms. The two veteran Climbers moved away and threw rocks at the red and purple mushrooms, successfully separating them from the rest. It was honestly a brilliant move, not sacrificing any resources while quietly gaining their attention.

Wyn didn't have time to be impressed, though. He had four mushrooms trying to kill him.

The green mushroom was far more physically intimidating than the others with their improved strength and reflexes, but the yellow mushrooms had weapons that increased their deadliness. Oddly, the blue mushrooms seemed to be a mix of the two, but it didn't wield any weapons as far as Wyn could tell.

Wyn turned to check the distance between himself and the mushrooms just in time to see the blue mushroom furthest back raise an arm and fire a large ball of magic from its hand. Wyn abruptly stopped and jumped back, dodging the bolt of magic as it slammed into the cave wall not ten feet behind him, exploding a huge brown mushroom into a plume of spores. The attack left a small crater in the wall. There was serious power within that magic.

So the blue mushrooms were weak to physical attacks but could cast magic. That was not good for his current strategy.

Wyn cursed and decided to go on the offensive. The green mushroom was the closest and would be his first target, and he had time to exchange a few blows before the yellow monsters would get close.

He raised his spear and stabbed out to the large green mushroom. It side-stepped the attack fairly easily and countered with a kick with its thick, trunk-like leg. Wyn tried to avoid the hit but couldn't dodge all of it due to the sheer size of the monster. Its green leg glanced off his shoulder, but it still knocked him to the side. He hardly felt the impact at all due to the magical armor taking the brunt of the attack, but if an attack actually landed he'd be in serious trouble.

Wyn recovered quickly and lunged out with his spear. Even though his spear gave him additional reach, the mushroom was still quick and strong, and several short jabs at the creature's torso barely connected. One strike was a solid blow, but the spear barely seemed to hurt it. There was no blood, no deep gash, no major reaction, or any real indication that Wyn made much of an impact at all.

Instead, the monster swung a wide punch that Wyn tried and failed to dodge. The force actually knocked him off his feet, sending him tumbling to the side and rolling on the cave floor. He took one deep breath, thankful it wasn't as pain-ful as he thought it'd be. It definitely hurt, but felt more like a bruised side than a cracked rib.

Unfortunately his armor was now completely gone on his left side, the attack using up the protective aura in that area. Fortunately he held on to his spear, years of training to always hold on to his weapon coming in handy.

Wyn stood up and realized two things. One, the other mushrooms were clos-ing in on him and would all attack him if he didn't move away. Two, this was a fight he absolutely was not going to win. Not with these circumstances, anyway. He wasn't equipped to be able to fight them all at once, and his teammates were handling their own tasks.

The blue mushroom raised its arm again for another ranged magical attack. Wyn started to run away at an angle, trying to maneuver himself in the square cave room so he'd still keep these monsters away from Marcy and Cedric. When the magical ball came at him again, one of the yellow mushrooms stepped in its path and took the force of the attack in its back. It lurched forward from the hit, one of its arms falling to the ground as its torso now held a large crater from the magic. The blue mushroom didn't seem to care that it hurt its ally. The others didn't even acknowledge the instance.

An idea suddenly crossed Wyn's mind. It was risky, but potentially a way for him to overcome these mushroom monsters.

First, he had to let the yellow mushrooms catch up. Despite their size they were slow to move but faster with their weapon attacks. The green mushroom mostly kept up with Wyn, and would be the biggest threat. If the others were gone, though, he felt more confident about handling just one mushroom instead of four.

It took several minutes and several more close calls with the green and yellow mushrooms almost hitting him, but Wyn was able to position himself to where the blue mushroom's magical attack defeated both yellow mushrooms. Only large, unneeded piles of their spores remained on the floor. The green mushroom was an aggressive annoyance, dodging both Wyn and the magical attacks of its brethren with relative ease. It needed to die next, though, so Wyn could kill the blue mushroom last. He had to run its precious blue spores to the pedestal right away once it was defeated, and couldn't run the risk of dealing with the green monster at the same time.

Wyn knew what he had to do. He just hated it.

At least he had a health potion to use after.

"You sure he'll be alright?" Cedric asked. He had his staff pointed forward, a spell ready in his mind. "That's four of those monsters chasing him around like hounds."

Marcy had an arrow nocked but hadn't pulled the bowstring yet. She stood right beside Cedric, waiting for the opportunity to attack the red and purple mushrooms that spotted them. "He has to be," she said. "He's trying to prove something to not just us, but himself."

Marcy drew back the bowstring and channeled a small amount of her mana into the weapon. It was hardly a noticeable amount, but too many of those magical shots would reduce her mana pool to a point where she couldn't cast the spells she might need. Plus, each arrow imbued with her bow's magic greatly reduced the chance of recovering it to use again. Even her enhanced arrows weren't perfect.

The arrowhead glowed with a dull blue, almost white in color, the telltale sign of non-elemental magic. It flew true and was placed well, hitting the fiery mushroom where its heart should be. Well, if it had a heart.

The magical mushroom momentarily halted its advance toward the two Climbers, its left shoulder dissipating into the air in red smoke. It screamed in rage and pain, an eerie high-pitched sound that sounded like nails on a chalkboard.

Then, it took in a huge breath as its stomach swelled. The flames on its head grew in size and strength, and a large whip of flame spun from where its shoulder should be.

It was suddenly a couple of feet shorter, but a new arm formed from its own power. It resumed its advance.

"Shit," Marcy said. "Only four arrows left. Have to make them count!"

"Take out fatty first," Cedric said.

The purple mushroom didn't seem to be offended by the insult. It lumbered behind the smaller and more agile red mushroom, its bulbous body and stubby appendages trying hard to keep pace. Its size looked to be more detrimental than helpful, but was surprisingly resilient to physical attacks and couldn't recover at all from magical ones.

Marcy relaxed her draw a few inches from her face. "I thought you wanted me to deal with the red one?"

"I think we need to focus on taking them out one at a time. So, big guy first!"

Marcy growled in frustration and turned her aim from the red mushroom not fifteen feet away to the large purple mushroom further behind it. The arrow glowed like before then shot forward and past the red mushroom. It struck the purple creature in the neck—an easy target from its size and slow movements—and it lurched backward as though hit with a sizable attack many times more powerful than a mere magical arrow.

Cedric's staff glowed with the familiar yellow light, runes forming just in front of the topaz at the staff's end. It wasn't as intense as before, the aura smaller and runes less complex. A small streak of lightning followed the arrow's trajectory, hitting the purple mushroom and dispersing in smaller arcs across its body.

The monster seized for just a moment before falling to the ground in a heap of spores, its magical weakness its final downfall.

The red mushroom closed the distance quickly, its body growing larger causing the flames and heat to grow in intensity. It was nearly in striking distance to Marcy.

Marcy anchored her arrow to her chin. She knew there'd be enough mana for one more spell after the one she planned to use, and it would have to do.

The spell left her mouth without hesitation. "***Drench***."

A green runic combination appeared in front of her arrow followed by the arrowhead being smothered in a brilliant blue glow.

The Ranger released the arrow right as the red mushroom expanded to twice its size not five feet in front of her.

CHAPTER TWENTY-TWO

The sounds of magic popping and cracking across the room tried to pull Wyn's focus from the mushrooms attacking him, but he forced his mind to stay at the task at hand. His magical armor still flickered and held, but not for long. Wyn only hoped it would protect him enough to not be a burden after his plan.

It wasn't a smart plan, but he didn't have time to sit and strategize further. Action spoke louder than hesitation.

Wyn tossed his spear away from him, noting the spot where it clanged to the ground. Even though he was risking his own safety, he couldn't run the risk of damaging his primary weapon. Drawing his dagger, he squared up to the green mushroom that stood between him and the blue monster further away. That was the true target, but it had to wait.

The green mushroom stepped forward in another attack, swinging a wild fist at Wyn's head. He ducked under it and stepped to the side, glancing to the blue monster. It just stood there, its arms by its side, watching like a judging referee in a sparring match.

Wyn silently cursed. The bastard needed to fire its magical attack again. There appeared to be a slight delay after each of its attacks, but the time was up. Why wasn't it attacking?

Wyn felt a heavy kick slam into his right hip that sent him sprawling onto the ground. He quickly got up but winced at the initial pain when he put pressure through his right leg. His magical armor was now gone there, but his leg still looked normal. At least it wasn't broken. Likely heavily bruised, but he could use it, still.

He refocused on the green mushroom. Several more attacks came his way, a combination of brawling attacks since the monster didn't hold any weapons. It was unfortunately both fast and strong, much more than the previous green mushroom earlier in the floor. When Wyn feinted to his right to dodge another strike, though, his leg gave slightly from the previous hit, slowing his movement. He couldn't avoid the attack and was punched heavily in his left side.

There was no more magical armor there to protect him.

Wyn yelled in pain as he stumbled back from the blow. He felt his ribs give under the heavy fist, and was sure he heard a few cracks from the hit. A painful deep breath confirmed his fear.

Holding his left side with his hand and dagger in his right, Wyn yelled at the blue mushroom that finally held a hand up, readying an attack.

"That's right, you bastard. Hit me!"

Another magical glow formed at the monster's outstretched palm. The green mushroom wasn't aware of the attack, just like before, though its quicker movements and Wyn's desire to avoid being hit both added to the monster not having friendly fire like its yellow brethren.

This time would be different.

Wyn baited the green monster into an attack and grappled it when it was close. Using his knife to solidify his hold, he stabbed it in the back of the creature up to the handle and held on. With all of his strength he did his best to maneuver the monster into the line of fire, fighting the wiggling creature. Its efforts to escape Wyn's grapple weren't enough, and Wyn's efforts to force it into the blue mushroom's path of attack were plenty.

A magical explosion rocked Wyn back and onto the ground, hitting him far worse than he anticipated. He knew it would be a powerful force but he previously hoped the remainder of his magical armor would protect him. Now he hardly thought about much of anything as his ears rang and his head swam. The stone floor was cold on his back, and his right leg tingled from his shin to his foot. Whatever injury he had before was worse now, and to top it all off, his **Arcane Aura** was completely gone.

Blinking dirt away, he opened his eyes to see his was alone, surrounded by a huge pile of green spores like ash from a bonfire.

A smile formed on his face. His plan worked after all.

The blue mushroom monster slowly walked toward, him, lumbering like a giant of impending doom. It lowered its head toward him, its glowing eyes a beacon of blue death.

His smile quickly left.

For all of his quick planning, he forgot to consider what might happen *after* he succumbed to a magical explosion. He still needed to handle the blue mushroom, after all. The very mushroom that was standing over him while he helplessly lay on the ground.

So much for his plan.

Marcy quickly nocked another arrow. Not that she needed it, of course, but she was paranoid now so close to the end. Her **Drench** spell completely washed the fiery red mushroom away in a torrent of water. She hadn't been able to use it on a fire elemental creature before, and the result was as satisfying as she hoped. Still, it required a chunk of her remaining mana, and she knew there was only enough left for one more spell.

Steam rose from the red spores that littered the ground, a harsh interaction from the two elements. It was too thick to see through and felt sticky on her exposed skin. Thankfully the mist didn't damage the precious spores that lay on the ground.

Confirming the monsters were dead, Cedric immediately began gathering the spores on the ground for the pedestals. If this was enough, they'd be finished and could return to Alestead.

A loud boom pulled both of the Climbers' attention. They saw Wyn fly several feet in midair, his magical glow shattering from the attack and thudding to the ground in a plume of green spores. He didn't move for a few seconds on the ground, then slowly stirred.

The blue mushroom began walking over to Wyn ominously.

"Damnit," Marcy said. "Cedric, get the spores. I'll help Wyn!"

Grabbing her two remaining arrows, she held one in her left hand and nocked the other on the bowstring while jogging over to Wyn. Hopefully she could recover them after killing the blue mushroom, or at least be able to leave. If they had to face another wave, they'd all die. She was sure of that.

Stepping around and behind the blue mushroom, she shot both arrows in quick succession at the monster. They sunk deep, nearly up to the fletching, but didn't stop its advance toward Wyn, who was still on the ground. Whatever maneuver he pulled cost him, but she couldn't think about that now. Only killing this blue bastard.

She dropped her bow to the ground and reached to her sides for weapons that weren't there. A foul curse left her lips, followed by an internal promise that she'd *never* climb without her primary gear again.

Looking around, she hoped for a rock large enough to bash it with. Instead, she saw Wyn's spear on the ground.

That would do nicely.

Wyn took a deep breath. This was it, then. The blue mushroom raised its foot as though it was going to stomp him before it suddenly jerked back with its shoulders. His spear poked through its chest, the metal head completely protruding from its body.

Then the weapon disappeared, yanked back out. The blue mushroom convulsed a few times before slumping and falling into a large pile of blue spores.

Marcy held Wyn's spear, heaving deep breaths at the same time. She started to say something before her face contorted after seeing Wyn on the ground, and words never came.

The spear clanged to the ground while she knelt beside him. "Shit, Wyn. Can you move?"

Wyn nodded, then tried to get up. Pain erupted all over his body, but he felt it most in his left side and right lower leg. "Barely."

Marcy grabbed Wyn's pack and dumped it. She grabbed the healing potion and gently uncorked it. "Aren't you glad you saved this? These injuries are exactly what these are for. Now drink."

Wyn didn't hesitate as Marcy tipped the slender vial toward his mouth. It was thick like honey but tasted nothing like the sweet syrup. It was more tasteless than anything, but the thought of it helping his injuries made it go down far easier. Instantly his breathing hurt less, and the pain subsided from his entire body. Everywhere except his right leg felt better, though not perfect.

When he stood he felt a much more tolerable jolt of pain from his right ankle, but unfortunately it was still there. He took a few hesitant steps.

"It's not perfect, but I can fight for a bit more. It didn't completely heal my ankle, but I can hold out."

Marcy patted him on the back. "They're potent, but that's only a tier 1 potion. If we had a tier 2 or 3 potion that would be a different story. But we'll get you healing when we get back."

Cedric trotted over beside them, quickly analyzing Wyn. "Good, you can stand. All the pedestals are filled except the main one. Look!"

Using his spear like a crutch, Wyn limped over and checked the portal. All of the bars were gone. The pedestals around the cave room were all glowing, completely filled as Cedric said. They obviously finished the challenge while Wyn was still fighting, and he wasn't aware how far ahead they'd gotten since he was still contending with the blue and green mushrooms.

A sigh left Wyn's mouth. He needed to realize he simply wasn't at their level of strength and power, but at least his distraction worked. And he was still alive.

"So that's it, then," Wyn said. "We just need to activate the portal so we can go home!"

"Yes, but how," Cedric replied. "We still need to do *something* with the last pedestal."

The white mushrooms still appeared like statues, unmoving and lifeless. It was unsettling as they were all facing the Climbers at the portal, staring at them with their fluffy white bodies and creepy eyes. Or, more accurately, they were facing Cedric as Marcy previously reasoned.

"Let's quickly talk this out," Cedric said. "I have a bad feeling."

"Okay. So the pedestals lit up based on their color," Marcy thought out loud. "We poured the colored spores in the bowl to match the color . . ."

". . . and it glowed, signaling it was right," Cedric finished. "But there aren't any colored pedestals left."

"But there is this one," Wyn said. He pointed to the main pedestal beside them in front of the portal. "It looks exactly like the others, only bigger and colorless."

"And we haven't tried pouring any spores into it," Marcy said. "Would it even take it, though? It doesn't have a color."

"Which is exactly what we need," Cedric said. "I finally remember!" He ran over to a pile from a mushroom they defeated and grabbed a handful of spores from it. It was dulled gray, the color long gone.

He walked over to the pedestal and poured it in.

The pedestal began to light up a softer gray, a faint magical aura emanating from the large stone. It only filled up a small amount, but it was obviously accepted. This pedestal would take much more than the others, two or three times as much based on the size difference.

"Cedric, you genius!" Marcy slapped him on the back, knocking him forward a bit.

Wyn smiled. That was the last puzzle to their challenge, then. They only needed to collect as much leftover spores as possible and fill this pedestal, and thankfully there were plenty of piles around the room to collect.

A rumble reverberated through the cave. The white statue mushrooms began to shake and move.

"Oh no," Marcy said. She pulled up her bow and nocked an arrow. Only one extra remained, held in her left hand. "That set something off!"

"Hurry, then!" Cedric yelled. "Wyn, get as much as you can!"

Wyn dropped his spear at the pedestal and ran over to the next pile of spores, wasting no time. His right leg screamed at him in pain, but he ignored it. If they could just finish this last task, they'd be back safely in the city and he could address his injuries. Now wasn't the time to slack off.

He began shoveling as much as possible into his hat. He kept sneaking glances, too, at the four white mushrooms. There was no telling what magic they possessed, and he had a feeling they were going to be the final challenge to face. His current job was to collect as much of the spores as possible and hope they could escape before they fought them, but if the mushrooms moved fast or shot magic at them it would be hard to avoid a fight.

One of the strange creatures began to elongate, growing legs and standing. It was nearly as tall as the last wave of mushroom monsters, easily ten feet to its large, mushroom-cap head. A yellow and blue mushroom on the ceiling shook their spores loose, and they traveled to the white mushroom like they were being magically directed.

The white mushroom absorbed the spores and began changing color, swirls forming inside it before coating its body.

The Climbers watched in amazement. What was once a white mushroom was now a blend of yellow and blue. It held a yellow sword in its right hand as well, growing from its body out of nothing. The rest of it was a hybrid of the colors, yellow and blue mixed around it like paints that couldn't combine on a canvas. Its eyes, previously small and black, were now glowing—one yellow and one blue.

"That's new," Marcy said. She kept her bow ready but didn't draw yet. She wanted to wait for the precise time and determined that time wasn't now.

"Yes, it is," Cedric said. "I don't remember them. What in the hells is going on?"

More mushrooms vibrated and released their spores on the wall and ceiling, various colors rushing to the cave floor all at once.

The next wave was starting, and it was going to be difficult. Maybe even impossible in their current state.

Wyn was already dumping the contents of his hat into the pedestal when the second mushroom stood and began forming new colors. The pedestal kept absorbing the spores, filling about a third of the way up. It was a lot, but he needed much more and several hatfuls.

His legs shook as he gathered the spores from the ground, trying to work fast with death looming. Spores flew into his hat as he scooped with his forearm on the ground before sneaking a look at Cedric. His shield was finally gone, too. Hopefully the Wizard realized it.

Wyn ran to the pedestal with his heavy hat and dumped more spores. It was now over halfway, and he was making good time despite the situation. His leg hurt more with each step, and he wasn't sure how long he could keep ignoring the pain.

"Marcy," Cedric yelled. He looked at her with wide eyes but a tight jaw.

He didn't need to say more. She understood.

Marcy stepped beside him and bent to the ground. "*Earthen Trap*!" A large rune spread out on the ground in front of them, covering the area in front of the portal. It was a larger placement than her previous one, too. She backed off, running away from the mushrooms for a pile of fallen spores she could gather to help Wyn.

All of the mushrooms were no longer white but a myriad of colors, and looked funny compared to the previously solid colors. They were bright and inviting, a stark contrast to how serious and deadly they were. All of them were lumbering their way toward Cedric at various speeds.

Cedric stayed away from the portal but directly behind Marcy's trap on purpose so he could escape when the timing was right, but he still needed to hold his ground. He cast out with his staff at the closest one, and lightning leaped from the topaz gem directly into the monster's chest.

This particular enemy was a mixture of orange and green, but just before Cedric cast his spell the colors swirled, and the front of it went completely orange as the green shifted to its back. It had large mushroom caps of armor that now layered its body, forming them just before it was attacked in a protective maneuver that highlighted more intelligence than the last set of mushrooms.

It took the lightning and halted its advance, but the mushroom caps softened the blow. It reformed its colors again, this time moving green to its legs to quicken it and keeping orange at its chest and head for additional protection.

It was smart. Almost *too* smart.

Cedric ran to the side away from the pedestal and portal, realizing they were in a dire situation. He only needed to outlast here, not defeat. He stole glances every few seconds to Marcy and Wyn to see their progress and knew they weren't quite ready. They were pouring another round of spores, and the pedestal was almost full, but not completely.

It would likely be full with this pour, though. They were almost free, ready to escape this hell of a day. Even though they were here at the end it felt like time was dragging in hours instead of seconds.

Marcy's rune activated with a loud blast. Ropes of stone and rocks settled around two mushrooms, holding them both in place. They struggled against it, shifting their colors of purple, red, and yellow to try to form a way to escape the magical trap, though Cedric knew the spell would hold long enough for them to be counted out of the fight.

That was two dealt with in the moment, but two more were right at Cedric. He didn't bother raising his staff to hold them off. The last blast of lightning consumed his remaining mana, and there were no charges remaining in his staff to defend himself.

He wouldn't be able to outrun them to the portal, but he needed to try. They were larger, smarter than before, and had several means to cut him off. He was used up, tired, and currently useless as a Wizard.

But he was still a Climber.

Turning as fast as he could, he lowered his head and sprinted. Marcy and Wyn had finished pouring their spores, and the portal was completely gray, signaling it was complete and ready to enter.

The pair smiled and hugged in celebration, then looked at Cedric. Their joy faded immediately seeing him run toward them with the giant mushrooms hot on his heels. Between the distance and time, they knew he wouldn't make it.

They ran toward him to help, though they were unsure what to do. Their minds were focused on leaving and escaping, and couldn't form a new plan to help him in the moment.

Marcy immediately shot both of her arrows at the closest mushroom, but the monster easily deflected both by swirling purple at its front. The arrows harmlessly bounced off its new, physically resistant surface.

Cedric met them not ten feet from the portal, though the mushrooms were there as well. The Wizard reached for them, extending his staff, hoping they'd pull him to safety. As long as he could just graze the portal he'd be gone instantaneously. Unfortunately he was caught by a green arm that grabbed his left wrist. He couldn't move, held in place by a mushroom giant.

He looked back and saw the other colored mushroom raising a yellow axe to cleave him.

Marcy yelled in defiance, trying in vain to pull her ally, her friend, away from death.

Wyn grabbed Cedric's forearm and tried to help Marcy pull uselessly, stuck watching the monster's yellow weapon ready to drop down. Cedric knew he wasn't going to make it into the portal. This was it.

Wyn refused to let another ally die no matter what. He changed his strategy by hooking Cedric's foot and shifting it to the side, twisting the Wizard's body at the last second to try to avoid a killing blow.

The axe fell.

Wyn was too focused on saving his teammate to watch the mushrooms. He and Marcy were able to pull Cedric away, dragging him back toward the portal. They had less than ten feet to go.

Marcy led into the portal first, dragging Cedric with a newfound strength. He didn't resist. He wasn't moving.

They had made it, though not unscathed. Not whole.

Wyn turned, taking in the sight of the final room one last time before he stepped backward into the portal to take him to the base of Alestead.

He saw, between the multicolored mushrooms standing nearby still pursuing them, Cedric's left arm lying on the ground. Behind it and the monsters stood the silhouette of an old woman. In only a brief second Wyn was able to see her, barely registering her features within the chaos and the magically lit room.

She had gray wispy hair and a wiry frame, and she didn't seem to be touching the ground. A witch, Cedric called her. A deeply unsettling smile was plastered on her face as she watched the Climbers scramble out of the cave.

Wyn continued to backpedal and felt the rush of the portal engulf him.

CHAPTER TWENTY-THREE

Wyn felt the pull of the portal like before, the tower sensing his desire of where to go. It was just as straightforward as the last time, though for many different reasons. Where he wanted to follow Lionel and advance to the second floor just hours ago, he desperately wanted to return to base this time.

In seconds he was standing in the hallway of portals. He saw all the various portals around him, nearly all red. But he wasn't interested in them right now. He saw Marcy on the ground holding Cedric, his body on top of her. He wasn't moving and was losing blood out of his left shoulder at an alarming rate.

Wyn flung himself down to the ground as he allowed exhaustion to take over. He wanted to help, but the one item he had that could potentially save Cedric from bleeding out was gone. He drank the potion just minutes ago, selfishly for himself. If only he would have saved it, his friend wouldn't be dying before his eyes.

"You made it!" a voice said. It was a woman's voice, soft but filled with relief. She had on the formal attire of the guild, an attendee for Climbers inside the tower's base. Her joyful expression quickly turned sour, and she gasped when she saw Cedric.

"I'll go get help!" She disappeared almost as quickly as she appeared.

Wyn clenched his fist and banged the floor. He despised feeling helpless. Maybe what others said about his class was true. He was too useless to make a difference.

The glow of his mark drew his attention. He'd been gathering mana during the final fight, but it wasn't enough. **Regen** needed more mana to be cast, he was sure of it.

But magic wasn't all he had.

Acting quickly, he tore off several strips of the remainder of his pants. He hobbled over to Cedric and turned him so he could have better access to his left shoulder.

Marcy just lay there, staring at Cedric's unmoving body as though she were catatonic. Wyn had seen that look before. She'd be fine eventually, but not now.

He wrapped the strips around Cedric's bleeding stump several times over, tying tight knots at the end of each strip to form makeshift tourniquets. Then he took his hat and covered his remaining arm, tying another strip over it to secure it in place.

The bleeding slowed. Wyn only hoped it would be enough.

For what felt like an eternity the three Climbers stayed there, two conscious and exhausted, one barely breathing without an arm. They didn't say anything else. No words seemed appropriate in the moment.

"Wyn!" a familiar voice said. Wyn looked up and saw Daniel. The older mentor was rushing from down the hallway with purpose. He seemed relieved, but his face quickly grew serious after seeing Cedric.

"Is he stable? Have you done anything?" Daniel knelt down beside Marcy and inspected Cedric's shoulder.

"I don't have enough mana to do anything else," Wyn said. "I just tried to stop the bleeding with what I had."

Daniel cupped Cedric's arm in his hands. *"Amplify Cure."*

A bright white glow enveloped Cedric, nearly blinding Wyn. It only remained for a moment before the magical light condensed and formed around his body like a protective coat. It was far denser and brighter than anything he'd seen before. To Wyn's relief, Cedric gained some color in his face, and his breathing slowed. To say that healing spell was a powerful one would be an understatement.

"He'll live, but he needs better expertise," Daniel said. "A more refined magical touch."

Daniel then turned to Wyn and flinched when he more closely inspected him. "Wyn, I'm so sorry." He cast the same spell while he gently touched Wyn's leg.

Wyn felt a wave of pure euphoria rush over him as the spell took effect. It felt like happy memories and romantic butterflies and the joy of belly laughing with friends all wrapped up in a singular sensation. Pure bliss didn't come close to how this made him feel, but relief followed immediately as he felt broken bones solidify and torn tissues mend.

"Thank you," was all Wyn could muster. He honestly didn't know what else to say.

Daniel smiled at him. There was a warm look in the older Ruby Magician's eyes. He was completely sober, too—Wyn couldn't smell any alcohol on him at all. "You did great. I'm so proud of you."

Daniel went to pick up Cedric, and Marcy stopped him, forcefully pushing his arm away.

"Don't touch him," she snapped. "Just . . . don't."

Daniel nodded. He understood her feelings better than most. The bond that groups shared when climbing the tower was strong in all situations. A deep sense of protectiveness radiated off Marcy like its own magical aura, and to Daniel it was palpable in the air.

"There's a large group of people waiting for you three," Daniel said, "after you didn't return with the other rookies. I passed an attendee on the way, and she said someone was seriously hurt. Help will be coming soon."

Marcy nodded this time, softening her expression. "Thank you," she whispered.

"The Tower Master will want an explanation of what happened," Daniel continued. "Preferably from a veteran." He sheepishly looked at Marcy, not wanting another scolding.

"Not now," she replied. "Not until I know he'll be okay."

A large clatter of boots and footsteps rushed them. They were immediately swarmed with people, all guild members. The officials were wearing various degrees and uniforms of clothes, but they all had the symbol of the tower on their chest signifying their status.

Four guild medics, recognizable by their white clothes and gloves, bent down to Cedric. Marcy waved them off, growling at them on instinct. She had a wild look in her eyes, and several guild members took a step back or gasped.

"Let them take him," a voice boomed. A tall and stout man loomed over them. He had an impressively groomed beard and well-cropped short hair, and his clothes made him the most well-dressed of the group. His demeanor gave off a sense of importance and gravitas.

When Marcy saw him, she relaxed and let the medics pick up Cedric. They placed him on a stretcher and took him off in a hurry. Marcy was right beside them, pushing people out of her way in order to keep up. She held Cedric's staff in her hand, and her bow was slung across her chest.

Daniel helped Wyn stand. "That is the Tower Master," he whispered. "Aureus."

Wyn straightened up. He realized he didn't know much about the tower and the world of being a Climber, but he absolutely understood rank and respect.

"Climber," the Tower Master said. He looked at Wyn. It was hard to gauge his emotion in the moment as his face was blank and expressionless.

"Sir," Wyn replied.

"I am Tower Master Aureus. You are a rookie, correct?"

"Yes, sir."

He waved a hand at Wyn and his face softened a bit. "No need to call me sir. Aureus is fine. Will you come with me?"

Wyn nodded. Aureus seemed stoic and fair, all things considered. Not asking to be called his rank with a less formal conversation was inviting and reassuring. Wyn only hoped he wasn't in too much trouble.

"And I am his mentor," Daniel said, with a bit of a stutter. He seemed flustered.

"Yes, Daniel, I believe?" Aureus said. "The Ruby Magician class mentor. You'll come as well."

The group gave a wide berth for the three of them, eyeing Wyn up and down. He felt uncomfortable, like a pariah. He didn't like it one bit. Aureus led them away, though not out of the base of the tower. It took several agonizing minutes winding around hallways Wyn didn't think could possibly exist within the building before they arrived at a very professional and ornate door.

Aureus opened it and held it open for the Ruby Magicians. "Please, come in."

Wyn tried settling into the chair, but it was uncomfortable. The entire office looked uncomfortable, but by the gods it was refined. Silver trimmed everything: the dark wooden desk with well organized papers; the similarly dark chairs with red cushioned seats. Even the window that peered out into the city of Alestead had silver trimmings around the frame.

"Ardwyn Thatcher," the Tower Master said. "Ruby Magician. From Rywood? I'm not sure I've heard of that town."

"It's small, sir," Wyn replied. "I mean—Aureus. A farming town, mostly."

Aureus smiled. "Take a breath, son. You've been through a lot. The room may look it but no need for formalities. I've been meaning to dull the place up a bit."

Daniel laughed awkwardly. He was seated next to Wyn and shifted even more uncomfortably than the rookie.

"You're right," Wyn replied. "I wasn't planning . . . well, all of that. I only wanted to join the rookie climb before the next season started."

"Yes, but you and the veterans who led your group went to the second floor. That's not only ill-advised, but against our rules for the veterans leading the introductory climb. Why did you do it?"

Wyn swallowed hard. How much should he say? This man was the Tower Master, after all, so likely the person with the most authority in the city. If Aureus found cause for him not following their rules—and lying about his first climb would be cause enough—he might be suspended or banned before he even truly started here.

"One of our group members stabbed another in the back at the boss of the first floor. He ran toward the portal and escaped, and I wanted to try to prevent that. The veterans followed me."

"Did that Climber say why he betrayed you all?"

Wyn thought to choose his words carefully. "He said he had an objective. That he was here to 'defend the tower, not climb it.' His exact words. He didn't say any more before he used a portal key and left."

Aureus was expressionless while he folded his fingers together on his desk like he was thinking. "And then what happened?"

"Marcy and Cedric, the veterans that led our group, entered the portal behind me. They didn't want me stranded or to get hurt so they followed me. Unfortunately they used their portal key just before when we defeated the boss, and we ended up being stranded after all."

Wyn thought to keep the two veteran Climbers' true reasons for going to the second floor secret. They wanted to find and kill Lionel just as much as him, but he didn't want them to get in trouble. And what he said wasn't necessarily a lie.

"I see." Aureus let the silence fester for several agonizing seconds.

Daniel sat still, taking it all in. He was as invested as the Tower Master, if not more. If he was shocked he did a good job of concealing it.

"So," Wyn continued, "we concluded our only choice was to finish out the floor and return back through the portal after the floor boss. Though the entire ordeal was my fault. I was the one who chased him. They only wanted to protect me."

The Tower Master sighed. "They served their role well, then. Any Climber who enters the tower should have a secondary objective of protecting their fellow Climbers. Always. Climbing Alistair is useless if we are pitted against each other, destroying ourselves from the inside. Healthy competition is one thing, but this . . ." He trailed off, not finishing his thought. He stood up and walked over to the window to look out into the city. His hands were neatly set behind his back in an officer's pose.

Wyn recognized that posture all too well and was instantly curious about Aureus's background.

"What happened to Cedric?" the guild master asked. He kept his back to them while still looking out the window.

"We made our way through the cave system," Wyn continued. "It was mostly a color puzzle, and we made it to the boss room. We were all low on mana and resources so we had to be smart, but Cedric figured out our task. The enemies were . . . strong. Much stronger than the earlier parts of the floor. Just before we made our way through the portal, one captured Cedric and held him down. The monsters closed in on us and were about to land a lethal blow. We . . . maneuvered him to where he only lost an arm instead of being cut in two." He blinked, trying to separate as much emotion from his report as possible.

Wyn's thoughts began to drift to the briefing he gave after the battle on the hill. The days after and his feelings of his men dying were clouded with regret, disgust, and anger. Dwelling in that headspace would do him no good here, and he needed to focus for this meeting.

Daniel shifted uncomfortably again in his chair. He tapped the armchair with his fingers nervously.

Aureus let out a deep sigh. "I'm sorry, Ardwyn. Unfortunately things like that happen in the tower. Climbers, especially rookies, forget how serious this life is. They get strong, wield magic, then they feel like they're invincible!" He placed his hands on the desk and leaned in toward the Magicians. "But they aren't. None of us are. And I don't need to remind you of that, Daniel."

Whatever composure Daniel had left was instantly deflated. He slumped in his chair, though he tried to maintain eye contact with the Tower Master. Beads of sweat began to form on his forehead.

"Anyway," Aureus continued, standing up with a sad smile, "I see no wrong on your part. In fact, I would have done the same thing, and you'd be damned to find another who'd feel differently. I hope you learned something from this, though."

"Yes, I did. Thank you." Wyn nodded his head in respect.

"Good. Then I'd encourage you to grab a bite to eat before heading to the infirmary. I know you're wanting to see your friends, but it would suit you well to have some food in your stomach first."

Wyn's stomach growled precisely at that moment. He instinctively touched it, realizing how hungry he was. He never had dinner and had definitely spent a day's worth of energy throughout the day, both with training and climbing.

Daniel stood first, and Wyn followed suit. They bowed and began to leave before Aureus cleared his throat.

"Oh, and one more thing," the Tower Master said. "You should stop by the reward center on your way out. It's normal after you climb, after all. I'm sure it'll surprise you what you earned having completed two floors today." He smiled, then sat down at his desk and pulled up some papers to read. "That'll be all. Welcome to Alestead, Ardwyn. I'm sure we'll meet again."

Wyn and Daniel walked in silence. Both were processing the information differently. Daniel couldn't believe his new student had been through so much so fast, and Wyn was still reeling from the events of the evening. He wanted to check on John and Cedric now, but he knew they were in more than capable hands. Both of them needed time to process the events, too.

"The reward center is pretty informal," Daniel said, bringing them both back to the present. "It's the desk before you enter and exit the hallway of portals."

"That was where all the rookies met earlier today, right?" Wyn asked. "The large room at the entrance?"

"Yes. Gods, that felt like just minutes ago."

Wyn stayed silent. He couldn't disagree more.

Soon they arrived back at the front of the base of the tower. Wyn was turned around several times, and was thankful Daniel was there to show him the way. Even Daniel had to stop at a few forks to figure out the exact way, though, but he hadn't completely steered them wrong yet.

At least the tower base wasn't fraught with traps or monsters like the cave. Wyn didn't mind a wrong turn or two here.

The large room was still as magnificent as before, more so now due to the emptiness. Wyn wasn't as distracted as earlier in the day with the many Climbers crowding the room, and it looked three times as large being more empty. It was still impressive, though he wasn't appreciating it nearly as much as before.

There was only one guild member behind the desk. Their head was down and snug in the crook of their folded arms. Wyn could hear soft, muffled snores coming from the sleeping lump.

"Excuse me," Daniel said, in the kindest tone he could offer.

The man jolted awake, startling the Climbers. There was drool all over his mouth that he promptly wiped with the back of his hand. He had bags under his eyes and looked like he hadn't slept for days.

"Whoa!" he said. "What is it?!"

Daniel shot a glance to Wyn and subtly pointed with his thumb to the guild member in a way that said, "*Go on, ask him!*"

"Umm, right," Wyn said. He pulled out his parchment, suddenly realizing he had nearly forgotten about it. It was strange having something magically record his progress, and he knew he needed to check it more, especially inside the tower. Hopefully it would become an easier habit to keep an eye on it.

"I just finished a climb, and I'd like my reward," Wyn said. "Right?"

The man let out a deep sigh. He mumbled something under his breath, but Wyn was too tired and didn't care enough to ask him to repeat it. He then put his hand out like he was wanting something. An awkward second passed.

"I need your parchment?" the man said, though he said it more like a sarcastic question.

Wyn handed him his entire stack of parchments.

"No, no," he said, and sorted through his papers. He folded most of them back and only kept one. "Only the summary page. I guess this is your first time. That page is where it tells you your rewards for the daily climb."

Wyn took the rest and went red in the face. He looked at Daniel, who gave him a reassuring smile.

"Whoa," the guild member said. His eyes went big. "You had a productive day, rookie." He smirked, obviously impressed, and walked off behind the counter. He disappeared through a door without another word.

"What did he mean by that?" Wyn asked.

"Well, if I had to guess, I'd imagine your rewards were better than others because you climbed the second floor in addition to the first. You earned much more than any other rookie today."

Wyn felt a smile forming and let it happen. It was the entire purpose of coming here, after all—amassing wealth to pay off his family's debts. He instantly wondered how much he'd earn for completing two floors. It likely wasn't very high since it was only the first two floors, and he didn't do *too* much while inside. Granted, they did have a smaller party for the first floor, and only three of them total for the second. Different things that added weight to what constituted a reward ran through his mind, distracting him.

While Wyn's mind raced with possibilities the man returned suddenly with a small chest. It had the same logo of the tower stamped at the top of the lid. It was well decorated and beautiful, and Wyn noticed it shimmered orange ever so slightly.

He set Wyn's parchment down and pointed to the bottom. It said **REWARDS** in a small summary under the goal of the floors. He hadn't noticed it before, but maybe it only showed up when a floor was completed?

"These are your rewards," the man said, "so you know we can't cheat you out of anything. Congratulations." There wasn't much enthusiasm behind his words, his initial excitement gone.

The man opened the chest and began pulling out coins. Wyn looked at the parchment at the same time. It clearly stated under rewards what he earned: 167 gold crowns, 39 silver cloaks, and 64 bronze boots. A ruby gemstone. One blue rarity magical dagger. One green rarity monster item. One green rarity magic item.

He thought about the items he found in the tower. Then he realized what the witch gave him was mysteriously not on the sheet. That . . . was concerning.

"Wow!" Daniel said. He was looking at the rewards, too. "For your first climb? That's incredible!"

The guild member set out the coins and handed them to Wyn. He grabbed them and put them in his backpack. Wyn quickly realized he would need a better coin purse to hold his earnings so he wouldn't lose them.

"The magical dagger, monster item, and ruby aren't here," the man said. "So I guess you got those in the tower. But reach inside for your magical item as your introductory climb reward."

Wyn looked confused but trusted him. He reached in and felt something inside. Strangely, he was able to reach all the way past his elbow. He shouldn't have been surprised it was magically deeper than how it looked, but the feeling was odd to say the least.

Sure enough, there was a physical item inside that he pulled out.

It was a belt. Standard and boring, just like the dagger, though it emitted a slight green shimmer.

"Oh, and these, too." He handed two glass eyepieces to the rookie. They were small enough to fit in the palm of his hand and emitted a white magical aura. "These are identifying glasses. You can choose to use them or not, but every rookie gets two. Thanks again." He closed the chest with a loud snap and walked off. He didn't return.

Daniel put his arm around Wyn. "I know this was a lot. You can always look at the items later. For now, would you want something to eat, or maybe to rest before you head to the infirmary?"

"Definitely some food," Wyn said. His stomach growled again as though on cue. "But then straight there."

Daniel nodded. They walked out of the tower's base together. In a stark contrast to earlier, it was dark and nearly pitch-black outside while the only light provided were the magical lanterns that lit the cobblestone streets and the twinkling of stars in the sky. Wyn wondered just how late it was, and also how close they came to running out of time on the second floor. The thought made him shiver with worry.

It was a cloudless night—beautiful, wondrous, and mysterious. Thankfully Wyn didn't have to walk it alone.

CHAPTER TWENTY-FOUR

The guild hall was almost empty except for Daniel, Wyn, and Wendy, who gladly served them. A few straggling Climbers were sitting by themselves at various tables with small stacks of books or notes. One Climber was snoring loudly, using a book as a pillow.

Wendy was kind and brought out leftovers from the day as the kitchen staff had long gone home, though Wyn didn't care. He was happy to have anything in his stomach, and he remembered the rations the military served.

Leftovers were a delicacy compared to that mess of food.

Wyn was also incredibly grateful for Wendy not pushing him by asking about his first day in the tower. She knew something happened, especially since he was here eating now so close to midnight, and he figured word would get around soon about what happened. He didn't care about talk or rumors, though. His thoughts were on his friends.

His friends. People he met only hours ago. It was funny how that worked in the heat of combat, though—he gladly called them friends as they were more than just teammates at this point. They'd been through more than most in a matter of hours.

Wyn contentedly ate in silence while Daniel sipped on some coffee. The older Ruby Magician didn't push the rookie for information, either. Wyn was thankful, and made a mental note that he would thank Daniel further, in one way or another, later.

After swallowing one last bite of potatoes, Wyn set his fork down neatly on the plate. His meal wasn't anything special, but it was hot and available. He looked at Daniel, who simply smiled at him, patient as ever.

Wyn took a deep breath. "Where is the infirmary?" He didn't return his mentor's smile. He was tired, anxious, and ready to make sure the others were all right before crashing for the night.

"It's close to the base but a short walk. Less than ten minutes from here." He set his coffee down and waved Wendy over.

Wendy flashed that same smile she presented earlier in the day. She carried bags under her eyes, and her hair was slightly messier, but she was as chipper as ever.

"Are you all done, sweetie?" she asked Wyn. She took his empty plate and dinnerware, and he nodded politely. He was finally satisfied after two plates.

Daniel went to pull out his coin pouch, and Wyn raised a hand. "Let me. You've done a lot for me today." He pulled out three silver cloaks and a gold crown and laid them on the table.

He wanted Wendy to like him, too, but he had a feeling she would whether he was a generous tipper or not.

The Magicians then went on their way, leaving the relative silence of the guild hall behind. At one point after passing some shops, Daniel started to offer some advice but stopped himself, choosing to instead give Wyn some peace. He figured the rookie wouldn't be in the right mindset to retain the information, anyway.

After no more than five minutes of walking, they arrived at the infirmary. Daniel's estimation of the time it took to cover the distance didn't account for Wyn's eagerness. He didn't mind, of course. He was just thankful the newest Ruby Magician was still alive.

The infirmary itself was bland, and Wyn had trouble telling it was even a medical building until he stepped inside. The building was two stories and matched the others around Alestead, and only the symbol of the medic placed above the door informed the public of what it offered. It was open hands under a red colored heart.

The inside was orderly and plain, a far cry from the base of the tower itself. It reminded Wyn more of military buildings than the fantastical areas in Alestead. A lone desk sat straight ahead, and a woman sat behind the counter. She was wearing the same guild clothing, including a medic hat. Her head was faced down, and she seemed to be writing in a book.

Wyn and Daniel approached her, and she still didn't take notice.

"Hello?" Daniel asked.

The woman yelped and shot her head up, startling them. She was attractive, with fair eyes and skin and had a distinct scent of sandalwood that reminded Wyn of home. He felt a rush of heat in his face as he took in the smell.

"Umm, yes, hello," she said, flustered. She smoothed out her uniform and adjusted her hat. "How can I help you today?"

"My friends are here," Wyn said. He shuffled his feet uncomfortably. "I'd like to check on them."

"Of course. What are their names and class?"

"John Gallows, Fighter. And Cedric . . . umm. Lightning Wizard." Wyn fumbled over his words. How could he not know Cedric's last name? A brief moment of panic flooded him as he realized he didn't know Marcy's or Tasha's last name, either. Maybe they would tell him on their own terms. Come to think of it, he didn't remember telling them his last name, either. Only John was comfortable enough baring it all, because of course he was. He was someone Wyn wanted around him. Needed, even.

The woman shut her book and pushed it to the side out of view. She promptly opened another, larger book that seemed like it held a log of information. She used her index finger to sift through names. Wyn noticed most of the names were scratched out.

"Ahh, yes. John is in Wing A. Cedric is in the intensive unit at this time, though. You won't be able to see him until he moves into the standard care unit."

Wyn let out a sigh. "Is he alright, though? Cedric, I mean."

The woman smiled. Wyn couldn't help but notice her smile was equally as attractive as the rest of her. "He is stable and recovering. We have some great medics here both with classes and without. If you'd like, we can arrange a courier to notify you when he moves out of the intensive unit?"

"Yes!" Wyn said, nearly shouting. The woman recoiled a bit with a bigger smile and slight giggle. "I mean . . . yes, thank you." He gave a slight bow and began to walk away.

Daniel bit his lip to stop himself from laughing.

"Umm, excuse me?" the woman said.

Wyn turned around, flush again. "Yes?"

"I need your name and class to inform the courier, please." She wagged the feather pen she was using to write.

Wyn swallowed his shame and walked back to her desk. "Wyn Thatcher. Ruby Magician."

She wrote down the information without any additional reaction. Wyn noticed that the mention of his class didn't seem to affect her at all. She was the first person to not immediately flinch or laugh in pity.

"Also, Wing A is the other way," the woman said. She pointed with her feathered pen and looked down at her book to try to hide her smile.

"Right," Wyn said. "Thank you. Again."

Wyn and Daniel turned around to walk further into the building, and Daniel couldn't help but chuckle a bit once they were safely out of the woman's earshot.

"Did you know Wing A was this way?" Wyn whispered, looking over his shoulder to make sure the woman couldn't hear him.

Daniel, still chuckling, pointed overhead. There was large lettering that read WING A over the hallway.

Wyn put his hand over his face. "You couldn't have pointed that out before? How embarrassing!"

"I'm sorry," Daniel said. "I didn't even think it was possible for you to be flustered like that. I just couldn't help it!"

"That's mean," Wyn said, smirking.

Daniel laughed.

Wing A was right around the hallway. The infirmary wasn't quite as big as Wyn thought, though he figured more of the space was for offices or larger rooms for the more injured or sick. The wing was lit by lanterns hung on the wall, and Wyn thought of the mushrooms that gave off the light in the second floor of the tower.

It was less colorful here but much safer. And that was enough.

Stepping into the main wing, Wyn was surprised to see how much it reminded him of the military infirmaries. There were beds made with fresh linens alongside simple bedside dressers lining both side walls, and curtains reaching half of the two-story ceiling separated each unit that could be pulled for privacy. A few beds further into the infirmary had their curtains pulled, and Wyn wondered if he had to pull each of them back to find John.

A few medics walked the makeshift hall in the middle of the wing. One man approached them, walking quickly. Obviously he read Wyn's mind and didn't want him intruding behind each curtain.

"Can I help you gentlemen?" he whispered, trying to keep his voice low.

"Yes," Daniel said. He matched the volume of the medic with a hushed voice. "We're looking for John Gallows. He's a Fighter."

"Ahh, yes," the man replied, "right over here." He pointed to the right, and sure enough, John was there in bed. The curtain wasn't drawn but he was sleeping.

"Wyn," Daniel said, "why don't I give you some time?"

Wyn took a deep breath, then released it over a few seconds. It was relieving, oddly, but welcomed, as though he'd finally had time to relax and his body finally got the message. "I'd appreciate that, Daniel. Thank you."

Daniel waved his hands in the air. "No need. Take as much time as you'd like. I'm heading back to get some sleep."

Wyn paused. "Speaking of, where am I staying tonight? I don't think I was ever given a room. And if I was, I definitely don't remember."

"You should've been given a key to a room at the guild hall. But we can sort that out tomorrow. When you're ready just come back to my apartment—I have a spare room you can sleep in."

"Are you sure?"

"It's not even a concern. Of course! I'll leave the door open and a candle lit so you know which room is yours."

Wyn put his hand out, and Daniel took it for a handshake. There was a key in Wyn's hand when he let go.

"For the outside door. I'll see you in the morning, Wyn." After a reassuring pat on the shoulder, Daniel decided to leave their goodnight at that.

Wyn was thankful for the older Ruby Magician. Daniel had done so much for him already, hardly knowing him at all, and was everything Wyn could have hoped to have as a mentor.

Wyn was far too critical of him when they first met. He'd need to make it up to him somehow. But maybe just heeding his advice and listening to his counsel would be enough for the time being.

The medic from before came over with a chair, placing it quietly beside John's bed. He smiled and walked off, leaving for his other tasks. Wyn appreciatively took the seat and looked at his new friend.

John was sleeping soundly, covers wrapped tight over his chest. It was haunting seeing him like that. Wyn instantly thought of his company in the field tents, the same white sheet covering missing limbs and gaping holes in his soldiers that wouldn't heal and who wouldn't return. He thought of the warmth the sheets provided in their last moments, or at least whatever little warmth the thin cloth offered. Then he thought of the sheet's next task of either keeping the now-hollow body hidden with no more warmth to hold, or sending them home crippled for an even harder life than the ease of death.

He thought of Cedric and his own white sheet. He wondered what its next task would be.

John stirred, moving ever so slightly. Wyn first thought to get up, to let him rest and recover. He only wanted to make sure he was okay and was happy to see him breathing and whole. He wasn't quick enough before John opened his eyes.

John smiled. It was warm and friendly.

Wyn smiled back. It was soft and sad.

"I'd ask if you're okay, but you were just stabbed in the back," Wyn finally said. "I'm happy to see your eyes open."

"Truth be told, magical medicine is pretty amazing. The wound was healed right away, but the medics said I lost a lot of blood. They said I should be completely healed by tonight."

Wyn's eyes went wide. "You're kidding!" He heard hushed voices shush him from across the wing. He hunched low in his chair, rebuked.

"Why would I joke about that?"

Wyn felt embarrassed. "You're right. I . . . I don't know."

John laughed, stretching his arms behind his head. "I'm just messing with you! I'm alright. Really." He sat up more in the bed and turned his body to fluff his pillows behind him.

Wyn looked him over and noticed he honestly did look fine, and seemed to be enjoying the rest. He was happy to see him alive and well, but he couldn't help but think of his own company. Anger rose inside of him for his soldiers who didn't have magical healing, who suffered and had to die or wish they were dead.

Cedric entered his mind, again. Maybe his white sheet would simply be a white sheet after all?

"Hello? Wyn?" John waved his hand in the air trying to get his attention.

"Hmm? Sorry," Wyn replied. "Did you say something?"

"Yeah. What in the hells happened in there! You *have* to tell me!"

"Shhhh!" came once again from across the wing. A woman held a finger up to her mouth and stared daggers at the Climbers.

John tried to hold back laughter before his smile faded, his face turning serious. "I heard from a medic that one of the rookie groups went to the second floor. What happened?"

Wyn didn't hesitate. "We chased Lionel into the portal."

John snickered and gripped the sheet, his knuckles turning as white as the draped cloth. "Lionel. That bastard."

"He escaped. I'm sorry about that, too."

John was quiet for a moment. Wyn tried to guess what he was thinking, but it was futile—he could be thinking of a thousand different things right now after confirming his own suspicions.

"But there was quite a bit that happened," Wyn continued. "Do you want to rest or—"

"Don't you dare hold out. You better tell me!"

"SHHHH!" was whispered loudly, this time from two medics. They were standing at different ends of the wing and were still able to be heard.

John and Wyn smiled, trying not to laugh again as giggles tried their hardest to escape.

"You're so eager for a healing Climber," Wyn said.

"I'm always eager, my friend. You'll see." He settled back into his bed and pulled the sheet up further on his chest. Wyn chuckled, thinking that John looked like a child waiting for his bedtime story.

Wyn told the tale of the second floor, sparing no detail. If there was anyone here he could trust, it would be John, and he had a feeling they would work together well.

All in all, Wyn was thankful that the sheet that covered John was only a sheet.

Wyn stumbled back to Daniel's apartment. It was late, and he was exhausted. He could feel his muscles ache, and his legs were heavy after climbing the stairs to get there.

He knew he had enough climbing for one day.

Holding his breath, he opened the door with the mangy and worn Ruby Magician symbol. He remembered Daniel's apartment and how dirty it was, and didn't have the stomach or energy to deal with it now. His plan was to simply rush to his room and close the door behind him, but he stopped after taking two quick steps into the apartment.

Wyn couldn't believe his eyes. The room was immaculate. The furniture was tidy and clean, the table dusted, and a fragrant scent hung in the air smelling of wheat and honey. He went back to the door and looked at the outside, wondering if he accidentally entered the wrong apartment.

Wyn then closed and locked the door. The rooms were past the sitting room at the entrance if he remembered correctly, and he walked in further to find the spare bedroom. Not far past the kitchen was a small hallway, and on the right was a cracked door with a bit of light shining through. He walked to it quietly, trying to not be too loud, and opened the door.

The room was fair and simple but cozy, perfectly suitable for a guest. The bed was made and a small desk sat beside it where some papers, a quill and ink, and a small lit candle occupied the space. The window on the far wall wasn't covered, the curtains pulled to the sides. The starry sky helped the small candle light the room, a mix of black night sky and soft orange light reminding Wyn of the cave and mushrooms that lit his path over the evening.

He blew out the candle and sat on the bed, satisfied watching the wisp of smoke float to the ceiling. He wished he had his sister's letter with him. Despite it being only one day, he missed her. If this first day was a hint as to what was in store for his new profession, it would be a difficult but likely rewarding road.

Wyn made a mental note to secure the key to his room tomorrow and get his belongings. He needed his own place to settle into, and he wanted to start logging what he needed to both survive the tower and help his family. There was much more to climbing the tower than simply having a class and gaining coins—if he was going to pay his father's debt back, he needed to be efficient and plan ahead.

Wyn carefully took off his boots and sat them beside the foot of the bed like the many nights in the barracks before this night. He undressed to his undershirt and pulled back the covers, relishing the thought of rest after the wildest day he'd ever had.

He let the night sky keep him company and welcomed sleep.

CHAPTER TWENTY-FIVE

Wyn woke up to the smell of coffee and eggs. His body was sore all over, and he instantly wished he could get more sleep. It was too early to wake up, and apparently magical healing still didn't do much about sore muscles and joints. The lone window in Daniel's spare room had light shining bright from outside, the sun high in the sky. He suddenly regretted not closing the curtains last night.

He shot up in bed. With the sun shining bright, it wasn't as early as he thought.

He grabbed his ragged clothes and threw them on haphazardly. He ran his hands through his hair and hoped to find a wash basin and bathroom soon to be more presentable.

A stronger scent of breakfast beckoned him once he left his room. He squinted, trying to let his eyes adjust after just waking up. With his eyes closed he could smell sausage and toasted bread, making his stomach growl. Footsteps pattered all around the kitchen before settling at the small table in the corner of the room.

Daniel was running around, trying to prepare the table for Wyn and himself. He sat down at the small table with the feast in front of him, noticing Wyn there with his hands up trying to shield his eyes.

"Good morning! I hope the noise didn't wake you." Daniel clapped his hands together in obvious excitement.

Wyn shook his head. "Not at all. The sun woke me, the smell brought me in."

Daniel laughed. "Good, good! It's all ready, and there's plenty!"

"Did you cook all of this?"

"I'm many things, but a cook is not one of them. I had Wendy bring it up for us. That woman is something else." He stood to grab a mug for Wyn in a cabinet and placed it on the table in front of an empty chair.

Wyn sat and began to make his plate of food. He rubbed his eyes one more time to help wake up. He was much slower than Daniel, who already had a full plate, steaming mug of coffee, and was tearing apart a piece of buttered bread. Wyn took his own bite of bread before pouring himself coffee out of the steaming kettle.

"So what are you planning to do today?" Daniel asked.

Wyn smiled. Daniel was much happier today than yesterday. He remembered how jittery and drunk he was, somber and negative. He began to warm up as he showed Wyn around Alestead, though, and Wyn hoped this was Daniel's true personality. His cheerful attitude suited him much better, even if it came while Wyn was still waking up.

"John and I decided we'd walk around Alestead. He still needs to claim his rewards from the climb, and we want to find some shops that could be useful for the next season. Not to mention I still haven't had a true tour of the city."

"That's a good idea, especially since you were too impatient to get going yesterday. There's an incredible amount of things to see and do here in Alestead. Just make sure you make it to the festival tonight."

Wyn swallowed a mouthful of sausage hard and too fast, stretching his throat uncomfortably. "I nearly forgot! With everything that happened yesterday it completely left my mind!"

Daniel chuckled over his cup of coffee. "Well, that's alright. Yesterday was not an ordinary day! Going to the second floor, one of your own group betraying all of you. That's too much for someone's first trip in the tower."

Wyn took his own sip of coffee. It was hot and nutty, much more enjoyable than the quality of coffee he was used to drinking. Obviously the amenities in Alestead were held in much higher regard than the military standards and farm life.

He took in the taste and smell for a minute, reflecting on the day before. Floors one and two all in one day. It felt much longer, and he was supposed to do this day-in and day-out for months. He wondered how other Climbers kept their sanity.

"Well," Daniel continued, "I'd love to hear the more detailed story of the climb. I'm sure there were some parts you decided to keep to yourself. And I'd be lying if I said I didn't want to hear about it. Plus, you made out like a bandit compared to the average for clearing floors one and two."

Wyn gave Daniel credit. The man wasn't easily fooled. "I know. It'd be good for me to fill you in, and I actually had some things I wanted to get your advice on, too. But is that not a typical amount? People come here for the riches, after all."

Daniel stopped chewing some sausage and grinned ear to ear. He was desired—wanted, even—by a new Climber for his expertise. He thought that maybe this time would be different. That Wyn would be different.

No. Daniel *knew* he was different, and he was excited to see this new Ruby Magician climb higher and reach new heights.

"I'll share anything I can and find out about what I can't. But no. A good average is about forty gold crowns for the first floor and twice that for the second. I wonder if it was because of your hardships and small group on the second floor that influenced the increased coin. Something to look into, I suppose."

Wyn never thought it was a possibility that there were so many factors playing into the rewards. Of course he didn't know much about being a Climber, not yet, but if finishing floors with fewer people increased his payout, he'd absolutely try that strategy. Whatever could get his debt paid off quickest would be worth trying.

"Thank you, Daniel. Maybe tonight after the festival we can discuss it? To prepare for the next season that starts tomorrow? I don't plan to stay out late partying. It's not exactly my area of interest."

"Splendid! Mine either. Though you should also go get your key and find your room from the attendant downstairs before you head out."

"Oh, gods, so much to do," Wyn said. He put his fork down, finishing a bite of eggs. He took a few more gulps of coffee, the mug having cooled, and stood up. "Let me wash up first, and I'll go get it before I meet John."

"How about you get your key and wash up in your own room? You can unpack a bit, settle in some before you set out. That way it'll be ready when you return tonight."

Wyn nodded in agreement. "That's a good idea. Would you mind helping me? I know you've done a lot for me already, but—"

"Nonsense," Daniel said, cutting him off. "That's a better idea, anyway." He put down his own coffee mug and threw on his Magician's robe. "The Ruby Magicians are off, ready for another adventure!"

Wyn laughed, nearly spitting out his coffee. Even though he had no idea what lay ahead, he knew today would be a good day.

Wyn's room was on the second floor of the guild hall, and his legs were deeply grateful. It wasn't a special room by any means, but his class symbol was marked on the middle of the door similar to Daniel's, only smaller and less worn. It was a basic apartment with a kitchen, small living area, and single bed, all in one large room. It was plenty for him, and much more than his communal bunk as a soldier.

Maybe one day he'd advance to a house further out in the city, or even a guild hall if his journey led to being in a guild. But that was a thought for another day.

He and Daniel worked to unpack his bag of clothes and gear. Daniel offered to help fill his small bookshelf with some books on magic, the tower, and general information that would be useful. Wyn gave him a spare key, and Daniel gave one to Wyn for his own apartment. Wyn didn't want to be intrusive and use it and figured Daniel would feel the same way, but the gesture was both kind and fitting.

Daniel left to enjoy the day for himself, though Wyn didn't quite understand. He mentioned he would scour the library and historical texts for books and information Wyn could use. But how could the library be *that* fun? Reading was helpful, sure, but spending an entire day in there and enjoying it? There was a reason Wyn joined the military and not the academy. To each their own.

After Daniel left, Wyn took a deep breath and fully took in his room. This was his. To some Climbers it would be a downgrade, especially if they were royalty, but for Wyn this was special. Even though he rented the space, it was an area he could call his own, not to mention the privacy he now possessed. It would be a great place for him to plan and recover to face the challenges that both Alestead and Alistair offered. Wyn initially thought the fee of two hundred and fifty crowns a month was absurd, but he'd likely make that in less than a week.

First, however, he needed to regroup with his friends after the events of yesterday. Realizing it was already after lunch, he hurried out to the infirmary. He didn't want to miss John getting out for the first time.

The streets of Alestead were bustling with people, both Climbers and tourists alike. Wyn thought the city had been busy yesterday, but it was nothing compared to the day of the festival. All of his preconceptions about trying to separate the Climbers and visitors in the crowd were also wrong, as there was no truly accurate way to tell them apart. People varied greatly in what they wore or carried, ranging from casual clothes to elegant dresses and no equipment to carts of supplies.

The crowd was nearly suffocating, too, and he was thankful it was likely only for one more day as people would hopefully leave after the festival tonight. They would come to explore Alestead for the day or weekend and enjoy the festival activities that evening to usher in a new cycle of exploration and trials. It was odd how they celebrated a new challenge that was just as defeating as rewarding.

At least he could ignore them and focus on preparing for the next month by really diving into being a Climber.

Wyn suddenly felt very lost, as he hadn't had a true tour of the city and what buildings were present. Daniel only showed him the basics and what he needed to know before entering the tower yesterday, but people flooded the cobblestone streets from the front gates to the tower base. There wasn't any rhyme or reason to their directions, and it was disorienting.

A pair of guild officials were standing in the middle of the streets handing out papers to anyone who wanted them. Wyn walked over to them to see what they offered, gently walking around people young and old.

He was grateful for their information, as they gave him a rough map of Alestead that highlighted the important buildings to visit as well as the various activities to be held that evening. The city held much more than he thought, and he decided to explore more when the crowd wasn't as heavy. The markets and trading districts were especially interesting, but he figured John and Tasha would be able to help guide him. He also figured there were housing sections and more desirable areas for the elite Climbers or nobility, and sure enough most of the surrounding land was for that purpose. There was enough room for thousands of people to live here, not to mention the hundreds that could live in the guild apartments and even more visitors from outside the city.

This would be an interesting new adventure.

Wyn continued to traverse the growing crowds on the way to the infirmary. It took longer than expected, but he made it nonetheless. When he entered, there was a woman behind the front desk, but she wasn't the same as the night before. This woman was older and frail-looking.

"Excuse me," Wyn asked. "Do you have any update on a certain Climber? I'd like to know how he's doing."

"Sure thing," she said. Her voice was rough and raspy like she'd smoked a pipe her whole life. "What's the name and class?"

"Cedric, Lightning Wizard." He knew it was a long shot of him being out of the intensive unit, but he still wanted to ask.

She ran her fingers down a log book. "Ahh, yes. He is still in the intensive unit. Sorry, but no more visitors allowed."

Wyn perked up. "No more?"

"One woman is already there visiting him. Has been there since last night, actually. We only allow one visitor per patient in the intensive unit."

Wyn smiled softly. "Thank you."

So they did allow visitors. The woman last night didn't mention that, but maybe she forgot? Or the woman visiting him was already there, and she didn't think to mention it.

"Wyn!" a voice said. Wyn turned, and John was standing outside Wing A with a woman beside him.

Wyn grinned. "Tasha!" He went up to her to shake her hand, but she threw her arms around him in a hug. He was surprised at first, but quickly and awkwardly returned the embrace.

She let go of him then punched him in the arm.

"Hey! What was that for?"

"John told me what happened. That was incredibly stupid of you to go to the next floor!"

Wyn winced. "I know, but—"

"But it was also brave of you," she said, cutting him off. "You're a good guy, Wyn."

John waved his hands in the air. "What am I, chopped goblin?" He started to limp and stepped closer to Tasha before putting his arm around her. "And I'm still recovering, you know."

"Oh, stop it," Tasha said, playfully pushing his arm off. "I basically healed you before we even came back! The infirmary was a formality. Don't act like you're still hurt."

Wyn laughed, then caught the look of the woman behind the desk. She had a look of displeasure on her face that Wyn couldn't quite place. It was definitely not as inviting as the woman from last night.

"How about we make our way outside," Wyn said, trying to avoid any more negative comments.

"So, what are we doing today?" Tasha asked. She held the door open for John, who gave a slight bow, then held his hands out in front of him after he went outside in an *after you* gesture.

"John and I were talking last night about it," Wyn said. "We want to go explore the shops a bit before we relax tonight. Maybe see more of the city, if possible."

"Yeah, like a good weapons and armor smith, a general goods store, maybe even a magic item shop?" John clapped his hands, giddy with excitement. "The basics, but important places. And we need to find some good ones to keep visiting for this next season!"

"Hmm," Tasha said. She held out a hand on her chin, thinking. "Then we should also look for a tailor, an alchemist, and a spell or scroll shop. If we're really covering our bases."

"That's a good idea," Wyn said, as he stepped around a family walking by with a large bouquet of flowers. The bundle was nearly as tall as the man, oddly. "But I don't know if we'll have time for all of that before tonight."

"We find the shops we might like, then ask around if they're even worth it," John said. "It'll be easier than getting around this crowd, at least."

"Are you going to buy anything with your rewards from yesterday?" Wyn asked.

John immediately stopped walking. "My rewards! I completely forgot to see what I earned after the climb!"

"Well, you were just stabbed in the back," Tasha said. "I don't think you had coins on your mind."

"Tasha, I *always* have coins on my mind." He looked at her with an obnoxious grin, making her giggle.

Wyn laughed, too. He was relieved that John really was okay, and with the three of them getting along so well, it felt *right*. He knew he had found the core of his climbing group, and only after one climb no less.

It was absolutely the worst way to start his time as a Climber, but Wyn was grateful. They didn't judge him based on his class like Daniel said, but rather by his actions.

John and Tasha would make excellent partners, though all three of them knew they needed more members.

Or did they?

"Wyn?" Tasha asked.

Wyn was thinking about a strategy to climb the tower. Would it work with only three of them? Could they survive? It was difficult with Cedric and Marcy, and they were veterans. They struggled just on the second floor. But what if they were better prepared? Both Marcy and Cedric admitted they were in the worst possible situations, and they still handled themselves well. Plus, Wyn wasn't keen on trusting a random Climber right now, so his options seemed limited.

"Wyn!" Tasha said, stepping in front of him on the street and waving her hand in front of his face. "Helloooo?" She drew out the word in a sing-song to get his attention.

"Hmm?" Wyn shook his head, and realized Tasha and John were standing in front of him staring. Tasha had her hands on her hips, her eyebrows scrunched up in confusion.

"I swear," she said, "you just disappear sometimes. You're in your head too much."

"I'm sorry," Wyn said. "What did you say?"

"Don't apologize," John said. "It's not a bad thing. But Tasha asked if you and her wanted to join me in going to the tower to get my rewards before we shop?"

"Oh. Of course," Wyn replied. "Maybe we can see about trading this dagger, too, for something useful?"

John's eyes lit up. "I'd love that! I'm so jealous you found it without me." He deflated a bit, his excitement leaving him in a rush. Instinctively his hand went to his belt, but he only grasped air. "I need a new weapon, too."

Wyn patted him on the back. "I know. We all need better gear. Let's see what we can find and we'll go from there. Maybe we can make a list?"

"A shopping list!" Tasha jumped up and down, joining in the excitement.

"And now she just made it boring," John said.

"For today," Wyn said, "I *love* boring."

CHAPTER TWENTY-SIX

John pushed his way through the door, excited to leave the bustling crowd. "Finally. A magical shop!" He began to wander around like a little boy in a toy store, wanting to see and grab anything that interested him. With each new magical item he spotted two more caught his eye, and he was bouncing around with glee like a puppy.

Tasha and Wyn were close behind, also happy to leave the ever-growing crowd but not nearly as ecstatic as John about the magic item shop.

"It's not like you'll be able to buy much with your measly forty gold," Tasha said, teasing John.

Whether he heard her or not, he continued his amazement over the different magical items the shop held. They ranged from scrolls to weapons to armor and potions, all with a brief description and colored tag to show their magical strength. It reminded Wyn of the colored mushrooms in the cave, though it was much more pleasing to the eye in the neat categories of the shop. Nearly all of them were green or blue, and Wyn wondered if the more powerful purple items that Marcy and Cedric mentioned were guarded somewhere.

A man appeared from around a corner, wearing an apron and fine cloth gloves. "Welcome to The Silver Step!" he said, his voice loud and smooth. He was objectively attractive, Wyn admitted, and well-groomed. His hair was styled, his clothes were neat and elegant, and he was wearing a bit of cologne.

Tasha gingerly walked up to him, drawn in by his charm. "I'm Tasha St. Clair," she said. "Your shop is lovely!"

The man gave a deep bow. "Thank you, my dear! Please, have a look around and let me know if anything catches your beautiful eye." He winked at her, then walked behind the glass counter at the end of the store. There were smaller, more detailed magical items set underneath it.

"You're a St. Clair?!" John said, louder than he intended. "You never told me that!"

Tasha bent over to read a description of a pair of jeweled earrings. "I didn't think I needed to. What does it matter?"

"It doesn't," Wyn said. He shot John a look. "But it does help explain your reasonings for coming here a bit better. And it's not often you find yourself in the presence of nobility."

"We can discuss all of that later," she replied. "Aren't we here for a specific reason? There are other places I want to see before the festival, too."

"Yeah, yeah," John said. "But I wouldn't be surprised if you're carrying more than your reward from yesterday. Are you looking to stock our bags and belts, St. Clair?"

Tasha didn't even look away from the earrings before waving John off like a fly. He simply laughed at his own joke.

Wyn wondered how much wealth John had, too. His family may not have been nobility but they all climbed and gained some form of fortune. He likely knew of ways to secure items most didn't, and he'd already shown a wealth of information that Wyn didn't think most rookies possessed. Wyn wasn't going to be the one to start asking for handouts, though—he would earn his place here and incur no more debts. Especially from those he called friends.

Walking around the room, Wyn was quickly growing overwhelmed with the magic items, their glowing auras, and descriptions of what they did. It was too much for him to mentally process right now as he studied each one he came across. He honestly didn't even know where to start. So, he settled at the counter where the charming man was patiently waiting with a smirking smile. Wyn felt a strange draw to him, though not a sinister one. The smell of cedar and smoke from the man's cologne filled his nostrils, and it was pleasant.

"I'm Ardwyn Thatcher, but you can call me Wyn. I'm looking for some information or advice, among other things."

"Hello, Wyn Thatcher! I'm Benedict Greaves. What information or advice, among other things, are you looking for? That could be one and the same or two very different matters." He bent forward toward the glass and rested his chin on his right hand, never losing the smirk on his face.

Wyn was a bit thrown off, but decided to go with it. Something was definitely different about Benedict, but he couldn't put his finger on what.

"Yes, well, first I would like to know about this," Wyn said, as he pulled the magical dagger from his backpack and gently placed it on the glass countertop. It shimmered blue, the magical aura visibly radiating when focusing on it. Magical items seemed to only give off their aura when viewed with intent. Otherwise the entire shop would've been a glowing headache of brilliant colors. As Wyn already discovered.

Tasha and John joined him beside the counter to watch, hoping to hear more information themselves.

"Ahh," Benedict said. He took the dagger and inspected it. He grabbed a small eyepiece from behind the counter and set it down, similar to the two Wyn received last night with his rewards. "What floor did you find it on, if you don't mind me asking?"

"Floor two," Wyn said.

"On his introductory climb, no less!" John added.

Benedict broadened his smirk into a genuine smile. It was as magnetic as the rest of him. "Now that is interesting! You must be the rookie that climbed to the second floor yesterday. My, my, I've already heard of you."

"I think everyone has by now," Tasha said. She mirrored Benedict, placing her chin in her hands on the counter across from him.

"That's me," Wyn said awkwardly. He wasn't used to that much attention and didn't know what else to say. "But I don't use a dagger. I primarily use a spear. Well, I do use a dagger, but only as a backup. And I don't even know if the magic in it would be useful to me." Wyn stammered a bit. He was caught off guard and oddly nervous. He felt strangely comfortable, though, which only added to his overall confusion.

"Hmm." Benedict took the dagger and held it up. "It wouldn't be practical to have a useful, magical backup weapon if your primary weapon is mundane. No, obviously the best option is to have all of your weapons and armor magical—but that will come in time, won't it?"

Both John and Tasha absentmindedly nodded yes.

"With that being the case," Benedict continued, "you have several options."

"I do?" Wyn asked.

"Why, of course! And I'm here to tell you about them. It's our duty to help our brave Climbers, after all!"

The three rookies smiled and looked at each other, eager to know more.

Benedict cleared his throat quietly. "First, if you want to identify the dagger, a few options follow. One option, is you then keep it and use it, which wouldn't be a bad idea if it's useful to you, but admittedly not recommended. Another option, is you could trade it at the guild's trading house to another Climber for a different weapon or item. Or, the last option, is to use a shop like mine to trade or sell it."

Wyn nodded, mentally noting his growing list of options. "Okay, and why wouldn't I want to identify it?"

"Ahh, that's a good question! If you choose not to identify it but still want to get rid of it, it's more of a gamble for either the seller or buyer. The magical properties could be useful or not, and there are quite a range of possible properties to be found."

"Which isn't quite as helpful for a lower quality magical item and new Climbers, but can be a larger risk or reward for a higher quality one," John added.

Benedict smiled. "Precisely. For a blue item, though, I wouldn't recommend it. Especially not at this stage of your climbing career."

"I'm inclined to agree," Wyn said.

Benedict laughed. It was hearty, warm, and infectious. "Excellent! Most Climbers who trade without identifying are well established and like the thrill of gambling items rather than coins. They like to . . . live a little." He winked again.

Wyn's cheeks flushed. He felt like he was under a spell.

Maybe he was?

"So I don't want to do that, then." He reached back into his backpack and pulled out one of the identifying glasses he received as a reward.

"No, no," Benedict said, "don't use yours. This one is on the house." He took his glass and gave it to Wyn. "Though you need to be the one to identify it. For your first time, and all."

"I can't wait until my first time," Tasha said. She stared right at Benedict.

"I'd be so honored," the shopkeeper replied.

Wyn's cheeks flushed with heat, and he did his best to ignore them, if it was even possible. John furrowed his brow, confused. He caught on far too late.

Wyn took the eyeglass and inspected it. Tiny runes lined the outer metal rim, and the glass was perfectly clear without flaw. It was gold where his two were silver, and he wondered what the difference between them was.

Not wanting to delay, he held it up to his eye, looking directly at the dagger. The magical sight revealed a completely different weapon. The blade was a darker metal and slightly curved like a hunting knife, while the handle was a mixture of gray and blue. Faintly glowing runes lined the hilt up to the short cross guard and gave off a small crackle of energy. There was a small topaz set in the bottom of the hilt, and as he kept looking at it he heard Tasha and John go "whoa" at the same time.

He took the eyeglass away, and the dagger maintained its new appearance, transformed after being truly seen and identified.

"That's incredible," John said.

"Look at your parchment for the effects," Benedict said, smiling. "This is always the best part, when new Climbers identify magical items for the first time." He picked up the dagger carefully, holding it like a jeweler would handle a precious item.

Wyn quickly pulled out his parchment and read the one labeled **ITEMS**. There, completely by the tower's magic, appeared a new paragraph. Wyn read it out loud for everyone to hear.

Stunning Dagger: This dagger is imbued with a topaz, helping give it the magical property of lightning. When struck by this dagger, the being has a small chance to become stunned, paralyzed by the lightning magic imbued within. The light but durable metal improves the wielder's agility by a small amount. Standard attacks will also electrify the target with small sparks to a minimal degree.

Benedict whistled. "That's mighty impressive! And two very useful effects, too. I can imagine there would be many Climbers who would appreciate having this as a weapon."

"Don't you think that would be useful, Wyn?" Tasha asked. She was inspecting the sheath, twirling it in her hands. It was identical to the dagger's hilt as a perfect match.

Wyn stared at the dagger in shock. His first thought was thinking back to the second floor. Would its effects have changed anything? It was an impressive weapon, but he doubted it would have made much difference.

Still, he couldn't have asked for a better effect and rarity on his first voyage into the tower, but he knew it wasn't what he needed at the moment.

"I do," Wyn said, "but I think a spear would be more useful for me right now. I'm sorry."

"Why are you sorry?" Benedict asked. He laughed again, short but sweet, and set the knife down. "This is a fine item and a valuable trade! I don't have an endless number of items here, but I do have many different kinds, with more in the storeroom. There's bound to be something to help you."

Wyn thought for a moment. "How about two weapons of slightly lesser value?"

Benedict clapped his hands and rubbed them together, startling the Climbers. "Ahh, you're thinking like a true Climber now! I love it!" The scent of his cologne hit their noses again, aromatic and charming like magic. "I would trade two green items for it—good ones, too!"

"Thank you," Wyn said. "Having two weapons for us instead of me having one really powerful one would be better."

"Wyn," Tasha said, "you don't need to do that. This is yours! We'll all find our own items in the tower eventually."

"I agree," John said. "And I already sent a letter to my family asking for a new sword!"

"You did?" Wyn asked.

"When I was in the infirmary I had some extra time on my hands. I explained the situation and even had the Tower Master sign it. They'll understand. It might not be as good as the sword I had before, but it'll be just fine, so don't worry about me!"

Wyn let out a satisfied sigh. "It's settled, then. How about a spear and a staff?"

"No, Wyn," Tasha said. She put the sheath back on the counter while Benedict hurriedly stepped away. "I don't need a magical staff right now. Spells are plenty for me."

"I don't think you understand. Either of you." Wyn looked at both of his team-mates in the eyes, emphasizing his point. "The second floor was *not* easy. I'm thankful that both Marcy and Cedric came after me, or I would've died in there. We need any useful resource we have, and sharing our capabilities is the best way to succeed."

"He's right, you know," Benedict said, holding both a spear and a staff. "What truly makes a rookie Climber become a veteran is how well they work with their team. A rookie group who works well together and communicates efficiently will be more effective than a stronger veteran group who doesn't."

Tasha let out an annoyed, relenting sigh. "Fine, fine, you win. What's a good staff for a Diamond Magician?"

Benedict looked at the staff he was holding, opened his mouth like he was going to speak, and then paused. "Wyn, what is your class?"

Wyn hesitated but didn't want to shy away from his class. He needed to own it if he was going to change other's minds. "I'm a Ruby Magician."

Benedict gave a pitied smile that he quickly shook away. He then left with both weapons in hand, and returned quickly with two others.

"I believe these will be to your liking," Benedict said.

Wyn noticed the spear first, and it was a beautiful weapon. The spearhead was longer than usual and more curved on one side, and there was a small feather that was attached with thin leather straps just under the blade. It still had a simi-lar height and appearance like a spear, but resembled more of a small glaive from the curved blade than the traditional spears he was used to fighting with.

The wooden staff he held in his other hand was nearly orange in color like young cedar, and the top was a large rounded knot that nearly formed a complete circle. It didn't look natural at all, but rather like it was magically shaped in a coil at its end. Runes were clearly etched on the upper half of the staff and throughout the circular top.

"Oh, those look impressive," John said. He was wide-eyed and smiling, eager to hear more about them.

Benedict handed the staff to Tasha and the spear to Wyn. "They certainly are, young man. Tasha St. Clair, that is a *Sunstaff*. It can cast the spell **Cure** three times a day, and by speaking a keyword it will light up brighter than a torch. In other words, it casts the spell **Torchlight** on command as often as you'd like."

Tasha gasped. "That's perfect! I used **Torchlight** a lot, and now I can focus on something else!" She held the staff and ran her fingers along it, feeling every inch of its magic.

"Excellent! It doesn't add to your magical abilities like some weapons, but I'd encourage you to find armor or accessories to fulfill that role. At least for now."

"Thank you for the advice," Tasha said. "I'll do just that."

"I have no doubt," Benedict said. "And for the spear—its name is *Windcutter*. It's magically imbued with the Wind element and is lighter than a regular spear.

Personally I think it's more like a small glaive, like how a short sword is to a long sword, but I'll let you be the judge of how to use it. You seem more than capable. But its real perk is the smaller, talon-shaped blade on the bottom."

Wyn twirled it around and inspected the butt end. Instead of a blunted shaft there was a small hooked blade, just a few inches long but curved like a claw. Runes sat above it in markings Wyn didn't recognize. Granted he didn't recognize most runes, but they were formed with harsh edges of squares and triangles rather than the more familiar layered circles he'd seen so far.

"What do these runes do?"

"You have a good eye, Magician! They cast the spell **Wingbeat**. It's not a common spell, only found on the Sorcerer's list. But it releases a sharp wave of air that cuts in a wide range over a distance of about twenty feet. It's used directly from the talon and twice a day."

Wyn spun it around in his hands a bit. Benedict had a brief look of shocked concern for his shop, but tried to contain himself. Wyn was well trained, and the spear felt natural in his hands despite the foreign appearance. He was right, too, as it was light and easily maneuverable but felt strong and firm.

"These are both great," Wyn said. "Thank you, Benedict."

"You are more than welcome! So it's a deal, then?"

"I believe so. These should serve us well."

Benedict clapped his hands together. "Then I hope my helpful suggestions will convince you to become regulars here! If you have other magical items you may always consult me. And, as a thank you, here is a small gift." Benedict reached behind the counter and pulled out a small pouch. It was a light brown leather and looked similar to a coin purse, but magical runes were easily seen on the bag's opening.

"What is it?" John asked. He held his hands out, practically begging for it.

"It's a magical pouch that is common for Climbers." Benedict handed the pouch to John. "It holds much more than it appears. Around the size of a large backpack in the convenience of a coin purse."

"I knew it! I tried to convince my parents to bring one but they refused, saying I needed to gain my items when I was an actual Climber. This would be very helpful, Benedict. Thank you." John immediately began to strap it to his belt.

"Can we keep these here and pick them up before we climb again?" Wyn asked.

"Of course. You shouldn't go to the festival carrying these, after all. You need hands to drink and flirt!"

Tasha giggled, and John stepped back toward the door.

"We should go to the tailor's shop next!" Tasha said.

"Girls and their clothes," John muttered.

Tasha shot him a look. They began to walk out, saying their goodbyes and thanks to Benedict.

"You guys go ahead," Wyn said. "I want to ask Benedict something real quick."

"We'll be right next door," Tasha said. "Come on, John. We need to find some matching clothes for us to wear if we're going to be a team!"

John gave Wyn a look of fear and walked out with the bouncing Tasha.

"I need a favor," Wyn said.

Benedict's eyes seem to sparkle as he lowered his voice. "Oh, favors. I like those."

Wyn pulled out his magical hunk of wood he received on the first floor. He gingerly placed it on the counter.

"My, my, you are full of surprises," Benedict said. "Another magic item. What are you interested in?"

"I'm not looking to trade. I'm looking for it to be crafted. Can you do that? Or know someone reliable who could?"

"I can. For a fee, of course. It's pretty straightforward to create something from a green rarity item. This doesn't have to be a favor either, though you owing me sounds much more fun."

Wyn scratched the back of his head. He honestly felt embarrassed. He wasn't sure what Benedict's talents were, but now that he knew he could also craft items, he was sure he'd be visiting him again.

"I have to ask, though. Is this for you or someone on your team?" Benedict asked.

"Someone else. It's for one of the veterans that helped me yesterday. I want to give a gift as a thank you to both of them, but only have an idea for one for now."

"That's very kind of you. What are you wanting?"

Wyn smiled. "Arrows."

CHAPTER TWENTY-SEVEN

Wyn took a deep gulp of the mead, letting the honeyed drink sit in his mouth a bit longer than usual. It was sweet and savory, a rare combination, like nothing he had experienced before. The small stall selling the mugs was quickly having people line up for more, and Wyn could see why. He paid the man behind the wooden counter and took his mug, making a mental note to bring it back in order to get a small refund. Not before getting another refill or two, of course.

The festival was about to kick off with the parade being the highlight of the evening. The markets and streets of Alestead had been busy all day, and after shopping for hours Wyn wanted to rest alone before he met back up with Tasha and John. He didn't know if shopping in the busy crowds all day was worse than the tower or not, but he felt like it drained him more than fighting. He was used to his life being in danger and relying on his own merits, but going from store to store looking through endless amounts of things was another challenge entirely.

He had decided to experience some of the festival by himself to relax, wandering around the Alestead courtyards. Where it normally was outdoor training grounds and popular hangout spots—at least according to his map and information from Tasha—the open fields were now bustling with activities and a steadily growing large crowd. There were many stalls of food and items, events, and general things to do, and Wyn was enjoying simply walking around to take it all in. The crowd migrated from the streets and markets, hoping to end the night as the parade would snake its way through the festival and people alike. It was a fun way to enjoy the festivities and company, so he was told.

The fields had been transformed, with banners flying, jugglers juggling, and bards singing. There was merriment everywhere, with the chaos of the people cheering, laughing, or singing along to the different songs that played in different areas. Most people walked around with food or drink in hand, and children ran rampant with ribbons and toys.

The three rookies had decided to meet at the food court, a small area where tables were gathered and stalls sold all varieties of food and drink. Wyn was trying to scout out a good table spot early when his stomach growled, persuading him to find food and drink instead. That was when he noticed the stall selling the mead, and he wanted to try it.

He walked around the fields sipping his drink, enjoying himself. There was a small crowd around a series of games, where people could pay a small price to play. He settled on watching a young boy run up to an area with dozens of bottles lashed together, holding small rings in his hand. The boy then threw the rings at the bottles, trying to get a ring around a bottle neck. He threw and threw and threw, but after eight tries was unsuccessful.

A man, probably the boy's father, walked up to the vendor and gave a few more coins. The woman gave out a handful more rings, and the man gave them to the boy. He instantly stopped crying and began laughing again, which made the father laugh, too. A woman then stepped beside them, dressed in combat gear with a sword sheathed on her waist. She put her arm around the boy's father, and the two of them fondly watched their son play another round of the game, this time succeeding twice.

It was a funny contrast, watching a Climber dressed for combat interact with her civilian-dressed family. The more Wyn looked around, though, the more he realized this festival was also for the many Climbers' loved ones to join them. He assumed they would take the opportunity as family and friends to gather and celebrate what they're doing, using the festival as a reminder of what they had and what they fought for.

It was heartwarming, but also filled Wyn with a sense of anxiety. His own family was struggling, barely able to feed themselves and riddled with debt. He thought of his sister, how she had abandoned her life to help their father after their mom left. He thought of his father, his health ailing him after his family nearly fell apart, now relying on his children for his own mistakes and poor judgment.

Wyn took a long swig of his mead, or at least he tried. It was empty, and he had a strong urge to fill it.

Back at the mead stall he was dismayed to see a line wrapping around the far corner. He sadly knew he wouldn't make it before they sold out. Instead, he opted to return the mug before looking for another source of drink.

Casually strolling back toward the food court, he saw Daniel and Wendy sitting at a table. They were smiling and laughing, giggling like they were children up to no good. Daniel had a mug in his hand, and Wendy was eating an apple on a stick, and it was coated in something thick like syrup. It looked strangely delectable.

Daniel caught him staring and raised his mug to him, very subtly nodding his head in a greeting. Wyn waved but didn't approach, wanting to be polite by saying hello but also not wanting to interrupt them. They seemed to be having a great time, and he didn't want to spoil it.

Wyn suddenly had an arm around his neck. He jerked away in response, then relaxed when he saw it was John.

"Easy, man. It's just me!" He pulled his hands back and held them up innocently, but was smiling his big, charming smile.

Wyn figured he could probably get away with most things based on that smile. He sighed in relief. "I'm sorry. I'm still jumpy, I guess."

"You're telling me. If anyone should be jumpy around here it should be me!"

Wyn took a deep breath. "You're right. But man, this festival is busy. It's almost as bad as the city."

John laughed. "Well, aren't most festivals busy? At least there are fun things to do."

"Yeah, I guess, but I didn't imagine it would be quite like this. I thought some Climbers and their families would be here, but it seems like it's much bigger than that. The rumors didn't do it justice."

"Oh, yeah. Plenty of people come out to see them and to watch the parade. It's wild—just wait!"

"I take it you've seen it before?"

"Dozens of times. When my family would climb, seeing friends who were climbing, when I wanted a vacation—any excuse I could make to come and see it I would."

Wyn looked around at the varying kinds of people, again marveling at how everyone meshed together despite their different backgrounds. Here they weren't a noble or a peasant. They were either a visitor to see the magical tower or a Climber to challenge it. Wyn had never seen such a cultural phenomenon, and had a feeling this barely scratched the surface of the wonder of both the city and tower. It was a refreshing break from the power struggle he was more familiar with.

"It's an entirely different world, here," Wyn said. "I had no idea."

John patted him on the back. "It's definitely different. But it grows on you in the best way."

John began walking away, heading to a table. Wyn followed him and saw that Tasha was sitting down with food and drinks already prepared.

"About time you showed up, Wyn! I was hoping we weren't going to have to find you in this crowd," Tasha said between a mouthful of food. She may have come from a noble house but she was eating like the poor soldiers who never had a full, hot plate.

"I don't think we ever would've found each other," Wyn said as he sat down at the table to eat. He grabbed a clean plate and began adding food to it. "But I'm glad we did."

"I'll drink to that," John said, raising a mug.

Wyn grabbed a cup, filled it with water from the pitcher, and toasted along with John and Tasha.

"No ale?" John asked.

"I already had a mug of the mead, and it was incredible," Wyn said. "Anything else wouldn't be as good."

"Not to mention we have to get back to climbing tomorrow, right?" Tasha asked. "It is the new season, after all. We might as well hop to it!"

John set his mug down after a long drink and stared at it. "I've given a lot of thought to that. You're right, of course. Though we haven't talked about what our plan is."

"What do you mean?" Tasha asked, cramming a chicken leg into her mouth.

"Well, we *are* here to climb," John continued. "But are we going to go just the three of us?"

Tasha put her now-cleaned chicken leg down and thought about it, licking her fingers clean. Wyn had already been thinking about it too, and now was the best time to bring it up.

"I think we should," Wyn said. "At least for now."

Tasha wiped her hands on a dinner napkin. "That's risky. I doubt we'd make it very far. I mean, no offense, but look at how you, Marcy, and Cedric did last night."

Wyn clenched his jaw, but reluctantly nodded his head, agreeing. "I know, I know. I could make excuses, but you're right. I just am having a hard time trusting anyone right now."

They sat in silent agreement, leaving their dinner for the moment. Wyn was right. They all had a hard time trusting anyone—but Tasha was right, too.

"Why the long faces?" a voice said at the end of the table while a mug of ale slammed down. Foam sloshed out of it, and the three rookies looked to see who rudely interrupted them.

Marcy stood there, one hand on her hip, wearing a tipsy smile and rosy cheeks.

Tasha jumped up and hugged her without a word, spilling Marcy's drink. The mug flew out onto the grass beside them as the Ranger couldn't hold on to it well enough. John stood up, too, and hugged her when Tasha let go.

"Yeah, yeah, settle down, settle down," Marcy said, her words slurring.

Wyn thought of Daniel and how drunk and depressed he was at the start of yesterday. He seemed to be wanting to sober up, though, to Wyn's delight. Marcy seemed to be going in the opposite direction, wanting to get drunk instead. Wyn understood her sentiment, as he likely would've kept drinking mug after mug of mead if John and Tasha hadn't found him first.

Wyn stood up and reached out his hand for a handshake. Marcy sized him up and firmly shook his hand before forcefully embracing him in a hug. She held him tight, squeezing him. He warmly hugged her back.

The four Climbers sat. After several awkward seconds of silence, Tasha was the one bold enough to ask what the others were thinking. "How's Cedric?"

Marcy grabbed a cup and poured water from the pitcher. She drank it and made a sour face. "Water? That's not what I want right now."

"It's probably what's best right now," John whispered to Wyn. Wyn kicked him under the table.

The rookies waited patiently for an answer. They didn't know if they should push the subject, but they were desperately wanting to know. Their curiosity didn't eclipse their disrespect, though, and waited for her to respond when she was ready.

"He's alive," Marcy quickly said. "So there's that."

A collective sigh was let out at the table. Leave it to a drunk Climber to answer promptly.

Wyn smiled and closed his eyes. Cedric was alive, and his effort to save him paid off.

"But he lost his left arm. They can't do anything about that." Marcy ripped off a piece of chicken and ate it sloppily.

Tasha held a hand over her mouth. John looked away, finding it hard to look at Marcy's face. Wyn knew he lost his arm. He remembered seeing it left behind, lying on the ground in the midst of the mushroom monsters who were still trying to kill them. What he didn't know, though, was if the medics could do anything about it with their magical healing.

Apparently they couldn't.

"Oh, and our group kicked us out."

"WHAT?!" collectively was shouted at the table, the young Climbers yelling in unison.

"Why?" "How!" Saying it out loud more than asking the question, they were baffled. Why in the hells would they do that?

"Cedric isn't really useful without an arm, so they say. They voted to leave him behind." Marcy banged her fist on the table, startling them. "I refused to do that. I will *never* leave *anyone* behind. So they kicked me out, too."

"Marcy," Tasha said softly, taking her hand into her own. "I'm so sorry. But hear me when I say this. We wouldn't be here if it wasn't for you and Cedric."

"I feel the same way," John said. This time he did look her in the eyes as his began to water. "I owe my life to Cedric. You, too."

Marcy sniffled as she wiped away tears that began to roll down her cheeks.

Wyn just couldn't believe it. They must've been a pretty pathetic group to simply cast away a member like that after something so horrible. But was that what Climbers do here? Were they so cutthroat to secure any advantage possible, that when a disadvantage rises they purge it right away?

A thought clicked inside Wyn that seemed to fall into place. It made sense, and was a perfect solution. "Marcy," Wyn said. "We're all thankful. Truly. And I have a proposal for you."

"What is it?"

Wyn looked at Tasha and John, who both tearfully smiled back, knowing exactly what he wanted to ask.

"Would you want to join our group? And Cedric, too, of course, when he's ready."

Marcy stared at them, dumbfounded. Then she laughed. It was small and quick, like a chirp, but then she laughed harder and harder, nearly falling out of her seat.

Wyn had a look of concern cross his face, hoping he didn't just insult her.

"I can't believe it," she said, wiping her hands on her shirt, smearing it with chicken grease. "A bunch of rookies wanting to pair up with a bum Wizard and an outcast Ranger."

"It's only fitting, considering I'm an outcast, too," Wyn replied. "But we work well together. You know that personally."

Marcy smiled. "I know. Yes, of course I will. Thank you for considering me."

Marcy barely got the words out before Tasha yelled in excitement and reached across the table to grab her arms. John and Wyn both exhaled in relief.

"What's the plan, then?" Marcy asked. "No offense, but I'm done being the responsible one for the time being. Don't want that burden for this coming season."

They all looked at each other, and eventually their eyes settled on Wyn. He was wondering that very thing, but had a feeling he would be their leader until someone else wanted to take the role or he messed up bad enough for them to take over. For now, though, he relished the thought of leading a group of warriors into combat.

Wyn made a personal vow to not make the same mistakes he'd made before. This time would be different. They'd be successful and meet whatever goals they set.

He took a deep breath.

"Let's figure it out tomorrow," Wyn said. "We can meet at lunch to prepare to tackle the first floor the next day. No rushing this time." He smiled, and genuinely felt happy.

They toasted in agreement and continued their meal as the night went on.

As a group, they made their way through the still-growing crowd to prepare for the parade. The people naturally separated into two sides, the middle being where the actual parade would take place. Everyone around seemed hopeful, joyous, and curious to see the actual display.

Wyn looked through the crowd at the people. He noticed some people were laughing and cheering, but some were serious or anxious. Several people, likely Climbers, had their weapons out and formally presented, like soldiers paying respects to officers passing by.

Or, which was likely the case here, respecting the memorial of a fallen ally.

Wyn remembered that the parade honored those that had fallen in the tower over the current season. He wondered how many previous Climbers had died, and how many more would die this coming cycle to the trials of the tower.

Interrupting his thoughts, the parade began with a pop of celebration as streamers of magic and toys began to fly through the air. The noise of the crowd instantly seemed to double. The parade itself was made up of various groups, some funny and some extravagant, all trying to entertain in different ways. All were succeeding based on the crowd reaction.

In the midst of some guild officials walking in the parade, waving and cheering back at the crowd, Wyn saw a strange figure on the other side of the crowd. The person was tall, robed, and wore a mask. Despite the flashing lights it wasn't easy to make out specific details, but the mask looked porcelain with a white blank face except for holes at the eyes.

Wyn's heart raced. It felt like the figure was looking right at him, unbothered by the crowd and parade.

Something felt strangely familiar but also foreign about the person, though a sinister emotion seemed to be pouring out of him. Wyn decided to act quickly, and he moved through the crowd, pushing people away but keeping an eye on the robed figure.

People called out in annoyance at being pushed away and interrupting the parade, but Wyn didn't care.

"Wyn?" John called out, but he was ignored.

The person was just on the other side of the parade, and Wyn knew he could get there quickly but he stopped his pursuit. He didn't want to make a scene and draw attention, and they stared at each other for only a second.

When a large, fake dragon passed by, actors underneath making it seem alive and roaring in the air, the crowd went wild. It blocked Wyn's view, though, and he tried to move around it to see. In seconds the dragon passed by, and then the figure was gone.

"Wyn, what's wrong?" John asked.

Wyn turned and saw his three teammates standing there, looks of confusion spread across their faces.

"I thought I saw something, but I guess not," Wyn said. "I'm sorry."

He tried laughing it off as a woman scolded him for blocking her view of the parade, and the others began laughing, too. Thankfully his friends didn't press him about it again, and he was grateful he didn't have to explain it further. He was sure he saw someone there, but he didn't want them to worry, especially if it was nothing.

The four Climbers continued their night, enjoying the parade and festivities in celebration before a new journey inside the tower began. It likely would be fraught with challenges both in the tower and out, but at least they would face them together.

As the parade finished and they began their walk back to their rooms, a lone figure in a porcelain mask watched them from afar. At their side was a familiar sword with an ornate hilt and sheath with gold trim, runes etched along the side. They tightened their grip on the weapon and widened their eyes under the mask, content on watching and waiting. For now.

The environment shifted from the musty cave to an empty, equally musty room. It was dark and oddly humid, smelling of mold and old linens. Lionel was breathing heavy, holding his face and neck. He could feel his skin being wet and warm and knew it was a mixture of sweat and blood, though hoped it was more of the former.

He pulled his hand away for a second, and felt a streak of liquid run down his neck into his shirt. A curse escaped his lips, and he recovered his upper neck with his hand, putting pressure on the wound.

That damned Ranger nearly killed him. If he hadn't gone through the portal and moved his body at the right time, the arrow would've struck his chest instead of grazed his jaw, and he'd bleed out before help could arrive.

He might still bleed out, but at least there was a chance he'd live.

A few slow, methodical breaths left the Fighter's still-quivering mouth. He blinked hard several times, panic rising inside him as the darkness wasn't changing whether his eyes were open or closed.

Did she blind him, too? No, that couldn't be right. The room must be nearly pitch-black, no source of light to be found.

Lionel jerked his head frantically side to side, looking for anything. He saw the faintest sliver of light under a door and stared at it for a few moments. The light centered him, and he started to see his surroundings better as his eyes adjusted to the darkness. Two old barrels sat against the wall, and a broom was leaning against it.

A chuckle escaped his smiling mouth. He was in a storage closet. Of all the places they could arrange for the other half of the portal to be, they picked a damned storage closet.

His mind rushed with the events of the afternoon. He knew he had to bide his time to fulfill his true purpose, and he succeeded. He didn't want to kill John, but it was necessary. It was the added bonus to his mission, and he knew he would be rewarded far more than what was promised.

Gaps of light formed and moved under the door. Lionel held his breath, afraid he'd be caught. The door suddenly opened, and an older, bald man stood hunched in the light. Lionel tried to move his other hand to cover his eyes from the sudden brightness, but stopped when he remembered he was holding John's sheathed sword. He alternated between squinting and trying to open his eyes from the influx of light.

"Incompetent," the man growled. He reached down and hoisted Lionel up with surprising ease.

Cold hands ran over Lionel's neck and face, and he didn't dare move his hand so he wouldn't bleed out. The man briefly fought with him, trying to make him move his hand.

"Move your damn hand, boy," the man spat. "I need to heal you if you're injured so you don't bleed all over the place. Can't be making a scene, now."

Lionel didn't recognize his accent, and he certainly didn't trust the man, but he wasn't in a condition to argue. He still could barely see.

Relenting, Lionel dropped his hand. In a flash, the man swiped some salve over his jaw. The cream was cool and thick, giving instant relief. He could feel his skin tightening underneath, and the cooling sensation turned warm as life seemed to return to him.

"Put this on," the man barked, twirling a cloak around Lionel's shoulders. He could only see it shimmering blue before his appearance began to shift, his hands tanning and clothes changing to robes.

"What are you doing?" Lionel asked. "Who are you?"

"Always with the questions," the man said, more to no one than at Lionel. "Shut up and follow me. *He's* waiting."

Lionel's heart skipped a beat. So this man was part of it, then.

Without another breath, the man pushed Lionel out of the room ahead of him. Lionel squinted and blinked hard and fast, trying to get his eyes to adjust quickly while being pushed to walk. He started to make out where he was after a few turns and hallways.

They were passing the hall of portals, at the base of Alestead.

For some reason Lionel thought that the special portal key he was given would take him to some secret place, not the actual tower. But maybe he wasn't quite worth that.

Not yet, at least.

The two men passed rookie Climbers still exiting the first floor, unaware of what he had done. He looked back to see the man guiding him along.

A smirk formed on Lionel's face. The stranger was wearing a vest with silver trimmings, and Alistair's symbol on the chest. Whether he was an actual guild member as a double agent or simply stole the outfit, Lionel didn't care. He was impressed. He was obviously important enough for all this effort, and that made his chest swell.

No one glanced twice at them as they walked. Lionel looked down and was shocked to see the sword he held looked like a staff, and his clothes like robes. For all intents and purposes, the cloak gave the illusion he was a Mage of some kind.

A grimace formed on his face. It was an insult to disguise him as some kind of Magician.

"Where are we going?" Lionel asked.

"Shut up," the man said, pushing him along. "No questions."

Lionel felt a sharp finger poke him in the back and push him forward. He gritted his teeth and kept walking.

They passed the front entrance at Alistair and turned off into an errant alley from the primary road. The way was dark and hard to see, but the strange man guided Lionel by the shoulder once they exited the main street of Alestead.

"Wait here," the man said. He stepped to the side out of view.

Lionel looked around. They stood at a dead end, the only thing around being a lone, small tree without leaves right beside him and a small patch of grass that rested under his feet. The area was surrounded by stone and brick of the walls from the neighboring buildings, trapping it from continuing. The area was unassuming and innocent, as though it were a perfectly secure place for a picnic.

Suddenly the ground under his feet shifted, and he backed away in alarm. A square patch of grass next to the tree flipped up and over, and the man was standing in the ground, only his head and shoulders visible.

"Come on," the man grumbled. "Not too much further." He climbed out of the hole and nodded his head toward Lionel for him to lead.

Lionel peered into the hole and saw a tall wooden ladder descending into darkness. It looked rotted and barely usable, but the man insisted, nudging Lionel's back. He relented and climbed down it, unsure how far down the ladder would take him.

Suddenly he felt the ladder shake, and dust fell on his face. He blew air out of the side of his mouth, trying to breathe without sucking in extra dirt. The man joined him at the top and flipped the grass cover back over them. The instant the cover was replaced, a dim light shone not far under his feet, and Lionel peeked under his boots to see the ground wasn't too far.

Landing with a thud, Lionel realized he stood in a narrow, carved pathway. It was all dirt and mud around him, completely underground though obviously manmade. Candles lined the walls every so often, barely lighting the path enough for him to see. Various patches of darkness made him cautious, but he didn't have anything to fear.

Not yet, at least.

After several minutes the pair arrived at a plain wooden door with a small square hole that was sealed from the other side. Bars covered the front of the hole in the door. The man pushed Lionel aside and rapped the door four times in a varied cadence with his knuckles.

The slot behind the hole flew open. A single eye peered through it and looked at both men.

"Aliyar's mercy," the man behind the door said.

"Is swift and unforgiving," the older bald man leading Lionel finished.

The hole was covered again, then a latch sounded behind the door. The wooden door creaked as it opened inward, and the man again pushed Lionel forward.

Lionel's mouth hung open when he stood inside the door, still clutching John's sword. Dim light completely filled a large open room with candles scattered around, either in tall iron holders, on tables, or just on the ground. There must have been over a hundred of them. The room was circular with various halls or doors leading out deeper into what seemed like the hub of catacombs.

Over two dozen people were gathered in the center of the room, all wearing dark blue hooded robes that covered their features. They faced away from Lionel toward a man sitting on a stone throne that held a multitude of candles, all dripping wax at different heights. The throne was elevated with several wide steps leading up to the gaudy and macabre display.

The man on the throne wasn't wearing a hooded robe, but instead a stark white cloth covering that looked like a bleached clergyman's outfit. He stood and waved Lionel over with a smirk.

Lionel hesitated. Was this *him*? The man who orchestrated this entire ordeal? It had to be. He was obviously their leader, here in the flesh. Lionel knew him only as a myth, and yet here he stood.

The older man pushed him forward yet again. "When you're summoned, you don't delay. Now go."

Lionel stepped forward, and the crowd silently parted to allow him passage. As he approached, the mysterious man's smirk grew to a wide smile.

"Lionel, my dear boy," the man said, his voice flowing like smooth honey. "Welcome to our humble abode. You have earned your place. I hope."

Lionel smiled and held John's sword in front of him. Despite feeling confident, the man gave off a strong sense of power. It was unnerving. "I have. I did exactly as you asked."

"*Commanded*," the man corrected, his voice stern and face expressionless. In another moment his features returned to before, smiling and inviting, as though a magical force shifted his demeanor in the blink of an eye.

Lionel scrunched his eyebrows. Something didn't feel right, but he couldn't put his finger on it. He was supposed to be welcomed, but this felt like a trial of sorts. He'd already undergone the trial and succeeded. This should be a formality more than anything.

"Alright," Lionel said. He looked around the room with quick glances and realized no one was looking at him, or even at the man in the throne. They were simply looking forward in the same direction, as though in a trance or under some spell.

"Please, tell me what happened," the man said, waving his hand toward Lionel. "I need to hear it from you. From your *soul*."

Lionel cleared his throat and recounted the events in the tower, sparing no detail. He didn't quite trust this entire ordeal, but he wasn't about to lie to this man in this place. He may have been many things, but a fool was not one of them.

The man sank down into his throne and closed his eyes as though Lionel was telling him news of dire importance, the kind that includes families being reunited with loved ones, or hearing someone lived when thought dead. He clasped his hands together in joy and let out a relieved sigh.

"Well, young man, you certainly went above and beyond," the man said.

"Yes, sir," Lionel said. He bowed his head in respect.

The man stood up quickly, his white robes flowing behind him like sheets in the wind. No one dared move in the chamber, and Lionel counted himself part of that group. The man stepped off from his throne and began to slowly walk down the steps.

"When our order discovered you, Lionel, we were hopeful we found our next lieutenant. Tall, strong, capable—everything we needed as a foundation to mold you." The man stepped down the steps slowly, accentuating his words. "You were receptive to us, as well! Your task, in order to join our order, was to betray an ally. To sever a bond you had made within the tower. Doing that would show you would stop at nothing for us, and ruthlessness is crucial for the role you'll need to play."

Lionel straightened his posture, though did not dare take his eyes off the man.

"You have succeeded at that task, and then went a step beyond."

The man snapped a finger, and three people in the crowd brought over a large stone basin of liquid. It was dark like the black of night, impossible to see through like standard water. It strangely appeared to swirl as the people placed the basin before Lionel, and he saw what looked like flashes of stars form and disappear over and over in the moving liquid. It was incredibly alluring, and Lionel fought to take his eyes off the mysterious substance in order to look back at the leader.

The man rested a hand on the basin and one hand on Lionel's shoulder, a sinister smile forming on his face. The rings on his hand reflected brilliant light in various metals and gems. "You not only betrayed your ally, but literally stabbed him in the back as well. *And* stole his sword! Incredible!" The leader lightly ran his fingers over John's sword before patting Lionel on the back.

"Not quite, my lordship," a familiar voice said.

Lionel snapped his head around to see the stranger who led him here sitting down eating an apple, his legs propped up on the wooden table in front of him.

"Excuse me?" the leader said. "What are you saying, Mathias?"

The older bald man—Mathias—finished his bite of apple before throwing the core in a small basin at his side. "Pardon me, my lord, but Lionel did *not* kill that Climber."

"What?" Lionel said in a low tone, growling through his teeth. "I stabbed him in the back. That Mage was out of mana. She couldn't heal him enough. No way he survived that!"

Mathias smiled softly. "He absolutely did. Apparently the Diamond Magician in your party was quite the healer. Or had more mana than you thought. She stabilized him and brought him back to the infirmary, where he's resting now. The healers are saying he'll recover completely."

Lionel's face softened and his eyes went wide. His plan to kill John failed. What did that mean for him here?

The leader clicked his tongue several times in a disapproving manner. "Oh, what a shame. So you didn't *quite* kill him. You tried and failed." He flicked John's sword, making Lionel jump. "You stole his weapon, though, and that's *something*. I guess." He turned hurriedly and walked behind the basin, raising his arms out wide. "Still, you have earned your original reward, despite not fully succeeding. A promise of power lies ahead." The liquid stirred in the basin as though prompted.

Lionel stared back at the basin, a hunger rising within him. Power was what he sought, and power was what he'd earned. He was inches from obtaining it, just within his grasp. His free hand, as though acting on its own, reached for the liquid. The dark liquid then pooled around his hand and wrist and began to trickle up his arm. It followed a strange path, swirling and turning without reason while causing runes to form on his forearm and bicep. Lionel could feel the liquid run up his shoulder and neck before settling on his face, all the while still rotating and moving like a miniature flowing river.

The liquid began to expand as though consuming his arm and shoulder. It originally felt cool and refreshing, but slowly turned warm against his skin.

The leader's smile faded, and his face was expressionless once again. The crowd all turned toward them, bearing witness to the event.

Panic rose inside Lionel. The liquid was now hot, and he could visibly see steam rising from his arm. He began to grunt and willed himself to manage the growing pain. His willpower was breaking far faster than he thought. The pain was unbearable, and he fell to one knee as the liquid scalded and burned his skin. A scream left his mouth, and he desperately wished for the experience to stop.

"Power does not come without sacrifice," the leader said, his hands resting on the basin as the excess liquid disappeared into his white robes.

Lionel kept screaming, his neck and face now sizzling from the liquid that still covered him.

"Power does not come without sacrifice," the crowd echoed in unison.

"You have earned your place with us!" the leader said, shouting above Lionel's screams of pain and agony. "You will come to know the might and power of the Great One, and all who she houses!"

The leader immediately grabbed Lionel by the shoulders, gripping them hard. The Fighter could feel the fingers digging hard into his flesh, harder than should be possible. It felt like a steel vise squeezing him—any harder and he'd pop. But from his touch the liquid began to cool. It was then drawn away from his face down his neck and arm into the white robes of the leader standing before him, completely bypassing the basin.

The room was completely silent except for Lionel's ragged breaths. His left arm twitched from the scalding liquid, and his eyes widened when he looked at it. Runes covered his entire left arm from his wrist to his shoulder, and he knew he must have some on his face, too. They felt like magical brands, seared into his skin by whatever kind of unholy liquid was introduced to him.

Lionel tried to settle his breathing down. Their lord was standing up at his throne now, his arms out wide. Three figures stood at the bottom of the stairs, just a few feet in front of where Lionel knelt. Two were on his left and one on his right. They all wore the same dark blue robes as the crowd though their faces were concealed with white porcelain masks.

He studied them for a moment. It was impossible to tell whether they were male or female, and they didn't seem to carry any obvious weapons or gear on their persons. Their masks had varying black marks—one had swirls of circles while another had only one triangle on each cheek, opposite each other like mirrors.

One of the mask-wearing acolytes walked toward him. Their mask had three thick black lines vertically running across the entire piece, one each over the eyes and the third over the nose. Lionel stood, unsure of what was about to happen.

"These are your fellow lieutenants," the lord said, his arms still out wide beside him and his white robe draped underneath him. "You are our fourth. You will make me proud, Lionel. And make Aliyar proud."

The masked acolyte reached into their robes and pulled out a blank, white porcelain mask similar to the ones the three wore. Lionel took it with a shaky hand.

"You will earn your marks," the lord said. "You are no longer a Fighter and no longer Lionel. Now, you will be known as *exactly* what you are. *Who* you are—the Betrayer."

"The Betrayer!" the crowd echoed.

Lionel stepped to the fourth and open spot beside the other masked acolyte, still breathing heavy. His arm and face pained him, though the pain was not without reason—he had done it. The Order had accepted him, and he was finally on his destined path.

The lord stepped beside him and leaned in awkwardly, speaking low enough only for Lionel to hear. "Do your duty or this power will be taken back along with more. Do I make myself clear?"

Lionel slowly nodded. The lord's words felt sharp, and a strange sense of fear mixed with excitement swelled within him.

Using this new power, he knew no one would stop him, and he'd make sure to finish the job he started.

CHAPTER TWENTY-EIGHT

Wyn anxiously looked around trying to find his team. He was standing at the base of Alistair, waiting to join them to finally enter the tower for the new season. They had decided at the festival two days ago to start the new season this morning to take their time on the first floor, leave after completing it, and analyze how it went. They wanted to take it a floor at a time for at least this week to get used to climbing while trying to minimize any problems.

It was slow, sure, but with their limited team of four and John literally getting stabbed in the back three days ago, they were understandably cautious.

Wyn took the time to focus and steady himself. They would show eventually, and they would be fine. He wasn't concerned about that. But after seeing the many different Climbers and their groups enter, he was feeling underwhelmed by his own group. They needed to be more cautious due to their shortcomings. If they had six members they could afford to be more risky, but as it stood now they needed to take it slow.

Which was unfortunate. He needed funds, and he needed them badly. Climbing slower meant taking longer to get them. Hopefully he'd find a way around that, but for now he was at a loss.

Wyn saw some other people standing around the base as well. They didn't appear to be involved in groups, though. One woman was wearing an explorer's hat and clothes with multiple pouches on her belt that seemed a bit excessive and unwieldy. She was looking around the room trying to survey the climbing groups for some reason.

Another one was a taller man, heavyset but obviously strong. He was wearing a large backpack and a war hammer was on his hip. He looked anxious, but wasn't studying the Climbers nearly as seriously as the woman.

"Are you looking for a group?" a man asked, startling Wyn. He had a shield on one forearm and a sword sheathed on his hip. His padded armor was green and black, and he carried a helmet under his shield arm. He looked like he led the climbing group behind him.

"Umm, no," Wyn said, caught off guard. "I'm waiting for my group to come."

"Oh," the leader said, "I'm sorry, I thought you were a Mapper."

"That's alright. Honest mistake."

"Are you a Fighter?" a man in their group asked. "I don't see many Climbers with spears, let alone a robe to go with it." He pointed to Wyn's spear that was leaning against the wall behind him.

This Climber had thinner leather armor on that was darker in color. A cowl was draped around his neck from his cloak, and Wyn noticed he had two short swords sheathed on his hips.

Wyn hesitated but decided to be honest. "I'm a Ruby Magician." He nervously fiddled with his backpack straps.

The Climber tried to suppress a laugh but failed. A woman in their group snickered.

"What's your class?" Wyn asked. He clenched his jaw, cursing himself for asking. He wanted this conversation to end before it picked up but foolishly kept it going.

"I'm a Rogue," the man replied. "It's not everyday you see a Red Mage out here."

"I guess not," Wyn replied. He looked around again, hoping that his friends were close. He was more than ready to get into the tower. Monsters were easier to face than ridicule.

"A spear-wielding mage," a woman said. "You're not the rookie that went to the second floor, are you?"

"No way," the Rogue replied. "Those are just rumors. He'd be dead if he actually went to the second floor."

Wyn declined to answer, choosing silence instead. One thing he learned in the military was it was often better to not talk back unless absolutely necessary. And it was absolutely *not* necessary right now.

The leader smiled. "Regardless, we have no room for you. We are only looking for a Mapper."

"Yeah, good luck in there," the Rogue said. "I'm sure you'll need it."

Wyn smiled back and grabbed his spear. He walked away, wanting to get as far away from them as possible. He hoped he wouldn't have to deal with them again.

Before long John and Tasha tore through the crowd toward him, and he thanked the gods they were finally here. He took a deep breath and donned his helmet. After discussing with Daniel, Wyn decided he wanted the protection rather than the appearance and comfort. The older Ruby Magician recommended finding a magical hat that protected him *and* was more comfortable, but until then, Wyn settled on the familiar helmet.

"Finally!" Wyn said when he was in earshot of the others. John smiled and Tasha rolled her eyes.

"Sorry, Wyn," Tasha said. "But this lazy ass just *had* to take his time with breakfast after we were already late."

"I can't help it," John said. "I need my beauty sleep and a full stomach to be of any use."

Tasha laughed. "You'd need a lot more for that."

John rolled his eyes. "Anyway. Have you seen Marcy?"

Wyn looked around, scanning the Climbers in the base. The crowd was new, most of them he'd seen earlier already entering the tower. He didn't spot her fur armor and bow and quiver.

"No, I haven't. I thought she might be with you guys."

"It's alright," Tasha said. "We can wait a little while longer."

The three of them nervously shuffled around, feeling out of place. It was a strange sensation. They were more confident for their first trip with Cedric and Marcy leading them, and now they were two less people without Lionel or Cedric.

"Are you guys as nervous as I am?" Tasha asked. She was fidgeting, fingering her potion belt and triple-checking the mana and health potions holstered in it. "It's a completely new layout. Who knows what it'll be?"

"That's the exciting part, though," John said. "Plus we have a plan. We'll be fine!"

"Exactly," Wyn said, agreeing. "There may only be four of us but we're healthy, ready, and not in a rush. After changing out **Ice Shard** for **Flamebolt** and adding **Cure** to my spell list, I'm in great shape. Our goal is to complete the first floor then come back to assess. Marcy has a key, too, in case we need it."

"Though we won't, since both of you can heal us," John said. "Not to mention Marcy could just obliterate anything on the first floor, anyway."

"I don't know about that," Marcy said, sneaking up behind the group, "but you're probably right." She put her arms around John and Tasha and smiled wide.

"About time," John said.

Tasha shot him an annoyed look.

Wyn smiled back at the Ranger. "Great. We're all here!" He started to turn to walk to the hallway of portals when he stopped and turned back around. "Wait a second. Are you wearing something different?"

He took a closer look at Marcy, who had on the fur armor she wore before, though it was more elaborate now. She had a wide belt at her waist that was new, and several potions were set in it sideways along with a pouch that was strapped to the side. A cowl was draped around her neck, and a matching cloak covered her back to her knees, both dark brown that matched her armor. Her quiver was full of arrows that had similar fletchings as before, though some were different colors.

She let go of John and Tasha and twirled a bit. "This is my normal climbing gear. I didn't wear it last time since we cleared the floor already, but let me tell you—I won't make that mistake again."

"Is it all magical?" John asked. He tried to touch her cape, and Marcy slapped his hand away.

"My cape, armor, belt, and boots are. Of course you know my bow and quiver are, too."

John whistled. "So basically everything you're wearing. Man. I can't wait to have that many magical items."

"Be patient. You'll get more in no time—trust me. You'll probably have at least two or three by the end of the month. Each of you."

"Can we go, already?" Tasha asked. "You can ask all the questions about her magic gear later. I'm tired of being anxious and want to just get it over with."

Marcy and John nodded, and they looked to Wyn. His heart raced when they did, knowing they were looking at him for guidance. He was their leader now. There wasn't any more room for errors or a lack of focus.

He didn't completely consider himself their leader, but when they planned this all out yesterday they certainly acted like he was. He was hoping Marcy would take over but she seemed distracted, and Wyn didn't blame her. She'd been checking on Cedric daily and probably would continue to do so. She had much more experience here in the tower, but he understood that she didn't want the pressure of being a leader right now.

Wyn took a deep breath and forged ahead. He led a company in the military, sure, but this was an entirely different beast. He wanted to make sure everyone would make it fine, and felt like he needed more experience before he felt like a true leader. Still, they trusted him, and Marcy did, too.

He didn't want to let them down or get hurt. Not like Cedric again. Or worse.

They arrived at the hallway of portals quickly. There were many other groups there, all steadily entering their own portal to climb the tower. Some of the Climbers were intimidating, reminding Wyn of Xander who led the rookies on his first climb, wearing scary looking armor and weapons. They moved silently, not paying attention to anyone else, only focused on the task at hand. Wyn realized other rookies noticed the veterans, too, as several groups cleared a path when more confident Climbers walked toward the portals.

Wyn's heart jumped when he saw the portals and wondered if it was anxiety, excitement, or a mixture of both. He stepped up to a portal and looked at it, waiting for his group. Tasha took a deep breath, and John was giddy with excitement. Marcy smiled, much more confident than the others. Not an ounce of fear was on display from her, but the other three held enough to share.

"Are you all ready?" Wyn asked. He looked around the portal at the others. They each nodded, and Marcy was the first to step in. Wyn quickly jumped in after her, and he hoped he would be able to tolerate the portal better than the first time.

He didn't.

When he emerged into the tower, his nerves got the better of him, and he began dry heaving to the side of the portal. Tasha and John followed behind him, and John threw up right away. Tasha kept it together much better than last time. She was taking deep breaths and small sips from her waterskin, though she stopped to laugh.

"Serves you right for eating a huge breakfast," she said, laughing at John.

John made a sour face at her, began to say something, then immediately threw up again. Tasha laughed harder.

Wyn took a deep breath and settled himself. It was better than the last time, but he obviously needed some practice.

He looked around and tried to process his environment. It was incredibly disorienting. He half expected to see the forest again, ready to fight spiders and wolves in the dark woods, but instead they were right on the edge of a thicket by a jungle. It was humid, the air sticky with heat and moisture. It was early morning, which was a nice change, but the large leaves on the trees and vines snaking around them made it nearly impossible to see too far into the nearby thicket.

Wyn decided to go ahead and put his overcoat and mushroom lantern into his backpack. The coat would be too hot to wear, and there was plenty of light, so he didn't need a magical light source.

He walked around a bit trying to take it in. The portal placed them in a small, open haven of a clear field. There was dense greenery all around them, every direction seemingly blocked by branches, bushes, or trees with leaves the size of people.

Worse, he was already starting to sweat, and they had just arrived.

Marcy was scouting ahead, taking in their surroundings. She started to look for any signs of a trail or path to start their trek. She went over to John to make sure he was alright before taking out her parchment to look it over.

Wyn thought that was a good idea to look at his parchment right away. He was curious what was on it, still impressed that it changed itself so often.

PARTY: 4/4
Floor 1

Quest: *There are rumors that a long forgotten temple resides deep in this jungle. Some locals claim that they see bright lights reaching to the stars at certain nights. Others swear they see a temple deep in the brush. You've been tasked with finding if these rumors are true.*

Wyn folded the parchment back up and put it away. The task seemed odd, but what about the tower *wasn't* odd? It seemed like his mission was to go deeper into the jungle and stay alive.

Easy.

The sound of John's sword unsheathing broke the silence of the group. He had his shield readied on his left forearm, too, and seemed to have his stomach more under control. The four of them gathered together to start their plan.

"Are we ready, then?" John said, pointing his sword toward the jungle. "I guess we need to start exploring. Find the set path and follow it to the boss area."

"I am," Marcy said. She furrowed her eyebrows and looked around. "I can't seem to find a path, though. Maybe it's deeper in the brush, but there's nothing to suggest a clear way in."

The four of them looked around, and Wyn pointed to a tree that looked a bit taller than the rest. "Let's start by that tall tree. We can use it as a starting marker."

"I just hope we don't get lost," Tasha said. "Marcy, how easy is it for someone to get lost in the tower?"

"It definitely happens, but usually you'd run into another group and keep going." She reached into a pouch on her belt and pulled out a portal key. "Though I do have one of these if we need it. Granted, we should keep trying even if we do get lost and use this as a last resort. Getting lost typically just makes the trip a lot longer, not impossible."

"And longer means spending more resources like mana and energy," Wyn said. "So let's stick together and take it a bit slower so that doesn't happen. Maybe map out our route if we have to."

"Plus, we have a veteran Ranger with us," John said, pointing his thumb at Marcy. "We're not going to get lost. So don't worry, Tasha."

Marcy laughed and shook her head. She started walking toward the tall tree, and the others followed. She stopped after a few feet of walking and took out a strange-looking dagger from her back that Wyn hadn't noticed before. It had a large, wide blade and was slightly curved. She began to swing it, using it to hack away at the vines, leaves, and bushes. The blade was clearing it relatively easily, and it appeared effortless, which Wyn considered was good so she wouldn't wear herself out.

John stepped beside her to do the same, using his sword as a makeshift tool similar to Marcy. Both of them created a wide berth of clearance for Tasha and Wyn to walk through. John was exerting much more effort than Marcy, and his sword wasn't as effective, but he was managing even if it was a bit slower.

Before long they all heard water running and rushed to see what it was. A river snaked its way through the jungle beside them with the water flowing steadily in the direction they were heading. It was murky and dirty, and the four of them weren't able to see what hid under the surface. It was a good sign, though, show-ing them that they were making some kind of progress.

They decided to traverse the jungle close to the river, hoping to find some-thing else, anything, that would direct them further with their task. The river curved and wound often, and the group was thankful that Marcy was leading their way since it was disorienting. Wyn wasn't used to traversing terrain like deep brush, and even then he wasn't the best at determining direction, choosing to use his guide during military marches rather than his own poor sense of direction.

The four of them continued this process for nearly an hour, stopping once to hydrate and take a break. As they were pushing forward, Marcy stopped mid-swing, looking around her.

Wyn had seen her do that before. He knew it meant her **Extrasensory** skill was activating. The others knew it, too, as they quickly alerted themselves to their surroundings.

Granted, their surroundings were dense foliage as high as them, and they couldn't see anything more than a few feet in all directions. That made for a ter-rible fighting environment and meant an ambush was all but guaranteed.

"Something's here," Marcy said, and shifted her knife around to hold it upside down. She left her bow slung around her chest, knowing it would be useless this close.

"Backs together," Wyn said, returning to his days as captain. He turned and took a few steps backward to the middle of the group. "Keep your eyes out for anything."

The others quickly caught on, the four of them able to see any threat in all directions. It was the best strategy for their situation, but still not perfect. Their hearts beat quickly as they felt blinded to enemies and each of them hoped they wouldn't be taken by surprise.

"Marcy, can you sense anything?" John asked in a hushed voice.

"Yeah, I think so," she replied. "There's two of them. Smaller, but moving quick." She perked up and turned her head around. "Wyn, in front of you!"

Wyn stepped forward and flipped his spear around, deciding to act fast. All he saw was the foliage rustle and shake, but that was enough for him to know enemies were close at hand. He took the clawed end and swung it in a wide arc, casting the spell at the same time: "**Wingbeat!**"

The spear briefly lit up, the green aura around it faint but noticeable. A strong rush of visible wind flew away from the spear, managing to cut down the bushes and leaves that clouded their vision. The force continued for nearly twenty feet, and they heard loud, piercing squeals as the wind cleared away a small section of the jungle.

Two creatures of similar appearance both fell over onto the cleared brush. They landed with several thuds, still and unmoving. Wyn and John hesitantly walked over to them, ready to attack again if needed. The creatures looked like giant lizards though were bipedal, almost like a human-lizard hybrid. Their torsos were separated from their chest and abdomen in a fine cut, Wyn's spell completely bisecting them.

Wyn and John looked at each other in shock. Wyn looked at his spear and had a newfound respect for the magical weapon.

CHAPTER TWENTY-NINE

W hoa," John said, still staring at the monsters lying dead in the grass. "That spear is wicked strong. Be careful where you swing that thing!"

"There's no way it's *that* powerful," Wyn said. "It's the least strong magical weapon out there."

"Yeah, but look at the flaming sword I had. I was melting spiders and wolves left and right!"

Wyn laughed. "That's a bit of a stretch, isn't it? Plus, your sword wasn't green."

John smirked.

They both heard a shriek and turned around to see Marcy and Tasha standing behind them. Tasha held a hand over her mouth, and Marcy nodded her head approvingly.

"That's disgusting!" Tasha said.

"*Impressive* is the word you meant to say," Marcy said. She patted Wyn on the back. "But don't think your spear is that strong. They must be earth-based, making them weaker to your wind magic."

"Ohhhhh, that makes much more sense," John said. "I knew it couldn't be that strong."

Tasha punched John in the arm.

"But still, nice job, Wyn," John said, rubbing his shoulder and glaring at Tasha.

The two creatures' bodies began to disintegrate like the creatures killed in the woods from the introductory climb, slowly returning to whatever plane of magic or existence they came from, if they even *did* come from something. The ground was just leaves and grass now, with no trace of the lizard creatures to be found. No blood, no body, no mess. It was strange, but made the environment less messy.

"So there are earth-based lizard creatures here, then?" Tasha asked. "At least Wyn's spear is strong to them. They didn't look too big, either."

"Oh, I'm sure there'll be bigger ones," Wyn said. "But I got lucky with my spear. I'm thankful they aren't ice-based or I'd be looking for another weapon. Right?"

"That's right," Tasha said. "It's not too bad to remember how the elements interact with each other. It seems pretty intuitive, if you ask me."

"You get used to it," Marcy said. "But yes, it's fairly straightforward. Fire is weak to water, of course. Lightning is strong against water. Earth grounds lightning, wind slices earth. Ice freezes wind and fire melts ice. That's how I've remembered it, at least. Oh, and do the opposite and you'll have a bad time. Trust me."

"You're right, that does make sense," Wyn said. "How often do the elements come up?"

Marcy laughed. "They play a constant role. It's partly why some of the more experienced Climbers have several sets of armor and weapons. They want an elemental advantage as much as possible. Often even an objectively weaker weapon or piece of armor is stronger based on elemental type advantage alone."

"Or, just burn things to the ground," John said. "That was my original plan with my sister's sword. It was so strong, even at an elemental disadvantage it would've been better than any weapon I would've found for a month or two. At least."

John whacked some errant bushes beside them with his sword. His frustration was obvious.

"I tend to recommend to rookies to find a weapon that doesn't have an element for their first two seasons," Marcy said. "The difficulties of trying to plan out elemental types with an already low number of items are just too high. Honestly Wyn, you got lucky the enemies are earth-based. Otherwise I would've suggested trading that spear for something else."

Wyn looked at his spear. What Marcy said made sense, which made the fact that Benedict didn't mention the elemental types concerning. Was he just trying to rid himself of the weapon, or did he not share the same opinion as Marcy? There was no way he could've known what enemies there'd be in the tower, either.

Whatever it meant, Wyn decided it didn't matter. His weapon was magical and strong, even if Marcy was right that he got lucky with the elemental advantage. He could use spells to round out his shortcomings, or find another weapon.

For now, though, he was satisfied.

"When we finish the floor we can plan if needed," Wyn said. "For now, let's keep going, yeah?"

"Couldn't agree more," John said. "We keep going the same way, right?"

"I think it's our best bet," Wyn replied. He began to walk back toward the path they were originally heading down before the monsters ambushed them from the side. "I hope we figure it out soon, though. This heat is rough."

"You're telling me," Marcy said. "This is the wrong armor for this season. I'm ready for a bath already." She walked ahead of Wyn, resuming her role of clearing brush.

Wyn could see the sweat beading on Marcy's arms and face, and felt it on his own arms and face, too. It was strange, this tower. They could be here all day in the blistering heat of the jungle then leave to return under the cool night sky back in Alestead. It was a weird concept that undoubtedly would take some time for him to adjust to.

John continued with Marcy, the both of them clearing a path in the thick jungle while Tasha and Wyn followed along. It was boring work, and the heat was exhausting, but they felt more confident now that they had a better idea of how to handle themselves.

The sound of the river came rushing back quickly, and they soon found themselves back at the riverbank. It was wider here and flowing more rapidly, the water smooth but steady. At the very edge of the river were small boats, crudely hewn, with paddles lying beside them.

"Canoes!" John shouted. He ran over to them, sheathing his sword. "I can't believe it!"

"I guess we know what we're supposed to do, then," Marcy said. She had a smile on her face, too. She inspected two of them for holes and found none, the hulls sturdy. Then she dipped her hands in the river and splashed water onto her bare arms and legs.

"We should probably go in groups of two," Wyn said. "Just in case. We don't want one canoe to fail and all of us drown."

"Hmm," John said, looking around. "I guess we should split up the healers, so Wyn and Tasha can't go together."

"And probably the same idea for being able to hit something from a distance," Tasha added, "so Marcy and Wyn need to separate."

"Alright, then Tasha," Marcy said, patting the canoe beside her, "here is the girls' boat!"

Tasha laughed and ran over to the canoe. She put her staff inside it to help Marcy push it out into the river.

"Wait!" Wyn said, nearly shouting. He startled the others. "When will we know to get out?"

"We'll go first so I can keep a lookout," Marcy said. "Just follow our lead. Easy."

Wyn looked at her hesitantly, then looked at John. They shrugged their shoulders at the same time, then prepared their own canoe for the river.

It only took a few seconds before both boats were setting out. They all had their own paddles though the river itself gave plenty of propulsion for them to move at a good pace. It was pleasantly cooler on the river, too, with a breeze forming from the ride cooling them all off, and a break from the thickly condensed air of the jungle foliage.

Tasha and Marcy handled their canoe easily, paddling every now and then to keep straight but letting the river do the work. They worked well together with Marcy leading and Tasha behind her, giving directions here and there when needed. The Ranger stood every thirty seconds or so, scanning around them for threats or signs to continue through the floor.

Wyn, however, cursed his luck. He wasn't used to being on the water and struggled, flailing his paddle back and forth on either side of the canoe to stay forward. He was a terrible swimmer, too, and his anxiety rose the instant they were on the water. He was afraid the current would sweep him under, and he thought that would be a pitiful way to die in the tower.

John was seated in back and kept chuckling at Wyn, noticing he was having trouble. He thought it was funny that the fearless mage's worst enemy was a canoe. After realizing he was seriously having trouble, he knew he had to help or Wyn would wear himself out.

"Slow down," John said, trying to get his voice above the sound of the river. "You don't need to paddle that much!" John seemed much more experienced in a boat, though any amount of experience was more than Wyn carried.

Wyn nodded, trying to listen. He looked back at John relaxing in the canoe and flushed red. How embarrassing. This was definitely *not* his specialty. He stopped for a moment to catch his breath and rest his arms. He saw how John would slowly put his paddle in the water and barely move it at all, like he had been on a boat all his life. The canoe would respond slowly but surely, straightening when needed with him steering from the back.

"See?" John said. "The river is doing the work for us. Fighting it is one battle you'll never win."

Wyn took a deep breath. John was right, after all. Their boat was keeping the course fine, and Wyn really didn't need to do any work at all. His anxiety and need for control had taken over in the worst way. He looked ahead and saw Marcy waving her arms, unslinging her bow from her chest and grabbing an arrow in a fluid motion.

Something was close. Wyn looked back at John who set up his shield as a makeshift barrier. It likely wouldn't do much, but could block an arrow before needing to be set up again. "I can steer the canoe," he said. "Just handle whatever is spooking her!"

Wyn set his paddle down and grabbed his spear. He instantly felt better with his weapon, though he really, *really* wanted to be on land. He felt trapped and out of control on the water.

He hoped whatever it was wasn't in the water, or else they risked flipping their canoe. He would be able to attack it, though, unlike something that would be on the bank. Marcy had the advantage with her bow, though Wyn knew he needed to be ready to cast a spell to attack, too. While he had limited mana and didn't want to use it all casting spells, she was far better equipped to handle enemies at range.

Wyn looked ahead to try to see what Marcy spotted. Further up the river he saw a group of lizard creatures standing on the bank, readying a makeshift barge to push out. It was crude and flat, several small logs banded together to make a platform to stand on but less efficient than a boat.

He turned and told John, who laughed.

"What's so funny?" Wyn said. His eyes were wide and his heart was racing. He was way out of his element. The thought of a fight on that rickety, cobbled together boat was frightening.

"Think about it," John said. He put his paddle down across his lap and stretched his arms. "If Marcy doesn't pick them off with her bow first, you'll just blast them out of the river. They have no idea what's coming."

Wyn turned back around, much less confident than John. He wasn't wrong, though. They could handle a few creatures well before they got close enough to pose a true threat.

He saw the creatures begin to push off, two of them holding spears and one readying a sling. Marcy fired an arrow at the one holding a sling, striking it in the shoulder. She purposefully waited until they were just off the bank for a reason. It stumbled back from the shot and lost its balance before falling off into the water. Its now limp arm was useless at trying to keep its head afloat, and it thrashed around before slowly working its way back toward the shore. The current was its worst enemy now.

The others hissed and screamed in anger, stabbing the air with their spears in defiance.

Marcy looked back at Wyn, held an arm out in an *after you* motion and smiled.

He shook his head. No way he was *that* accurate with his spells. She'd gone mad!

"Come on, Wyn," John said. "Let loose!"

Wyn relented. At least this would be good practice.

He held his left arm out toward the creatures who were using the current to steadily float toward them, nearing their canoe. He saw their beady eyes and forked tongues lash at them, holding their spears ready to stab at them in seconds.

Now was his chance. They weren't moving and their path was fairly predictable.

"Dyadcast: Flamebolt!"

A large magical rune appeared in the air just in front of Wyn's hand, the Ruby Magician sign overlapping the rune for the spell. Two small bolts of fire shot out of Wyn's hand toward the lizards. He aimed directly in the middle of them, hoping the spell would split evenly and hit both of them. One flaming ball of magic struck the creature on the left, burning an apple sized hole into its chest, and the other one hit their barge right at their feet.

The lizard that was hit dropped, falling on its back and tipping the barge. The other one took a couple of steps back from the fire that was forming in the middle of their boat, further rocking the craft. The magical flames weren't being dowsed by the water whatsoever.

The Climbers watched, opting to see how the events unfolded rather than continuing to use resources to kill them. In a matter of seconds the monsters' makeshift boat was coming apart, the fire destroying several logs and lashes that held it together. The remaining lizard fell into the water, flailing about with its spear while the other one slid off and floated on the surface motionless.

Wyn and John kept watching them to make sure they were completely out of commission before they heard a loud whistle. It startled both of them, but they looked ahead and saw Tasha and Marcy pulling off the main river onto a small stream. The stream ended into a small pool of water, and there seemed to be a mostly cleared path leading away from the river that was free of bushes and tall grass.

Wyn looked back at John, unsure of how to steer the canoe that hard and precise.

"Paddle on the left!" John said.

Wyn followed his instruction and quickly paddled, trying to get as much water behind him as possible. Their boat began to veer right, though if they didn't steer it well and fast they would miss their exit.

"Now the right!"

Wyn flipped his paddle over, hitting the side of the canoe in the process and spraying water all over him and John. The current was making it much harder to paddle at his current angle, but he was determined to get out of this damned canoe. He was giving it everything he had, trying his best to use his strength and energy to pull themselves out of the raging river.

Their canoe oscillated like a fish's tail, but it diverted toward the bank, following the girls and making it off the main river. They just narrowly avoided turning too much, risking a capsize and nearly losing control of their boat, but they made it. The offset stream had barely any current to it and they floated gently for a moment.

Wyn took a deep breath, thankful to almost be off the river. There was a small moment of peaceful waters outside the main river that Wyn soaked up.

Marcy and Tasha got out of their canoe and pulled it to the bank. There were a few other canoes there, and they pulled theirs beside them to form a line. They were laughing the entire time.

As the boys pulled up and Wyn hopped out, John laughed with them.

Wyn looked around, not sure what was funny. "What is it?"

"It's you," John said. He pulled the canoe onto the bank and grabbed his shield. "You were trying *so* hard!"

"I didn't want to miss the exit!" Wyn said. "Or flip over!"

John laughed harder.

"You don't have much experience on the water, do you?" Tasha asked. She was leaning on her staff and giggling.

Wyn flushed red and grabbed his spear. "They tried me out for the military on a boat, and I promptly threw up and panicked. So . . . no."

John laughed even harder, and Marcy snickered too.

"Aww, well, it's alright," Tasha said, and walked over to pat Wyn on the back. "You can't win them all."

Wyn sighed. "I just feel much better on the land, thanks."

"Just think," Marcy said, "you'll get much better at it the more you do it." She unsheathed her dagger and walked over to the cleared brush, ready to move on.

"I hope not. I'd like to avoid it if possible."

Marcy turned around wearing a sinister smile. "You're in the tower, now. You know how many times you'll likely be repeating this floor?"

Wyn's heart sank. The realization of repetition in the tower's floor hit him like a mace to the stomach. John and Tasha laughed out loud, much harder than before.

"Oh gods," Wyn said. "I didn't even think about having to do this floor again."

"And likely many times at that," John said. He wiped away tears from his red cheeks.

"Maybe we should just go on to the second floor, then," Wyn said. "Finish it and then start there next time? Didn't you say that's how it works?"

"Not a chance," Tasha said. "We agreed to take it a floor at a time, after all."

"She's right," Marcy said. "Not to mention, this is your first season. It's standard that new Climbers run the first few floors over and over their first full month, which means you'll be seeing this floor for weeks to come."

"We'll be fine," John said. "In all seriousness, we just need to take our time and not rush it. You'll be fine the next time we do this, too. Don't worry."

"Easy for you to say," Wyn whispered. But they were right. They all agreed to take it easy this month, both to gain experience and to be on the safe side.

He just really, really hated the thought of going back out on that river. But that was a worry for another time.

CHAPTER THIRTY

Marcy and John led the way again as Tasha and Wyn kept a lookout behind them. The path was easier to traverse, having been cleared already with leaves and brush littering the jungle floor in a wide swath.

It was cut cleanly with a blade as Marcy had pointed out, just like how she and John were forging a path through the floor before the river. This clearing was wider than they were cutting and looked like three or four Climbers were doing the work.

"So a group is directly ahead of us, then," Wyn said, picking up a large leaf that was cut and looking at it closer.

"It seems that way," Marcy said. "But it shouldn't be a problem. It happens. Especially early on when all the groups are having to clear the early floors to get to the tier and floor that will actually challenge them."

"That makes sense," Tasha said. "Like it's oversaturated right now with Climbers?"

"In a way, yeah."

"Will we miss out on enemies and treasure?" John asked.

Marcy laughed. "No, don't worry about that. The tower will add more enemies to accommodate for the increased number of Climbers on the floor."

"I would've been fine without knowing that," Tasha said. "You just *had* to ask, didn't you, John?"

"Of course," he replied. "I need those sweet, sweet magical items."

Marcy stopped and held up a hand signal for them to stop. She looked back at them. "Something's coming. Get ready."

"Tasha," Wyn said, "remember what we planned for!"

Tasha nodded, grabbed her staff and settled behind John. The Fighter raised his shield and readied himself to fight at the same time. Marcy went to grab her bow but thought better of it and kept it slung across her chest. The jungle was not suitable to longer distanced combat. Not that she was ineffective with her bow at close range, but she decided to keep more of a lookout role while the newer Climbers worked their strategy.

On second thought, she unslung her bow and nocked an arrow just in case. She'd let the other three go as long as possible, but after her last climb she wanted to be absolutely sure they'd be safe.

Marcy and Wyn formed a triangle with John then scanned the jungle while Tasha was protected in the center. Just like before, it was hard to see past the dense bushes, grass, and trees, but they tried to be as still as possible while on high alert. Wyn turned his left forearm over and quickly checked his mark. **_Lucidity_** had recovered little of his mana from using **_Dyadcast_** on top of his spell, but he was still over half. He could cast any of his spells if needed.

They all heard leaves rustle and sway before seeing low-hanging branches move in John's direction. Wyn and Marcy shifted a bit for a better angle, and John stepped forward with his shield raised. He was going to take whatever emerged first and didn't hesitate in the slightest. Preparing himself, he breathed deep and let out a firm exhale, loud and strong like a bull before a rush.

Tasha tapped her staff on John's back. "**_Arcane Aura_**!"

The staff glowed while a multitude of runes lit up in the air in the space between her staff and John. John instantly had a visible aura of white magic surround him. The magical armor overlapped his own, and he stood a bit straighter as confidence swelled up inside him.

"**_Focus_**," John said quickly with another exhale of his breath. A red wave-like aura spilled out of his torso, covering his body under the armor spell that protected him. It pulsed like a beating heart, the aura trailing off and thinning under the white armor that enveloped him. It was duller in brightness than the armor's aura but appeared more dense.

Wyn glanced at John and sensed something different about him. A chill ran over his arms. He hadn't seen him use one of his skills before. The blood-red aura seemed like visible bloodlust. Wyn knew John had to have several other skills, too, but wondered how many the Fighter had since he couldn't cast spells. It had to be enough to be balanced compared to the magical classes, or at least each of the skills strong enough to be powerful all on their own.

The large leaves suddenly moved and parted, pulling Wyn out of his thoughts. Nearly as quick as it emerged, John moved forward, bashing the first creature that came through to his left. He moved much faster than Wyn expected, his reaction and strength higher than he'd previously seen from the Fighter.

Just what, exactly, did that skill increase?

The lizard creature, bigger than the previous ones they'd met, held a jagged dagger in each of its hands. It stumbled to the side, knocked over in surprise from John's shield. Unfortunately being bashed to the side cleared a path for its allies to emerge as more barreled out of the foliage. Another monster leaped from the bushes, this time a sword slicing down toward the Fighter. John met it with his own in the air, parrying it with a loud clang.

Wyn decided to act while John was keeping the other one distracted. He stepped forward and lunged at the staggered lizard monster with _Windcutter_, aiming for its chest. The spear struck true, sinking in and through it completely, the wind-element weapon showing its advantage. The lizard let out a shriek and coughed blue blood, coating Wyn's boots and pants. It was dark and bubbly, a clear sign Wyn had pierced its lungs.

To his surprise, the lizard swung wildly at him with its daggers, still trying to attack him in a frenzy despite it clearly dying. Thankfully the spear was keeping it just out of arms reach, and Wyn pulled it out of its chest inflicting a deeper cut. It lurched forward from the momentum, trying for one last flurry, though Wyn spun the weapon around and used the clawed end of _Windcutter_ to hook it and sling it to the ground out of harm's way. He doubted he'd be able to succeed with that maneuver on one of the monsters who wasn't on the brink of death and sputtering blood, but he was thankful for the advantage when he had it. One final stab to its chest on the ground sealed its fate, a perverse cry leaving its jaws before going still.

A loud thud made Wyn turn back to the group, hoping John wasn't being overtaken. He should've known better, though, as he saw one of the creatures lying on the ground beside the Fighter trying to get up. John had moved to a third monster further in the grass, where he took another blow on his shield from a large hammer that caused the loud noise. This lizard was the largest of the group, even taller than John, and looked to be the strongest, too, as it swung its large hammer to attack. The weapon looked as though it should be wielded with two hands, but the monster made it look easy holding it in one. Its body was lean with muscle, too, comparable to any warrior Wyn had seen who'd trained for months to enhance their physicality.

Wyn was sure the blow would've hurt John's arm, seeing the force needed to move the heavy weapon, but the Fighter absorbed it without flinching. He figured the red-aura skill aided the Fighter in his physical ability, but he was shocked to actually see it in action. He doubted John even needed the magical armor around him. John, not missing a beat, swung his sword back, too quick for the lizard to react and cleaved its arm off at the shoulder.

It was gruesome, Tasha even yelping at the sight of it, as she turned her head away and closed her eyes.

The second lizard monster on the ground, meanwhile, was up and about to strike John from behind. Wyn started to rush forward to help but stopped midstride when he heard the whoosh of an arrow fly beside him. It struck the monster hard on the back of its shoulder, and it whipped around to see who attacked it.

Spittle flew from the monster's mouth as it growled in anger, a deep, rumbling noise escaping its reptilian jaws.

Two more quick arrows silenced it, one hitting it in the chest and another in the neck. It sputtered blood as it clawed at the arrow shafts sticking out of it, breaking them both as it ripped them free from its body.

Wyn promptly slashed and stabbed at the creature while it was recovering, peppering it with quick blows. The attacks caused it to bleed profusely, and it let out one final angry roar while dropping to one knee.

A fourth arrow pierced its open mouth and exited the back of its head, killing it.

Behind it, the largest lizard dropped its hammer and held its empty shoulder, screaming in a fit of rage. John promptly stepped forward and stabbed it with his sword, the blade emerging from behind it. It was silenced quickly as John retracted his sword and stabbed it again. It toppled over in death.

In a matter of seconds all three lizards were dead and bleeding, the ground in their area more blue now than green from the jungle floor.

Tasha gagged and wiped her eyes before taking a deep breath. "Is everyone okay?"

John breathed deep one more time and wiped his sword on a large leaf before sheathing it. "Should be. They weren't that bad."

"Tasha, are *you* okay?" Wyn asked. He walked over to her and grabbed her shoulder. "Were you hurt?"

"No, I'm alright," she replied. "It's just . . . I wasn't expecting it to be that gruesome."

"You mean all those wolves and spiders weren't enough for you?" Wyn asked.

"This was much worse than that, and you know it," Tasha replied. "I could handle spiders being killed all day long. But these reminded me of people."

"That's the tower for you," Marcy said. "Monsters can show up like anything. But this is real. Don't forget that. And I hate to break it to you, but *life* is gruesome."

Tasha took another deep breath to settle herself. "I know. I just have to get used to it. But John—I'm speechless. That was incredible!"

"Yeah," Marcy said. "Where was that last week? That was . . . a bit terrifying. In a good way."

John smiled at the compliment. "I wanted my first time to be skill-free, purely on my own training and abilities. But yeah . . . that *was* special." He flexed his arms, enjoying the rush of his skill and finding himself unable to be still from his physical surge.

The lizard creatures all began to dissolve and the blood along with them. Where the leader lay was a small item glowing with a green aura. Tasha was the first to spot it.

"Hey! Another magic item!" Tasha ran up to it and went to grab it but paused. There were two items rather than one. "Even better—there are two! How should we split them up?"

Wyn walked up beside Tasha and looked at the items. They were a lizard tooth and claw, both much larger than the lizards themselves possessed and giving off a faint green aura. Both were the size of his palm. He picked them up and handed them to John.

"I think you deserve these," Wyn said. "They kept wanting to attack you, not anyone else. They saw you as their biggest threat and you *were*. And, you handled them easily."

John grabbed them and put them in a pouch on his backpack. "Thank you. I don't quite know what I want to do with them yet, but we can figure it out later."

"What could you do with them?" Wyn asked.

"Well, I could sell them or have them crafted into something. Nothing too great since they're both green items, but maybe a potion or basic item. My mother told me some crafters are able to break down items into raw materials that are more readily used, so even green items like these have *some* value."

"Or the guild will buy them from you for a flat amount of coins," Marcy said. "Something like ten gold per green item, I believe. Nothing too much, but they can definitely add up."

Wyn thought about that. That would certainly be another way to supplement his needed income.

"But like we said before, we can discuss all of this outside the tower," Tasha said.

"Agreed," Wyn said. He twirled his spear and slung the excess blood off the blade. "I assume we just keep following the path that was cleared?"

"I would think so," Marcy said. "If a group ran into a dead end, they would've retraced their steps, and I haven't seen or heard anyone yet."

"Then we keep following it," Tasha said. She grabbed her staff sheepishly and stepped beside Wyn. "But I would still like you two to lead."

"Alright," Marcy said, "then let's keep going."

A loud scream suddenly filled the air. Tasha jumped with a slight yelp then held a hand over her mouth.

"What in the hells was that?" John asked.

"I don't know," Marcy replied, "but it doesn't sound like it was very far away."

"And it was definitely further down the path," Wyn added. "We should hurry!"

The others agreed without another word as they followed the scream at a light jog. Wyn was impressed again at how well John was keeping up in his armor, but he had to remind himself that he had been training for this long before he came to Alestead. He knew a lot of soldiers who wouldn't be able to keep at that pace and still be useful once they stopped. He wondered just how well his Fighter skills expanded his already improved physical talents. A passive skill or two was likely helping him like how **Lucidity** was helping Wyn recover mana.

"Once we see what it is," Wyn said, still running, "we help, but stick together. No one separate." He wasn't used to running and talking at the same time, but he managed to get his words out between huffs of air.

"Good idea," John replied. "Tasha should stay back with Marcy, and Wyn back me up!" He was running just as fast as the others and didn't seem to need to take a break to talk while running.

Wyn felt a pang of jealousy. John was basically showing off, now.

They could all see from the cleared brush a larger area ahead and heard more commotion. Yells, another scream, and loud thuds all hit their ears over the noise of their own gear as they ran. In seconds they came out of the cleared path and emerged into an open field full of chaos.

There were two giant lizard creatures, both holding heavy, huge weapons they wielded in their hands. One was a large club and the other a large axe. They easily stood over ten feet, dwarfing the previous enemies they'd met so far. They had cloths that scantily covered their bodies and war paint on their chests, arms, and faces that looked menacing.

Unfortunately, they were fighting a group of Climbers who weren't doing well.

Four members of the group were at the edge of the clearing, one lying on the ground and another holding him in a way that seemed like they were comforting or healing him. The third was standing nearby with a staff in hand and didn't seem too engaged in the fight. The last member was just standing there with a large backpack on and not moving.

Three more Climbers were facing the lizards, engaged in direct combat. Two of the climbers were tall and dressed in armor like John, holding shields in one hand and a weapon in the other, while the third held two short swords and was working hard to mostly dodge strikes or reposition themself. They weren't doing much attacking back.

Wyn couldn't make out their exact details, but he knew they were in trouble. The frontline Fighters looked exhausted and beaten, and they all looked ragged and worn to some degree.

Behind the two large lizards was the portal for the next floor. It was still red, the Climbers' task not yet completed to gain entry.

"Rally!" one of the Fighters yelled. "Don't give up!" He stood firm, beating his shield with his sword two times before thrusting the blade up toward the sky in a cheer. A wave of red aura left him, covering over his allies in combat and shrouding them, similar to John's aura. It was less intense but familiar. The skill was obviously a strong and useful one as it was able to spread to others, and Wyn instantly wondered what benefits it gave. The Fighter looked back and saw Wyn and the group standing at the edge of the clearing.

"Reinforcements!" the Climber who held the short swords yelled, smiling and waving the weapons frantically. His head was covered by a dark cowl, and his thinner armor was darker than what the other Climbers wore.

"Stay focused!" the rallying Fighter yelled back. "We don't need their help!"

One of the lizard creatures swung its club across in a wide arc, and nearly all of them missed it by jumping back out of the way or ducking. The Climber who held the two short swords was too focused on Wyn and their group instead of the fight at hand and didn't even realize it happened.

The club caught him in the side of his torso and threw him several feet in a loud crunch. It sounded like dead wood splintering apart. The woman on the back lines screamed the same scream that pierced the jungle minutes earlier.

The Climber lay still, not moving. One of the Fighters moved to guard him with his shield from the lizards. His sword arm and legs visibly trembled.

The lead Fighter growled and turned back to the monsters. "Forget about him! Kill these bastards, now!" His armor was more easily seen now, green and black in color that stood out from the mundane colors of regular armor.

"Come on," John said. "We have to help them!"

"Let's do the boss formation," Tasha said. "I think we can do it."

Wyn looked at them and nodded, agreeing. They *could* do it. He didn't have a doubt in his mind at their abilities. His concern was the lack of discipline and obvious skill of the other Climbers.

The woman from the other group ran over to them crying and screaming. She didn't have her staff in hand as she left it back at the other Climber who was still lying on the ground. Her breathing was fast and inconsistent and her movements were jerky as she was frantic and panicking.

"Please, help us!" she cried, stopping as she got nearer to them. "Oh, gods, we're all going to die!"

Wyn recognized her as she ran closer, able to see her features in more detail. She was the woman who laughed at him just hours ago at the base of the tower for being a mage wielding a spear. The familiar look of the rest of her group clicked into place in Wyn's mind. The Fighter with the green and black colors wielding a sword and shield. The Climber with dark armor and two short swords.

This was the group who ridiculed Wyn. And now they were failing miserably.

CHAPTER THIRTY-ONE

The group separated without another word, already knowing their roles. They had prepared for this, planned ahead, and gone over it multiple times in the training room the day before. They wanted to be ready, work together effectively, and be more efficient despite their smaller group size.

Wyn and John ran directly toward the fight, going to help out. Marcy and Tasha followed the woman to the back line where Marcy kept an eye out for any additional enemies. She already had an arrow nocked with her bow in hand, her attention pulling away from the boss fight. There was something out in the woods that was making her *Extrasensory* tickle the back of her neck. Was it another threat like a champion group? She couldn't tell at the moment. And she needed to focus on the immediate threat.

Tasha, meanwhile, bent down to inspect the Climber who was on the ground. The man was stable but unconscious. She didn't see any wounds that needed to be healed and felt him breathing when she placed her hand beside his mouth and nose. The woman, a Diamond Mage too, was breathing loud and quick, nearly having a panic attack. Tasha stood back up and squared up to her, grabbing her shoulder with her free hand. She stared into her eyes with a determined but calm look.

"Look at me," she said. "Take deep breaths. You *have* to calm down and help. He is stable, breathing, and alive. But you have to help with the others who might not be."

The woman took a deep breath and nodded quickly, settling down a bit though her eyes still flittered around the area. "O-o-okay," she said, stammering her words. She wiped away a tear that had fallen down her cheek.

Tasha bent down and picked up the woman's staff and handed it to her. She took it with a bit of hesitation, but Tasha was giving her courage. "You can do this. The others will handle the enemies. We only need to heal the wounded. Just follow my lead, okay?"

She nodded without another word.

The other mage, wielding a staff with a garnet set in the end, stepped forward. "*Flamebolt*!" he yelled, pointing his staff to the lizard monsters. The spell lobbed to the side and well short, missing them entirely before erupting in the jungle and setting a bush on fire. He sheepishly looked around and cleared his throat. He was too nervous to join the fight, opting to stay a safe distance away.

Marcy saw the large Climber wearing a similarly large backpack. His jaw was set, and he was sweating, his fists clenched by his side. He looked like he was paralyzed.

"Are you alright?" she asked him.

He turned to look at her, and his expression softened a bit. "No. I want to help, but Frederick said to stay out of it." His voice was surprisingly soft for his size and demeanor.

"And you listened to him?"

He turned away and looked back at the fight. "He said he'd have me banned from the tower if I did, disobeying a direct order. I'm only a Mapper, not a Climber, and don't have the authority. According to him." He grabbed the war hammer on his belt and squeezed it so hard his knuckles went white.

"Well, he's a fool that's going to get his group killed," Marcy said. "Stay here with me and keep an eye out. With us joining the fight, it's only going to get worse."

She looked over at Tasha who nodded back at her, her face serious and posture straight. She was more than ready—she was determined. Marcy smiled and pointed with her head toward the fight. Tasha pulled the other Diamond Mage behind her, nearly dragging her, and they set off to join the chaos. Their groups needed them. Marcy only hoped that nothing was lurking deeper in the jungle.

Wyn's thoughts ran to the war, thinking about his men scattered on the ground in various states of life and death. He thought of his inaction, where he wanted to move but felt as though he were a statue set in place.

He willed his thoughts out of the past, shaking his head. Now was *not* the time to lose focus. He chastised himself. That was the past, and this was the here and now. People needed his help, and they needed it right away. His group couldn't afford for him to not act. Not again.

"I'm going to get him out of there," Wyn said, jogging alongside John. They were rushing into a dangerous situation with people they weren't familiar with and dangerous foes, but they were confident in each other. The other Fighters, though, could very well get in the way, being more trouble than helpful. The two Climbers both knew it without saying it out loud.

"I'm going to distract them," John replied. "Just don't take long!"

In seconds they were across the field. Wyn split off first, stabbing his spear into the ground twenty feet before the lizards and Fighters where it stood on end. He noticed the Fighters look at him, and the lizard monsters looked, too. The monster that held the great axe swung down at the two Fighters trying to hit them both at the same time. The weapon was as big as a person, and the swing was forceful but slow. They both stepped out of its attack awkwardly, with the Fighter guarding the downed Climber falling to the ground, and the other stumbling but staying upright. He cursed and stared at Wyn.

"You! Red Mage!" His eyes were furious, his mouth in a snarl.

Wyn hoped he was angry at the situation and not him personally, but it honestly didn't matter. He saw the unconscious Climber and guessed he was likely a Rogue. He bent down to grab him and realized the jungle floor was soaked in blood, his armor wet and slick. His left arm was bent at a strange angle, and what he assumed was a previous gash on his side had opened considerably.

Wyn didn't know how close he was to death. There were still the faintest signs of breath as his chest slowly rose and fell, but it was weak. Wyn wasn't a medic and didn't know the true extent of the man's injuries. What he did have, though, was magic.

Wyn touched his side gently. "*Regen*," he said, hoping his spell would help keep death away. He saw the white aura envelope him and hoped it would be enough. The Rogue's swords were lying on the ground, but they weren't important right now and would just get in the way. Wyn slipped under his good arm and heaved him up, trying his best to run away from the fight so he wouldn't get smashed in the back.

He saw Tasha and the other mage coming across the field and met them in the middle. The woman gasped and went white, taking a step away in fear. At least Tasha stood resolute at the gruesome sight. Wyn set the man on the ground as quickly and gently as he could.

"I don't think *Regen* is going to work fast enough," Tasha said. She inspected him like she did the other Climber, feeling for a breath and seeing what wounds he had.

"It's all I have," Wyn said. "I was hoping you could take care of the rest." He stood and watched as the other mage threw up.

"He's still alive!" Tasha yelled, turning back to the other woman. She placed a hand on the man's chest. "*Stabilize*."

The white aura around the Rogue increased in size but decreased in intensity. Wyn couldn't tell if the man's wounds were closing or not, but he trusted Tasha and her abilities to heal.

A crack in the jungle made Wyn whip his head toward the noise. Nothing moved. What was that? More monsters? Marcy should have alerted them if more monsters were nearby. And they likely would have attacked before Wyn came over when the others were more vulnerable.

Something moved in the jungle's edge that looked like the size of a person. Another group, then? Why hide and not join to help?

"He's barely alive, but I got it from here," Tasha said.

"Good," Wyn replied. He shook off the noise and refocused. "I need to go back. I'll yell if we need you."

Tasha held out her staff and tapped Wyn on the shoulder. "***Arcane Aura***," she said, casting another spell. The aura enveloped him in magical armor while she went back to tend to the Rogue. She touched her staff on him, now— "***Cure***." The staff glowed for a moment before creating the familiar runic structure at its tip. This spell was cast using the energy from the staff itself as the runes in the air didn't have Tasha's Diamond Magician signature. The white aura now grew exponentially as multiple spells of healing magic flowed into him.

His arm was now right again, and his side was nearly whole. The gash had mostly healed but was still open, though the ***Regen*** spell was still active. It was closing the wound up slowly.

The Rogue stirred and coughed. The other Diamond Mage gasped and cried.

"Come get me, you bastards!" John screamed while banging his sword against his shield. He was standing off to the side away from the other Fighters, working to get the giant creature's attention. One of them turned, its eyes black and full of death, and lashed out with its tongue in a feral cry. In two large steps it was within striking range as it held up its axe and swung it at John.

He sidestepped nimbly, avoiding the blow of the weapon as it lodged into the ground and kicked up grass and dirt. He rushed forward and slashed at it several times, leaving small cuts across its upper thigh.

Its skin was as tough as armor, and his sword was basic. In this moment he really, really missed his magically flaming sword. At least he still had his shield.

He stepped back quickly, putting some distance between the monster and himself to reassess. He knew he just needed it distracted and their numbers would overwhelm them eventually, but he didn't want to be directly under it.

Or did he?

"Hey, jackass, stay out of this!" the other Fighter yelled. He pointed his sword at John. "We are handling it!"

"Like hells you are!" John yelled back.

The Fighter turned to strike at the other lizard creature as he and his ally were taunting it. Their strategy fell apart almost immediately as the lizard swung at them with its club and they dodged it in the same direction, the leader tripping and nearly falling over the other. He cursed again, pushing his teammate away from him with his shield in frustration. The other Fighter stumbled back a bit, caught off guard by being shoved.

John realized how poorly they were working together. This was just the first floor, and they looked like they just held a weapon for the first time yesterday. They'd likely never make it as Climbers. He pitied them.

The axe-wielding monster raised his axe again to strike. John stole a quick glance back and saw Wyn running toward them, and he knew it wouldn't be long before he would join and they could take them out. His ally might be a Red Mage, but he was more competent than even most of the Fighters John trained with.

He just needed to survive until Wyn joined the fight. His idea was going to test that fact, but he wanted to try it.

"*Focus*!" he yelled, and the same red aura covered him again. He felt its effects immediately, like a surge of adrenaline but more stout and effective. He charged forward at the monster right as it swung down with its axe. Narrowly avoiding the weapon, he sidestepped it and parried it at the same, using his magical shield to redirect the force. The axe struck the ground once more, and John stabbed the monster's lower torso several times.

The blade sunk deeper and was more effective than before, his skill working to improve his strength. Dark blood seeped away from the gashes, but they weren't as deep as he would've liked. He ran around the giant to the opposite side of the other Fighters, hoping to at least turn its attention away.

"Come on, come on," he said, taunting it.

Wyn picked up his pace across the field after seeing how the other Fighters were hurting themselves more than helping. Their communication was terrible. He was thankful his own group had a plan and knew they would be able to make it far despite their smaller party.

John decided to draw an attack to give Wyn the chance to strike by surprise. The other two Fighters would just have to deal with one of the large beasts while he took on the other by himself. He realized the shielding spell Tasha placed on him was starting to fade, as the auras from his own skill and her spell had blended together before but now the red was overtaking the white. In a desperate effort he decided to use what was left to his advantage.

He stabbed at the monster several times, more to taunt it than actually cause damage. The creature roared in frustration, the noise deafening, causing the Climbers except John to flinch. He was too zoned in to be distracted himself. The monster let go of its axe and swung with a backhand to John as though he were swatting a fly.

John didn't want to sidestep it this time—he used his shield to take the blow.

The magical shield combined with his stacked magical effects took the entirety of the force. He held his ground, keeping his stance together, but was shoved to the side several feet. There were marks in the jungle floor where his boots dug in and pushed out the ground from the force. He stabilized himself behind the shield and stood tall and proud at absorbing the blow.

Wyn plucked his spear from the ground without slowing down as he closed the distance. He twirled his spear around and sliced in a heavy arc at the back of the creature's knee that was attacking John. He felt the flesh give out and saw a spray of blood burst from its leg, covering the side of his clothes and the ground beside him. He couldn't even tell its skin was hardened like armor, his wind-based spear cutting through it like a hot knife through butter.

The creature fell to the ground on its knee, screaming in pain. It dropped its axe and clawed the dirt in pain and anger.

"Now!" Wyn yelled.

John ran forward and stabbed it in the side, hoping to do whatever damage he could. Wyn, however, let out a flurry of slashes and stabs, all of them gouging and opening the flesh of the monster. It cried in agony and pain before Wyn put one final blow into its torso, feeling the entire blade sink in where its heart should be, causing the beast to go still.

As he pulled out the spear it fell to the ground in a loud thud.

Wyn and John smiled at each other, happy at their success.

A loud clang shook them from their brief celebration. They looked and saw the other group's leader stabbing at the remaining lizard-giant while his teammate was on the ground, his shield cast off to the side. He was holding his arm and yelling in pain.

Wyn ran to him, checking his mark on the way. He still had some mana left, but it wasn't enough to cast **Regen**. His lack of available mana while climbing was becoming detrimental, not just a nuisance. Whether it was mana potions or equipment or both to increase his ability to use spells and skills, he decided right then and there he needed it to be more effective.

"That bastard!" John yelled, rushing to help, directing his frustration at the Climber. He couldn't heal the other Fighter and knew his role was to help deal with the monster directly.

Wyn looked back at Tasha and saw that she had already come to help. She pointed her staff to the Fighter and used its magic once more. "**Cure!**" she yelled, and a flash of white magic overtook the Climber and began healing his wounds.

Satisfied that Tasha was taking care of the injured Climber, Wyn looked back at the beast and held out his spear. He knew it would be over quickly, but he almost wanted the other Fighter to manage it on his own just to add insult to injury.

No. He wouldn't stoop to their level. If he was going to show them what being a Ruby Magician entailed, he needed to prove himself and the power of the class.

He hurried forward beside the other Fighter.

"Stay away!" the Fighter yelled. His eyes were crazed, and spittle flew from his mouth when he spoke. "We don't need your help, *Red Mage!*"

Wyn looked in his eyes and promptly ignored him.

The beast raised its club again to attack, and the Fighter wasn't even paying attention. He was only looking at Wyn, furious that he would even try to help. Wyn ran to him and shoved him out of the way to the ground just as the giant swung in a wide arc with its club.

It caught Wyn in the back as he fell to the ground, flinging him further away several feet. He blinked, shocked at the hit, and tried to move his body. He stood up, thankfully, and hoped his adrenaline wasn't taking over and masking an injury. He looked down and noticed his white aura was completely gone.

It absorbed the blow for him and dissipated. Whatever strength was in that swing and however it contacted Wyn was enough to completely use up the magic inside it. The thought of being hit without that magical protection made Wyn shudder.

Angered with new resolve, he ran toward the beast with a battle cry. The monster just roared back in a challenge. He saw John beside it, readying his sword, wanting to help however he could.

"***Wingbeat!***" he yelled, hooking his spear as though he was pulling something from thin air with the clawed end. He aimed it in a diagonal arc so it would miss John instead of catching him in the spell. Hopefully it would react as intended. The magical wind cut through the air at the creature and sliced across it exactly how he'd hoped, catching its right leg up to its left shoulder. It left a large gash across its body, causing it to rear back. It dropped its club and clawed at its chest as blood poured out of its wound.

It fell back onto the ground in pain. Wyn ran forward and forcefully stabbed it in the neck, nearly beheading it from the blow.

The field was silent for a moment except for the Climbers' deep, fast breaths from exertion.

"Whoa," John said. He lowered his sword and walked over beside Wyn.

"I'll say," Wyn replied. "You were amazing, John. Even better than expected."

"I meant you, Wyn. Look at them! They're nearly in pieces!"

"I . . . can't believe it," the Fighter said, his eyes wide in amazement. He was lying on the ground and looking up at the carnage. "But you're just a . . . a *Red Mage.*"

"It's not about the class, you idiot," John said. "Look at you. You nearly got your teammates killed, and you're supposed to be a Fighter! You should be able to handle these types of enemies well enough!"

The Fighter looked back and saw what was left of his group. The others had gathered around Tasha and the Rogue, staring at the scene at the end of the floor. They were all shocked, barely aware of what had happened.

Suddenly a loud crash hit on the edge of the field. Another giant lizard stepped out, this one holding two swords. It had the same war paint and torn linen on its body, and it roared at the Climbers for a fight.

An arrow protruded from its eye socket in a flash in a sickening thunk, immediately silencing it. The beast paused and went still. Suddenly the arrow exploded in a flash of fire, and a now-headless giant lizard creature fell to the ground with a loud thud.

All of the Climbers looked to the direction where the arrow came from and saw Marcy standing there with her bow. She shrugged and slung it around her chest, unbothered.

Wyn wondered if that was the other creature in the jungle. But it couldn't be. It was far too big. What he saw was more of a person. Now that he thought about it, they were darkened, almost as though hidden by a cloak.

He didn't want to jump to conclusions, but it was definitely an odd experience. Something to be on guard for if he noticed it again, at least.

The portal past the boss changed color to gray, showing they had successfully completed their task and were allowed to proceed.

Wyn, setting aside his concern, walked over with the rest of his group, celebrating their success.

The other Climbers stood there dumbfounded, staring at the small group in disbelief.

"Hey," the Rogue said. "Who in the hells are you guys?"

CHAPTER THIRTY-TWO

The group felt the pull of the portal, the strange sensation of every fiber in their bodies twisting and turning over in a second. They appeared back at the base in Alestead one by one, Wyn and his group appearing much more intact than the other group of Climbers.

John inspected himself when he emerged, checking for any wounds or bruises. The adrenaline and skill both now worn off, he only felt the drag of fatigue and not any extraneous damage. He breathed a sigh of relief, thankful this time he emerged without needing to dash to the infirmary. Hopefully that was a one-time occurrence.

The Fighter and Rogue who were both hurt were standing, at least, but decided to take themselves to the infirmary to make sure there wasn't any additional damage they couldn't see. Tasha healed them nearly on her own without the other healer's help, and she wasn't trying to seek any form of payment or thanks. Still, the frantic pair wanted to leave almost immediately when they entered the base.

The woman, a Diamond Mage, stammered over her words when she tried to thank Tasha. "You . . . you saved us. And . . . you saved . . . me. Just . . . thank you!" She bowed low to the ground, nearly dropping her staff awkwardly.

Tasha snickered. "I did what I needed to do. But this isn't a place to mess around! You *have* to be ready to help when you can." Her cheeks were flushed, hot with nerves and a brief flash of disdain.

The mage recoiled. "I know. I . . . I'll be better."

"Good." Tasha softened a bit and sighed. "Just . . . *try*, okay? It'll get easier. But you're their lifeline. We can heal injuries but only to a point. Don't let it get out of your control."

The mage nodded her head and sniffled. "Words to climb by. Thank you."

"She's right, it will get easier," John said, putting his arm around the woman. Her face grew even redder than Tasha's. "But don't worry! Just heal first and throw up later."

"Easy for you to say," Tasha said. "You still throw up going through the portal."

John blanched. "I really shouldn't have eaten those eggs this morning."

Tasha laughed, and the other mage nervously laughed along with her, John's arm still resting on her shoulders.

"You idiots!" the Fighter yelled, stepping up to Wyn. He was shorter than Wyn but held his chest high with arrogance. His face was blood red. "You nearly got us killed!"

"*We* nearly got you killed?" Wyn said, standing firm. He held his spear at his side and felt his knuckles pop from his tightening grip. "We saved you and your group! If it wasn't for us you would've had two dead Climbers, maybe more."

The Fighter leaned more into Wyn, nearly at his face. "We had it under control. *I* had it under control!" He threw his hands to the side and yelled in frustration. He backed off, turning to face his group before they completely left the hallway of portals. "If you all would've just listened to me! *I'm* the leader here. You take orders from ME!"

The Fighter and Rogue stopped before they completely left the room, turning around to face him.

"Are you serious, Frederick?" the Rogue said. His face was contorted between disgust and laughter. "We basically hobbled our way through that floor. We had a full group! And it was only the first floor!"

"And that speaks about the leader more than anything," the Fighter added, "more than the group as a whole, at least. You made awful calls, rushed us, and nearly got us killed."

"Yeah, they saved us," the Rogue said. "You should be thanking them!"

Frederick slowly walked toward them, putting a hand on the hilt of his sheathed sword. "You ungrateful fools," he started, but was promptly cut off. He stopped moving immediately, an arm appearing under his chin in a flash.

Marcy held him in place, twisting his arm behind his back and choking him at the same time. She was calm, her hands steady and face neutral. His already red face grew redder, his eyes nearly bulging out of their sockets in rage.

Her mouth was right behind and above his ear, though she leaned in for more effect. "I would advise you to calm down, Climber. You won't like the outcome if you draw that sword."

Frederick struggled for a few seconds but relented. He either realized he was outmatched or out of place. She was strong, and he didn't expect it, but his emotions were also raging with intensity. He raised his hands slowly, taking deeper, slower breaths. "Alright, alright." He struggled, his face now purple.

Marcy let go and stepped beside him, eyeing him suspiciously. He coughed a few times and rubbed his throat.

"At any rate, I'm done with you worthless, weak excuses of Climbers," Frederick said, his voice now hoarse. "Find your own leader." He walked off, pushing past the other Fighter and Rogue, who stepped out of his way.

"What in the hells is his problem?" John said. He looked down and realized he had grabbed his own sword hilt in response, subconsciously readying himself if things went worse. His hand quickly jerked away.

"He thinks he's a somebody because he's rich," the other Magician said. He shook his garnet staff mockingly.

"A noble, actually," the Fighter said. He sighed. "From Caryn."

"A nobody, actually," the Rogue added, "is what you meant to say. He's a piece of dirt and doesn't deserve to lead a group."

"Well, he won't lead us," the Diamond Mage said. She walked over to the rest of her group. "We can manage without him. This time we find someone better and do it right."

"That's the spirit!" Tasha said. "I'm sure it will go much smoother next time."

"Thank you," the woman replied. "We owe you guys."

"Yeah, like our lives," the Rogue said. He walked over to Tasha and extended a hand. "You saved my life. Thank you."

Tasha waved his hand away. "You shouldn't thank *me*! Wyn was the one who pulled you away and healed you first."

"Who is that?" He looked over at John, who only smiled back, then waved sheepishly.

"He's our leader, I guess," Tasha said. "Though we haven't exactly decided. He's the Ruby Magician."

The Rogue jerked his head toward Wyn, shock evident on his face before changing to serious as he relaxed and set his jaw. Wyn smirked but quickly shook it off. There wasn't any need to gloat. Not now.

"It's no big deal," Wyn said. "I'd hope anyone would do the same for me."

The Rogue walked up to Wyn and held a hand out. "I'm sorry for earlier. That was . . . pretty shitty of me. Thank you."

Wyn took his hand and shook it firmly. "It's alright. I'm just glad you're okay."

"I will be, I'm just . . . embarrassed. I'm sorry. I obviously need to be a better judge of character."

"Both good and bad," John said, pointing a thumb toward the exit where Frederick stomped off.

The Rogue sighed. "Right. Well, we should be going. I might take a few days off, but I hope to see you all again. Truly."

"Yes!" the Fighter said. "Might be worth grouping together in the future. I know we could definitely learn a thing or two."

John walked over and clapped the man on the shoulder. He introduced himself and made another joke, further lightening the mood. The Fighter introduced himself as Travis, and the others exchanged names and pleasantries as well. The Rogue—Devon—seemed to lighten up the most, and Wyn was grateful they were friendly. There were good people here, after all. After a few more minutes of talking, the others finally said their goodbyes.

"Maybe another time," Maven, the Diamond Mage, said. "Dinner would be nice, but we need some time to think. Thank you all again." She herded the other Climbers like sheep.

The group hobbled away, reminding Wyn of himself, Marcy, and Cedric after they left the second floor. He thought of the scene right before they left, where he saw Cedric's arm lying on the ground and the witch standing in the distance. He knew the Lightning Wizard would be changed forever, but he didn't know to what extent. Hopefully he'd be able to see him soon—he'd been wanting to talk to him, to make sure he's doing alright. Sure, physically he lost an arm, but he had no doubt he was alive and stable. He was wanting to make sure mentally he wasn't falling apart. That was far too common in his background, and he had a strong feeling that it was common here, too.

"I think I'm ready, too," John said. He stretched and took a deep breath. "That wasn't that bad, but I lost my breakfast before we even got started."

Tasha laughed. "I'm sure you're starving. I can get some food with you before we meet at the training hall." She walked over to him and playfully nudged him in the side. He yipped, more in surprise than pain. "If you don't mind the company?"

"Escorting a noble to a meal?" He bowed to her in a large, grandiose way. "Not at all, m'lady. May we collect our rewards, first?"

Tasha laughed. "Stop it. If you act like that I'll kick you out to the streets!"

John returned the laugh, and they walked out of the hallway of portals toward the base entrance. Marcy shook her head and followed them out, wondering how in the hells she ended up in this situation.

Wyn began to follow them out before he saw the Mapper awkwardly standing to the side, holding onto the straps of the large backpack he wore. He was trying not to be nosy, but he stood just far enough away to go unnoticed. He caught Wyn staring at him and jumped a bit, straightening up his posture.

Wyn walked over to him, having to look up at him to look him in the eyes. "Are you alright? I didn't really see you in the fray back there."

The Mapper cleared his throat and spoke. His voice was higher than Wyn expected for someone his size, though not comically so. "Yes, thank you," he said sheepishly, avoiding eye contact with him.

Wyn waited for him to continue, but he didn't. "Well . . . alright, then. Good."

The two stood there for a moment, Wyn not knowing if he should speak further and the Mapper wanting to avoid conversation entirely. The man started to walk out of the hallway toward the tower entrance, and Wyn walked with him.

"You know," Wyn said, trying to fill the void of silence, "people like that don't deserve to lead a group. I hope he wasn't unkind to you in the tower."

The Mapper didn't reply, only readjusted his backpack straps and continued walking. They passed groups of Climbers here and there, some entering the tower late and others leaving, heading back to the front entrance. Wyn found he had to step slightly faster to keep pace as his legs were slightly shorter, though the Mapper didn't seem to be in a hurry. He was just set on where he wanted to go.

"Regardless," Wyn continued, "I'm glad you're okay. It seems like most of their group suffered rather than improved under him. Hopefully they will find a better leader and you a better group."

The Mapper looked at him for a second then turned away. His face was kind but serious, almost sad in a way. "I hope so, too. No one should have to deal with an attitude like his."

Wyn smiled. "I agree. My name is Wyn. I'm a Ruby Magician."

"I figured. About your class, I mean. No way I could've guessed your name."

"How's that?"

The taller man shrugged. "You used a healing spell and then rushed in to fight. No base class has the ability to heal along with being confident enough to fight directly except for Red Mages. I just put two and two together."

Wyn looked at the man again. There wasn't anything that stood out on his person except for the backpack that looked like it could hold Wyn. Everything else—his clothing, armor, and war hammer on his belt—looked perfectly normal here in the tower. He obviously knew much more than he let on, and Wyn liked those kinds of people.

"Well, you're spot on," Wyn said.

The man chuckled, laughing with his whole body. "My name is Caloman, but you can call me Cal."

Wyn stopped and put his hand out in a formal greeting. Cal stopped, too, and shook it. His hands were huge and strong as Wyn was barely able to squeeze his hand for the handshake. "Good to meet you, Cal. If we need a Mapper, I hope you're available for us. We're a new group, but we work well together."

"I'll make sure I'm available if you need someone. Just put in a request at the desk at the entrance, and I'll be sure to see it. And I can tell you all have *some* experience, at least. Better than Frederick and his group."

"Well, this is our first official season and only second time in the tower, but I'd like to think we're preparing ourselves well."

"Huh," Cal said, and kept walking. "I would've thought this would've been your second or third season. Did you all know each other before you came to Alestead?"

"No, actually. We met just a few days ago, but we seem to get along well enough. I think we'll go pretty far together."

"I think you will, too. I know a good group when I see one."

Wyn smiled. Whether he was looking for it or not, he was glad to have some validation about their group. Sure they were small, and most would likely judge them as not being capable with their smaller number, but he felt good about them working well together. Hearing it from someone else didn't just feel good. It felt *great.*

The sound of conversation grew quickly around them as they entered the base of Alistair. Climbers were still readying themselves to enter the tower, people who left were collecting rewards at the desks, and some groups were catching up with others at the start of the new season.

Cal waved bye to Wyn as he walked back toward the wall where the other Mappers stood to be hired for a climb. Wyn waved back, glad to meet a new Climber and potential ally in the future.

He saw Marcy, John, and Tasha standing beside the desks, laughing at John's antics. He was waving his arms in some big show, and Wyn was sure he was making some kind of joke. John saw him and waved him over.

"Hurry up and get your rewards," John said as Wyn approached them. "We need to grab some food then head to the training hall already!"

"Oh *now* you're in a rush?" Tasha asked, pocketing her parchment in her robes. "This morning you dragged your feet to come to the tower!"

"It's all about the food, St. Clair! I basically missed lunch, so now I have to stack up enough for lunch *and* dinner."

Tasha sighed audibly. "Of course it is. But that actually makes sense in a weird way."

Marcy laughed and crossed her arms, leaning on the desk.

"You guys go ahead," Wyn said. He pulled his parchment out of his pocket. "I'll get my rewards and meet you at the training hall."

"What? Why?" John asked.

"I want to talk to someone here about Frederick. Someone like that shouldn't be allowed to lead a group. He could've gotten them killed." He also wanted some time alone to process what he saw at the end of the floor, but he didn't know if he should share that, yet. He had no idea how John might react if he suspected someone was around and watching them. Wyn didn't want to panic the others by telling them he thought it may be Lionel, at least not without proof."

John looked at the women. "Yeah, but is it our business?"

"He's a Climber like we are, so yes, I think it is. If we won't, who will?"

John sighed. "Alright, alright. You make a valid point. But I'm *starving*. Can you handle it without us?"

Wyn laughed. "I think I'll be fine. Like I said, I'll meet you guys after."

"I'll go with you," Marcy said. "It would be good to have an eyewitness with you."

"And Tasha and I will grab some food," John said. He visibly brightened. "Perfect!"

"Always food with you," Tasha said. "Sorry guys. I'll bring some food to the hall for both of you."

"Thank you," Marcy said. "It won't be too long."

John nearly dragged Tasha away, and Wyn could only shake his head.

"I'll show you who we need to talk to," Marcy said. "But I doubt it'll amount to much."

"Really? How so?"

"Climbers like that are everywhere. John knows it because he knows more about the tower than most rookies, and I've personally seen it many times before, sadly."

"That's . . . not fair," Wyn said. "The guild should know when Climbers could jeopardize the lives of others. Can't they take disciplinary action to punish them or expel them from climbing?"

Marcy barked a laugh. "Technically Frederick didn't break any laws. Incompetence isn't the same as a crime."

"I don't see it that way. If this were the service he'd be demoted and forced to clean boots for a week."

"Wyn, this isn't the war. The same rules don't apply. If nothing else, you need to understand that simple difference."

Wyn shook his head and sighed. "Maybe so."

"The guild is an organized entity to help regulate us, but they definitely don't operate the same way. They'll make sure no crimes happen but they tend to leave the dealings of group squabbles to the group to work out."

"That was more than a squabble. But I see your point. Still, I want to tell *someone*."

"Yeah, it won't hurt to have his name on record, just don't be disappointed if nothing happens."

Wyn thought about that. It wasn't fair that Frederick wouldn't at least be disciplined for his shitty leadership. Wyn had seen that too many times before for less offensive actions. He'd even felt the sting of shame and failure and paid terribly for it. His mind drifted back to the hill and his soldiers' deaths, the aftermath of the scolding and punishment he took for simply following orders. Being a lower officer, even if he led a company, still meant he took orders, and meant that he also took the fall for failures that shouldn't have been his.

Being a Climber was being part of a new world. He couldn't use his previous experiences to completely relate to this new position. There were still plenty of things for him to learn.

"Alright," Wyn finally said. "I know I still have a lot to learn here. Thank you for talking it out with me."

Marcy smiled warmly. "That's what friends are for."

Wyn nodded, and they walked on in silence. He noticed something with her was off since they faced the boss. Not wanting to beat around the bush, he decided to just ask. "You seemed a little distracted during the boss fight. Is everything alright?"

Marcy glanced at him before avoiding someone walking a little too close to them on the street. "I think so, but I'm not entirely sure. I noticed something in the jungle when we helped the group fight the boss. It probably wasn't anything, though."

Wyn felt a strange mixture of relief and worry. Relief that he wasn't going crazy, but also worry that what he saw was likely true. "I wouldn't be too sure about that. I saw something, too."

Marcy stopped, ignoring the people now having to walk around them. "What do you mean?"

"I caught a glance of something past the foliage. Or someone. Like a person, hiding and watching."

"Not a monster?"

"I don't think so."

"Strange. If it's other people, maybe they were just curious. Why not help, though? That doesn't make sense."

Wyn shrugged. "I'm not sure. But it might be something to be on the lookout for in case it happens again."

"Maybe. The odds are low, but I understand your concern. Don't stress yourself out, at least. Alright?"

"Alright. I'll do my best to somehow be less stressed than I already am."

Marcy laughed. "That's all I can ask for. Now come on. John might be the one who loves food, but I'm hungry, too."

CHAPTER THIRTY-THREE

I'm ready whenever you are," Marcy said, smiling wide with her hands on her hips. She was walking with Wyn to the training hall, their pockets deeper with their rewards and stomachs growling from lack of food.

Wyn sighed in frustration, delaying his eventual response but knowing she was going to get it from him one way or another. "It's getting pretty tiresome saying it all the time."

"For you, yes, but I'll *never* tire of hearing that phrase." She skipped ahead, then turned around and walked backward to face him while keeping their pace. "Come on already, spit it out!" She eyed him teasingly.

"Fine! You were right." He shook his head and smirked, pleasantly annoyed. The guild member whom they spoke to was no help. When Wyn informed her about Frederick, and even had Marcy corroborate his story, she politely but dismissively told him they would note it and cut him off. She wrote his name and class in a bound book but inquired no further, shooing him away so she could move on to other matters.

Wyn knew that interaction well from the reports he gave in the service. They were logged somewhere as a formality, but never released to the lower grunts or officers again. There the change was obvious as soldiers would be gone from their company or officers reassigned or shipped back home, but here was different. Nothing would change, and the problem would remain. He had hoped the politics at the tower would be better, but he was unfortunately sorely mistaken from this simple interaction. Marcy was gloating while he stewed.

She turned and stepped beside him. "That wasn't so hard, was it?"

"I don't care to admit you were right. It's the fact that nothing will change and he'll just keep doing whatever he wants in the tower."

Marcy sighed. "I know. It's awful. But, think about it this way—no one here is under orders to commit to one group or do something they don't want to do. Just like the Climbers before, they're free to leave and find another group as they like."

"I guess that's true."

Wyn felt a cool breeze tickle his neck, the newly summer air pleasant and warm. Spring was gone now entering the third month of the year, and hopefully a harsh summer wouldn't be found in the city. The sun wasn't as hot as it would be in the coming weeks, and the swarming clouds were helping to keep the air mild. They turned a corner at the end of a block and saw the entrance to the training hall in front of them. Climbers were steadily entering and exiting, dressed in their full gear to train and ready themselves for the real challenge.

"I know it's true," Marcy said. "He'll have a horrible time finding a team that sticks with him and is successful unless he changes his attitude, and the rest of them are better off finding someone else anyway."

"I just hope no one gets hurt from him in the tower."

"Don't we all hope that. But how about we worry about our own group?"

Wyn opened the door to the hall and stepped to the side for Marcy to enter first. "True. I'm just trying to find the time to tell John I suspect that it was Lionel following us earlier.

The two Climbers walked past the crowd that stood at the front entrance, working their way to the hallway that led to private rooms. They all decided to meet in the same room they used yesterday when planning for the new season, the second furthest room to the left. Marcy knocked on the door three times, and Tasha answered it with a jolt.

"Finally," Tasha said. "I was afraid your food was going to get cold!"

"Sorry," Wyn said, and set his spear on the weapons rack when he stepped through the doorway. John's basic sword was set beside it in the scabbard, and Marcy set her bow and quiver on a rung beside Tasha's staff. "I had to do it."

"I guess it didn't go well, then?" John said. He was sitting down with his elbows on the large square table in the center of the room. Pieces of paper and stones for weights were strewn across it, and he had a quill he twirled with his fingers. "Based on your gloomy face I gather that it wasn't a pleasant conversation."

"No. You were right, too."

John smiled sadly and shook his head. "I don't take any pleasure in that. I'm sorry, Wyn."

"At least someone doesn't," Wyn said, taking a seat beside John. He grabbed a hunk of bread from a platter of food on the table.

Marcy snickered.

"How did you know it wouldn't work, John?" Tasha asked. She took a seat at the table and pulled a piece of paper in front of her.

"My family told me about things like that. They know all about the ins and outs of the politics here. My parents climbed over four years, and my sister almost three."

"That's pretty incredible," Tasha said. "I guess you're an expert, then?"

"Not exactly. It's like when you learn everything you can about something and then go out in the world to practice it. It's not quite the same, and you have to see it for yourself to really understand it."

"That's true," Wyn said. "Like in the military, you can only learn so much in training. The real lessons are out on the battlefield."

Marcy grabbed a mug of ale and raised it in a toast. "And that's why we're here, to prepare ourselves for the real training. To Alistair, the climb, and the Climbers themselves."

The others raised their own mugs in a similar fashion before all taking a drink.

They set their drinks down except for Marcy, who kept hers in hand for a longer drink, nearly finishing the cup in one gulp. Wyn plucked a handful of berries from the platter of food and munched on them periodically. "So let's pick up where we left off yesterday."

Tasha banged a fist on the table and startled the others. "Alright, then! So we want one day off in the week to rest and recover. That'll be Torday."

"We can get supplies, change strategies if needed, or just relax and recover," Marcy added, taking another drink from her mug.

Tasha nodded. "Exactly. Which gives us two more days in the tower before then after today."

John was writing something down on a piece of paper. He picked up his quill to dip it in the inkwell, not looking up to disturb his focus. "Plenty of time to practice the first floor again. It honestly was easier than I expected."

Wyn wiped his hands before grabbing his mug to wash down the tart aftertaste of the berries. "I agree with John. And now we know the theme of the first tier is a jungle and earth-based enemies. Marcy, what do you think would benefit us the most?"

"I think I need to ditch my fur armor and wear something cooler," Marcy said, as she rubbed her hand over her armor and bristled the fine hairs that lined it. She poured water into her mug from the pitcher on the table. "Your wind spear is great, Wyn, though none of you have the resources to change gear like seasoned Climbers just yet. I'll grab some different arrows and weapons that should help and change a few spells, too."

"What arrows and spells?" Wyn asked. "We need to know everything, remember? Lay it on the table. Maybe Tasha and I can pick other spells, too."

Marcy sighed. "It's a bit overkill, but alright, then. My fur armor is too dense for the warm air in the jungle. I have a light leather set that'll keep me more cool and boosts my hand-to-hand combat ability. My kukri is good for the dense jungle, and I'll grab another, too. Some fights might not be the best with my bow in that dense shit. I'll get some wind arrows, another exploding arrow, and change my one spell away from lightning since they'll resist that. Maybe a **Wind Trap** spell, instead."

"That's helpful. Would there be anything different we could use for spells?"

"Both of you are still only on the first level of Magician spells. You don't have access to much, and I still don't even know what a Ruby Magician can use. Once you hit the next tier you can see about more, but you'll be fine for now. Don't worry about it."

Tasha took a deep breath. "That's helpful, but I'd love to have access to more spells that could be useful. John, when are you getting your new sword?"

John picked up his paper and inspected it, turning it in different directions. "I just mailed the letter on Faesday before the festival, but my family should be mailing it as soon as they get it. Hopefully by the end of the week? Or next Solday? So I'll have to manage this week without it."

"That's nice that they are doing that for you," Tasha said. "Do you have an endless amount of magic items at home or something?"

John laughed. "No, though that would be awesome! It's the sword I trained with at home, actually. The other one was a gift and more powerful. Mine is a water sword I can freeze to become ice-based, and it's a blue aura sword."

"Oh, impressive. I can't wait to see it!"

"It'll feel good to have it again, that's for sure. This basic sword just doesn't feel right. And we are wanting to go to the second floor this week, right? I know we said only the first floor for now, but that was easier than we expected. I think we could handle it."

"I still would like to only stick with the first floor for now to be safe, but this is a group decision," Wyn said. "Marcy has a key if we need it, too, but I would only feel good about it if we spent very little resources on the first floor. I'd want us as healthy as possible entering the second floor."

"That's reasonable," John said. He put his quill back in the holder and folded his hands to rest on the table. "Plus, don't forget that the higher we climb the more rewards we get. I only made about thirty gold today, and I'm sure your rewards were similar. We need to be climbing higher to really make any sort of good coin."

Wyn sighed. John was right, of course, and Wyn had been thinking that very same thing. Still, it was going to be a slow process, especially in the beginning without any experience, items, or real power under their belt. "I know. I think about that a lot. We'll get there, I just don't want us to get hurt in the process. No amount of gold or silver is worth us jeopardizing our safety."

The others nodded while Marcy took another drink. "We're being almost *too* cautious. We'll be fine! If anything big sneaks up on us, I'll kill it. And both you and Tasha can heal, so I'm not worried at all. My vote is to move on."

"Yeah," John started, "shouldn't you be leading us, Marcy? No offense, Wyn, but she has a lot more experience here than we do."

Wyn sat back in his stool before grabbing more food from the platter. "I've already tried to get her to lead. She said no."

"Really? Why not?"

Marcy stood up and pushed her stool under the table. "Because I'm no good at making those kinds of decisions. I'm a good little soldier and will do my role well, but I don't want to be the one to make the plan. No thanks." She walked over to the weapons rack and grabbed her bow and quiver, slinging them on her back.

"Are we done?" Tasha asked. She fiddled with the hem of her robe, watching Marcy get ready to leave.

"Looks like it," Wyn said. "There's not much else to discuss, at any rate."

"Almost," Wyn said. "I wanted to mention that I saw something in the tower lurking in the jungle. Or possibly someone. I think they were watching us."

"How do you know?" John asked, looking up from his paper.

"I saw it too," Marcy said. "Certainly odd, but not really anything to be concerned about."

"Not at the moment," Wyn said. "But maybe something to be aware of. I found it strange enough to point it out."

"Then we'll keep an eye out," Tasha said. "More than usual."

"Good. And John, you want to share what you've been writing?"

John smiled and showed the group his piece of paper. Marcy waited to leave until after she saw it, being as curious as the others. "Tada!" The paper was a crude drawing of them fighting the lizard creatures, with John standing over one with his sword raised high in victory. Marcy and Tasha laughed, while Wyn just shook his head.

"I'm glad I saw that before I left," Marcy said, already halfway out the door. She closed it gently behind her.

John folded the piece of paper and put it in his pocket. "Well, I guess that's that. I'll be saving this as a reminder of our first victory!"

"You are ridiculous," Tasha said. "But I can appreciate the sentiment. That'll be nice to look back on one day."

"I think so, too. It'll go in my collection of rewards from here!"

Wyn stood up from the table and took one more roll from the platter. "That's a good note to end on. I'm going to train for a bit before calling it a day. See you guys in the morning." He walked over and grabbed his spear, following Marcy out.

"And on time, please!" Tasha emphasized to John, who was standing up to leave, too. "Bright and early, Climber!"

"Alright, alright, damn. Are you sure you weren't an officer in the war?"

Wyn laughed, and he knew Tasha was giving John a harsh look without even looking.

He had a good feeling about this month.

Wyn opened the door to his room with a shaky hand. He was surprised the floor only took the morning and early midday, and opted to train for several hours more. He practiced some spells and fighting on the dummies in the training hall, trying various combinations of things while allowing his mana to recover at the same time. He still didn't quite have a grasp for the timing of his recovery, but the exercise was helpful to see which spells he could cast with however much mana left, and being more familiar with the spells themselves was always helpful.

He stepped inside and set his spear against the wall, shedding his clothes and grabbing a cup of water. He was ready to turn in, wanting to rest for tomorrow. The books on the bookshelf Daniel provided goaded him into learning more, but he was physically too tired. He decided to crack one open tomorrow.

The window was open, but Wyn had no light in his room. He quickly lit a candle and looked out the window. It was cloudy and moving quickly, with lightning strikes lighting the sky in the distance. He hoped it would avoid Alestead, but then realized he wouldn't be in it, anyway. The tower has its own weather and environment.

He moved with his candle across the room. The desk beside his bed had a few sheets of paper, a quill and inkwell, and he sat at the stool with sore legs. Unfolding his pieces of parchment, he sat and reflected on the magic that was his class, skills, items, and spells.

Ardwyn Thatcher
Citizen of town Rywood
Resident of Jahnin
Tower Alistair: Climber
Class: Ruby Magician
Growth: Any
Passive Skills: Lucidity, Armored Spellcasting, Spellcasting (Ruby),
Tower's Blessing
Active Skills: Dyadcast, Speed Up

<u>SKILLS</u>

__Lucidity__: Allows passive recovery of mana. Your mark will show the current status of mana and is a guide to your expected amount of recovery time from empty to full. When your mark fully glows, you are empty and currently recovering. When your mark is dull and gray, you are full. Current time to fully recover: 3 hours.

__Dyadcast__: Allows you to cast a spell twice for only one and a half the mana cost. Speak the skill followed by the spell to engage the ability.

__Speed Up__: Increases your speed a bit temporarily. Speak the skill or mentally will it to activate. Costs a smaller amount of mana.

__Spellcasting (Ruby)__: Allows the use of spells. Ruby spells are selected from other classes at the cost of a lowered amount of spells, slightly higher mana consumption, and decreased overall mana capacity. You may select spells from the Sapphire, Garnet, Topaz, Amethyst, Emerald, Diamond, and Aquamarine Magician list only.

__Armored Spellcasting__: Wearing armor does not interfere with spellcasting. Passive skill and always active.

__Tower's Blessing__: A gift from the Avatar of Alistair. Provides one additional spell slot that may be used from any class at your tier that uses spells.

SPELLS

__Flamebolt__: A damaging spell that allows you to fire a small ball of fire in the direction you point. This has the ability to catch fire. Consumes a small amount of mana.

__Arcane Aura__: A protection spell that coats the user or target in a magical shield of armor. Currently provides basic protection that will last a short amount of time. Consumes a moderate amount of mana.

__Regen__: A healing spell that will heal the user or target over a period of time. Heals basic wounds, not able to cure diseases or remove poisons. Currently takes more time to heal and consumes a less moderate amount of mana.

__Magic Weapon__: A utility spell that coats a weapon in magic for a small amount of time, increasing damage, durability, and overall effectiveness. Consumes a less moderate amount of mana.

__Cure__: A healing spell that heals the target instantly. Heals basic wounds, not able to cure diseases or remove poisons. Currently consumes a less moderate amount of mana.

ITEMS

Windcutter—This magical spear possesses a hooked claw at the base and curved blade at the tip. Wind elemental magic runs throughout the weapon. Able to cast __Wingbeat__ three times per day.

**__Wingbeat__: fire a sharp slice of wind a medium distance.*

Mushroom Lantern—A handful of rare, luminescent mushrooms reside within this magical jar. When shaken, the mushrooms activate, shining bright in their own colors. Provides dim light up to sixty feet. Will stay active for one hour, may be shaken again immediately. Colors can change with each activation.

Wyn sighed. He didn't love his **Cure** spell as Tasha provided more than enough healing, but he was at a loss of what spell to actually take. Hopefully Daniel had some better insight into choosing a good spell. Wyn had decided to swap **Ice Shard** before the season, but that was his only change so far, unsure of how to proceed. This was still an entirely new experience, but relying on his mentor for advice was the best option for now.

Wyn folded up his parchments, closed his eyes, and grabbed one of the blank pieces of paper. It was unfolded but crinkly, and he flattened it further on the edge of the desk. He read it once more, trying to keep his eyes from getting misty reading his sister's words.

Arabelle. She was worried, and rightfully so.

She wrote him that their father's health was declining, that he recently fell and broke his ankle. He'd pushed himself harder on the farm from the injury though and wasn't doing well. Which meant he'd be worse to Arabelle than he already was, forcing her to pick up more around the farm than she was probably already doing. Hopefully the useless man didn't treat her any harsher than normal, which Wyn thought would be false hope.

Arabelle was worried about him and asked him to come home, to forget about the debt. He knew it was impossible to leave. It was frustrating, in a sense, how ignorant she was about the situation, but she was inside it, and he was seeing it from the outside. It's harder to notice when you're living it, and Wyn hadn't been living at home in years. He'd visited some but wrote constantly, keeping tabs on their land and his family, but he was still trying to live his own life. It was a strange dichotomy between becoming your own self and living how you're told.

Wyn wanted to correct his sister and tell her how serious this was, that he was helping them when they couldn't help themselves, and how things would get so much worse if they couldn't produce the funds for the debt. He didn't, though. The quill moved quickly on the paper, ink barely drying before he started a new word, a new sentence, a new paragraph.

He told her that he would continue getting them money for food, for supplies, and for their debt. He told her not to worry, that it wasn't so bad and they would make it just fine. He told her he would visit soon, that their debt was manageable.

He told her lies. This was to comfort her, and to encourage her to keep her head up and do whatever work she could do to help herself, their miserable father, and their land.

He told her he loved her, and that he would secure the funds to pay their debt and help them survive. That he'd find a way to get her away from this situation to be able to live her own life that their father was robbing from her. That he was always thinking about her.

He told her the truth. This was to comfort him and to give him the motivation to keep climbing Alistair to help her, their father, and their debt.

Wyn finished the letter in minutes. He signed it with his name and two drops of tears that ran their course down his cheeks.

He set the quill back in the inkwell, set the paper aside, and grabbed a sheet that was set to the side.

He took the quill and wrote his rewards for the day: 31 gold crowns, 19 silver cloaks, and 27 copper boots. He needed to keep climbing, to keep earning money for his family. Every day was a step forward, but he wanted to take leaps instead of steps.

"Don't worry, Arabelle. You'll be alright. I'll make sure of it."

Wyn withdrew for the night and slept in a deep sleep.

CHAPTER THIRTY-FOUR

Wyn saw Daniel eating by himself in the busy guild hall. Climbers were everywhere, tables full of groups readying themselves before they entered Alistair and the difficulties it would present to them. Wendy walked over and brought him a new pitcher, taking his old one off on her tray.

"May I join you?" Wyn asked his mentor, walking around him so he wouldn't startle the middle-aged man.

His face soured for a brief second then softened. "Of course, of course. Wendy will bring something out for you shortly." He took the pitcher and poured it into his mug. It was dark and hot and smelled earthy.

"Thank you, Daniel. How are you? It's been a couple of days since we've spoken." He grabbed a mug and poured himself some coffee, too. He decided to wait to let it cool as it warmed the mug almost instantly, content with his hands absorbing the heat and smelling the fragrant aroma.

Daniel grabbed a piece of bacon and ripped into it, void of manners. "I've been well, thank you! But I'm glad I saw you. I've been wanting to talk to you about what you saw in the tower on the second floor."

Wyn set his mug down on the table, wishing he had some food to eat so he could stall. Blowing on his hot cup would only get him so far. He knew Daniel would ask about it at some point, but he had other things on his mind for the morning. There were moments when he completely forgot about it and other times when it was the only thing that occupied his mind. Daniel probably felt the same way, though for likely different reasons.

As if on cue, Wendy appeared with a plate of breakfast. "Here's some food for you, dear! If you want something different let me know, okay?"

Wyn graciously grabbed the plate of food and set it on the table. "This is great, Wendy, thanks."

"Wendy! Refill, please!" a voice yelled across the hall. Wendy seemingly flew between the tables to the customer, nimble as could be.

Wyn began to coat a piece of bread with jam from a jar. He smirked, thinking about how lavish the food here was compared to the slop he ate in the service. If someone needed to prepare themselves for a day of training or climbing, this was certainly the type of food to keep the body going.

"I know it's a sensitive topic . . ." Daniel started, toying with more bacon.

"It's alright. We need to talk about it. Maybe another time, though, when I have more time and my head is a bit clearer?"

Daniel's eyes went wide, and he laughed once, obnoxious and loud like a chirp. "Oh of course, of course! You're climbing today! Yes, I'm sure you want to eat and meet your group. Silly me. Another time, then." He put the bacon down and grabbed a slice of bread, eating it in large chunks.

Wyn felt a pang of guilt. He didn't want to avoid the topic. He just didn't want to dwell on it now before climbing the tower. "I do need to meet them soon, but maybe we could have dinner to talk about it?"

Daniel swallowed his large bite of bread hard. "I'd like that. How about tomorrow night? I was going to go to the archives to research what you told the guild master. It would be good to have a better idea of what's going on, after all."

"That's a great idea. I was wondering if something like that was here in Alestead. I guess it's at the library?"

"Oh, yes! The archives are full of history around the tower and surrounding region, as well as uncovered magic, environments, and past seasons in the tower. It's not as vast as the mage college, mind you, but it's worth looking into since it's here. Some people swear there are patterns to how Alistair presents the new seasons and challenges, but nothing's been substantiated."

Wyn nodded along, not really caring about theories or research. Daniel obviously enjoyed it, though, so there was no sense in being rude. "I think it's absolutely worth looking into, too. Would you want me to come along?"

Daniel smiled. "No, no, you have other things to do. I'm here to be your mentor, and I believe this is how I can best serve at the moment. Let me worry about the boring research!" He took a long drink from his coffee.

"Why do I have the feeling it's not quite boring to you?"

Daniel barked a laugh again causing a Climber at the neighboring table to jump. "But I see you're not wearing your Ruby Magician cloak. Is it because of the new season?"

Wyn finished his jam-covered bread and moved on to the sliced sausage on his plate. It was absolutely delicious, but he knew he needed to be careful to avoid eating too much and throwing it all up like John did yesterday. "Yes, it's jungle themed. Humid, sticky air, and I just took it off right away. Too warm."

"Hmm." Daniel took another sip from his mug before he set it down on the table. "I was hearing rumors yesterday that that was the first tier. I believe it gets better in the second and third tiers, but you're not quite there yet, I'm afraid. Some Climbers are having problems with their heavy armor, having to rethink their strategy. It might end up being too late, but maybe you should have your cloak enchanted to be weather resistant? It's fairly common, you know. Unless you're looking for other magical items first, which is more than reasonable."

Wyn blinked and stopped just before taking a bite of sausage. "Huh. I didn't even think you could enchant items. I thought they had to be found in the tower."

"Oh no, my boy! You can use magical essence to magically enhance a mundane item. There are several steps and factors involved, but if you find some items in the tower you don't want or need, you can have them broken down into essence. There are classes out there that specialize in it as well, mostly Magicians or Sorcerers who leaned away from the perils of climbing and toward more mercantile professions."

"That's great information. Thank you again, Daniel. I'll be sure to think twice before I quickly get rid of them."

"It's what I'm here for—to help you grow and learn!" Daniel plucked a few grapes from his own platter and popped them into his mouth. "I'll grab a book or two for your shelf so you can read about the different properties and outcomes, too."

Wyn smiled awkwardly, grateful for his gesture, but thinking about the tedious act of reading textbooks. He made a mental note to ask Benedict about it when he would visit the market on their rest day. Surely he could help him, or point him in the right direction. Maybe the shopkeeper was a former Climber, too?

"Daniel, I keep hearing about more classes. I thought there were only five classes?"

"Ahh, that's a more advanced topic. When you clear the fourth floor of each tier, the fifth tier is a sort of rest and advancement floor. You'll get to choose an upgrade for your class that is presented by the tower. It's the only way Climbers could manage the third and fourth tiers, for example. They're far too dangerous to manage with only base classes."

"That makes sense. How far did you advance?"

Daniel stopped mid-bite of a grape. He swallowed it thoughtfully before answering. "I made it to the third tier and chose not to proceed any further. I still call myself a Ruby Magician because I chose an upgraded path that expands on the core of the base class, like an enhanced version. Climbers who want to be mentors or guides often go that route. Be cautious, though, Wyn, when those options are presented to you. Please consult me before you make a decision. As Ruby Magicians, there are far more potential options of upgrades than other classes. There's no telling what classes you'll be presented, and there are numerous books about class upgrade paths to be found."

Wyn rubbed his temples. There was a lot of information to still be learned about being a Climber, and he felt a headache coming on from Daniel. He knew there was magic and that it would be complicated when he came, but he started to doubt if he made the right decision jumping into climbing so quickly. Maybe taking his time to learn some of this would've been a better option.

No. That wasn't Wyn's style. Plus, he couldn't afford to wait weeks before making more coin. He made the right call. Learning on the fly was just going to have to be part of his experience these first few months.

"I appreciate you sharing that. It's a lot to think about, and we can definitely talk about it more tomorrow night."

Daniel smiled softly and nodded, taking another sip of his coffee.

Wyn finished his bite of sausage and reached into his pockets for some coin. He placed some cloaks and one crown on the table, then stood to leave for the tower. Daniel stood up to politely dismiss him and the two Ruby Magicians exchanged their goodbyes before parting.

Wyn felt his stomach turn when he was pulled through the portal, his breakfast churning inside him. He willed it to stay down, trying to not emulate John's situation yesterday.

When the group emerged back into the jungle they all took a second to compose themselves except for Marcy, who walked toward the jungle and began to orient herself. Her leather armor set was less bulky than her previous fur armor but covered a similar amount, and she moved gracefully and with purpose in the lighter set. There were likely other benefits to it, both magical and mundane, and Wyn was envious of her setup. Her leather headband held her auburn hair off her face, giving her more ability to see in her periphery as well as keep her head cool.

John coughed a few times and spat on the ground before breathing a sigh of relief. "Thank the gods breakfast stayed down this time." He shook his head and rubbed his stomach, patting it for thanks that it agreed with him.

Tasha walked over beside Marcy and stared into the thick jungle. "Whoa. This feels incredibly strange."

Marcy withdrew her kukri and nodded in agreement. "It definitely is. It's disorienting seeing the similar terrain and having memories of a specific path, but then it's laid out completely differently. Like a foggy memory that feels both right and wrong at the same time."

"That's exactly how I'm feeling. It's a wonder people don't get lost."

"Oh, they do. You just have to approach it like it's brand new, because that's exactly what it is. And tell yourself that it's *not* the same path as before. Over and over. It'll get easier the more you climb."

Wyn and John joined the women at the edge of the jungle. Wyn looked around now and tried to orient himself though found it hard. The leaves and thick brush looked the exact same, but the trees and layout itself were just . . . different. He couldn't wrap his head around it but trusted it would get better. It'd be easy to get lost, though, as his instincts told him to follow one path that wasn't the right way anymore.

John took a deep breath and drew his sword. "I'm just going to cut down whatever path you say. This is . . . strange."

Marcy smiled. "We've all been there. Try to see it as a new day, a new journey."

John walked up and slashed a tall, thin tree from the bottom. "Like a new jungle ready to be explored!"

"That's the spirit," Wyn said. He patted Tasha on the shoulder. "We'll be fine. It's the same challenge as yesterday, and we did great!"

Tasha sighed and used her staff as a walking stick to follow Marcy and John. "I know, I know. Let's just make it through."

"Find the river and make it past," John said. He looked back at Wyn, pausing from cutting through the thicket. "That's what Wyn is looking forward to most, after all!"

Wyn blanched, nearly forgetting about the river. He hated the thought of traversing it again in the canoes and instantly dreaded the experience.

It was necessary, though. He'd overcome his fear one way or another.

In what felt like half the time as before, they heard the sound of running water and made their way straight to it. Unfortunately they didn't find any canoes, but they knew they only had to walk the bank until they did find them.

John started humming a tune while they walked, thankful that he didn't have to clear brush on the riverbank. It was jolly and upbeat, and he whistled in certain parts when he didn't hum. Wyn recognized it right away. It was a common song bards would sing about merry times and adventuring guilds seeking fame and fortune. It was a popular song in the barracks and out in the field at war, a song to remind young soldiers out of their depth of far away happiness and hope in the midst of strife and stress.

During John's third iteration of the song, Wyn spotted something strange out of the corner of his eye. He stopped walking and looked back toward the jungle. It was a plant, much smaller than the foliage around it but still an impressive size, though what stood out most was that it was colored yellow and bloomed in a vertical spiral. He had never seen anything remotely similar to it.

"Wyn?" Tasha asked. "What is it?"

Wyn walked over to the plant and looked at it closer, bending down to inspect it. It had a faint magic shimmer to it. He couldn't believe it. It was magical.

Tasha snuck up beside him and put her face right beside his. "Whoa! That's beautiful!"

"And magical. I didn't know if we would find anything like this here, but here it is right in front of my eyes!"

"A plant? That's it?" John said, standing with his sword resting on his shoulder. "Boring!"

"Plants like that can be useful," Tasha said. "Alchemists or Herbalists can use them, you know. You could sell it for coin at least!"

Wyn reached low to the base of the stem and plucked it, trying to preserve as much of the entire flower as possible. "Thanks, Tasha. I'll find a use for it somehow, I'm sure."

"I wonder what it's called?" the Diamond Magician asked.

"I'm not sure. Maybe Marcy knows?"

"We always ask her everything. I'd like to figure things out on my own for once." Tasha walked back to the river's edge, following behind John.

Wyn understood her point and felt the same way. He appreciated Marcy's experience and expertise but didn't want to keep annoying her by asking questions all the time. He wanted to explore and learn the ins and outs of the tower on his own to the best of his ability.

He stopped again, struck with an idea. He pulled out the parchments from his pocket. Shuffling through the papers, he pulled out the one labeled **ITEMS**. He saw his dagger, his spear, and their descriptions, his leather armor, helmet, backpack and supplies, and now the flower.

Sun Spiral: a flower that grows in a spiral toward the sun. It gives off magical heat when in full bloom, deterring potential predators from eating it. It continues to grow throughout its life, and the heat is more intense the larger the flower.

Wyn smiled. "Huh. It's called a Sun Spiral, Tasha." He shuffled the papers again but noticed something different. There was more text on the main page. He looked at it and saw a new paragraph under the Quest description.

Secondary Quest: Sun Spirals are uncommon but not unheard of in the jungle. The magic society finds them very valuable, though they have been mysteriously disappearing in this area before being harvested. There have also been reports of an increase of weird sightings around patches of flowers, such as glowing eyes in the dark and large, reptilian footprints.

1/8 Sun Spirals

"Whoa," Wyn said. "That's new."

"What is it?" Tasha asked.

"I have a secondary quest. I didn't even know that was possible."

Tasha excitedly skipped over to Wyn to see his parchment. "I didn't either! Can I read it?"

"Sure. But I wonder if it applies to all of us or just me?"

Tasha's eyes grew wider as she read the description. She promptly pulled out her own parchment and gasped. "I have it, too! I can't believe it!"

Marcy stopped walking and wiped her brow, slinging sweat away from her onto the jungle floor. "What are you two going on about?"

"Marcy, did you know about secondary quests?" Tasha asked.

"I haven't heard of them before. What is it?"

"Look at your parchment!"

Marcy looked over at John, who already had his sword sheathed and parchment open. He was intently reading it, and he scrunched his face while trying to piece together the new information.

Wyn scanned the area to make sure no enemies were around but then thought that Marcy would've alerted them if there were. That was an old habit that wouldn't go away anytime soon. "So it's another quest within our main objective. My parchment says I have one out of eight, probably to finish the quest. Do you all have that, too?"

John nodded and folded his parchment before placing it back into a pouch at his side. "Yeah, it was the same for me. So we could find more flowers and finish another quest? But it doesn't help toward getting to the next floor."

"No," Wyn replied, "but it might offer the chance at getting more rewards."

"Which means more coin," Tasha added. "I wonder how hard it would be to find more?"

John sighed. "I don't know, but I'd rather keep pushing our main quest. Since we're deciding to go through this floor several more times I'd like to keep practicing at it. I still feel turned around."

"I'm with John," Marcy said. "No offense, but slogging through the first few floors sounds more like a chore than anything. The quicker we get to the next tier the better. And we'll get better gear and items as we climb."

Tasha looked at Wyn, who shook his head and put his parchment away. She slumped her shoulders. "Alright, alright. Then we keep going. But this is definitely something to look into further, especially since you aren't familiar with it, Marcy."

"I'm with Tasha on this," Wyn said. "If we find some flowers along the way then we'll grab them. Maybe we can finish it by the time we complete the floor. Otherwise, we can look at it more when we get back. Deal?"

John and Marcy relented before turning back to the brush ahead of them to continue their clearing.

"Deal," Tasha said. She picked up her staff and walked with a smile, more intrigued than before and curious about their new revelation. Wyn felt the same way. This new discovery could be an incredible resource for him. There could potentially be a lucrative opportunity in whatever these secondary quests held, and the more chances he had at making coin the better.

CHAPTER THIRTY-FIVE

John slammed his sword into his sheath before leaning back against a tree. He groaned and wiped the building sweat off his forehead with a lazy arm. The sun was beating down in various patches within the jungle, and the foliage only served to contain the warmed air instead of cooling it off.

"I can't express how badly I want to get out of this jungle," John said. He drained his waterskin before throwing it back into his backpack. "And now I'm out of water. Perfect."

Marcy stood beside him on the tree also leaning against it. "You need to get some magical armor. That gambeson isn't helping cool you at all. I don't know how you're functioning in that."

"I know. But chainmail is a bit too heavy for me to use comfortably, and leather armor is too light. I think I'd rather have new armor at this point than my new sword. If we can just progress to the next floor, hopefully we can get out of this hotbox."

Marcy laughed. "I have a feeling the next floor will also be hot, so you'll need to rethink that strategy."

John groaned even louder than before, then sat on the ground to rest. "Great. You're probably right! But what in the hells is taking them so long?"

"Wyn! Tasha! Hurry up!" Marcy yelled into the forest. She also took a long drink from her own waterskin before offering it to John. "Here. It's enchanted to refill over time and stay cold."

John's eyes lit up as he graciously took the leather waterskin. He drank a seemingly endless amount and poured some over his head when his mouth had had enough.

"Almost done!" Tasha yelled back from behind a large bush. She reached down and plucked a large flower while shielding her face from the flower's heat. They felt like miniature torches without giving off a flame. Her back was hot and sweaty from the other flowers she stored in her backpack. "I think this was the last one! Wyn, did you get all of yours?"

Wyn put away his waterskin after both quenching his thirst and cooling his head. He had removed his helmet hours ago, though his hair was still wet from both sweat and water where he had attempted to cool himself off not long ago.

Despite John's and Marcy's desire to finish the floor quickly, Wyn and Tasha convinced them to complete the side quest of gathering Sun Spirals before they fought the final lizard enemies. Their curiosity about the rewards gained from finishing the side quest was just too great, and the heat and energy expenditure of clearing thick brush finally broke down both John and Marcy to take an extended break. John and Marcy were also wondering about finishing the quest, but their desire to escape the heat far exceeded their interest in flowers that were named after the sun.

Wyn was searching through thick brush with Tasha just outside the clearing that they determined held the final enemies before the floor's portal. Both of them wanted one final opportunity to find the flowers, and they were elated to find a patch of several of them this late in the floor. Wyn was developing a theory that they were more abundant deeper into the floor and jungle overall, and would see if he was right if the second floor was still jungle terrain and held more flowers.

After what felt like hours in the heat, Wyn spotted the eighth and final flower he needed to fulfill the quest in a matter of minutes. "I see my last one! I'm nearly finished!" Just as he had been doing, he used his helmet to block his face from the intense heat of the Sun Spiral before plucking it and adding it to his backpack. He was ready to dispose of them so his back would cool off, though the thought that each of them were potentially worth more coins helped convince himself to deal with the heat they exuded.

Either way he was happy to be finished, and rejoined Tasha with the others with a full but hot pack.

"Finally!" John said, throwing his hands in the air in celebration. "Can we get through the floor already? I don't even think I want to climb again today. I just want a cold bath and a cold drink."

"Yes, we can finish now," Wyn said. "Even though you aren't the one holding the little fires like me and Tasha. I can barely stand it."

"I know," Tasha agreed. "I'm going to be mad if the reward is puny."

"I have a hunch it'll be worth it," Wyn said. "But John's right, let's finish out. I'm curious to see what the reward will be, too."

The group readied themselves before quickly entering the final clearing. Just like yesterday, they immediately spotted two of the large lizard monsters that separated them from the portal that would take them back to the base. Unlike yesterday, there was no group already engaged with them to make the fight even more complicated.

"Just like before?" Tasha asked. She held her staff with more confidence and a steadier hand than her last two climbs.

"Just like before," John answered with a malicious grin. "I'm ready to—"

"**Windstrike**!" Marcy said, cutting John off. A series of runes appeared in the air in front of her arrow, and she released the arrow as the spell was cast.

It flew with blinding speed between the group of Climbers as a small gust of wind rippled in the path of the arrow. All three of the rookies covered their faces from the aftermath but still tried to peek at the trajectory of the attack.

One of the large lizards faced them after hearing Marcy cast the spell, and right as it turned the arrow struck it directly in its chest. The impact caused a crater to form in its chest as though a huge rock was launched into it by a catapult. The wind element showed its power over the monster's earth element, and it was knocked backward onto the ground with a hole in its body so large it was nearly bisected.

It lay still, obviously dead from the Ranger's attack.

The three Climbers slowly turned to look at Marcy, their eyes wide and mouths open in surprise.

Marcy furrowed her brow. "What? I'm just as ready to be done as you! It's too damn hot here!"

The others looked at each other with amazement. They still didn't know the actual power Marcy possessed, and she kept letting small glimpses appear like this attack. It reinvigorated their drive to push on and advance, and they all pushed toward the lone giant standing before the portal.

Wyn had all of his mana remaining as they barely spent any of their resources on this climb, not to mention the recovery time from him and Tasha collecting the Sun Spirals. If only one more obstacle stood in their way, he figured he could be more liberal with his magical energy.

"John," Wyn said. "Let's see how quickly we can take the other one out!"

John smiled. "What do you propose?"

Wyn held his hand out toward John's sword. "**Magic Weapon**," he said, casting his spell. White light instantly began to glow from John's mundane sword.

John simply nodded. "**Focus**," he said, as a red aura enveloped his body. He breathed in deep, then out with a hefty force before launching himself toward the final enemy. His empowered body shot him forward with large steps that covered the distance much quicker than a normal person.

Wyn opted to let his friend take the lead in direct combat and would support him when possible with his spear. He didn't want to get in John's way or be a liability, and he could help survey both their fight and the battlefield as a whole by keeping a perceptive watch.

A loud thud interrupted Wyn's thoughts as the other lizard monster fell, its lifeless body smacking the ground. He blinked a few times trying to process what happened, wondering if Marcy ended the fight early again.

John wildly yelled into the air in victory, pumping his magically radiating and bloody sword into the air over and over.

"What happened?" Wyn asked. "That took no time at all!"

"I feel invincible!" John replied, screaming into the air. "It was much easier with a proper magical weapon!"

"I don't remember you taking care of the wolves and spiders so easily last week!"

John laughed. "I didn't use skills then! Not to mention my style is more suited to big dumb beasts like this guy."

The two large lizard bodies began to dissolve, though nothing was left from their corpses. The portal they guarded immediately turned gray, signaling their success yet again at completing the first floor.

"That was fast," Tasha said. She and Marcy joined them while John calmed down.

"Not as fast as me, but still impressive," Marcy said. "You have a good technique."

Wyn was happy for his friend and teammate at his success, but upset he missed the brief fight. He didn't even know what techniques John used.

"I guess all my training paid off," John said. He sheathed his sword and started walking toward the portal. "Though I'd like my sword already so I don't have to rely on that spell. No offense, Wyn."

"None taken," Wyn replied. "If it'll free up another spell for me to use, I'm all for it. I've been thinking about some others to use for the second floor, anyway."

John stopped walking and quickly turned around to Wyn. "Does that mean you're open to going to the second floor already?"

Wyn looked at Tasha and Marcy, who both shrugged as though they had no say in the matter. "Well, that did go much better than planned, but I'd like a few more magical items before we climb the second floor. Or at least another key or two."

"Like trading our one magical item we got on Faesday for our first climb?" Tasha asked. "Weren't we going to go to the markets on Torday to trade them for something better?"

"Maybe we can go tomorrow morning instead and make that our day off," Wyn said. "Or even this afternoon if we want. Test them, practice with them, then aim for the second floor on Faesday?"

John clapped his hands together. "I love it! Even though I won't have my sword by then, I say we go for it!"

"About time we moved on!" Marcy added. "But let's finish this back at the base. It's still too damn hot."

John shook his parchment at the guild official like a banker trying to collect payment. He was itching to get the rewards for their climb, hoping that his performance at the final boss was enough to help get him a few more gold crowns. The official brought out their signature orange glowing chest that magically gave out the rewards from the tower. The others were waiting at the desk, too, eager for their own rewards but listening to John as his was brought out first.

"Alright, here you are, sir," the woman said with a smile. She flipped open the chest and began reading John's earnings from his parchment. "You earned 51 gold crowns, 36 silver cloaks, and 12 copper boots for coins. You found a Lacert Tooth and Lacert Claw, both green rarity crafting components. Congratulations!" She stood awkwardly beside the chest for a moment while the Climbers stared at her. "Oh, right!" Her cheeks flushed red as she reached into the chest to procure John's coins for him.

John smiled. "That was more than last time, *and* the climb was easier. This is great!" He rubbed his hands together while the official finished gathering his coins, eager to pocket them.

"Here you go," another guild official said. He placed an identical orange glowing chest onto the desk in front of Tasha.

Wyn suddenly wondered how many chests the guild possessed to give out rewards to Climbers and if it took any special magic to open and pull items out of them, or if it was purely a business protocol that only guild officials could manage them. Regardless, the magical portals of coins and rewards opened for Tasha, and they were all surprised at the result. The most surprised, however, was the guild official.

He originally had a nearly blank stare and emotionless face, just there to do a job rather than having a passion for the work. When he read Tasha's parchment, though, his eyes shot open, and he audibly gasped. The change of demeanor immediately caught the attention of the four Climbers, and they wondered what made him react like that.

"Is something wrong?" Tasha asked.

"No, ma'am," the guild official responded. "You just completed a secondary quest section and rewards! It's the first time I've actually seen it!"

"You're kidding!" John replied. "How is that possible? Are you a new employee?"

The official yanked his head toward John with a disgusted look. "I've worked here for nearly eight seasons, thank you very much. This was a new discovery this season, and we are still as surprised as the Climbers to see it in person!"

"A new discovery? Like the class advancements a couple of years ago?" Marcy asked.

"Yes, exactly," the guild official responded. "We are noticing an increasing amount of new things Alistair is giving to us recently. It just so happens one of the top Climbers discovered the incident of these side quests on Solday, which were never part of the tower before. Now, though, more and more Climbers are finding out about them."

"Are they on every floor?" Tasha asked.

"Not that we've seen. But the rewards are impressive, even for the basic tasks like yours."

Tasha stood there shocked, a large smile quickly forming on her face. "Well, show me, then! What did I get?"

The guild official opened the chest on the desk and flattened her parchment beside it. "For completing the first floor, you are rewarded 38 gold crowns, 44 silver cloaks, and 8 copper boots. For completing the secondary quest, you are rewarded 25 gold crowns and 8 Sun Spirals, which are green rarity herbs. Congratulations!"

John's jaw dropped as Tasha yipped with excitement. "Wow!" Tasha said. "That's nearly as much as completing the floor itself!"

"I'll say," John said. "You were right. I'd say that was definitely worth it!"

Wyn was just as elated as Tasha. The reward was impressive, just as the guild official said. It wasn't quite as much as completing the floor, but accomplishing both was nearly as good as completing the floor twice in a day. The payoff for the amount of work needed was enormous, and it didn't require him to risk his safety in combat. He instantly wondered about secondary quests on other floors and the rewards they offered.

It also solidified the fact that climbing higher would obviously yield more rewards for the effort and danger. Sure, anyone could stay on the first several floors and clear them several times each day for an impressive amount of coin that couldn't be guaranteed elsewhere in the world. That process, however, would be both boring and less efficient than climbing higher floors for better rewards. It would be safer, but Wyn couldn't exactly afford the safest option.

While the guild official took Wyn's parchment and began to tally his earned coins, he began to do some math in his head. If he cleared the first floor twice in a day and completed the secondary quest each time, he could net over 100 gold crowns easily. It would be monotonous but safe. If he did that every day, it would also be exhausting, and the risk of failing by getting hurt or dying goes up when a person is exhausted in this line of work. Doing that every day for a month? He'd make well over 3000 gold crowns, and anyone could find themselves rich doing that for a year if the other seasons had similar secondary quests.

It was nowhere near what he needed, though. Wyn knew he needed to clear nearly 13,000 gold crowns a month to pay back his family's debt by the year's end. He wasn't foolish enough to believe he could make that his first month, and hoped to find a way to submit some form of deposit or good will to his debtors initially before making up the sum later. At his current rate, he was looking at more of about half of that if he pushed himself and sold off some items.

Interrupting his thoughts, the guild official slid his earned coins across the desk, where Wyn promptly stashed them into his new coin pouch. It was obviously magical, and he was incredibly thankful for it—the stack of additional coins added no more weight or substance to it, as it held them inside a magical plane of existence. Or at least that's what the description on his parchment read, and he found out it was true when he was able to magically procure any coin he possessed by simply reaching into it and thinking of the coin he wanted. It didn't have the ability to hold anything else, but it was still an impressive piece of equipment.

"So what now?" John asked. He hoisted his shield onto his back over his backpack and stretched at the new weight. "Are we wanting to go back into the tower this afternoon or something else?"

Marcy groaned, throwing her head back and slumping her shoulders. "I'm normally all for climbing the tower, but damn this first floor is rough. I don't think I can go back unless we clear the first floor to move on to the second floor. It's just too hot for me, even with my lighter gear."

"This is really affecting you," Wyn said. "Haven't you had something like this in one of the other seasons you've climbed?"

"Not at all. I can stand colder weather—and my first season a few months ago had us literally climb a mountain in a cold climate—but this heat is frustrating me. I'm sorry."

"My mentor mentioned something about enchanting your armor to be weather resistant. Do you have something that can ward off heat?"

Marcy smacked herself in the forehead. "By the gods—no, but I know Cedric does. I'll see if he'll let me borrow it. My mind has been everywhere lately."

The group all looked at each other. "Will he let us see him?" Wyn asked.

Marcy sighed. "Not yet. He's still pretty shaken up. If nothing else, he values his privacy."

"I understand. I don't want to be disrespectful. If anything, I'd like to thank him and actually pay my respects."

"I know. In fact, I'll go see him this afternoon. I'll ask about the cloak he has and if you all can come see him."

The rookies all visibly brightened. They each wanted to see Cedric but Wyn had more personal reasons than the others. He did save the Wizard's life, after all, even if it meant for Cedric to lose an arm.

"That leaves us three, then," John said.

"Instead of climbing, why don't we go finalize our gear?" Wyn asked. "We can try to trade the items we earned on Faesday and see if these Sun Spirals can get us anything, too. I've been wanting to see the trading district anyway."

Tasha clapped her hands. "That's a great idea! We might not have enough worth to trade, but I'd like to try."

"It's definitely worth trying," Wyn said. "If we can't trade it, we'll head to The Silver Step and see Benedict."

"I like it," John said. "Off to the markets for our first trade!"

Wyn smiled. He was told the trading district was a high-energy and highly magical place as Climbers and merchants both tried to trade gear or advertise themselves. Getting better items could make the difference between giving them an edge over the lower floors as their basic items were rapidly becoming less useful. He had to sacrifice another climb or two in the meantime, but that was a necessary sacrifice. Better equipment could mean a faster improvement in the tower *and* better rewards to boot.

Wyn had a new goal in his mind for him and his group. They'd succeed in the first tier and advance the entire five floors, ready to tackle the second tier for next month. It was fast progress, but urgency still motivated him.

He'd get his gold as quickly as possible. Arabelle just had to hold on.

CHAPTER THIRTY-SIX

Wyn and Tasha stood by the auction house doors impatiently waiting for John. They all agreed to have lunch and grab the items they wanted to trade before meeting in the trade district, though John was unsurprisingly late.

"I swear, no one is worse than him at being on time," Tasha said. Her arms were folded, and she kept pacing a small distance, huffing with deep sighs every few minutes. "Is it really that hard to be punctual?"

Wyn could only smile. He was a bit more patient than Tasha, enjoying the warm early summer air and still marveling at the city. "For some, yes. There was one man in my company who always slept in, was always the last to meetings, and always had to be reminded about times for everything."

"Really? You'd think being in the military would force you to have more initiative. Did you whip him into shape? Scold him? Make him clean the floors and dirty dishes?"

Wyn shook his head. "No, I let him get away with it. He was never *that* late, and the other soldiers always gave him enough friendly grief about it. It kept morale up and gave them all something to laugh at. I didn't think he needed his commanding officer to rip into him and disrupt that."

Tasha stopped pacing. "That's very kind of you, Wyn. I'm sure other officers in your position would've enjoyed having the excuse to put him in his place."

"Probably. But being at war, I didn't want any of us to have another reason to loathe our situation. I'd rather have the respect than resentment."

Tasha took another deep sigh. "I guess you're right. It's not always fair, and it's not like we're pressed on time."

As though on cue, they both spotted John walking up to the trading district. He was looking down on the ground and walking slow.

Wyn immediately thought something was wrong. Normally John was jovial and energetic, but now he seemed down in the dumps. Tasha must've picked up on it, too, because she shifted her posture and her face softened, looking worried more than upset.

"What is it?" Tasha asked John. "Are you okay?"

"I'm not getting my sword from home," John said, his head still lowered facing the ground.

"Really?" Wyn asked. "Why not?"

John managed a deep sigh. "My sister wrote back to me. She was upset I lost her sword and told me I needed to earn my next one. *And* to bring her a sword back to replace the one she let me borrow!"

"Oh, John, I'm so sorry," Tasha said. She placed a hand on his shoulder.

"Even the word from the Tower Master didn't help! But what am I going to do now? I was relying on that sword. Now I have nothing."

Wyn pointed to the markets behind them with his thumb. "Good thing we're in a place where we can find you a new one. We can pool our items together for one if we find a good deal."

John waved his hands across his body. "No way. I'm not going to ask you to trade for me a sword."

"John, remember what Wyn told me in the Silver Step?" Tasha asked. "We're a team. You having a magic sword will help push us forward, so that's what we look for. Plus, the item I earned from our first climb doesn't fit me, anyway."

"Me, too," Wyn added. "I was looking to trade the belt I have. If it means getting you a better sword I'm all for it."

John smiled his usual warm, inviting smile. "Alright. I trust you guys. I'm just pissed about losing my sword to Lionel, but thanks." He instantly brightened a bit and hugged both of them before stepping forward to the trading district. When he opened the door to the markets, it was as though they opened a portal to a hub deep in the city.

Wyn remembered once helping guard a nobleman's family for an event at their estate. It was an auction of expensive artifacts and items, some even magical, coming from the towers around the world. His company was hired to provide security services for the many royals attending the event, and he thought about how proper the affair was while priceless magical items were exchanged before their very eyes.

Standing here in the markets within the Alestead trading district he felt a very different atmosphere despite a similarly impressive situation.

There were Climbers littered across the many tall tables in the open lobby, and chaos was as close to a descriptive word as Wyn could find. Loud conversations, occasional shouts, frantic hand waving, and even displays of magic all scattered around the large hall. It looked like an auction house but five times larger. Individual areas were being used to trade items, and the rookies had no idea where to even start.

Wyn was intimidated by the Climbers and their gear as they looked even more menacing than the ones he saw during the festival just a few days ago. It looked

as though they had slain great beasts in the tower and immediately came to bar-
ter and trade afterward. Large weapons and blood splattered armor covered the
various people in the crowd.

Thankfully for the inexperienced Climbers, a row of desks lined the back wall,
and guild officials were waiting on standby to assist Climbers as needed. The group
worked their way through the crowd toward the guild members, hoping to find
some direction.

"First time in the house?" the guild official asked, raising his voice to be
heard over the noise. He had a smirk on his face and leaned on his elbows on the
desk.

"That obvious?" Wyn asked.

The man laughed, but they all saw it rather than heard it. He laughed like Cal
more with his body than his voice. "You first time Climbers always have the same
bewildered look on your faces. But it's alright. You'll be at the tables arguing and
trading in no time!"

Tasha leaned in toward the official and scrunched her face, cupping her hand
over her ear. "What did you say?"

"I said, welcome to the trading house! How can I help you?"

Wyn and John couldn't suppress their laughter. Tasha obviously had no idea
what he actually said and continued on none the wiser.

"We're looking for some items," Wyn said.

"Is it always this loud?" Tasha asked.

"Mostly at the start and end of the floor cycle," the official said. "Are you looking for items directly or from the logs?"

"The what?" Tasha yelled.

The man held up a finger without another word. He reached behind the
desk and pulled out a large book. It was easily the largest book Wyn had ever
seen, and very obviously magical. The cover was leather with stacks of tiny
runes lining the edges, and they all briefly glowed at random times. It looked
like miniature lights randomly flickering on and off. The spine was thick with
more runes, as it needed to be thick and powerful to hold the hundreds, possibly thousands of pages inside. Wyn instantly assumed that the book was from
the tower, but how something that massive could be found was beyond his
understanding.

A sudden shout erupted from behind them. Two men squared up to each other,
yelling about some trade. They looked like they were about to begin fighting while
other Climbers in the house either cheered them on or yelled at them to stop. The
place somehow became even more chaotic than before.

Instantly a large, visibly magical barrier appeared around the two separating
them from the crowd. The space inside the barrier began to shrink, causing both
of the men to fall to their knees as though commanded by their king to bow. The

crowd hushed. Another guild official, a woman dressed in their similar attire but carrying both a clipboard and sense of purpose, calmly walked to the troublemakers.

The crowd moved to give her room to walk without any instruction. Her power was purely the gravitas she carried, let alone whatever actual power she possessed. Wyn knew she was someone important as the other Climbers seemed to know her.

"Don't worry about that," the man with the log book said. He didn't need to raise his voice anymore as the trade house was much quieter. "Unfortunately it happens a lot. But what kind of item are you looking for?"

The three Climbers did their best to ignore the situation behind them and focus. John kept staring, though, curious as to the outcome. The woman was muttering something to the Climbers in the barrier, who were still on their knees. It looked as though the barrier was pressing some form of magical weight on them, as though it took every bit of their strength to even stay on their knees instead of being pushed to the floor. The crowd around them made it hard for him to see or hear what was fully happening.

"We're looking for a magical sword, preferably a blue rarity one," Wyn said. "We have some green rarity items to trade for it. Are we allowed to trade several items for one?"

The man smirked again. "You can attempt to trade for anything! It solely depends on if anyone will accept it. I'm merely a middle-man. But let's sort by blue rarity swords first." He opened the book with a heave, and then the magic began. The pages began turning by themselves, quickly fluttering by blocks of pages.

Both Wyn and Tasha were mesmerized. They knew magic was intertwined with a fair amount of things in life, especially in the noble courts, but here in Alestead it seemed as though magic was part of literally everything.

In seconds the book fell to an open page. Some words on the page were glowing, and they were all a blue aura.

"Here we go," the guild official said. "Blue aura swords offered for trade. Would you like to peruse through them to try to find one you like?"

"Sure!" Tasha said. She quickly grabbed the book and began sorting through the lines of description with her finger.

Wyn read the lines along with her. Each one held the name of a sword and a brief description of its effects, and the name glowed blue signifying its rarity. After the description was the name and class of the owner, followed by a short summary of what the seller was seeking for trade.

"John, do any of these catch your eye?" Wyn asked. He turned to see John still watching the group behind them. "John?" Wyn shook John's shoulders.

"Hmm?" he responded. "Oh, sorry. What?"

Tasha sighed. "Always distracted. Can you look and see if there is a sword you'd want? There're so many!"

John's eyes grew wide seeing the magical lines of text. "Wow. All of these are blue rarity swords, I'm assuming?"

"If you were paying attention, you'd know the answer to that," Tasha said.

Wyn smiled. Tasha may have been timid in the tower and in combat, but she was definitely not shy when it came to manners and social etiquette. That was her familiar battleground, always confident and reliable. She likely had more experience in that area than both of the men put together.

The new Climbers took several minutes to debate and search for different swords John would find useful that they could potentially trade for. They discussed swords that cast spells, swords that enhanced skills and martial abilities, and even swords that changed their physical makeup to grow longer or wider. John had a hard time deciding on the magical components.

One in particular caught Wyn's eye, and it wasn't because of the sword itself but rather what the seller wanted in exchange. The summary said they wanted 25 Sun Spirals in exchange for a blue rarity sword. Other offers asked for two or three green rarity pieces of equipment, but this was the only description Wyn noticed that asked for a green rarity item that was not a piece of armor, clothing, or weapon.

"Look at this," Wyn said. He pointed to the line with his finger. "This is the first offer I've seen like this."

"And the sword is pretty good, too," John said. "The name is _Sword of the Elementalist_. It says it can change its sword to become any element. That's incredible!"

"The owner's name is Cara, class Sorcerer," Tasha said. "So how do we find Cara? Or make the deal?"

"We can help locate the owner to negotiate," the guild official said. He was idly standing by while they waited to decide. "Her name is glowing which means she's here in the trade house. I'll find her and point you in her direction."

John fidgeted with his backpack. "It said we need 25 of those flowers. How many do we have?"

"Both Tasha and I have 8," Wyn said. "So we're short. But let's at least talk to her to see if she'll accept another item or something similar."

John nodded, satisfied with the answer.

"Here we go," the man said. "She's at a back table. Follow me, please."

The guild official raised a portion of the desk on a hinge that allowed him to walk through. He led the three Climbers through the crowd to a table that was more isolated. The crowd began to grow loud again, though the auction house was large enough that the area they were heading into was more spread out with tables. There were far fewer Climbers here, too, as it seemed to be less of an active and volatile trading area and more relaxed or professional.

A woman sat at a table by herself reading a large book. She was wearing a tall brimmed black hat and a black mage's robe with many pockets with gold ornate trimmings on everything. She was obviously a well-seasoned Climber.

"This is Cara," the guild official said. "Cara, here are some potential buyers for one of your trades." The man bowed to both parties and promptly returned to the desk.

Cara kept reading her book and didn't even acknowledge the trio. They all looked at each other, then John shrugged.

Tasha cleared her throat. "Excuse me—"

"Yes, yes," Cara said, cutting Tasha off. She kept reading her book, her eyes not leaving the pages. "You're here for the *Sword of the Elementalist*. Do you have the Sun Spirals?"

Tasha blanched, taken aback. "Umm, yes, that's right. How did you know that?"

Cara sighed. "Don't ask stupid questions, girl. It's unbecoming."

Tasha's face quickly turned red, and she opened her mouth to respond, but Wyn put a hand on her shoulder.

"Let's get back to the matter at hand," Wyn said. "Obviously you're busy. Why are you looking for Sun Spirals?"

Cara looked up at Wyn and then scanned each of them. Her eyes darted from head to toe, randomly and without any pattern. "Sun Spirals are a new herb found in the tower. I'm wanting to continue to research them. Plain and simple."

Tasha seemed to relax a bit. She looked at Wyn, who nodded back. She knew she couldn't take offense—this wasn't a test of politeness or formalities, but a business exchange, pure and simple. She readjusted her robes and held her head high.

Tasha pulled out the flowers from her backpack and held them. "We have 16 Sun Spirals right now, but—"

"Then you don't have enough," Cara said. "Goodbye." She returned to her book and flipped the page she was reading.

Tasha didn't move. "We can get you another 16 by tonight, totaling 32. If you guarantee us the sword now."

Cara stopped reading and looked back at Tasha. The boys looked at each other, their eyebrows raised. Tasha apparently had some gumption for bartering, too.

"That's an interesting offer," the Sorcerer replied. She closed her book with a loud thud and crossed her legs. "32 green rarity items for one blue rarity item doesn't seem like too good of a deal. For you, at least."

"These flowers aren't much use to us at the moment, but the sword is."

Cara laughed. "So you want the sword for your Fighter. That's obvious. However, I'm guessing you don't know the flower's true power, do you?"

Tasha stood still, determined to appear like she wasn't completely inexperienced in matters regarding magic and climbing. Cara was playing along, though, much more interested than before.

"Honestly, no, I don't," Tasha replied. "But if it doesn't help me now, why should I care that much? I'd rather have an item that can help me live and climb for today, than something that *might* help me tomorrow, when no tomorrow is guaranteed."

Cara stopped smiling and stood up. She stepped around the table and faced Tasha directly, intimidating them by her sheer height alone. She stood taller than Wyn and John, though the boots she wore also had high heels, betraying her actual height. The Climbers thought that Tasha might've said something wrong, offending the Sorcerer. Wyn's heart raced, thinking they just blew their chances when Tasha was gaining ground in the conversation.

"You're wiser than most rookies, Mage. That mindset will carry you far." She reached into a pocket on her robe and pulled out the hilt of a sword. The weapon continued to elongate out of the seemingly endless pocket before completely revealing itself. The sheath was basic and unmarked, but when Cara drew the sword it had a brilliantly mirrored sheen to the blade. If he didn't know any better, it looked more suited to decoration than fighting.

Wyn recognized the sword's style. It wasn't a traditional longsword but rather a broadsword, possessing a slightly wider blade closer to the hilt that became more pointed toward the tip. It was more commonly used to slash with the wide blade, but it was still a popular style of sword. The entire weapon from pommel to tip was beautiful, though, and John's jaw dropped when he saw it.

"This sword is blue rarity because it can become any element you wish," Cara said. She turned the sword over and showed them the hilt. It appeared to have a socket directly where the hilt overlaid the blade, though it was currently empty. "If you place a gemstone in the hilt and infuse a bit of your mana into it, it will become the element that represents the gemstone. The elemental magic will be stronger based on the clarity and rarity of the gemstone. With some limitations, of course. You can read the full descriptions on your parchment." She handed the sword out to John who hesitated before grabbing it.

"Go ahead," Cara said. "You have a deal."

John now excitedly grabbed it, inspecting every inch the moment it was in his hands. Wyn knew he was now tuned out of the rest of their conversation, too.

"Meet me here at nine tonight," Cara added. "You have until then to bring the rest of the Sun Spirals. Or I will get that sword back, one way or another."

Tasha put her hand out. "We accept the deal and will meet you tonight."

"This is better than I could have hoped for!" John said, hugging the sheathed sword. "What monster did you kill for it? Was it the boss on floor nine? Or from a group of champions? In an ancient temple, or maybe a secret underground cavern?"

Cara let go of Tasha's hand after shaking it and smiled a wickedly sharp smile. "I didn't find that sword. I made it."

CHAPTER THIRTY-SEVEN

The three Climbers had one more stop before they returned to the tower. After John finished admiring his new weapon, Cara gave him the matching sheath along with more information. The elemental properties of the sword were activated via mana using an ability called ***Elemental Shift***. According to John's parchment, all he had to do was infuse his mana into the weapon while it contained a gemstone similar to his skills. It only took a small amount of mana, and the blade literally changed properties to mimic the gemstone. It could stay like that for an hour before he needed to infuse it again, though he was confident he wouldn't have an issue between keeping the elemental property active and using his other skills. He didn't need to keep it active all the time, either.

The group also decided to purchase a portal key at the Silver Step before going back inside Alistair so they could promptly leave the tower at any time. John also wanted to be included on the rewards this time, opting to gather flowers, too, to also complete the secondary quest. They realized the Sun Spirals held some value after Cara wanted a bunch of them and felt they would be useful to sell. They didn't have the crafting ability the Sorcerer had, but they could always use the money, especially Wyn.

John also brought up an interesting point as they were nearing Alistair.

"I think we'll be fine if we decide to peek at the second floor," the Fighter said. "If we're going to use a key to portal out of the floor, why not see what the second floor looks like first? If we don't like it we can just leave right away. No harm done!"

Both Wyn and Tasha had reservations about going to the second floor with just the three of them. They were arguing about even finishing the first floor since Marcy wasn't with them, but John was making a compelling point that they had had no trouble so far, and his new sword gave them both offensive power and confidence.

They entered the base of Alistair and watched the various groups enter and exit, still working in and out of the tower in the early afternoon. They stood there with their gear, not entirely sure of themselves with their three-person party. All three of them thought the same thing, though they didn't speak it. Not at first.

Wyn finally broke the silence of them watching other Climbers and waiting. "Maybe we should group up with another team for this afternoon?"

Tasha and John didn't immediately disagree with him, and he knew it was because they agreed instead. They just didn't want to outright admit it.

"Hey!" a voice said from behind them. "Red Mage!"

The group turned around. Wyn's heart skipped a beat as he was obviously being called out. Someone either recognized him or guessed he was a Ruby Magician, and he wasn't too keen on either option. How they'd guess his class was beyond him.

Three Climbers pushed through the crowd all looking a bit worse for wear. They were headed straight for Wyn, intent in their eyes.

Wyn immediately recognized them as part of the group they saved in the tower yesterday. It was Devon the Rogue, Maven the Diamond Mage, and the Garnet Magician, though he couldn't remember his name.

John and Tasha softened a bit seeing them. "Hey guys," Tasha said. "I see you've been climbing. Did you find someone to lead you?"

"Not exactly," Devon said. "I decided to lead us instead. Travis decided to take a couple of weeks to train more, so he left, but we wanted to keep climbing. But damn if the tower isn't hard for a smaller group! We've barely been scraping by on the first floor."

John smiled. "We understand that! But luck seems to be on our side today. Were you all going to go inside again for the afternoon?"

The other group looked at each hesitantly. "We were, yes," Maven said. "We really want to get better to clear a few more floors this season."

"Right, and we need the practice," the Rogue added. He flashed a sleek, dark gray short sword for them to see. "I just got a new weapon, too, so I'm eager to try it out."

John laughed, taking the Climbers by surprise. "Well, fortune really is shining on us today! We only have three members are looking to climb one more time. Should we party together?"

The other group collectively breathed a sigh of relief. "I think that would be great," Maven said. "Having two healers would take the burden off me. I still don't think I'm reacting as fast or as well as I need to."

"We'll see how much we'll be needed," Tasha said. "I didn't have to heal us this morning. It was a bit boring, to be honest."

The Garnet Magician gasped. "You're kidding! I nearly used all my mana just trying to kill those lizard things!"

"I think we'll manage fine," Wyn said. "Weren't there more of you, though? Besides Travis, I mean."

Devon deflated a bit. "Yea, but he left our group, frustrated with how we're doing. I'm worried Travis might do the same. So it's just us now."

Wyn looked at his friends, who just nodded. "Well, you have us for now. So why don't we discuss strategy while we head in?"

All of the Climbers walked and talked, eager to share their abilities. Well, the other group did, at least, hoping to establish a bit more confidence in the more successful team of Wyn, Tasha, and John. The Garnet Magician, William, completely used offensive fire-based spells, though had trouble both aiming and timing them. Devon had several skills that gave him an edge in combat for movement and attack speed, as well as general perception in the area, but the group as a whole was sorely lacking melee combatants since their other two Fighters left.

The other group was also surprised at the mention of the secondary quest and were immediately interested. Completing the quest could afford them additional opportunities to advance their gear or hire members until they found a lasting group. They all decided to attempt to find the Sun Spirals, though Wyn secretly was afraid they wouldn't have enough flowers to satisfy their own quests with six Climbers total looking for them. If it was a quest presented from the tower, though, there had to be enough. Worry just seemed to flood his mind far too easily lately.

After the initial jaunt through the portal the group set off both to find flowers and the path leading through the floor. They decided to let Tasha and Maven take the lead looking out for flowers, and Devon was the best equipped to help find the path they needed to take. The others assisted where they could.

John swung his sword around, excited to try it out, before stopping mid-swing and audibly groaning.

"What is it?" Wyn asked.

"I completely forgot—I don't have a gem to socket for the sword!" John said.

"Yes you do," Tasha said. She was peeking behind a bush while looking for Sun Spirals. "You got that jade gemstone from our first trip, remember?"

John smacked himself in the forehead. Without another word, he pulled out the gemstone from his backpack and placed it inside the hilt of his sword. Concentrating and infusing it with a bit of mana, the gemstone fit inside it like it was perfectly made for it, and wouldn't budge when he tried to pull it out. The blade began to shine a mirrored green, matching the gemstone exactly.

"Whoa," Devon said. "That's impressive. I'm assuming it's elemental, too?"

"You have a good eye," John responded. "It should be the earth element, now. At least these guys aren't wind-based. I need to find more gemstones just in case, though."

"In due time," Wyn said, as he patted John on the shoulder. "Let's just worry about the here and now." He continued on their path, looking around for flowers and enemies more than the path itself. Marcy wasn't there to alert them to danger, a fact he realized they had become accustomed to having, and he didn't want to be caught off guard.

"I think I see something," William said. He raised his staff and pointed it deeper into the jungle.

"Nice eye, William," Devon said. He drew his other sword and turned toward the jungle. "Fire some bolts into the woods, just in case!"

Wyn's eyes went wide. "No! Don't do that! Save your mana for when you actually see them!" He looked into the thicket, too, and saw nothing. "You don't want to accidentally hit another Climber or waste your mana!"

"Or scorch a flower," Tasha said. She was finishing picking another Sun Spiral from a small patch she found. "Don't be so on edge!"

John had his sword and shield drawn, holding it out in front of Devon placatingly to hold him back. "Relax. Take deep breaths. Don't consume your resources so quickly and without true reason."

Wyn eyed the split group. In this moment he was incredibly proud of Tasha and John. It was obvious John had training before coming to climb the tower, and his actions and words proved it. Tasha was level-headed and more confident than their first climb, and they had only climbed a couple of times at that. Albeit they hadn't climbed past the first floor together, but so far their ability to work as a team was far and above these other Climbers, who looked like they hadn't faced any form of combat or training in their lives.

Were these the kind of people who became Climbers? Wyn suddenly understood why Daniel was so insistent on taking weeks to prepare before actually climbing. If they were the average, it was a miracle more people didn't die.

The bushes suddenly rustled in front of John and Devon, and they all saw three of the Lacerts, as they were called according to their parchments, emerge from the thicket. They were the average-sized monstrous lizards that didn't pose much of a threat before. Two were carrying clubs, and one was unarmed, though their sharp claws easily counted as weapons.

William immediately pointed his staff at the group and yelled a spell—"*Flamebolt*!"

A large ball of flame shot from his staff, narrowly missing Devon and striking one of the Lacerts that held a club. It singed the ragged cloth it was wearing and scorched its leathery skin.

"Careful, William!" Devon yelled. "That was too close!" He sprang to the side away from the Fire Mage and toward the other Lacerts. His feet pattered against the grass as he moved much quicker than the other Climbers but far quieter. In seconds he was directly in front of the enemy attempting to strike it.

Unfortunately, John was already moving toward the same monster, acting faster than Devon but not reaching the target as fast due to his lesser speed.

John was caught off guard by the Rogue's fast movement and abrupt positioning, backpedaling to avoid being caught in the direct melee. Wyn was watching the entire debacle unfold, shocked at the mistakes the others were making. "Watch your positioning! Give each other room to fight!" He wanted to join them but knew he'd only get in the way at the moment. An obvious choice that didn't seem so obvious to Devon or William. He could help directly if the fight were more serious, but he knew this would be a good learning opportunity that wasn't *too* deadly.

John reluctantly turned to fight the other enemy after giving himself some room from Devon, though was unfortunately a second behind. That Lacert wielded a club and swung it down in a surprisingly fast arc, though John was ready with his shield. His shield absorbed and redirected the blow, causing the enemy to briefly stumble.

Taking the opportunity, John reached out to stab the Lacert directly in the chest. It was both a direct hit and a powerful strike, and the magical sword impaled the creature deep into its torso. John felt the body go limp on his sword, and he freed his weapon before the body hit the ground.

Devon yelled in frustration, exchanging blow for blow with the final and unarmed monster. The Rogue's arms and torso were cut up, the claws from the creature acting like small daggers slicing his skin with shallow cuts where his armor didn't protect him. He had the upper hand, though, as his swords were making far greater and deeper gashes into the scaled, leathery hide.

With a few more strikes the Rogue felled the creature. As the body began to disintegrate into the jungle floor, Devon breathed heavy and was already sweating through his clothes. The existing grime, sweat, and dried blood was coated with new layers.

"Maven, can you heal me?" Devon asked. He sheathed his swords with effort and inspected his arms. Dozens of cuts were randomly strewn about, and he sighed at his shredded skin.

Without another word, the Mage held a hand out to the Rogue and began to heal him, casting her *Cure* spell that closed his wounds but left his clothes in tatters.

"Not too bad, right?" William said. He held his staff awkwardly. "At least I hit that lizard!"

"No," Wyn said. "That *was* bad. I'm honestly surprised you three are still alive."

Devon snickered. "Look, I know we're not as good as you three, but that's a bit much. I think we did alright."

Wyn sighed. "It's the truth, and you all need to hear it."

"What, in your opinion, made that so bad, then?" William asked. "We're alive. Healed, even, in top condition! The enemies are dead, and we barely struggled!"

Wyn looked at the Fire Mage and straightened his posture. These Climbers weren't his soldiers, but he needed to channel his inner captain in order to show them the error of their ways and to help them prevent the same situation in the future. He wanted to do his best to leave his commanding behind, but his friends trusted him to lead them.

In order to lead, sometimes you have to scold.

"I can give my opinion," Wyn said. "Let's review. Devon, you asked William to attack an unseen enemy without knowing what was truly there, potentially hitting an ally and wasting mana on a low chance of hitting an enemy. William, your position was bad to attack from range. Your spell nearly hit Devon, and based on the last time we saw you climb, your aim could use some work. The hit you made was a lucky shot."

Wyn walked around the small battlefield, pointing and waving his arms to emphasize his point. "Devon, you were forced to move your position, but you stepped in front of John, who was already beginning to engage with the same enemy you rushed to attack. Despite you saying you have a high perception you didn't see your ally's movement or attack, becoming a liability. That caused John to relocate to the last enemy, causing a delay of precious seconds to defend himself. All of that and you still traded blows with the enemy, needing to be healed right away, who is the most basic of basic enemies in this tower. This is the first fight on the first floor, and every single enemy past here will be stronger, faster, and tougher."

The other Climbers were dumbstruck, even Tasha and John. They had no idea Wyn possessed the strategic analysis skills he shared, and after hearing it laid out from a fight that took less than a minute, they didn't know how to respond.

"Oh, and one more thing," Wyn added. "Your mana use needs work. Getting hurt, Devon, caused you to need to be healed, costing Maven her mana to heal you. And she'll need that mana for later on in this floor. This fight should've been over without *any* mana expenditure, and little energy used, too. I am far from an expert at climbing this tower, and even less so with being around magic, but I do know my way around a battlefield."

Devon and William looked at each other. Their smiles faded long ago, and their shoulders slumped to a depressing degree.

"I . . . don't know what to say," Devon said.

"Me, either," William added. "I had no idea there was even that much to consider."

"Well, you do now," Wyn said. "It's important to reflect on your performance and recognize where you can improve. This isn't a child's game. This place is serious, and you *will* get seriously hurt if you aren't careful or smart with how you approach it."

William pounded his staff into the ground and straightened his robe. "You're right. We can do better! We *will* be better!"

Devon smiled and crossed his arms over his chest. "That was still harsh, but appreciated. We'll do better. We have to, after all."

Wyn smiled back. "Exactly. I'll be the first to admit I'm not perfect. My first climb here was basically a disaster in more ways than one. But I will force myself to be better to make sure all of you live to see another day. So, next fight, how about you watch how we handle enemies. Then you critique us and see where we could improve."

Maven laughed, putting her hand in front of her mouth. "Now *that* would be something. I wouldn't even know where to start!"

"It's a good learning technique," Wyn said. "You'd be surprised what you notice when you're trying to."

"Speaking of noticing things," Tasha said, interrupting the other Climbers. She walked over to a thick patch of tall leaves and vines, away from the path they were following to advance. "Here's another patch of Sun Spirals!"

The others all gathered to collect whatever flowers they could find. Wyn was thankful they found as many as they did just starting out on the floor, and was quickly gaining confidence they could find enough for all six of them.

Taking the time to pick the patch, Wyn heard a rustling outside their contained area. He saw that Tasha noticed it, too, and was on alert looking around. There wasn't the sound of a group of Lacerts growling or scheming, and they weren't jumping out to attack. Which meant it was likely something else.

Or *someone* else.

This may be a more serious climb than he thought. And of course it was happening while they were paired with a trio that could barely call themselves Climbers.

Still, they were more than capable themselves, even without Marcy with them. They just needed to be more aware of their surroundings. Hopefully it was just someone watching them rather than an enemy. Though Wyn wouldn't take that chance, and was prepared to act in the worst case scenario.

He made a mental note to be on guard for the rest of the climb. His and the group's lives likely depended on it.

After they picked the entire patch, they moved on, eventually finding the river and canoes that allowed passage through the rushing waters. Nothing else showed up despite Wyn diligently keeping an eye out.

"Here is where you really want to watch Wyn's ability to navigate," John said to the other Climbers, elbowing Wyn in the side. It was obvious he was trying to keep the mood light. "You should give him some feedback on the water!"

Tasha laughed while the others looked confused. Wyn's cheeks quickly flushed red, but he cleared his throat and relented with an awkward smile. No sense in trying to appear like he was good at everything, and it could make him more relatable if the new Climbers saw him bad at something. Not that that would be difficult.

Grabbing their canoes, Wyn reluctantly stepped into one with John, who was still laughing to himself.

"You think you're so funny, don't you?" Wyn asked.

"No, I *know* I'm funny," John replied.

Wyn couldn't help but crack a smile at the Fighter's charmingly disarming personality.

"But, Wyn," John added.

Wyn turned around to face John. "Yeah?"

"I'm really glad you're in our group. And even happier you're leading us. I know most Climbers are pretty rough when they start, but . . . I'm excited to see where we go with you at the helm. I feel a lot better climbing at your side."

Wyn was shocked. He expected another joke, not for John to be serious. Still, it was an incredibly generous thing to say, and Wyn's confidence grew even more. Along with his trust in his new friend. "Me too, John. I know I'm very lucky to have all of you in a group."

"Good. Now—don't have a heart attack here on the water. I might just laugh instead of save you."

Wyn sighed. It was going to be a long canoe ride.

CHAPTER THIRTY-EIGHT

Wyn took a deep breath, thankful his boots were once again on dry land. He had wondered before if practicing this floor and being forced to navigate the river would help alleviate his fear of the water, but he found himself just as afraid and nervous as ever.

The other Climbers—even Tasha and Maven—all had caught on to his discomfort and teased him in some form, though it was nothing he couldn't take. His soldiers gave far worse insults. He was simply grateful his boat never flipped. They hadn't seen any Lacerts, either, which Wyn thought was suspicious, but he quickly remembered it was the afternoon and the floor had likely been cleared and thinned of enemies throughout the day.

He assumed that was the reason, at least. The other possibility was that they were staying away to fight something else. Or someone else.

The group was nearing the end of the floor in less than an hour after navigating the river, and they had completely filled their quota of Sun Spirals to both complete their quest and for Cara, too. It had been a fruitful, straightforward climb.

"I feel like this is cheating," Devon said. "I haven't even found a track of an enemy since the beginning of the floor. And we're nearly done, I think."

"Yeah, we definitely are," Wyn said. "The end wasn't far after the river where the large enemies guarded the portal. It's so strange how little Lacerts there are."

William was inspecting a large tree, craning his head to see the top. "So that's what they're called, huh? Lacerts. I've never heard of that word."

"It was what the guild official called the components we earned," John said. "But don't keep your guard down. You never know what's around the corner."

Devon suddenly shot up from his crouched position while trying to find more tracks. A sword-wielding Lacert shot through the jungle thicket with impressive speed, slashing at him in a surprise attack.

The Rogue nimbly sidestepped the swipe at the last second. "Help!" he yelled, unsure of what else to say in the moment.

John and Wyn both rushed to cut off the creature from Devon, hoping to intervene without issue. This Lacert was wearing leather armor that covered his body in addition to its scaly hide, along with bracers and thigh guards. They immediately recognized it was a stronger enemy and that more were likely not far behind.

"Tasha, protection!" Wyn yelled, organizing his group. They had rehearsed scenarios in the war room for various situations during their day off before the season started, and this one was one of their more basic strategies. It was simple but effective.

Without hesitation, Tasha raised her staff and pointed it at John while remaining behind the closer ranged fighters. "*Arcane Aura*!" she said, casting her protective spell. The white magical aura enveloped him in the familiar glow as the new layer of armor protected him.

John simultaneously activated his *Resolve* skill to increase his power and endurance. The red aura radiated around him under the white magical armor, and he breathed in deep before exhaling loud in a crouch.

Devon stepped back, surprised by the Fighter's sudden change. John looked like a bull breathing heavily while covered in a magical aura, and his presence took on a new feel. It was as though the surrounding air was more dense with arcane energy accumulating heavily around the Fighter. He didn't hesitate before engaging with the Lacert.

Wyn took note of the surroundings, finding two more similarly equipped Lacerts behind the brush ready to attack with one on either side of their current position. It seemed as though they planned to pin the Climbers. They looked identical, all holding swords though no other weapon or shield. "*Speed Up*," he said, mostly to himself and not loud enough for others to hear. The soft red glow enveloped him like John, though to a smaller degree. He felt new power surge through him, knowing the mana fused into the skill was fueling a newfound speed.

Their strategy was straightforward. John would distract and fight the strongest enemy while Wyn and Marcy would handle the weaker and more numerous ones. John could easily handle himself, and Wyn was more suited to literally running around while Marcy could choose her targets easily. Tasha would stay in the middle of the group to be able to intervene anywhere, keeping her eyes and ears open to heal or support where she could. Unfortunately they'd have to deal without Marcy being around, but Wyn felt confident they could handle it.

Wyn ignored the noise of metal clashing between the monster and John and pushed to the jungle's edge right as the Lacerts stepped into their small clearing. He took the first one by surprise with his speed and weapon, slashing down in an arc at a safe distance, thanks to the spear's reach before the Lacert could even raise its sword. The slash cut deep, the element showing its superiority by opening an even greater gash that Wyn didn't expect. He followed the strike with a quick stab to the chest, his skill increasing his follow-up speed to a degree that still surprised him.

His moves felt fluid and body quick, like every intent to move was met with a near instantaneous response. It was a true testament to using magic, as he was so used to fighting at a standard speed that his enhanced speed still took some adjustment.

He wasn't fighting a trained or even skilled opponent, though. The spear went straight through the creature, and he pulled his weapon out before the body fell to the ground. He sidestepped around John toward the third monster, giving him information as he passed by. "One left!"

John parried a sword attack easily with his shield before striking back with a forceful swing of his sword. He had held back the entire fight, performing his role of drawing out the engagement with ease. The sword came crashing down through the lizard-like monster, all but ignoring the leather armor it donned, and cleaved its arm off at the shoulder. The Lacert's scream, though, was cut short with another strike from the Fighter that killed it with relative ease.

Wyn, still rushing to the third and final Lacert, had to cover more ground as the enemy ignored the two frontline combatants and charged at the rest of the group. The three new Climbers simply stood by, remembering that Wyn asked them to only watch but were also paralyzed by fear of the enemies.

Tasha stood her ground, though, holding her staff in front of her as though she would smack the creature the instant it came close. Instead, Wyn cut it off, his heightened speed giving him more than enough time to intervene.

Before the creature even stepped into its sword range to attack Tasha, Wyn was beside it. He swept its legs with his spear and nearly cut them both off at the knees with a brutal hit. The monster screamed, a bloodcurdling sound that made the Climbers standing by recoil. The monster fell to the ground, dropping its sword and clawing at the jungle floor with its hands to crawl to the closest Climber, relentless in its pursuit.

Wyn promptly stabbed it in the back. The creature then lay still, ceasing its advance.

For a few seconds there was only silence in the clearing where everyone stood before the sound of John sheathing his sword broke the lull.

"That was pretty good, even without Marcy," Tasha said, tapping the dead Lacert in front of her. Its body began to dissolve back into the tower leaving no trace of its existence.

"I definitely learned even the champions are probably a bit of a pushover now," John said, wiping some blood off his padded armor. "It's actually easier to fight these monsters than the pack of wolves or weird tree monsters from last season!"

"We haven't been overrun, yet," Wyn said, taking steadying breaths. He mentally canceled his skill, the red glowing aura dissipating around him. The increased sense of speed withered, too, causing a slight hitch in his first couple of steps. "There haven't been packs of enemies here like before. Which is odd, but I'm not complaining."

The other Climbers all stood unmoving, shocked at the display. Devon and William looked at each other, and the Fire Mage simply shook his head side to side.

"How in the hells can you lot do that," Devon said. "That was . . . something else."

"There's no way you're new Climbers," Maven added. "Surely you've climbed into the second tier already. You made that look far too easy."

John laughed, and Tasha hit him in the arm in response. "What?" the Fighter asked, still laughing. Tasha gave him a stern look. He just sighed.

"This is our third day in the tower, but we've been planning a lot," Tasha said, still staring daggers at her teammate. "I do believe we're more than capable, though."

Devon laughed this time. "You don't say?"

Tasha nodded her head, accepting the compliment.

"So what do you think we could improve?" Wyn asked. He straightened his simple leather armor and wiped some dirt off his boots. "Any feedback would be helpful."

The new Climbers looked at each other before Maven and William shrugged.

Devon walked further on the path, continuing deeper into the jungle and first floor. "Not a damn thing," he said, as he walked by them.

John, Wyn, and Tasha all looked at each other, accepting the answer but not satisfied. They all then continued their trek on the floor, one more patch of enemies dealt with.

Over the next hour Wyn became increasingly concerned about not seeing any enemies. He wasn't sure what was happening. While the others continued to prattle on about their good fortune of an easy climb, he wasn't so sure. It felt wrong. Like something was interfering with their climb. Was it the Avatar guiding them to an easy victory? No, that couldn't be right. Wyn dismissed that thought almost immediately.

He quietly shared his thoughts with John and Tasha when able, and they both agreed to be on the lookout. Not having Marcy around meant their primary scout was gone, and they needed all eyes possible to make sure there weren't any hidden threats.

But, no one revealed themselves as they continued. Wyn wondered if it was just him being worried.

Soon they all reached the familiar clearing that held the portal to the next floor and giant Lacerts that guarded it. Wyn checked his mark and saw that it was entirely gray. He was completely full of mana, only having used his skill once and barely spending any to use it at that. He knew he could be liberal in the coming fight if he wanted but thought that saving enough for a few spells on the second floor would be prudent—just in case.

"Should we form a plan?" William asked, whispering behind a bush. The entire group had stopped just outside the clearing, and three large giant Lacerts stood guarding the portal. The six Climbers all hid behind the jungle foliage in order to not alert the giant monsters.

"We absolutely should," John said. "And that's good that you realize that!"

"Well, the way you three handled the last fight seemed too easy," William said. "Maybe this could be easy, too."

"It definitely can be," Wyn said. "Maven, do you have the **Arcane Aura** spell?"

Maven nodded her head yes, not taking her eyes off the giant guards.

"Good," Wyn continued. "So you and Tasha cast one each on John and Devon before we rush in. The plan is to take them out one at a time. If we spread our focus over all three, it'll take longer and leave more threats."

The other Climbers nodded in agreement, letting Wyn instruct them. This was what felt more familiar to him than anything else, even in direct combat. He knew he was more than competent in a fight, but he enjoyed the strategic aspect of a good plan more, and climbing in the tower afforded him many chances to exercise that strength.

"John, you focus on one like before," Wyn continued. "Devon, attack the same one as John, and don't worry about holding back—just finish it as quickly as possible. You should have plenty of chances with both of you attacking it."

"What about the rest of us?" William asked. "I can fight!"

"You're joining me by being the distraction this time. We need to keep the other two off John and Devon, annoying the giants enough to try to attack us and not gang up on the fighters. Once John and Devon kill it, they'll move on to the next one, and then we distract the last one. When there's only one left, we just kill it, though don't cast your spells at an enemy if there's one of us fighting it. The chance of you hitting an ally is too high."

"Do me and Tasha just stand there?" Maven asked. "You left us out."

Wyn glanced back at the giant bosses. They were still unaware. "Do you have any spells to attack enemies or support us in the fight?"

Maven knitted her eyebrows together. "Not at the moment, no. Just the **Shield** spell, **Arcane Aura**, and more healing."

"Look at it this way," Tasha said. "We help setup the fight and provide healing if needed. If it's not needed, then as a group we're all the better for it."

Maven sighed and held her staff close to her body in a hug. "That's true, I guess."

"So you can cast **Shield** to block any attacks that look too threatening, too," Wyn added. "It would be good practice for you. Same for you, Tasha." From their downtime and planning, Wyn learned that **Shield** was a spell that quickly erected a curved barrier to block physical attacks. Its counterpart, **Shell**, blocked magical attacks, but that wasn't a popular spell choice in the first tier since so few monsters actually used magic. He had decided against exchanging one of his spells for it but wondered if he chose wrong.

One of the giant Lacerts grunted and turned toward the group. It didn't seem completely alert but suspicious at the noise.

"Maven, Tasha, armor up!" Wyn whispered. "William, stay on the left side of us a bit away, and aim your spells this time!" He grabbed his spear and fanned out to the right side in a slight jog, waving his spear around frantically, hoping to pull the Lacert's attention to him.

The move worked. All three giants turned and howled at Wyn, waving their weapons or fists at him.

The rest of the group set out in motion and began their advance. After gaining their sets of magical armor, Devon and John rushed straight into the clearing, immediately gaining the attention of two of the Lacerts. William mimicked Wyn and fanned out to his side, and though he was slower than the others he didn't need to cover as much ground.

William planted himself at a distance he felt comfortable and pointed his staff at the leftmost Lacert while it was still advancing toward the melee Climbers. "**Flamebolt**!" he yelled, and the spell hit his target in the thigh. It was a well-placed spell, though fairly weak against the boss as it did hardly any damage. The Lacert giant yelled in anger before stopping and turning toward William.

William initially cheered at his success, but quickly realized the gravity of what was happening. He had a giant monster now running toward him and began to panic again. Keeping his staff pointed toward the beast, he immediately cast three more spells in quick succession. They all hit the giant in various places, and it stopped its advance to cover itself with its large arms from the onslaught of globs of flame. It began to retreat not long after, its leathery skin smoking and body missing pockets of flesh from being burned away. The spell might not have been too strong, but several of them hitting back to back definitely added up.

William held his ground and tried to steady his increasing heart rate. He didn't know if he should continue attacking it or wait, then realized he didn't need to decide at the moment.

Wyn, on the other side of the clearing, was slicing the large Lacert across its entire body, leaving relatively shallow gashes that opened up deeper from the magical wind element of his spear. He was doing his best to keep an eye on the other two giants at the same time and found it not too difficult—the large monster's swings with its club were easily avoided. They were heavy and shook the ground when they fell, but their wind-up and attack was predictable and obvious.

Wyn saw William fend off the attacking Lacert and smiled when it retreated. The middle one wasn't faring much better, nearly dead already from Devon and John's combined attacks. In less than a minute they had all performed their roles nicely, even better than Wyn had hoped.

Stepping to the side to avoid another club smash into the ground, Wyn saw Devon split away to begin attacking the burned giant Lacert. John was about to deliver a final blow on the monster that was a bloodied mess. Cuts and puncture wounds covered its legs and torso like a gruesome training dummy. The blood was seeping from the wounds at an alarming rate, and it seemed unnatural.

Wyn began to maneuver himself closer to John, drawing his giant to the middle of the clearing. A loud thud suddenly reverberated across the jungle as one giant Lacert fell to the ground dead. John immediately rushed to the next enemy and slashed the monster fighting Wyn in the back, causing it to roar in anger. The Fighter nodded to Wyn with confidence, and Wyn knew he could handle it from then on.

Wyn looked down at his mark, wondering about his mana. Of course it was nearly full as he had only used one skill and no spells. Their journey had been easy, and he was thankful they were able to manage with minimal resources. The tower was quickly appearing less and less intimidating, even if they had only traversed the first floor.

A crash into the soft jungle floor pulled Wyn from his thoughts. Devon lay on the ground not far from him, the magical armor around him gone. His sword was cast off to his side, and he immediately coughed up blood. There weren't any obvious injuries, but Wyn knew he needed help fast.

The Lacert picked its heavy club back up to rest on a shoulder, now trying to close the distance between itself and the Climbers. It had knocked Devon back quite a bit, making solid contact with its attack that the Rogue was unable to dodge.

"*Regen*," Wyn said, the instant he was beside the still-coughing Rogue. A magical white glow enveloped him, but he struggled to get up. His left arm was bent terribly, but Wyn didn't see any other obvious injuries. Everything must have been internal.

Wyn pushed him to the ground and held him in place. "Don't get up. Stay here." He looked back at Tasha and Maven, who were already rushing to their side. Tasha was nearly dragging Maven, both looking frantic though Tasha less so and for different reasons.

Knowing the Diamond Mages would take care of Devon, Wyn needed to take the monster down. Another bolt of fire hit the Lacert again, William attacking from the side. He seemed confident and focused, a far cry from his demeanor the last time they were in this situation against the same enemies. At least his spells were hitting the intended target.

Wyn raised his spear and wanted to settle this fast. He swung it in a wide arc, casting the **Wingbeat** spell at the same time. A visible line of magic swept out and across the creature, slicing it across its chest and hip. It caused a deep gash to form and blood to pour, and several burned areas appeared to open up as well. It roared in pain before another bolt of fire silenced it, hitting it directly in the face.

"How's Devon?" William asked. He trotted over to the Climbers, sweating. Wyn could've sworn he saw the Fire Mage shaking a bit.

"I'll be fine," Devon said. He was still glowing white, though more pronounced now. "And that **Regen** spell of yours definitely helped."

"Happy to hear that," Wyn said. He smiled seeing the Rogue in better spirits.

Another thud interrupted them, and they all turned to see John standing beside the last Lacert that had just fallen to the ground. The portal the monsters guarded was now open, as well.

The Fighter turned around and waved them on, not waiting to bask in the glory of their success. He then turned to face the portal and eyed it seriously.

Everyone gradually gathered together in front of the shimmering portal that taunted them with its clear swirls of magic. They silently stood there staring, knowing they weren't heading back to the base but rather to the second floor. The only member in their party who had entered the portal to advance to the second floor was Wyn, and he had done so for very different reasons than purely scouting ahead.

Though they had been excited about seeing what mysteries beckoned them further into the tower, they hesitated. All it would take was a key to open a portal back to the base and they would safely return—but it was still a daunting thought of the harder, and more dangerous, floor of the tower that stood before them. This was their entire reason for being a Climber, though. Like that first trip into the portal, it would get easier in time. But the first time was always harder.

John turned his head and smiled at all of them. It wasn't his usual confident, charming smile but rather a feigned appearance that betrayed his nerves. Wyn smiled back, strangely comforted by his friend's hesitation.

Wyn then patted him on the shoulder in reassurance before stepping forward toward the portal. He mentally told himself he wanted to progress to the second floor, throwing his caution to the wind. Gripping his spear tighter and patting the key in his pocket, he continued his steps through the portal and felt the magical pull of the tower's magic once again.

CHAPTER THIRTY-NINE

The members of the party all exited the portal one by one, being spit out around the starting area randomly. Tasha and John ended up next to each other looking ahead into more dense jungle. After a few seconds to allow their heads to stop spinning, they both looked at each other in confusion.

"I imagined being out of the jungle, at least," John said, scratching his chin. "I guess we have to slog through it some more."

Tasha turned around, her eyes widening and jaw opening. She tugged at John's arm without a word.

"What?" the Fighter asked, before turning around to see what she was gawking at. His face quickly matched hers. "Whoa."

The rest of the group had already been enamored by the second floor's environment. Jungle brush still coated the edge of the initial starting area, but it was obvious they would leave the dense foliage behind for the entirety of the second floor. This was obvious due to the fact that an incredibly large ancient temple stood in the not so distant background, and ruins covered the path from the jungle to the steps that made up the bottom portion of the temple.

Cracked arches and broken sandstone littered the area separating their small grove and the temple that looked eerie. It was a literal maze before the cult-like building, though. Wyn assumed the floor would be a trial of puzzles similar to the cave system of mushrooms during the last season, and it looked like he was right at first glance. So far, the second floor seemed to have a goal of completing a puzzle to advance rather than just killing the monsters on the path.

They all had their hands on their foreheads, covering their eyes to be able to see the path past the bright sun. It rested high in the sky, no clouds in sight to offer any form of reprieve from the light and heat.

"The path looks dense," Devon said. He pointed with his sword to the forest of sandstone and rock. "Tight corridors, small pathways are likely. Though the sky looks to be open the whole way to the temple, so we won't feel *too* claustro-phobic without a roof."

"And that means the temple is the third floor," John said. "That's not terrify-ing at all."

"One floor at a time, please," Tasha said. She gripped her staff tight and held it close. "My **Torchlight** spell won't be too useful right now. It's so bright."

"When we get into the temple, though," Wyn said, " I have a feeling we'll be glad you have it."

William and Devon stepped forward out of the safety of the grove. The Mage turned toward them and smiled. "One floor at a time, right? I have a feeling we'll be lucky to make it to the temple this season at all."

Devon laughed. "Don't count us out yet. There's an entire month left. This is only the first week!"

The group slowly made their way toward a large sandstone arch signaling the entrance to the ruins. It was nearly as massive as the entrance into Alestead, and resembled it, too, with pillars bordering the open path. Here they were in tatters while the ones in Alestead were pristine. The ground beneath their feet abruptly shifted from grass to sandstone, small rocks and dust coating the area like a blan-ket. Behind the arch was a small sandy courtyard, a desolate entry into the maze that called them further.

"How far are we wanting to go?" Maven asked. She was standing close to Devon, whipping her head back and forth to survey the area. "I feel like I've seen enough."

William laughed. "We just stepped into the ruins, Maven! It wouldn't be a bad idea to know if more lizard things were here or something else, too."

Devon threw his hand out to the side, forcing the group to stop. He bent down to the ground and ran his hand over it gingerly, as though he was trying to feel energy radiating from the sandy floor. His hand suddenly stopped, and he felt the stone with his palm. A sigh escaped his lips, and he grabbed a larger rock, inspecting it closer.

"I'm not worried about the enemies at the moment. Traps line the path. I'm sure of it." He tossed the rock about ten feet ahead of them, and an arrow flew across the courtyard from left to right.

Maven yelped, jumping back. The group all readied their weapons, unsure of what to expect next. Devon stood up and wiped his hands together, a small plume of dust rising above him.

Wyn couldn't make out exactly where the arrow came from but spotted mul-tiple holes between stones on either side of their immediate path. There were likely more areas of the path that would cause additional arrows to be shot, but whether it was from a specific spot or just general movement he wasn't sure. Nothing else in the courtyard gave any indication of being triggered.

"This will make it more challenging," Wyn said. "But nothing we can't handle. You spotted it almost right away, Devon. Is it certain spots on the stones or something else?"

Devon carefully stepped forward. "I believe it's just as we move forward. I'll stay to the front." He kicked another rock forward and another arrow flew across them in a similar manner, also from the left.

Wyn looked at John, who nodded back at him with a smirk. The Fighter was serious but confident, and Wyn had a rising feeling inside him that warmed him. It was unusually calming.

He didn't know how, but he knew they could do this. They could make it through the floor with their group as Marcy had a higher degree of perception than Devon, and they could take their time to map it out.

Wyn kept repeating that in his mind over and over. They could do this. They could continue climbing the tower.

The memory of the colored mushrooms flooded his mind along with Cedric mapping out their path. He hoped the Wizard was recovering well and vowed to ask Marcy right away when he could see him next.

In minutes they were across the small courtyard, carefully advancing while Devon made sure they were safe. It took several agonizing minutes and they only crossed about fifty feet, but thankfully no traps were set off by the group following Devon. It was as though once the traps were sprung they were done, much to the group's relief. The area ahead was more narrow and covered, and multiple paths branched away to lead them further.

They all stood there, anxiously waiting, checking each path to see if there was a difference.

"Which looks less menacing?" John said.

"That might be the most dangerous," Wyn responded. "But we aren't looking to complete the floor. Let's just pick the middle path and see what we find. Any signs of too much trouble, and I'll activate the portal to get us back."

The group nodded and let Devon lead them slowly, carefully checking for traps along the ground. It was a laborious process and incredibly time consuming. It took them the better part of an hour to just go a small distance further from the time they entered the ruins, taking a few turns here and there with no signs of enemies or more traps.

Everyone was becoming more impatient with each step. Devon was being less careful with his approach, the heat causing him to sweat more and groan with each new open hallway they entered.

"This is getting frustrating," the Rogue said. "If the whole floor is like this it'll take ages!" He kicked a rock forward, hoping to set off a trap—anything to break the monotony.

Nothing happened.

John joined him in an exaggerated groan. He wiped more sweat off his forehead and slung the moisture onto the ground. Their morale was waning, and the weather only contributed to the lethargy of the lengthy maze.

Wyn couldn't help but chuckle. They had barely entered the second floor, and everyone was already hot, tired, and complaining. They certainly weren't soldiers. Otherwise they'd have kept their feelings to themselves and pressed on, following orders as given. They were Climbers. Barely even adults and definitely not trained to withstand such discomforts. Not yet, at least.

Devon began to walk with a tired gait, flailing his arms and torso to the end of the short path before it turned again. He suddenly straightened and whipped his hand to the pommel of his sheathed sword.

The group stopped walking, unsure of why the Rogue was alerted but readying themselves for a fight.

"I hear something," Devon said, his voice short and hushed. "A group moving ahead."

Wyn tried to silently tiptoe on the other side of the pathway beside Devon, his spear ready to strike.

A group of monsters appeared at the end of their path from the left-hand turn, walking in a structured marching formation. They were Lacerts, though much more well equipped than the ones on the first floor. The first two wore heavier armor and chain mail with helmets, along with halberds that were double their height. Behind them was a new creature. It looked like a hybrid between a giant snake and a human, with a long, muscular tail beginning at the hip and recognizable features from the head to navel. Well, recognizable except for the slitted nose and snakelike head and scaled skin. It stood heads taller than the Lacerts and taller than any man Wyn had seen, likely seven or eight feet. There were two swords strapped to the snake-man's back in a cross formation, and it slithered along between the two Lacerts in an undulating motion.

Wyn's heart raced. He knew there'd be all sorts of monsters in the tower, but this was definitely frightening. It was much more humanoid and looked fierce. Even though there were only three enemies, they seemed to be much more capable than the previous Lacerts, likely even the floor bosses. Walking in a formation showed both intellect and teamwork, and the weapons and armor they wielded were intimidating.

Devon took a nervous step backward. Wyn saw his hand quiver above his sword, hesitation evident in his posture.

Hesitation could be the difference between life and death, and it was crucial to act when necessary. Wyn knew this all too well, though was afraid his teammates wouldn't be as prudent with their decisions.

"William, fire!" Wyn said curtly but quietly. He trotted forward, trying to close some distance between the enemies. He didn't want to be caught off guard and was afraid the snake monster would be fast.

There was a pause. The enemies turned toward them and yelled something, the Lacerts pointing with their giant weapons. A rough snarl left the snake-man's mouth, and he drew his swords from his back in a rush.

William still hadn't attacked. Wyn stole a look back and saw the mage was frozen in place, Tasha shaking his shoulders to stir him to action.

John appeared beside Wyn, his sword glowing from the gemstone and shield raised in a defensive position.

Wyn immediately sliced his spear horizontally to cast **Wingbeat**, trying to hit all three monsters. The spell flashed through the air, catching the hybrid snake monster off guard. It recoiled for a moment, trying to block the spell with its sword. To Wyn's surprise, the swords actually deflected the strike, though not entirely. Two large cuts formed on the outer edges of the creature's torso from the magical slice of air.

The Lacerts also fared surprisingly well. They braced themselves from the spell, the air cutting across their armor and forearms. Their chainmail took the majority of the attack, and though they were knocked back several feet and arms slashed, they remained standing.

Wyn's heart sank. These enemies were even stronger than the champions from the first floor. The difference in power was startling, and he knew they would be in trouble if they couldn't handle them quickly. Half of their group was more of a liability than help.

"William, *fire*!" Wyn repeated, a slight hint of desperation in his voice. "Hold those two back!"

He stayed focused on the immediate threat, not risking a glance back at his teammates to see if they were coming around or still wrestling with inaction. If he was distracted for even a second, his climbing career would be over here and now.

The half-snake monster whirled its two swords around like a dancer, graceful and with ease. The blades were wide and curved, a far cry from the standard longsword so common to soldiers and Climbers alike. Bright flashes glinted off the metal, reflecting the sun's rays in a dizzying display when the angle hit Wyn's eyes just right.

In seconds the creature slithered toward him, its body writhing side to side as the large tail guided it along the ground. It was hard to predict where it would stop and attack. It wasn't like a usual person or Lacert attacking straight on, and its movements were smooth and fluid, unusual for fighting.

"**Arcane Aura**!" Wyn yelled, wanting to desperately protect himself as he was unsure whether he would be able to defend with only his spear. A white flash of magical armor enveloped him. He took a few steps backward and stabbed out with his weapon, hoping the extra reach he possessed would be enough to counter the monster's height and movement.

When Wyn would stab in one area, the monster simply twisted its body to avoid the spear tip, and appeared to do so easily. He jabbed at it several times in various areas, but each strike hit only air as the monster utilized its snake half well to slither out of harm's reach. John similarly tried to swipe and stab at the monster but it deflected each hit with one of its swords.

A sudden loud pop interrupted their fight. The creature looked back to its allies, and Wyn couldn't help but see what caused the noise, too. Small fires were scattered around the two Lacert soldiers, and they were both rolling on the ground trying to put out the flames that now covered them.

William had finally cast his spell, and it worked beautifully.

The snake monster roared in anger, and its voice was piercing in the noiseless ruins. Wyn recoiled, wincing at the sound. He recovered quickly, however, hoping to utilize the brief window of time that the creature wasn't focused.

Wyn swept in an arc with his spear, aiming for the lower, scaly half of the monster. It hadn't dodged or deflected the blow, currently focused on fighting John, and the spear cut a large gash across its reptilian body. Blue blood poured from the wound, and the snake-man writhed in pain.

The movement only caused the wound to seep more blood, though it quickly attacked with a fury. Wyn was able to block one sword strike with the shaft of his spear, but he helplessly stared as the other was coming down on top of him. He couldn't maneuver his spear to block the next attack as well and hoped his ***Arcane Aura*** spell would protect him.

A clang rang out as a shield blocked the sword from Wyn's shoulder. John was beside him and absorbed the blow with his magical, runed shield. A red glow surrounded his body as he was empowered with his Fighter skill, activated at some point during the fight. He sidestepped around the monster and began to attack it from the side. The snake-man was unable to completely keep up with both warriors, and in the span of several more exchanges of blows was cut down from magical spear and sword alike, but not without landing a few hits of its own.

John and Wyn looked at each other over the lifeless body, both panting, mostly from fear. John's armor was cut up from the creature's swords and Wyn's spell was nearly spent. It alone had landed more attacks than any creature they'd faced so far. It was quick and deadly, and Wyn knew they'd be in far worse shape if they had to fight it alone. The thought of fighting more than one at a time made Wyn shudder.

Tasha rushed over and inspected them quickly. She had a frantic look in her eyes, her pupils darting over them as her head turned on a swivel. "You both seem okay," she said finally, taking a deep breath. "The difference between them and the monsters on the first floor . . ."

"Is scary," John finished. "Thankfully there were only three of them."

"One, you mean," Wyn said. He looked over at Devon and William, who were both standing over the Lacert's charred corpses. Devon pulled his sword out of one of the bodies. He had finished them off while they burned on the ground, William's spell doing most of the damage. "They took care of the others."

"Imagine if there were more," John said. He tightened his grip on his sword, steadying his shaking arm. "If I didn't have this skill, I wouldn't have been able to keep up. I can't use it every fight, though."

"I know," Wyn said. "We need a different strategy for this floor. These fights won't be easy."

"It should be easier with Marcy," Tasha said. "She can help with traps and help take down anything like that." She pointed with her staff to the lifeless corpse of the snake-man hybrid.

John and Wyn looked at each other. Wyn knew what the Fighter was thinking—Marcy would be incredibly helpful, but they were still limited with the four of them. This floor wouldn't be easy, and it only spelled increased difficulties further into the tower, too.

They desperately needed to fill their group to six members, and fast. He wondered about the three currently joining them. They seemed to have a good rapport and had improved quickly with proper guidance.

"I'm sorry about that," William said. Using his staff as a walking stick, he walked over to the rest of the party along with Devon. "I . . . froze. Again." He fiddled with his robes, his eyes darting between the other Climbers.

"Me, too," Devon said. He scratched the back of his head and stared at the ground.

"It's alright," Maven said. "We'll do better next time. Don't be hard on yourselves." She smiled awkwardly, holding her staff close.

Wyn looked at all three of them. Devon and William had shameful looks plastered on their faces, and Maven seemed more fearful than ever. And yet, despite that, they were still here. The three of them didn't run or hide and eventually acted to help the group. It was better than when he first saw them, and he knew they'd improve in time as long as they were smart and stayed alive.

However, they still didn't act right away, and those precious seconds were costly. They'd be fine Climbers eventually, but for now—they weren't the party members his current group needed.

"Wyn, what did you think?" John asked.

Wyn shook his head, lost in his thoughts again. Everyone was staring at him. "Hmm?" he asked, unsure of what he was being asked.

Tasha sighed. "Here we go again, lost in thought! We asked, do you think we should keep going?"

Wyn nodded slowly. "Ahh . . . well, no."

The others seemed to give out a sigh of relief. John and Tasha simply nodded their heads in understanding.

"I think we saw what we needed to see," Wyn continued. "No sense in chancing anything further. We can collect our rewards and call it a day."

"Exactly what I was hoping," William said. "Time for supper and a good book!"

Devon and Maven chuckled, though Wyn only smiled awkwardly. It felt like they didn't respect the tower, not fully realizing the danger present. They wanted to leave as quickly as they wanted to climb. If anything, it only solidified Wyn's thoughts about the contrast between them and his own team.

"And we should be going, too," John said, sheathing his sword. "But, thank you all for joining us. I'm glad it worked out."

While the others talked, Wyn took the portal key out from his pocket. He turned it over in his fingers several times. If only he had something like this the last time he was on the second floor. Then Cedric wouldn't be in the position he was in. And Lionel might not have escaped so easily.

The sound of a portal opening pulled Wyn's attention. None of the others held keys in their hands, and he hadn't used his yet. But the sound was unmistakable. Turning around, he froze.

A large, nearly black portal opened in the area behind them roughly thirty feet away. It looked like a corrupted floor portal but larger and flatter.

"What in the hells is that?" William asked.

John eyed the portal and drew his sword, and Wyn dug out the portal key in his pocket. He hadn't heard of a portal like that before. If it was something dangerous, he'd rather escape than fight.

A person stepped out from the portal, hidden by a large navy cloak. Wyn suddenly put the puzzle pieces together. A hidden figure just outside their group watching them, never revealing themselves. A figure also wearing a porcelain mask with a familiar sheathed sword on their hip. One that was brought to be used by someone else, stolen after an act of betrayal.

Beside Wyn, John growled. "*You*." The words came out like venom. "That's my sword."

The figure looked down at their sword and slowly unsheathed it as the blade was engulfed in flames. They pointed the sword at the group as William, Maven, and Devon stepped back. John, Wyn, and Tasha held their ground.

Behind the cloaked figure another person stepped through. They also wore a fine blue cloak with a hood over their head, masking their head and most of their face. Then two more people immediately stepped out behind them, each of them wearing identical cloaks. One was as tall as Lionel, while the other two were of average height. All of them were mostly hidden. Wearing the same cloaks with a masked Lionel leading them made them give off the appearance of a cult.

"How?" Devon asked, his voice quivering. "Those are people!"

"Steel yourselves," Wyn said. "They're still enemies."

A red aura engulfed John before he yelled, running forward to fight.

CHAPTER FORTY

Trying to think quickly as John ran forward, Wyn knew he needed to act. John more than likely wasn't going to think straight, so he needed to be the one to think for him. The Fighter likely could handle Lionel on his own, though he had no idea about the other three. Were they warriors? Mages? Were they even first tier Climbers, or Climbers at all? Opening up a black portal like that was beyond any sort of magic Wyn knew about, even with his limited knowledge. They likely possessed powers different even from what Climbers considered normal.

There were too many unknowns to make any kind of rational decision. So, there was really only one option. Try to take them down as quickly as possible before they could potentially gain the upper hand.

"Tasha, protect, heal, and guide Maven," Wyn said, while mentally activating *Speed Up*. "Devon, William, attack the others with everything you have!"

Devon and William were frozen, stunned by these people's sudden appearance. Wyn mentally cursed at their inaction but didn't dwell on it further. Instead, he rushed forward to help John, all while hoping they would support them.

As he ran, he quickly scanned the people in front of them. There were four of them total, which was good. Having six people in their own party gave them a numbers advantage. Two were purely support with Tasha and Maven, but the four enemies could have a support healer as well. If not, then they'd be at an even greater disadvantage.

John was nearly at Lionel when magical armor enveloped him. He then clashed with Lionel who raised his flaming sword to defend himself. A loud twang of ringing metal echoed before John moved to attack again. Each swing was accompanied with a growl, and Lionel was immediately on the back foot. One of the others, the larger one, pulled out a club from under their cloak and swung it at John, but he deftly blocked it with his shield.

Wyn was nearly at the group when he decided to distract the rest of their group. If all of them ganged up on John, he'd be overwhelmed right away. "***Dyadcast: Flamebolt!***" He pointed an empty palm ahead of him as his Ruby Magician mark appeared just in front of his hand. Two small balls of fire fired from the runic circle directly at the grouped opponents. One of them dove to the side avoiding the hit while the other was pelted in the leg. They screamed with a high-pitched feminine voice, then fell to the ground while trying to pat out the flames with the non-burning part of their cloak.

As the person took off their cloak Wyn saw that it was a woman about his age. She wasn't wearing anything special, just simple clothes with a metal rod attached to her side where a weapon might be. A mage, then. Either she wasn't a healer or she was too flustered to think, as she kept writhing on the ground from the ball of fire that was already snuffed out.

Wyn moved to the one who dodged his attack and stabbed out with his spear. To his surprise, the person avoided the blow, jumping back just out of reach from the spear tip nearly piercing his stomach. They then drew a short sword from their side and threw the cloak off their back, revealing themselves. It was a man, younger than Wyn, likely John's age. He scowled but didn't look any different from anyone else walking around the city.

Wyn steadied his breathing. It had been some time since he fought someone seriously, as climbing meant only facing monsters. But this wasn't a normal climb. And these enemies weren't normal. Lionel betrayed them and nearly killed John, and now he was back.

Anger swelled inside him as he knew what needed to be done. He had killed before, and sometimes it was the only option. Though he didn't necessarily want to kill all of them. Only Lionel. Siding with him, though, put them all in a position where it may be necessary. They were attacking them, after all, and they very well could try to kill them.

Which meant Wyn needed to have the same mindset. These may be people, but it was just another day of killing monsters.

The man grunted as he stabbed forward, elongating his body and stretching his arm out in a stabbing attack. Wyn easily stepped to the side and avoided it. The move wasn't anything special, and the man was in a far inferior position. His short sword was a poor matchup for Wyn's spear, and Wyn was enhanced with his speed skill.

In a single move, Wyn stabbed the man through his foreleg as he cried out in pain. He pulled his spear free and prepared himself to stab the man in the chest but then paused when the enemy did something unexpected.

He dropped his sword and clutched his leg while falling to the ground. His face scrunched in pain while his eyes widened in surprise, and he immediately ignored Wyn while helplessly holding his bleeding thigh.

Was he *that* inexperienced? Just who were these people?

A whooshing sound followed by a thud and cry pulled Wyn's attention. He looked over to see the cloaked mage once again on fire, except this time the flames completely enveloped her. Two small globs of fire were burning on the ground around her, and she cried from the fire burning her while shedding her cloak.

Wyn turned back to the man on the ground but he wasn't there. Instead, he was hobbling away back to the portal, still clutching his leg.

Ignoring him, Wyn ran to the fight to help John. Devon was there, now, fighting with the large man who seemed to be holding his own fairly well with his club. They were locked in a game of cat and mouse, with Devon rolling or dodging hits though not effectively striking back. He seemed to wear armor under his cloak, and was more skilled than the others.

John was still locked with Lionel as strands of flames whipped around them from John's stolen sword. John didn't look injured, but Lionel looked just as healthy. They were evenly matched.

Wyn moved to John's side and lashed out with his spear against the masked man. He wanted to tip the scales to their favor. Lionel swiped the spear away but missed John's attack that sliced across his torso. Lionel grunted in pain though no blood was shed. Looking closer, Wyn could see thick padded armor that covered his body, and he looked even better protected than John.

That wouldn't protect him for long, though.

Another series of quick exchanges left Lionel bleeding from his hip and arm. His moves were becoming sloppy as his anger grew. Throughout the brief encounter Lionel kept pointing his left arm forward or to the side, as though he was trying to cast magic. Nothing happened, though Wyn found it concerning. At least it was useless at the moment. Annoyingly, Lionel's mask was still on his face, as though it was magically placed or equipped, and never wavered despite the man's rough movements.

"Go!" Lionel yelled. "Get the others!"

"He's different," John whispered, trying to make sure Lionel didn't hear him. "Stronger. Tougher. Not sure why."

Wyn didn't know what kind of new powers Lionel could have possessed. It wasn't obvious that he had any new magical items, but there was likely some strange magic he had from this cult. Whatever it was, Wyn needed to be fully on guard.

The injured mage near the portal Lionel didn't hesitate at his order, immediately scampering back and disappearing through the black void. The hobbling man was there, now, too, quickly following her to wherever they came from.

Wyn cursed. He didn't care so much about the pair leaving, but he was concerned about who would come through the portal. Would it be more capable and magical people of this cult? Or just more bodies to help cover Lionel?

"Why did you try to kill me?" John yelled more than asked, parrying a wild swing from Lionel and then bashing him with his shield. The move only served to break the masked man's posture rather than give any kind of injury while he ignored John's question. But John pressed him with the sudden advantage.

Wyn refocused and moved to help before he was turned away by a scream. He glanced over to see Devon lying on the ground with the larger man standing over him. His club was on Devon's chest, and the Rogue sprayed a mouthful of blood to the side. He suddenly glowed with a white aura, but the man raised his club to hit him again. No amount of healing from Tasha or Maven would actively stop Devon from continuously being beaten.

Directly in front of him, though, Lionel was cornered. If he could press him, along with John, they could finally end this. But ignoring Devon meant he would endure a torturous amount of pain, if not an outright death.

Split second decisions could make or break someone in the heat of battle. Nothing was ever clear about what was the right or wrong move. What was clear, though, was doing nothing. Inaction meant certain death. Unfortunately Wyn had seen that time and time again. He couldn't stand there and take precious seconds to decide. So, he acted.

Lionel would have to wait. John could hold his own, but Devon would suffer or die.

Wyn rushed over to help Devon and stabbed at the large man's back. Being closer, he could see the faint red aura of a Fighter skill. So a Climber, then. Which meant he was dangerous.

While he was fast, he wasn't quiet, and the man turned in time to force the spear off course. Instead of a direct blow it was more of a glance, and Wyn both felt and heard the familiar scrape of metal armor under his spear's blade.

The man, standing easily a head taller than Wyn, raised his club to attack but was too slow. Wyn swept with the butt end of his spear to the man's legs, hooking his ankle and throwing his balance. The man faltered, nearly dropping his club, before Wyn continued his spear's momentum and slashed at his arms. The man feebly raised his arms to defend himself, suffering a sliced hit across both of his forearms. He grunted in pain as he stumbled. Wyn slashed again and again, aiming for any part of the man exposed. His thighs, knees, and arms were the only parts not armored, and Wyn cut or stabbed into all of them.

But each hit caused far less of an injury than was normal. The man had some Fighter skills that Wyn was unfamiliar with, something that seemed to enhance his skin or body. He was so durable that his own metal spear tip reduced the slices and hits to mere shallow cuts.

Wyn dodged a wild swing from the large man's club, then struck back with his spear. Annoyingly the man was well armored on top of his already tough body, and was bulky enough that Wyn's strikes weren't doing much. He wasn't trying to outright kill the man, but maybe that needed to change. Lionel was still engaged with John, and he wanted to join to make sure John won.

After another avoided club swing, Wyn saw that Devon was on his feet. Maven and Tasha were nearby, both providing support with William directly in front of them. They all looked terrified. It was one thing to fight monsters, but other people? That required an entirely different mindset. And Wyn didn't blame them. This wasn't their choice.

Devon helped Wyn by slashing at the club man's back, and he was distracted long enough for Wyn to act. Bringing up his spear, he aimed for the man's chest and drove his spear deep with as much force as he could muster. He felt the resistance of armor but then continued to push his weapon, sinking the blade halfway into the man's side. Despite him pushing with all of his strength, the spear still only dug in a few inches. It was enough, though, and he yelled, both from shock and pain. Then he dropped his club and fell to the ground, heavily bleeding from his side.

The man was a brute, but he didn't have much willpower. That blow would be detrimental but was unlikely to be fatal, and he writhed on the ground as though he was struck hard enough to be killed. Was he used to being healed by a group member? Or just not experienced enough to know what that kind of pain felt like?

The other man Wyn fought gave up just as easily. Was their cult new or something? Nothing made sense.

Devon turned and threw up, dropping his sword. Wyn looked away. He'd seen warriors do worse in lighter situations.

Ready to engage with Lionel, Wyn saw three more people come through the portal. He cursed. Reinforcements. If this fight dragged on, they would lose if more enemies came to help. They needed to be sent back or killed, and fast.

Redoubling back to the group, Wyn again used his **_Dyadcast_** to cast **_Firebolt_**, hoping to at least distract one or two of the new enemies. Of the three who came through, one carried a spear with both hands, one had a wooden shield and hammer, and the third a bow. They all had the same navy cloaks, too, though none had any obvious active skills at the moment.

Defending themselves from Wyn's magic, the one holding the shield started waving it in the air as it was ablaze, and the archer beside them caught fire on their leg. They both screamed.

None of these people were suited for this fight. Except maybe Lionel and John. And that was where Wyn needed to be.

Lionel's sword was still on fire, and he was now covered in a red aura similar to John, whose magical armor set was now completely gone. They commanded a large space to move and fight, and their clashes sounded like loud bangs with every parry or block. The third person to come through the portal held a spear and was helping Lionel, successfully attacking John and keeping him on his back foot.

Before rushing forward, Wyn quickly checked his mark. It was glowing a little over halfway, which meant he still had a small majority of his mana left. He didn't want to endlessly throw magic at Lionel, and his weapon was already magical, which meant a solid choice was to boost his and John's defenses.

When he reached the fight he carefully slid behind John and touched his back. "***Dyadcast: Arcane Aura***!" He knew that would be the last of his usable mana, but it was well worth it. Magical white armor once again enveloped John, and an identical set covered Wyn's body, too. Both of them being magically defended meant Lionel would have a much harder time against them.

Lionel, seeing this, paused. He raised his flaming sword and held it with two hands while crouching into a low stance. "You damn Red Mage. Always interfering!"

Wyn ignored him and moved to the newcomer. He was tall, broad shouldered, and had a fierce look in his eyes. Worst of all, he had a red aura around him reminiscent of a Fighter. He eyed Wyn and shifted his focus, moving to attack.

Any other weapon would have a disadvantage against a spear due to its reach, but it didn't come without flaws. If someone was too close in hand-to-hand combat range, for instance, a spear was nearly useless. It was too long to be useful at that point and would end up being more of a burden than a help. And if someone wasn't used to fighting with one, that weakness was exacerbated.

Knowing this, Wyn moved directly toward the man, dodging a spear thrust that went wide. He used the hooked portion of his spear's butt end to pull the man's front foot off balance, causing him to stumble. Then he moved in close and drew the dagger from his lower back with a practiced move, stabbing it directly into the man's side.

The man's eyes bulged as he realized his position, and he then wailed in pain. He quickly let go of his weapon and punched out, hitting Wyn in the shoulder. The blow felt more like being hit with a hammer as he was knocked backward with ease. The aura must have improved his strength, but it didn't matter now. The man was holding his side, bleeding. And Wyn was fine as his magical armor took the entire blow.

"***Wingbeat***," Wyn said, slicing his spear across the man's torso once he gained his footing. A magical cut of wind quickly flew across the air and struck the man, fully knocking him to the ground. He likely wouldn't get back up anytime soon, and Wyn checked on the other two near the portal.

They were beating out more flames around them as William was casting fire spell after fire spell, keeping them both distracted. A few actually hit them and were burning them, and Wyn was thankful the mage was acting.

That freed Wyn up to help John, and without hesitation he moved to help.

Stepping into the fight, Wyn analyzed the man. He was big, bigger even than John, and strong. With his Fighter skill active he was equally as effective as John, too, whom Wyn knew to be a great combatant in his own right.

But Lionel also had several disadvantages. He wasn't as skilled with a sword and was reckless, easily giving away his intent before each strike was executed. And while he was strong, he wasn't as fast as Wyn. Wielding a sword against a spear gave him less reach, too.

Wyn ducked and rolled under an unskilled horizontal swing while slicing out with his spear. It grazed Lionel's leg without any purchase. Stabbing back out, he connected with Lionel's hip, though his spear only sank into flesh a few inches. Lionel yelped in pain before lashing out with his sword, causing a wide arc of flame to erupt around him. The magical armor around him absorbed the fire, and Wyn readied himself to launch a counter attack.

As he did, he smiled. Now came Lionel's most grievous disadvantage. He was outnumbered. None of the other cult members were able to help, either incapacitated or currently on fire.

John cut heavily across Lionel's back, severing his cloak and causing a spray of blood to paint the ground beside him. Lionel was knocked off balance from the hit but then completely stumbled forward when John followed the strike with a bash from his shield.

Together, they both struck out Lionel in quick succession, and the man who stabbed John in the back began to fall to the many hits littering his body. Occasionally he raised his left arm to them, but nothing happened. He was nearly done.

Then Lionel yelled with a great fury, ignoring the many injuries on his body and sweeping his flaming sword out all around him, causing both John and Wyn to step back. He started lashing out far more wildly than before, swinging the sword more like a club than a sword, not even bothering to try to hit with the edged portion of the weapon half the time. But each hit came at nearly the same speed as Wyn from his speed skill, and Wyn was afraid his own aura would soon be gone. John was now on the retreat, pushed back while defending each of Lionel's strikes.

He and John were gaining the upper hand so quickly that Lionel was growing desperate, and he was spiraling.

Whatever desperate magic Lionel drummed up was helping turn the tide, and John was in trouble. Some of his magical armor was already gone, too. Wyn ran to Lionel's back and stabbed at him, but Lionel turned and caught his spear with his left arm. Wyn's eyes went wide at the realization. Raising his sword with his other arm, Lionel nearly struck him down, but John was there, stabbing into Lionel's front. The man grunted in pain but didn't let up, instead head-butting John in the face and pulling Wyn in to kick him in the side.

The impact felt like a horse stomped into Wyn's ribs. It made the other man's punch feel like a hit from a child. His breath caught in his throat, and he was sent onto his back from the sheer power of the hit. His own magical armor left his side from the kick, and Wyn knew he would've broken several ribs had the spell not been around him. Then worse after Lionel would have followed up on the attack.

Two things quickly went through Wyn's mind. One was what in the hells happened to Lionel? And the second was that John was incredibly tough for taking as many hits as he did.

As he sat up, he realized the other two were just as injured. John was covering his face with his hand, stumbling around, while Lionel was on a knee holding his side. Blood dripped heavily onto the floor from his stomach, and his breathing was ragged as each breath caused his body to hitch.

This was their chance. Wyn stood with effort, realizing that maybe his ribs really were broken as pain shot through his right side. Doing his best to ignore it, he moved forward with his spear ready, hoping to stab Lionel one final time.

That was when the black portal expanded, pulling all of their attention. The cult members still fighting the flames were immediately engulfed, and the man on the ground Wyn defeated was suddenly overtaken by a black cloud.

Lionel took the moment and ran toward the expanding void, leaping in and disappearing.

Wyn decided it was best to let him go. That unknown magic was dangerous, and going after him would be a death sentence now.

"You coward!" John screamed. "Still can't even finish what you started!"

Wyn fell to a knee near John, who was taking deep breaths. He spat blood to the side, and Wyn realized his nose was broken and lip busted. The rest of their group was there soon, and Tasha and Maven immediately began healing them.

Devon, William, and Maven were all silent after the black portal closed and the cult left. The only sounds were John's frustrated breaths and his equipment clanging as he couldn't stand still. Wyn understood. He wanted retribution, too.

Tasha motioned to Wyn, and he moved over toward her and John. She spoke quietly so the other three wouldn't hear. "We could have killed those people."

"If needed, I would have, too," Wyn said, keeping his voice equally quiet.

Tasha gave him a surprised look but didn't answer. Wyn didn't blame her. How can anyone deal with the possibility of watching people die? But Wyn had a strong feeling it would only get worse. And likely sooner rather than later.

CHAPTER FORTY-ONE

The strange dichotomy of leaving Alistair and the brutal realities of fighting and killing only to return to a pristine and safe portal room at the tower's base wasn't lost on Wyn. Each time they entered the tower to climb the expectation to fight and kill was there, but normally it was only monsters. Not other people. Being a soldier at war was a life he wanted to leave behind, but he was oddly thankful for the experience. It helped keep his mind sharp and his focus true when pressured. And facing Lionel and his cult was definitely pressure.

As the others stepped through the portal around him, he was also struck with a sense of thankfulness at his own teammates. The people he was quickly calling friends. Tasha and John did well, both acting and supporting as needed. They were trustworthy, capable, and good to be around.

Wyn didn't have the heart to feel the same about the other three that joined them.

Not that they were bad people. They fought as true allies and came out alive, after all. But they had a bit of a ways to go as Climbers, both with their skills and their mentality. He sincerely hoped they would keep improving, though. At their core they were solid people and would be great friends otherwise.

As they settled together, the six of them didn't quite know what to say. John and Tasha looked to Wyn for support, and he pulled everyone to a part of the room where they were more alone. Climbers were still entering and exiting infrequently and likely wouldn't bother them, but it was still prudent to maintain some discretion.

Wyn tried to explain the situation as best he could without worrying the three others. Seeing their faces change between fear, anger, and anxiety throughout his explanation didn't give him any assurances that it worked, unfortunately.

"So you're sure that was the same Climber that betrayed you and stabbed John in the back?" Devon asked.

Wyn nodded. "Yes. I had my suspicions but they were confirmed just now. I'm sorry you three were dragged into this."

William rubbed the back of his neck. "I know climbing isn't easy, but I wasn't really prepared to be fighting other people. I could have killed some of them. A few times I thought I did."

"But if you hadn't helped they likely would have done worse to us," Wyn countered.

"I might take some time away," Maven said.

Devon nodded his agreement. "Might be good to go back to training and search for some others to make a full group before we go back inside, too."

"That's a great idea," Tasha said.

"And, you know, it's not like it's always safe when you climb, whether it's monsters or people," John added.

Both Tasha and Wyn glared at him and the Fighter's half smile was quickly wiped away.

"I think what John's trying to say," Tasha said, "is that overall you still did well. You're here, after all. Don't forget that."

"Should we talk to someone about them?" Maven asked. "They seem dangerous. What if they attack other Climbers?"

"They shouldn't," Wyn said. "Lionel seems to only have it out for us. But if it would make you feel better, you can tell the guild about it. Though I'm not sure what they could do."

"You don't want to do that?" William asked.

"I don't want to bring more attention to this than needed. And the last time I reported something it fell on deaf ears, so I'd prefer to deal with the situation on our own. I have a feeling Lionel will show up for us again."

That seemed to assuage the others as they didn't ask anymore questions and quickly said their goodbyes. Wyn did hope to see them again. Having allies was important, even outside their group. Hopefully they would take the situation in stride and seek to improve rather than quit.

But that wasn't his responsibility. What was, though, was making sure he was as capable as possible. He already had a few ideas on how to make that possible.

Leaving Alistair's base, the three walked together mostly in silence. The streets of Alestead were darker than usual, though surprisingly not empty. Many Climbers and civilians alike still filled the streets, conversing while the night continued. The night sky was cloudy, the normally illuminating stars above covered and hidden. Magical lamps were the only light source tonight, and despite not fearing anything in the city's streets, the three Climbers stayed closer together out of habit and comfort.

"I still can't believe what just happened," Tasha said after some time. "I know you warned us but still. It's not the same as actually seeing it."

"I just wish we would have done better," John said. He punched his palm with a fist. "I can't believe he got away. That bastard."

"I have a strong feeling we'll get another chance," Wyn said. "He's likely going back to their little organization or cult or whatever and being punished. If his goal was to kill us or even hurt us, he failed on both accounts."

"Good," John said.

"I hate that the others were caught up in that," Tasha said. "It wasn't their fault or their choice. Just climbing with us put them in danger."

"Like we said with them, every time we climb we're in danger," Wyn said. "Whether it's monsters or people. Remember Cedric?"

Tasha sighed while John nodded. They understood. And Wyn understood what Tasha meant, too. He also hated that they were caught in the middle of their own mess. They didn't deserve that.

The three continued to walk in silence before Tasha spoke again. "You probably didn't get much of that in the military, did you? Choice, I mean."

Wyn laughed. "Not at all. Do this, go here, say that. It was all orders until I left. Now I have the freedom of choice but still feel tied down."

"You mean your debt?" John asked.

"Yes. I can choose my team, my equipment, when to climb or rest. I can even choose my spells with my class, but still have to climb at the end of it all." Wyn sighed. "Bottom line is I need money. Badly."

"We'll help you, too," Tasha said. "With your debt."

"No," Wyn said curtly. "I can't take on another form of debt. I'd never ask you to do that."

"It's a good thing you aren't asking," Tasha said. "And didn't you just say you have the freedom of choice? Well we do, too."

Wyn looked at her. She stared at him intently, no signs of playful banter whatsoever. "You're right." He smiled. "And, I've been meaning to tell you—you've really proven yourself, Tasha. You seem much more comfortable and confident in the tower."

John let out a snort. "Yeah, a far cry from our first climb last week. No offense, but you definitely seemed out of your element!"

Wyn could see Tasha's cheeks turn red, even under the dim light.

"I had to grow quickly if I wanted to hold my own," Tasha said. "I think seeing you like that, stabbed in the back and bleeding . . . I just . . . I'm going to prevent that from ever happening again."

John put his arm around her shoulders. "That sounds like the best plan I've heard yet."

Wyn could've sworn he saw Tasha lean into John's embrace before she slightly shook her head and shrugged him off. Then she jabbed a finger in his side.

"Still," Tasha said, "I've been feeling a bit more useless this season. I hate watching you both do everything."

"Your **Arcane Aura** spell has been incredibly helpful," John said. "I feel invincible with it! And don't take any nasty injuries."

"I'm with John," Wyn said. "Taking the load off of me for that spell is invaluable. I'm not sure I even need it, now."

"I guess," Tasha said. "But I wish there was more I could do."

"Are there other spells to help support us?" Wyn asked.

"Buff is the term Climbers use," John interjected. "Buff for support and debuff for afflictions on enemies, though that isn't nearly as common."

"I think so," Tasha added. "I'll have to look over the spellbook again. I can only support, not afflict, but there are some others to use. We're so limited right now with only tier one spells and abilities, though."

"Wait," Wyn said. "You mean we get more spells?"

Tasha and John laughed together.

"Of course!" Tasha said. "Even I know that. Didn't you read the spellbook?"

Wyn felt his face rush with blood. He kept telling Daniel he'd look over the books he graciously placed on his bookshelf but honestly hadn't even opened one. The thought sounded boring, and he wanted to either climb, search the markets for items, or train. But obviously he'd missed out on crucial information. Magic was a part of his skill set, and he needed to utilize every piece of it. He made a mental note to brush up on the magic available to him as a priority.

"Not . . . yet," Wyn said.

Tasha sighed. "You're a Mage, Wyn, you need to know this! When we upgrade tiers and classes we'll have access to more spells *and* more mana. It will definitely make things easier."

"And combat classes get more skills," John said. "A lot more, too. It tends to even out some since I can't use spells."

Wyn mentally chastised himself. He came rushing into the tower, thinking his training and experience in the military would've been enough to start and climb, but he was wrong. Very wrong. This process was complex and challenging, and if he wanted to succeed he needed to be better.

"Alright, then," Wyn said. "I think I should catch up on the intricacies of being a Ruby Magician tomorrow instead of going to the markets."

"Are you sure?" John asked. "It'll be a better day than today, though that wouldn't be too hard."

"I think so," Wyn replied. "I was only planning to try to trade my magical belt, and if you both still go you can do it for me. I don't quite think an embroidered silk belt that makes me less of a target for enemies is the right fit. And Tasha's right, after all—I really do need to learn more about the magic here."

"I think it's the right move," Tasha said. "And we can look for another item for you while you catch up."

"You're already looking for more magic items?" a figure said. They were leaning against the trading house wall in a spot between two streetlights, hidden in the dark.

John and Wyn crouched, ready to attack. Wyn grabbed the knife on his back ready to draw it. Tasha jumped and gasped.

The figure stepped out from the light, laughing. It was Marcy.

"That's not funny!" Tasha said. She stomped her foot on the ground in emphasis.

Wyn and John relaxed, both sighing in relief.

"It was a little funny," Marcy said. "But what else do you need for the first two floors? You three are getting magic items quicker than any rookie I've seen."

"My mentor told me about some enchanted robes that can help with the extreme weather," Wyn said. "I think it'd be helpful in the heat."

"No kidding," John said. "I'd take anything to cool off in the hot jungle. It's miserable."

Marcy shook her head. "No, no. Trust me, you don't want that. That's just an enchantment that helps comfort. You'll want something more impactful."

Wyn furrowed his brow. "I didn't have another idea right now. What would you suggest?"

Marcy grinned. "It'll be a surprise. I can go with you two tomorrow and help sort through some good trades."

Tasha bowed at the waist. "That would be so helpful. Your expertise and experience would make it far easier. Something for each of us and Wyn, too?"

John shot a worried look at Wyn, and he was sympathetic. He was sure Tasha would want to check all of the shops again, and John would be dragged along willingly or not. More importantly, though, having a day off to de-stress and not think about Lionel would be good for them. Wyn hoped to do the same.

"We need to catch you up on today, too," Wyn said. "You missed a lot."

"Yeah?" Marcy said. "I came here with news, too. Cedric asked about all of you. That climb really took a toll on his mentality, but he wants all of you to come by on Faesday to see him."

"That's great," John said. "I'd love to thank him for saving me."

"And he wants to thank you, Wyn, for saving him," Marcy said. "Among other things."

"What other things?" Tasha asked.

Marcy shifted her feet and shook her head. "Like say goodbye. He's leaving Alestead. For good."

* * *

Wyn rolled over in his bed as the sun beamed in through his open window. He kept his eyes closed and soaked in the morning light, taking deep breaths to help himself wake up. A smile slowly formed on his face. He enjoyed the leisurely mornings of Alestead where he could wake up when he wanted and perform whatever morning routine he wanted, too. When he was in the field with his soldiers he had strict routines, times, and harsh living arrangements.

Still, despite the bed being cozy and morning warm, there was work to be done.

Thankfully breakfast was just downstairs, and he opted to satisfy his hunger before he'd strain his mind. He didn't relish the thought of sifting through books all morning but knew it was both necessary and important. Having food in his stomach and more in his room for later was important.

It took him less than an hour to get ready and eat, Wendy serving him as usual. She was particularly speedy this morning, both serving him food and cleaning up. Wyn wondered if she had a sixth sense about her customers or if she was just used to quick turnover in the dining lodge due to the number of Climbers wanting a large breakfast before they disappeared for the day. Regardless, she was as pleasant as usual, and another bright part of his day before the slog of reading began.

Wyn straightened up his room, periodically looking over at his small bookshelf that was mostly empty, save for the few books Daniel provided him. He was seriously procrastinating reading them, and tidying or cleaning anything he could find. A speck of dust there? Gone. Dripped wax on his desk? Scraped off. Clothes thrown about his room? Placed away to be laundered.

Another few minutes drained away. He looked out his window again and sighed. How could this be so difficult? It was only reading books. The information was interesting, too, and he knew it would capture his attention once he started. But that was exactly the problem—without being told what to do, starting was never easy.

Reluctantly, he growled out loud to himself to get it done. His friends were busy with their tasks, even if theirs were much, *much* more enjoyable.

He lumbered over to the bookshelf and skimmed the spines. A few of the books he picked up and read the summary. There were books that covered any topic he'd need as a new learner. They included the history of Alistair, the history of Alestead, the basics of climbing, magical items, classes, tiers and upgrades, magic as a whole, spells . . .

His finger stopped on the spine of the one book he was familiar with. *Magic of the Ruby Magician*. It was the book he reviewed with Daniel the very first day, when he had his mark placed and chose his first spells. He flipped open the pages and began perusing the book. It wasn't a very thick book, but he was never one to sit down and read from cover to cover, whether reading for pleasure or education. He was suddenly happy the size was more easily digestible, otherwise he'd be looking at a migraine later in the afternoon.

The beginning of the book helped explain what he already knew. His mark allowed the use of spells as a catalyst instead of the usually complicated method of using gemstones, knowing the rune formations, mana requirements, etc. It was a complicated process, and he blinked several times trying to process the dense information. Thankfully, being a Climber afforded him a much easier method of using spells than the Wizards of the world like Tasha's father.

He skimmed the book further to find the spells listed inside. It was broken down categorically by tier, which was a simplified magical progression. From what he skimmed, there were four categories total, belonging to four different tiers of classes. When a Climber finished the first tier, they were able to upgrade their class and progress to the next tier, where more spells and skills became available to them. Wyn wasn't sure about the exact process, but the information was easy enough to follow.

This book only had information on the first tier of spells, and it mentioned how he could grow his mark much more than that, though higher ranked spells were more difficult to come by and had more books to explain them and their use. Those spells used more mana, had more effects, and were of course far stronger. Lower tier spells were also upgraded as a Climber grew with their class, and each new effect was slightly different based on their new class. This was obviously a beginner book meant to inform rather than provide true research and study as it didn't explain further. Wyn didn't worry about it, though. He'd cross that bridge when necessary.

A sigh subconsciously left his lips. More reading, and more studying. It was never his strength, but now it was a necessity.

He kept looking through the available spells the book listed. There weren't many, which confused him. In fact, most of the book was an explanation of the how and why of the Ruby Magician class as a whole, rather than the exact spells he could use. Some of the spells listed were the basic ones he'd seen before and used, like **Cure**, **Ice Shard**, and **Arcane Aura**, but he didn't see **Regen** on the list and knew he could use it.

The pages flew under his fingertips as he reviewed the spells again, more carefully this time. **Regen** still wasn't there.

"Huh," he said out loud. "That's strange."

He scoured the beginning of the book again to try to find an explanation. When he skimmed the pages before, he didn't realize that more than half of the book was a summary, and just skipping around from paragraph to paragraph obviously made him miss some important information.

He began to read the book from the beginning, finding a comfortable spot in his chair to settle in. Straining his brain was already harder for him than training his body, but it was an exercise all the same.

In just under an hour, he leaned up from the chair. Finally, a relevant part of the book stood out to him, and his heart raced to find the answers. The paragraphs showed him that the Ruby Magician is a unique spellcaster, able to utilize the spells of other classes. He already knew that, but figured he had a specific list he could use. Instead, a brief sentence read that the book wouldn't list all the spells he could use because they were already listed under the other Magician's book, and he would need to scour the spellbooks of other classes for compatibility. This book mentioned only the most commonly used. Apparently under the spell description was a small mark of the Ruby Magician, showing it could be used by his class.

He groaned. That meant he'd have to individually search through other books to find the spells he could use. It could take hours, possibly days, and he just didn't have the time, mental capacity, or desire for such an undertaking.

It was another question to ask Daniel, and potentially another task if his mentor was gracious enough to find the spells for him. He'd pay him if he had to, but Wyn just couldn't stomach the thought of searching through so many other books for potential spells that he may or may not even use. Daniel likely had many of the spells already memorized anyway, and Wyn decided to simply ask for a brief list based on what he wanted to do as a Climber.

The book thumped on the small table as Wyn set it down, still open to the page he was reading. He stood and stretched, basking in the warm light through the window above his small kitchen area. This was the perfect time for a small snack, and a break would be appreciated.

So far, his choice of spells had been mediocre at best. He didn't have many options, though. Or at least he didn't think he did. Daniel helped guide him about the basic spells to use, but Wyn didn't press him last week—he only told his mentor about what kinds of spells he wanted to use, and Daniel helped him from there. Based on his party makeup, though, he wanted to rearrange a few things.

He grabbed a clean cup from a cabinet and filled it with water from a pitcher, staring out the window. The view wasn't great as he only saw the side of a building, but the change of scenery was nice enough. This was far better than the mudfloors of his tent out in the fields, or the barracks during training with soldiers in bunks and no privacy for weeks.

Wyn then took a deep breath. There wasn't any point to delaying what needed to be done. He was here for a reason, and his and his team's survival was partially dependent on his ability to perform well in Alistair. His physical capability would only go so far—he had the means to cast spells and he needed to capitalize on that.

Not only that, but a dreaded fight loomed in his mind. One that he needed to be as prepared for as possible. He needed to protect his friends, and he didn't want to rely on them. He wanted to be the one they looked to for protection.

He strode over to the bookshelf and looked for more books. He saw similar books for Diamond Magicians, a book that covered the elemental magic the various Magicians use based on their gemstone that was basically a thick tome, and a book detailing magical theory and history.

Wyn sighed again before picking up the largest book of them all—*Magic of the Elemental Magicians*. He settled back into his comfortable chair, slid the last book to the side, and cracked open the monster of a book. His eyes flittered through the pages, and his fingers swept over sentences and paragraphs with a renewed sense of determination. That feeling didn't last long, however, and Wyn's pace began to slow as the minutes dragged on.

A knock at the door stirred Wyn. He jolted from his chair. The room was darkened as the only source of light he was using was nearly gone. The sun was almost completely set, a faint orange and purple glow creeping into Wyn's apartment.

"Shit," Wyn said, as he realized he fell asleep reading through the large spellbook.

Another knock rasped the door, this time louder and more pronounced. A muffled voice came from the other side, drowned out by Wyn scrambling to put the books away and be more presentable.

"Coming!" Wyn said. That bought him a few seconds as the knocks stopped and he rushed to the door. He jerked it open, and Daniel stood there smiling.

His mentor barked a laugh. "Have you been catching up on some well-needed sleep?"

Wyn rubbed his eyes and tussled his hair. "I was reviewing some books and fell asleep." He yawned absentmindedly.

Daniel smirked and put his hands behind his back. "Dinner is ready in my apartment. How about you meet me there?"

Wyn nodded gratefully. "It'll only take me a few minutes to look more presentable. Thank you."

Daniel waved a dismissive hand at him with a chuckle. "That worn out already? You've barely started climbing?"

Wyn shrugged. "It's already been quite eventful. And I have a feeling it'll only get worse."

Daniel nodded. "Such is the Climber's life. I look forward to hearing all about it." He patted Wyn on the shoulder before leaving.

Wyn sighed. So much for looking over the spells—he barely remembered what he read. Apparently he fell asleep soon after looking more spells up.

He'd settle on asking Daniel over dinner about some guidance and advice. There was so much now open to him, so much to this life that he needed to grasp. Magic. Betrayal. Death. Coins. Good or bad, this new life he chose was full of complexities that he never imagined. He only hoped he could be capable enough to survive, protect his friends, and earn enough to cover his family's debt.

For now, though, that would have to wait. He needed to wipe the drool off his face first.

EPILOGUE

Landing back in the dank candlelit cave was miserable. Lionel hit the ground with a hard thud, and his body was already delicate. Cursing his luck, he punched the ground underneath him.

What shame and embarrassment. He was supposed to wipe the floor with John and that damned Red Mage. Instead they actually put up a decent fight, and he was held to a standstill. Why? And how? He was given power. Though it didn't work as intended. What was he missing? It should have activated like any other magical ability originating from Alistair—with a thought and directly on command.

Also, he was given recruits! Those damned good-for-nothing shit stains weren't even helpful! Half of them were just fodder, and the others could barely hold weapons. Harold was the only one who actually did his duties, though even then he was put down by the Red Mage. There might be potential for him, but Lionel couldn't see it right now.

A snarl formed on Lionel's face thinking of Wyn. The Ruby Magician. It was frustrating that he was so capable of a fighter, *and* had the opportunity to wield spells. When Lionel came to Alestead, he had the barest of training, and improved rapidly as a Fighter.

Not that he started out as one. But he knew in his heart the tower made a mistake about his first class choice. No one took that class except for Wyn, the smug bastard. And being a Fighter was who he was, even if he didn't have any growth because he changed his class. That was partly why he sought more power, to make up for Alistair cheating him out of what should have been his all along.

Though now he was being made a fool.

"Healer!" Lionel cried.

Several people met him immediately on exiting the portal. The first few were the acolytes that originally joined him and were injured, including Harold. More people were tending to them while a couple were casting magic to heal their injuries. Lionel forced his way through the crowd to one of the healers, ignoring every look he received.

"I'm injured," Lionel said. "Heal me."

"These people are injured, too," the woman said, pointing to a man with a wrapped thigh. It was bloodied, and he was pale.

"I'm your lieutenant," Lionel growled. "I'm priority."

The woman opened her mouth but didn't respond. She curtly nodded then moved her staff to him.

Lionel closed his eyes while the white healing aura engulfed him. Every second was agonizing as he replayed the fight in his mind. Every mistake. Every failure.

"Betrayer," a voice called.

Lionel grimaced. He was wondering when they would show up. He had hoped he could at least face them completely healed, first. Looking so pathetic was . . . well, pathetic.

"Slayer," Lionel said, slightly nodding his head in a greeting.

The masked and cloaked man laughed. It was haughty and grating. His head bobbed up and down while his white porcelain mask gave away no obvious expression. "You've seen better days, it seems."

Lionel wanted to punch the damned man in the face, but knew that would be incredibly frowned upon. And he might actually fight back. The man was annoying, but he was also skilled. He had earned his title and proved several times it wasn't for show.

"So I have," Lionel said.

"What happened?"

Lionel hesitated but knew it was pointless. He'd need to fess up eventually. "I found my mark and followed him. I tried to catch him off guard to finish my task, but these useless people didn't help for shit."

"What do you expect? Over half of them are just citizens in the city. We told you that. The others who have classes have barely climbed the first two floors. Didn't you say it was a few rookies? Why should they give you trouble after what Aliyar blessed you with anyway?"

Lionel looked at his left arm. It was mostly hidden from his armor, but he knew the runes that covered his skin. The power he was given didn't work. "I wasn't able to harness it as intended."

Slayer hoisted Lionel to his feet and brushed him off, ignoring the surprised looks of the others who were slowly backing away. He looked up at Lionel, his face still hidden. "Performance issues happen to all of us. Well, not me, but you get the point."

Lionel growled and balled his fists. Slayer responded by sending a brief pulse of magic at him, a solidly black aura that engulfed his body and made him feel weaker. As though his strength was being sapped from his body. He relaxed, knowing the intent.

Slayer was telling him to back off. Lionel would comply. For now.

"Betrayer," another voice called.

Both men turned their masked heads to see the other two lieutenants walking toward them. Slayer instantly let go, and Lionel felt his tension relax. No one would do anything with all of them together, especially to one another.

The two walking toward them were women, both very different. The one in the back, Terror, was anything but. She was timid, quiet, and weak, according to Lionel. He had no idea how or why she earned her name. The one in the front, and their leader, was Gouger.

Like the other woman, he had no idea why she was given that name. And a large part of him didn't want to find out.

"Yes, Gouger?" Lionel asked.

The masked woman looked around, and no one else was left around them. She pointed with her head behind her. "Come with me."

Lionel heard Slayer snicker and ignored him. Reluctantly, he followed the woman. Why in the hells was he already being summoned? Did their leader already know about his failure? Or maybe he wanted to know why he left so suddenly and took a number of their people with him?

It didn't matter. The point was that he failed. There had to be consequences.

"Do you know what this is about?" Lionel asked.

The woman turned a corner in a hollowed tunnel, then paused. The only light was a series of torches set along the walls. It cast an eerie glow around her.

"Did you finish your original task?"

Lionel grit his teeth then forced himself to relax. "No. There were some . . . complications."

Gouger slowly nodded. "Your abilities haven't realized yet, have they?"

Lionel felt an odd pang of worry. How did she know that?

She huffed a laugh. "It happened to all of us at first. Zarath's magic takes time to take hold, and you were impatient."

"Damnit," Lionel muttered. "How long?"

"However long it takes. It's strange magic. It works by how much he trusts you and sees you as an actual follower of Aliyar. A follower of him, too. Since you've yet to prove yourself, your runes haven't taken effect."

"That's a bunch of bullshit."

"You don't believe me?"

"No I do, I think it's bullshit that his magic works that way."

Gouger shrugged. "It is what it is. All magic is from Aliyar, but this magic was granted to Zarath directly. That he passed on to us. So it's not to be taken lightly. Prove yourself, and power will be yours."

As they continued walking through the tunnels, Lionel wondered what she meant by that. All magic was from the tower, and by proxy Aliyar. Of course he was loyal to him. He had seen the power that magic provides, and the truth about what the tower represents. About Aliyar's purpose and how misguided everyone else was. What else was he supposed to do?

Power does not come without sacrifice. He hadn't considered what else he needed to give up besides his own body and comfort. Was it his loyalty? He had given that already. He was here, after all. But was his mind here? Was he going through the motions instead of actually believing what he wanted? Did he mentally resist that much, even after everything he had seen and was promised?

He focused his mind and tried to calm himself. His purpose was to further Aliyar's will. John was a thread that kept being pulled, but ultimately he wasn't the true reason he was here. Or the true reason he was given power. He was stuck in his own past and needed to look forward to advance.

A strange pulse reverberated across his left arm and shoulder. It took him by surprise when it lingered. But it was undeniable.

It was the runes Zarath bestowed on him. The power he had been craving.

Gouger suddenly stopped, and Lionel nearly walked into her as he was focused on his arm. They were in front of a wooden door, and she knocked twice, paused, then once.

"Come in, lieutenant," Zarath said on the other side.

Lionel followed Gouger inside to where Zarath was seated at a simple wooden desk. He didn't bother looking up.

"Gouger, you may leave," Zarath said. "Thank you for showing Betrayer the way."

The woman bowed then promptly left. She really was a loyal follower. Likely the most loyal besides Zarath himself. It was no wonder she held the position she did.

Zarath was writing something on some stacks of paper while Lionel just stood there. He didn't know why he was brought there, so he waited.

"I see that two very interesting circumstances happened today," Zarath finally said, still not bothering to take his eyes off the papers. He paused to dip his quill in an ink bottle before continuing to write.

"Sir?" Lionel asked.

"The first interesting situation was that you hastily returned inside Alistair to confront the man you failed to finish. And didn't succeed. Correct?"

Lionel felt a lump form in his throat but forced it down. "Correct."

"The second was that you realized your dormant power, which is now awakened."

"Yes. Also true."

Zarath put the paper he was writing on to the side and set his quill down. He finally looked at Lionel, his eyes piercing. It was unsettling, but didn't seem to carry any anger. At least not that Lionel could see.

"I'm disappointed you rushed back to failure without awakening your power first. That would have been more prudent."

Lionel reluctantly agreed. He couldn't hide anything from their leader. It would be better to be honest anyway. "Yes. You're right, of course. I hoped that the power would show itself when I was pushed, or under stress."

"Ahh." Zarath leaned back in his chair and took a deep breath. "That wasn't a bad idea. Pushing ourselves to the very edge helps us move that very edge, increasing our resolve, our strength, and our capabilities. But the power I shared with you doesn't work that way."

Lionel nodded.

"Which leads me to the second circumstance. That you just awakened it. Did you have a realization? Some epiphany that led you to see Aliyar's truth?"

Lionel held up his left arm. Despite it being covered, he could sense the power it contained, now. And he had a feeling Zarath did, too.

"Yes. I thought I knew of his truth before, but now I know for sure. I was stuck in my own past and need to bring forth his future."

Zarath's placid face slowly turned into a large smile. "Yes. Now you see! There is more work to be done than just your own. Which, I will say, will come in time. You will have the opportunity to correct your mistakes. But not before pursuing and accomplishing other goals set before us."

Lionel bowed. He understood, now. He needed to be patient. It wasn't easy for him, but he needed to fight his own negative tendencies and embrace his positive ones. He was strong. Powerful. Capable. And would prove it.

And, eventually, he would show John and the Ruby Magician the truth. A truth that only came in death.

"Yes, sir," Lionel said. "I am at Aliyar's command. What would you have me do?"

Acknowledgments

Thank you again to Katy, supporting me through all the early mornings and late nights. You never stopped encouraging me, and this book wouldn't have happened without you.

Thank you to Melanie, the president of my fan club. You very well might have marketed this book single-handedly more than anyone else.

Thank you to my Royal Road readers, providing views, follows, rates, comments, and support. Y'all have been wonderful and have helped bring this story to fruition.

Thank you to my Patreon subscribers who went above and beyond to support me. You showed me there was potential in people wanting to pay to read more of my story, and I'll always be grateful for you.

Thank you to Podium for giving me the opportunity to become a published author. Writing a book is only a small portion of actually publishing one, and y'all gave an unknown writer a chance to become an actual author. I can't thank you enough!

And thank you, reader! Your support by reading this book is incredibly appreciated. If you have any questions or comments or just want to reach me, feel free to contact me on reddit (u/drhudgins).

About the Author

D. R. Hudgins is the author of the Ruby Magician series, originally released on Royal Road. A daydreamer, lover of the fantasy genre, and avid enjoyer of good stories, he spends his free time watching movies and reading books from his ever-growing TBR list. Hudgins lives in Nashville, Tennessee, with his wife, two boys, and dog.

RESPAWN YOUR CURIOSITY

follow us on our socials

 podiumentertainment.com

 @podiumentertainment

 /podiumentertainment

 @podium_ent

 @podiumentertainment